ACCLAIM FOR
LETHAL AND **SANDRA BROWN**

"Pulse-pounding...a relentless pace and clever plot."
—*Publishers Weekly* (starred review)

"The amazingly prolific Sandra Brown does not disappoint in this new Louisiana-set novel that's a perfect mix of thriller and romantic suspense...If a portrait could be painted of a Sandra Brown fan it would look something like this: a reader sprawled on a couch or curled up in a chair, tea or coffee within easy reach, a look of complete satisfaction on his or her face. It's all about stealing away."
—*USA Today*

"Read just a chapter of LETHAL and you'll figure out in a hurry why the Texas-born author has written so many *New York Times* bestsellers (sixty, in fact). She sets the stakes high and early—and you can't help but keep reading...A master at building suspense, Brown is especially good at keeping her readers guessing...Get ready to raise your blood pressure a few notches...and I dare you to guess the identity of the villain."
—*BookPage*

"Sandra Brown delivers a Hitchcockian thriller that reads like a bullet...No one is better in the genre than Brown, and she has written her best book to date."
—Associated Press

Novels by Sandra Brown

SANDRA BROWN

LOW PRESSURE

GRAND CENTRAL
PUBLISHING

New York   Boston

Grand Central Publishing
Hachette Book Group
237 Park Avenue
New York, NY 10017
www.HachetteBookGroup.com

Grand Central Publishing is a division of Hachette Book Group, Inc.
The Grand Central Publishing name and logo is a trademark of Hachette Book Group, Inc.

The Hachette Speakers Bureau provides a wide range of authors for speaking events. To find out more, go to www.hachettespeakersbureau.com or call (866) 376-6591.

The publisher is not responsible for websites (or their content) that are not owned by the publisher.

Printed in the United States of America

Originally published in hardcover by Hachette Book Group
First international mass market edition: January 2013

10 9 8 7 6 5 4 3 2 1
OPM

To

Mary Lynn and Len Baxter

with everlasting gratitude for your belief in me,
your enduring friendship,
and your unqualified love

A.K.A.

LOW PRESSURE

Prologue

The rat was dead, but no less horrifying than if it had been alive.

Bellamy Price trapped a scream behind her hands and, holding them clamped against her mouth, backed away from the gift box of glossy wrapping paper and satin ribbon. The animal lay on a bed of silver tissue paper, its long pink tail curled against the fat body.

When she came up against the wall, she slid down it until her bottom reached the floor. Slumping forward, she removed her hands from her mouth and covered her eyes. But she was too horror-stricken even to cry. Her sobs were dry and hoarse.

Who would have played such a vicious prank? *Who?* And *why?*

The events of the day began to replay in her mind like a recording on fast-forward.

"You were terrific!"

"Thank you." Bellamy tried to maintain the rapid pace

set by the publicist for the publishing house, who functioned as though her breakfast cereal had been laced with speed.

"This show is number one in its time slot." Her rapid-fire speech kept time with the click of her stilettos. "Miles ahead of its competition. We're talking over five million viewers. You just got some great national exposure."

Which was exactly what Bellamy wished to avoid. But she didn't waste her breath on saying so. Again. For the umpteenth time. Neither the publicist nor her agent, Dexter Gray, understood her desire to direct the publicity to her best-selling book, not to herself.

Dexter, his hand tightly grasping her elbow, guided her through the Manhattan skyscraper's marble lobby. "You were superb. Flawless, but warm. Human. That single interview probably sold a thousand copies of *Low Pressure*, which is what it's all about." He ushered her toward the exit, where a uniformed doorman tipped his hat as Bellamy passed.

"Your book kept me up nights, Ms. Price."

She barely had time to thank him before being propelled through the revolving door, which emptied her onto the plaza. A shout went up from the crowd that had gathered to catch a glimpse of that morning's interviewees as they entered and exited the television studio.

The publicist was exultant. "Dexter, help her work the crowd. I'm going to get a photographer over here. We can parlay this into more television coverage."

Dexter, more sensitive to his client's reluctance toward notoriety, stood on tiptoe and spoke directly into Bellamy's ear to make himself heard above the Midtown rush-hour racket. "It wouldn't hurt to take advantage of the situation and sign a few books. Most authors work their entire professional lives—"

"And never receive this kind of media attention," she said, finishing for him. "Thousands of writers would give their right arm for this. So you've told me. Repeatedly."

"It bears repeating." He patted her arm as he steered her toward the eager people straining against the barricades. "Smile. Your adoring public awaits."

Readers who had become instant fans clamored to shake hands with her and have her sign their copies of *Low Pressure*. Being as gracious as possible, she thanked them and smiled into their cell-phone cameras.

Her hand was being pumped by an enthusiastic fan when she spotted Rocky Van Durbin out of the corner of her eye. A writer for the daily tabloid newspaper *EyeSpy*, Van Durbin was standing slightly apart from the crowd, wearing a self-congratulatory smirk and giving instructions to the photographer accompanying him.

It was Van Durbin who had uncovered and then gleefully disclosed that the writer T. J. David, whose first book was generating buzz in book circles as well as in Hollywood, was, in fact, Bellamy Price, an attractive, thirty-year-old woman:

"Why this native Texan—blue-eyed, long-legged, and voluptuous, and isn't that how we like them?—would want to hide behind an innocuous pen name, this reporter doesn't know. But in spite of the author's coy secrecy, *Low Pressure* has soared to the top of the best-seller charts, and now, apparently, Ms. Price has come out of hiding and gotten into the spirit of the thing. She's eschewed her spurs and hat, abandoned the Lone Star state, and is now residing in a penthouse apartment overlooking Central

Park on the Upper West Side, basking in the glow of her sudden celebrity."

Most of that was a lie, having only filaments of truth that kept it from being libelous. Bellamy did have blue eyes, but she was of average height, not noticeably tall, as his description suggested. By no one's standards could she be considered voluptuous.

She did have a cowboy hat, but it hadn't been on her head for years. She'd never owned a pair of spurs, nor had she ever known anyone who did. She hadn't abandoned her home state, in the sense Van Durbin had implied, but she had relocated to New York several years ago, long before the publication of her book. She did live on the Upper West Side, across from the park, but not in a penthouse.

But the most egregious inaccuracy was Van Durbin's claim that she was enjoying her celebrity, which she considered more a harsh glare than a glow. That glare had intensified when Van Durbin wrote a follow-up, front-page article that contained another startling revelation.

Although published as a novel, *Low Pressure* was actually a fictionalized account of a true story. *Her* true story. Her family's *tragic* true story.

With the velocity of a rocket, that disclosure had thrust her into another dimension of fame. She abhorred it. She hadn't written *Low Pressure* to become rich and famous. Writing it had been therapeutic.

Admittedly, she'd hoped it would be published, widely read, and well received by readers and critics, but she had published it under a non-gender-specific pseudonym in order to avoid the spotlight in which she now found herself.

Low Pressure had been eagerly anticipated even before it went on sale. Believing strongly in its potential, the publishing house had put money behind its publication, placing transit ads in major cities, and print ads in magazines, newspapers, and on the Internet. Social media outlets had been abuzz for months in advance of its on-sale date. Every review had been a rave. T. J. David was being compared to the best crime writers, fiction and nonfiction. Bellamy had enjoyed the book's success from behind the protective pseudonym.

But once Rocky Van Durbin had let the genie out of the bottle, there was no putting it back. She figured her publisher and Dexter, and anyone else who stood to profit from sales, were secretly overjoyed that her identity and the backstory of her book had been exposed.

Now they had not only a book to promote, but also an individual, whom they had deemed "a publicist's dream."

They described her as attractive, well educated, well spoken, not so young as to be giddy, not so old as to be boring, an heiress turned best-selling author. She had a lot of "hooks" to draw upon, the chief one being that she had desired anonymity. Her attempt to hide behind a pen name had, instead, made her all the more intriguing. Rocky Van Durbin was relishing the media frenzy surrounding her, which he had helped create, and, never satisfied, continued to feed the public's voracious curiosity with daily tidbits about her, most of which were either blatantly untrue, speculative, or grossly exaggerated.

As she continued to sign autographs and pose for photographs with fans, she pretended not to have noticed him, but to no avail. He rudely elbowed his way through the crowd toward her. Noticing his approach, Dexter cautioned her in a whisper, "Don't let him get to you. People are watching. He'd love nothing better than to goad you into saying something he could print out of context."

When the so-called journalist came face-to-face with her, making it impossible for her to ignore him, he smiled, revealing two rows of crooked yellow teeth, which she imagined him filing in order to achieve that carnivorous grin.

Looking her up and down, he asked, "Have you lost weight, Ms. Price? I can't help but notice that you're looking thinner."

A few weeks ago she'd been voluptuous. Tomorrow she would be suffering from an eating disorder.

Without even acknowledging his sly question, Bellamy engaged in conversation with a woman wearing an Ohio State sweatshirt and a Statue of Liberty spiked crown made of green rubber foam. "My book club is reading your book now," the woman told her as they posed together for a snapshot taken by her equally enthusiastic husband.

"I appreciate that very much."

"The rest of them won't believe I met you!"

Bellamy thanked her again and moved along. Undaunted, Van Durbin kept pace, furiously scribbling in a small spiral notebook. Then, stepping between her and the next person waiting for her attention, he asked, "Who do you see playing the lead roles in the movie, Ms. Price?"

"I don't see anyone. I'm not in the movie business."

"But you will be before long. Everybody knows producers are lined up to throw money at you for the option on *Low Pressure*. It's rumored that several A-list actors and actresses are campaigning for the parts. The casting couches have never had turnover this brisk."

She shot him a look of pure disgust.

"No opinion on the subject?"

"*None*," she said, stressing the word in such a way as to discourage any more questions. Just then a man wedged himself between two young women and thrust a copy of her book at her. Bellamy recognized him immediately. "Well, hello again. Hmm…"

"Jerry," he said, smiling broadly.

"Jerry, yes." He had an open, friendly face and thinning hair. He'd come to several book signings, and she'd spotted him in the audience when she lectured at a bookstore on the NYU campus. "Thank you for coming out this morning."

"I never pass up an occasion to see you."

She signed her name on the title page, which he held open for her. "How many copies does this make that you've bought, Jerry?"

He laughed. "I'm buying birthday and Christmas presents."

She suspected he was also starstruck. "Well, I and my publisher thank you."

She moved on and, while Jerry fell back into the crush, Van Durbin boldly nudged people out of his way so he could stay even with her. He persisted with the question about a possible movie based on her book.

"Come on, Ms. Price. Give my readers a hint of who you see playing the key characters. Who would you cast as your family members?" He winked and leaned in, asking in a low voice, "Who do you see playing the killer?"

She gave him a sharp look.

He grinned and said to the photographer, "I hope you captured that."

*   *   *

The rest of the day was no less hectic.

She and Dexter had attended a meeting at the publishing house to discuss the timing of the release of the trade paperback edition of *Low Pressure*. After a lengthy exchange of opinions, it was decided that the book was selling so well in the hardcover and e-book formats that an alternate edition wouldn't be practical for at least another six months.

They'd gone from that meeting to a luncheon appointment with a movie producer. After they dined on lobster salad and chilled asparagus in the privacy of his hotel suite, he'd made an earnest pitch about the film he wanted to make, guaranteeing that if they sold him the rights, he would do justice to the book.

As they'd left the meeting, Dexter joked, "Wouldn't your friend Van Durbin love to know about that meeting?"

"He's no friend. T. J. David's true identity was supposed to be a carefully guarded secret. Who did Van Durbin bribe to get my name?"

"A publishing house intern, an assistant to someone in the contracts department. It could have been anybody."

"Someone in your agency?"

He patted her hand. "We'll probably never know. What does it matter now who it was?"

She sighed with resignation. "It doesn't. The damage has been done."

He laughed. "'Damage' being a matter of opinion."

Dexter had dropped her off at her apartment building with a warning: "Tomorrow's going to be another whirlwind day. Get some rest tonight. I'll be here at seven a.m. to pick you up."

She'd waved him off with a promise that she wouldn't be late, then entered the lobby of her building. The concierge had called to her from behind his desk. "A package for you was delivered just a little while ago."

It had looked innocent enough when she'd set it on her dining table along with a stack of mail. The box had been sealed with clear packing tape. She'd noted that the label was printed with her name and address, but not the sender's information. That was curious, but she didn't think too much of it as she split the tape, folded back the flaps, and lifted out the gift-wrapped box inside.

She never could have prepared herself for the hideous surprise it contained.

Now, sitting on the floor with her back against the wall, she lowered her hands from her eyes and looked at the box with tissue paper blossoming out the top of it. That festive touch was so incongruous with the contents it had to have been planned that way as part of the joke.

Joke? No. This wasn't funny. It was malicious.

But she couldn't think of anyone whom she had offended, nor of anyone who would hold her in such contempt. Would Rocky Van Durbin, even having *Sleazy* as a middle name, do something so low-down and dirty as to send her a dead rat?

Slowly she worked her way up the wall, sliding her spine along it for support as she unsteadily came to her feet. Standing, she was able to see the rat nestled in the shiny paper. She tried desensitizing herself so she could look at it. She tried to objectify the corpse, but because each of its features was so grotesque, they seemed extraordinarily detailed.

She swallowed bile, chafed the goose bumps on her

arms, and by force of will pulled herself together. It was only a dead rodent, after all. Rats were a common sight in the subway stations. Seeing one scuttling along the tracks had never caused her to have this kind of violent reaction.

She would replace the lid on the box and carry it to the garbage chute at the end of the hall. Then she'd be rid of it; she could forget about it and go on about her business, having refused to let the prankster get the best of her.

Steeling herself, she took a step forward, and another, and another, until she was almost upon it.

And then the rat's tail flicked.

Chapter 1

Dent answered the phone with a grumble. "What?"

"You're still in the sack?"

"What time is it?"

"You sound drunk."

"Do I need to be sober?"

"If you want the job."

"Today?"

"Soon as you can get here."

"I was afraid you were going to say that. Is it worth my trouble?"

"Since when can you afford to turn down a charter?"

"Okay, okay. How much?"

"Two thousand, down and back."

"To?"

"Houston Hobby."

"Overnight stay?"

"No."

Dent sat up and placed his feet on the floor, testing his level of sobriety. He raked his fingers through his hair then left his hand there, palming his muzzy head. "Twenty-five hundred plus fuel costs."

"The guy's sick. He's going to MD Anderson for chemo."

"Twenty-five hundred plus fuel costs."

An unintelligible mutter about greed, then, "I think I can swing that."

"You do, and it's a deal. What's the weather like?"

"Hot, muggy, Texas in May."

"Precip?"

"Possible scattered thundershowers late this evening. Nothing you can't dodge, nothing scary." After a hesitation, "You're sure you're okay to fly?"

"Gas up the plane."

On his way to the bathroom, his bare foot hooked the electrical cord of the gooseneck lamp and pulled it off the nightstand. It fell with a thud, but fortunately the bulb didn't break. He kicked the lamp and a heap of discarded clothing out of his path and stumbled into the bathroom, cursing the cold glare when he switched on the light.

He shaved by feel in the shower, brushed his teeth bent over the sink, and decided to let his hair dry naturally rather than use the dryer. Any grooming inconveniences these shortcuts imposed were preferable to looking at himself in the mirror.

Back in the bedroom, he dressed in his flight uniform: jeans, white oxford cloth shirt, black necktie, which he knotted but left loose beneath his open collar. He stamped into his boots, then scooped his wallet, keys, and aviator sunglasses off the dresser. At the door he paused to look back at the naked woman in his bed. She, whatever her name was, was still out cold. He considered leaving a note asking her to please lock the door when she left the apartment.

Then his bloodshot eyes swept the place, and he thought, *Why bother*? There was nothing in it that a thief could possibly want.

Morning rush hour was over, so traffic was reasonably light. The one remnant of Dent's former life was red, equipped with an after-market-enhanced 530-hp engine, six-speed transmission, long tube headers, and a Corsa titanium exhaust. Punching the Corvette up to eighty whenever he had a clearing, he sped it beyond Austin's northern city limit to the private airfield.

He could have kept his airplane at a fancier FBO, one with a control tower, but there were loyalty issues to take into account. Besides, this one suited him better.

His airplane was parked on the tarmac, which formed a concrete apron in front of the corrugated metal hangar. It had seen better days. It had seen better days twenty or so years ago, when Dent had first started hanging around.

Johnsongrass grew like fringe around the base of the rusted exterior walls of the hangar. The faded orange wind sock was the only one Dent had ever seen there, and he figured it was the original that had been attached to the pole shortly after World War II.

Parked in back, out of keeping with the rundown appearance of the building and Gall's beat-up pickup truck, was a shiny black Escalade with darkly tinted windows.

Dent drove the Vette into the hangar, jerked it to a stop with a squeal of tires, cut the engine, and got out. Gall was seated behind the cluttered desk inside the hangar office, which amounted to one cloudy glass wall overlooking the hangar's interior and three other walls constructed of unpainted, untaped Sheetrock. The enclosure was ten feet square, and it was jam-packed.

Maps, diagrams, topographical charts, and yellowed newspaper clippings of aviation stories were thumbtacked to the walls, which were pocked with pinholes. Outdated flight magazines with curling covers were stacked on every available surface. Sitting atop a rusty, dented file cabinet was a stuffed raccoon that had cobwebs over its glass eyes and bald spots in its fur. The calendar above it was from 1978 and was stuck on Miss March, who wore nothing except an inviting grin and a strategically placed butterfly.

When Dent walked in, Gall stood. Planting his fists on his hips, he looked Dent up and down, then harrumphed in undisguised disapproval and rolled his unlit cigar from one side of his stained lips to the other. "You look like hammered shit."

"Got my money?"

"Yeah."

"Then spare me the insults and let's get to it."

"Not so fast, Ace. I brokered this charter and take responsibility for the safety of the three passengers."

"I can fly the goddamn plane."

Gall Hathaway was unfazed by Dent's tone. He was the only person on earth Dent would answer to because Gall's opinion was the only one that mattered to him. The old man fixed a baleful stare on him, and he backed down.

"Come on, Gall. Would I fly if I wasn't fit to?"

Gall hesitated for a few moments more, then slid a

folded check from the pocket of his oil-stained coveralls and passed it to Dent.

"A check?"

"It's good. I already called the bank."

Dent unfolded the check, saw that it was drawn on a Georgetown bank for two thousand five hundred dollars payable to him and signed. All seemed to be in order. He put the check in his wallet.

"I pumped in ninety gallons of gas," Gall said. "She'll cover the fuel bill when you get back."

Dent gave Gall a hard look.

"I trust her. She left her credit card as collateral." Gall opened the lap drawer of his metal desk. In it were stubby pencils, bent paper clips, orphaned keys, a Bic pen with a fuzzy tip, and an American Express Platinum card. "She assured me it was valid. I checked anyhow. It is. For two more years. What FBO do you want to use? She left it up to you."

Dent named the one he preferred.

"Cheaper fuel?" Gall asked.

"Fresher popcorn. Ground transportation?"

"She asked me to arrange for a limo to be waiting. That's done."

"They're waiting in the Escalade?"

"She said it was too hot and stuffy inside the hangar."

"*She* seems to be running the show."

"I guess you could say." Gall was suddenly having trouble looking him in the eye. "The old man is awful sick. Be pleasant."

"I'm always pleasant."

Gall snuffled. "Just remember, you can't look a gift horse in the mouth."

"Anything else? Mother?" Gall snarled, but Dent headed off whatever he was about to say with a question about coffee. "Still hot?"

"Ain't it always?"

"Tell them I need twenty minutes, then we'll take off. Anything they need to do in the meantime, go to the bathroom, whatever—"

"I know the drill." Gall mumbled something Dent didn't catch, which was probably just as well, then he added, "Before they see you, squirt some of that stuff over your eyeballs. They look like road maps."

Dent went into the hangar proper and sat down at a table where the computer stayed linked to his favorite weather Web site. He made a note of the storms forecast for that evening, but the skies were presently clear.

He had made the flight to Houston Hobby many times. Nevertheless, he reviewed the information he needed for the flight portion of the trip as well as for the airport. He had Garmin in the cockpit. The Airport Facilities Directory for each state, plus FBO data, were downloaded onto his iPad, which he could access from the cockpit. But as a safety precaution he always printed out and carried with him information pertaining to takeoff, the destination airport, and an alternate airport. Lastly, he called ATC and filed a flight plan.

Outside, he went through the preflight check of his airplane, even knowing that Gall already had. He got under the wings to drain gasoline from five different locations, checking the glass tube to be sure no water had collected in the fuel tanks. It was a time-consuming chore, but he'd known a guy who'd failed to do it. He'd crashed and died.

Satisfied that his plane was ready, he signaled Gall with

a thumbs-up. "Good to go if they are." He went into the restroom, where he splashed cold water on his face and washed down three aspirin tablets with the dregs of his coffee, which hadn't been as hot as Gall had boasted but was double the recommended strength. And, as advised, he put in eye drops guaranteed to get the red out. All the same, he put on his sunglasses.

When he emerged from the building, his three passengers were waiting for him on the tarmac, standing shoulder to shoulder.

It was easy to pick out the patient. The man was tall and dignified, but had the yellowish-gray complexion of someone suffering from cancer and its harsh chemical treatments. He was dressed in casual slacks and a sport jacket, both of which looked several sizes too large. A baseball cap covered his bald head.

In the middle of the trio was an attractive woman, slightly younger than the man, but well into her sixties. Something about her...

Dent's footsteps faltered, then he came to a dead standstill. His eyes swung back to the man and tried to picture a healthy version of him. *Son of a bitch.* It was Howard Lyston.

There could be no mistake because beside him stood his wife, Olivia, looking as well put together as Dent remembered her. She was a pretty woman who took the time and trouble to stay that way. She was still trim, although her weight was distributed differently now, a little more around the middle. Her hair was lighter. The skin around her mouth and beneath her chin was looser than it had been nearly two decades ago. But her haughty expression was the same.

Dent stared at them for several moments, then swiveled his head around. Gall was lurking in the doorway of his office, obviously watching to see how this scene would play out. Under Dent's glare, he scuttled back into the office and closed the door. Dent had some choice words for him, but they could wait.

He came back around and regarded the Lystons with contempt. "Is this a joke? If so, I fail to see the humor."

Olivia turned her head and spoke to the younger woman standing on the other side of her. "I told you this was a dreadful mistake."

The younger woman took two steps toward him. "It's no joke, Mr. Carter. We need to get to Houston."

"There's a superhighway that runs between here and there."

"Daddy can't travel that far by car."

"*Daddy*?"

She removed the large, dark sunglasses that had been covering easily a third of her face. "I'm Bellamy. Remember?"

Yeah, of course he remembered, but this was *Bellamy*? Susan's kid sister? Like a nervous cat, always ducking out of sight whenever he came around. Skinny, gawky, braces on her teeth and pimples on her face. This was her?

Her bony frame had since been padded in the right places. Her complexion was now unblemished, her teeth straight. She was dressed casually but expensively, and there were no split ends in the dark, glossy ponytail that was draped over one shoulder. Altogether a nice package.

But you couldn't melt an ice cube on her ass.

She emanated the same snooty attitude as her parents. Directed especially toward Denton Carter. Olivia was looking at him as though he hadn't showered that morning. The old man was either too sick or too indifferent even to speak. As for Bellamy, she had an imperious manner that rubbed him the wrong way, and they'd only exchanged a few words.

He wasn't going to take their shit. Not a second time.

"There's a commercial airport southeast of downtown," he said, addressing Bellamy. "Maybe you've heard of it? Big shiny airplanes? They fly them several times a day to and from Houston."

She responded to his sarcasm with a smile that was equally caustic. "Yes, well, thank you for the suggestion. But it's an ordeal for Daddy to go through airport security and all that that entails. I was told"—she glanced beyond him toward the hangar, where Gall was playing hide-and-seek—"I was told you have an airplane for charter. I've agreed to your terms and paid in advance for your services."

Dammit, he needed that payment.

Two and a half grand was pocket change to the Lystons. To him it meant electricity, groceries, and a loan payment on his airplane. He could have kicked himself for not charging more. He could kick Gall even harder for not telling him who his paying passengers were. Setting him up to be blindsided like this, what was the old fart thinking?

For that matter, what were the Lystons thinking? Why had they selected him out of all the charter options, including private jet service, which they could well afford? He doubted they wanted to form a friendship circle.

He sure as hell wanted nothing to do with them.

But, unfortunately, what Gall had said about gift

horses applied here. If they could stand his company, he could stand theirs. Houston was a short flight.

Dent turned to Howard Lyston, forcing him to acknowledge his existence. "What time is your appointment?"

"Two o'clock."

"I'll have you there with time to spare."

"Good," Bellamy said. "If there's nothing else, could we please get under way?"

Her condescension was all too familiar, and it made Dent feel like grinding his teeth. Instead, he smiled and indicated the steps leading into the cabin of his airplane. "After you."

The flight was smooth. The only difficulty they encountered was getting Howard Lyston into and out of the airplane. Not only was he so weak he could barely muster the strength to move, it was apparent to Dent that he was in pain. When he settled into the backseat of the limousine that was waiting for them when they arrived, he seemed pathetically relieved to have gotten that far. Olivia slid in beside him, solicitous and protective, just as she'd always been.

Bellamy held back with Dent, shouting to make herself heard above the noise of airplane engines and a stiff Gulf wind. "Invariably the staff and doctors are running behind schedule, so I can't predict how long we'll be."

The opaque sunglasses were back in place, but the lower part of her face was taut and tense, which, Dent supposed, could be attributed to concern for her father. Or maybe she had the same low regard for him that her parents did. God only knew what she'd heard said about him over the past eighteen years.

"I'm on your clock, so I'll be here whenever you get back." He gave her one of his business cards. "My cell number is on there. If you give me a heads-up when you leave the hospital, I'll have the plane ready to go by the time you get here, so we can take off immediately."

"Thank you." She hesitated for a moment, then opened the deep shoulder bag she was carrying, dug out a hard-cover book, and extended it to him. "Have you read this?"

He took the book from her. "*Low Pressure*. T. J. David."

"A.k.a. Bellamy Lyston Price. Did you know I'd written a novel?"

"No." And he wanted to add, *Nor do I give a damn.*

But he withheld that because she was looking up at him, her head tilted at an inquisitive angle. He couldn't see through the lenses of her glasses into her eyes, but he got the feeling she was carefully gauging his answer. "No," he repeated. "I didn't know you'd become a writer. Price, you said?"

"My married name."

"So why T. J. whatever?"

"I picked it out of the phone book."

"How come?"

Olivia called to her through the open door of the limo. "Bellamy? Coming?"

To Dent, Bellamy said, "The book may help pass the time while you wait for us."

With that, she turned and joined her parents in the limo.

As it pulled away, Dent stared after it, cursing beneath his breath. Entering the building, he took out his cell phone and speed-dialed Gall, who answered with, "Make it fast. I'm busy."

"What the *fuck*, Gall?"

"You can afford to be particular about passengers? In this economy?"

"It should be up to me who I fly. Had I known it was them, I'd have stayed in bed."

"You're scared of them."

"Why are you trying to piss me off even more than I already am?"

"You needed the charter. Their money is good. Tell me where I'm wrong." After a silence, he grunted with satisfaction, then said, "I got work to do," and hung up.

In days past, Dent had loved hanging out at airports of any kind, be it a major hub or a county airfield with a grass landing strip used mostly by crop dusters. He liked nothing better than talking shop with other pilots.

Now, he avoided conversation with them. Nor would any want to talk to him once he introduced himself by name. He went into the pilots' lounge only long enough to grab a couple of newspapers, then made himself comfortable in an armchair in a remote spot off the main lobby. He read both sports sections. Tried to work a crossword puzzle, but didn't get very far. He idly watched a five-year-old soccer game being telecast on ESPN.

When lunchtime rolled around, he picked up a cheeseburger at the grill and took it outside to a patio eating area. He ate the burger while watching planes take off from Hobby. Each time one soared off the runway, he felt that familiar and thrilling tug deep in his gut. As much as anything, maybe even *more* than anything, he missed the adrenaline rush of jet propulsion, the thrust that was virtually sexual. It had been like a drug to him, and he'd quit cold turkey.

Eventually Houston's sultry heat drove him back into the air-conditioned building. He returned to his spot and, out of sheer boredom, opened Bellamy Price's novel and began to read.

The prologue left him numb with disbelief. After five chapters, he was angry. By the time he came to the last chapter, he was seeing red.

Chapter 2

———⟡———

It was the calm before the storm, otherwise known as dinner at Maxey's.

Sister restaurants in New York and Boston had already established its reputation, so almost as soon as Maxey's Atlanta opened fifteen months ago in the tony Buckhead area, it became a choice spot for the well-heeled and beautiful—and wannabes—to see and be seen in.

Co-owner Steven Maxey was seated at the brushed-chrome bar, reviewing the chef's specials for the evening and mentally gearing up for the onslaught that would begin as soon as the doors opened at five-thirty. When his cell phone vibrated, he glanced at the caller ID and, with a sense of dread, answered. "Hello, Mother."

"I know you're busy."

"Never mind. Is it Howard?"

"We're in Houston. We came down to see what our options are in terms of further treatment."

Their viable options were dwindling, but neither had the heart to say so out loud. "Give him my best," Steven said.

"I'll be sure to. He's napping now. Bellamy's sitting with him. I just stepped out to phone you."

He could tell she had more to say, although for several seconds a hollow silence was all that came through the line. Then, "We flew down in a private plane."

That statement, while seemingly innocuous, vibrated with a portentous note. Steven waited.

"Bellamy chartered it. Guess who the pilot was."

Steven's gut clenched. "Please tell me you're not about to say—"

"Denton Carter."

He placed his elbow on the bar, bent his head toward his hand, and rubbed his forehead with the pads of his fingers in an attempt to ward off the migraine this information would no doubt bring on.

"I tried to dissuade her," Olivia continued. "She was determined."

"For crissake, why?"

"Something about getting closure, mending the past. You know how your stepsister is."

"Ever the mediator."

"She wants everything to be ... nice."

"Was *he*?"

"Nice? No. No happier to see us than we were to see him."

"Then why did he agree to fly you?"

"That old man who owns the airfield—"

"He's still alive?"

"He arranged it, apparently without telling Dent who'd booked the charter. When he realized who we were, he was as unpleasant and arrogant as ever. There's no love lost on either side."

"Did he know about Bellamy's book?"

"According to her, no. But he might have been pretending, or being obtuse. Who knows? We have to fly back with him when we're finished here." Steven heard a sniff and realized just how upset his mother was. "I never wanted to see that boy again."

She continued to bemoan what an untenable situation it was. Steven understood how she felt. His emotions ran the gamut from dismay to alarm to anger, as they'd been doing since the day *Low Pressure* was published. His anxiety had worsened when Bellamy's identity and the biographical nature of the book became public knowledge.

William Stroud, his business partner, tapped him on the shoulder and signaled that it was time to open. The receptionist had moved into place inside the door. Waitstaff were scattered throughout the dining room, putting finishing touches on the table settings. The sommelier was standing by to answer questions about the extensive wine list.

"Mother," Steven said, cutting in, "I'm sorry, but I must go. We're about to open for dinner."

"I'm sorry, I should have realized—"

"No need to apologize. Naturally you're upset. Bellamy shouldn't have subjected you to seeing Denton Carter, not on top of everything else."

"She's apologized a thousand times, Steven. She never intended for anyone to know that her book was based on . . . fact."

"I'm sure her apologies are sincere, but what good are they? She chose to write the book. She risked her identity becoming known. But she also risked exposing the rest of us. That was very unfair."

"She realizes that now," Olivia said around a heavy sigh. "But in any case, it's done."

"Yes, it's done. But the last thing you needed was another reminder in the form of Dent Carter. Put it out of your mind and focus on Howard. Don't forget to give him my regards."

He hung up before more could be said, then moved to the end of the bar to make room for eager first arrivals. Unobtrusively, he asked one of the bartenders to pour him a vodka on the rocks. He watched the dining room fill, watched the bar become three people deep. After the initial flurry of activity, William joined him and must have discerned from the drink and his broodiness that the recent telephone call had rattled him.

"Your stepfather took a downward turn?"

Steven related the latest about Howard's condition. "That's bad, but there's more. Denton Carter has now entered the picture." William knew the history, so there was no need to explain or elaborate on why that was disturbing. "At Bellamy's invitation, no less."

Steven told him how the reunion had come about. William shook his head in disbelief. "Why on earth would she contact him now? Since leaving New York and returning to Texas, she's suspended all the publicity for her book and virtually disappeared from the public eye. Why is she stirring things up again?"

"For the life of me, I don't know."

Concerned, William asked, "What are you going to do?"

"What I've been doing most all my life." Steven tossed back the remainder of his drink. "Damage control."

Bellamy guessed Dent had been watching for the limo from inside the building. Even before the car glided to a halt, he was there, beating the chauffeur to open the rear door. As soon as she alighted, he brandished the copy of *Low Pressure* in her face.

"I want to know why in the name of God you wrote this damn thing."

She wondered if his bristling anger was a good sign, or bad. Good, she supposed, because it indicated that he'd told her the truth when he claimed not to know anything about her novel, which made it unlikely that he was the one who'd sent her a rat wrapped in silver tissue paper.

But he was irate, and she needed to defuse him before attention was drawn to them and someone recognized her. She'd returned to Texas to get out of the spotlight. So far she'd succeeded.

She walked around him and entered the terminal. "I apologize for not calling you as I left the hospital. It slipped my mind." Noticing the tables near the snack bar, she said, "I'll wait over there while you do whatever it is you have to do before takeoff. Let me know when you're ready."

She started in that direction, but this time he sidestepped, blocking her path. "Don't brush me off. I want to know why you wrote this."

She glanced around self-consciously. "Will you please lower your voice?"

"To make money? Daddy's fortune isn't enough for you? Or did your husband blow through your inheritance?"

"I'm not going to talk to you about this, not in a public place, and not with you yelling in my face."

"I want to know—"

"Now isn't the time, Dent."

Maybe it was her raised voice and sharp tone, or perhaps the use of his name, or he could have seen the tears start in her eyes and that made him realize that she was upset and had returned alone.

He backed away, shot a glance out the window toward the departing limo, then came back to her and stated the obvious. "Your parents aren't with you."

"Daddy was checked into the hospital. Olivia stayed with him." He said nothing to that and she took advantage of his momentary calm. "I'll be waiting over there."

She went around him and didn't even look back to see if he was following. Angry as he was, he might take off without her, leaving her stranded and forced to return to Austin on a commercial flight. That would be all right, too. In fact, it would probably be best.

As Olivia had remarked several times throughout the day, reconnecting with him after all these years had been a mistake. Bellamy had thought it necessary to her peace of mind, but now she regretted not having taken Olivia's advice to leave well enough alone. She'd made another enemy.

At the dispensing machines, she filled a paper cup with ice and Diet Coke and sat down at one of the tables, relieved that no one else was currently in the snack bar area. The day had been emotionally draining. Her nerves and emotions were raw. She needed a few moments of quiet in order to reinforce herself before the inevitable clash with Dent.

Through the large windows, she watched as he went through his preflight check with her book tucked under his arm. She knew nothing about airplanes, but his was white with blue trim and had two engines, one on each wing. He oversaw the fueling of it and checked something on the left wing. He squatted down to inspect the tires and landing gear. Standing, he dusted off his hands and walked around the wing to the tail section. All his motions were practiced and efficient.

How old was he now? Thirty-six? Thirty-seven?

Two years older than Susan would have been.

Bellamy had been curious to see how the years had treated him, if he had developed a paunch, if he'd gone bald, if he was letting himself settle comfortably into middle age. But he bore no drastic signs of aging.

His light brown hair was still thick and unruly. At the corners of his eyes were squint lines from staring into the sun through cockpit windshields for the better part of his life. Maturity—and no doubt years of hard living and late hours—had made his face thinner and more angular. But he was no less attractive now than he'd been at eighteen, when he'd made her tongue-tied and self-conscious of her acne and braces.

Check complete, he gave the ground crew a thumbs-up, then, in a long and purposeful stride, walked toward the building. A gust of wind accompanied him inside, causing the young women behind the reception counter to stop what they were doing and watch appreciatively as he impatiently jerked his necktie back into place and smoothed it down over a torso that was still trim and flat. He removed his sunglasses, carelessly raked his fingers through his windblown hair, then made his way over to where Bellamy was waiting.

He got himself a cup of coffee and brought it with him to the table. As he sat down across from her, he dropped the book onto the table. It had the heft of an anvil when it landed.

For a momentous amount of time, he just stared at her, still seething. His gray-green eyes she remembered. Flecked with brown spots, they were the color of moss. Those qualities were familiar. The anger in them was new.

At last, he said, "He's bad off?"

"Daddy? Very. His oncologist prescribed another round of chemotherapy, but it's so debilitating he and Olivia are wondering if it's worth it. Either way, the doctor thought he was too weak to return home tonight."

"More chemo might help."

"No," she said softly. "It won't. With or without it, he's going to die soon."

He looked away and shifted uneasily in his chair. "I'm sorry."

She took a sip of her Coke and waited until he was looking at her again before saying, "Don't say things you don't mean."

He ran his hand over his mouth and down his chin. "Gloves off? Okay. It's a shame anybody has to go out like that, but your daddy never did me any favors."

"And vice versa."

"What did I ever do to him? Oh, wait. If I need to know, I can just read your book. It will enlighten me." He gave the book an angry poke.

"If you read it through—"

"I read enough."

"—you know that the character patterned after you—"

"Patterned after? You did all but use my name."

"—comes across as a victim, too."

"Bullshit."

He'd been leaning across the table toward her, but after that succinct statement, he flung himself against the back of his chair and stretched out his legs, not even apologizing when his foot bumped hers beneath the table.

"Why'd you dredge it up?"

"Why do you care?" she fired back.

"You have to ask?"

"It happened a long time ago, Dent. It impacted your life for what, a few weeks? A couple of months? You moved on, went on with your life."

He made a scoffing sound.

"Do you have a family?"

"No."

"You never married?"

"No."

"You own your own airplane."

"Working toward owning it."

"You're obviously still close with Mr. Hathaway."

"Yeah. Until today. Gall is currently every name on my shit list."

"He didn't tell you it was us?"

"No. Not even when he gave me your check."

"The name Bellamy Price didn't mean anything to you?"

"I only looked to see if the amount was right."

"I thought you might have seen me on TV."

"You've been on TV?"

She gave a small nod.

"Talking about that?" He hitched his chin toward the book on the table.

Again, she answered with a nod.

"Great. That's just great." He raised the cup of coffee to his mouth, but set it back on the table without drinking from it and pushed it aside so hard that coffee sloshed out.

"For several weeks, there was a lot of media coverage." In a murmur, she added, "I don't know how you missed it."

"Just lucky, I guess."

Nothing was said for a full minute. People drifting through the lobby for one reason or another moved on without coming into the snack area, as though sensing the hostility between them and affording them privacy to sort it out. Each time Bellamy glanced toward the women working the counter, she caught them watching her and Dent with ill-concealed curiosity.

It was he who finally broke the charged silence. "So why'd you book a charter with me? You could have got your daddy down here some other way. Private jet. You didn't need me and my lowly little Cessna."

"I wanted to see how you'd fared. I hadn't heard anything about you since the airline...thing."

"Ah! So you know about that?"

"It made news."

"I know," he said drily. "You gonna write a book about that, too?"

She gave him a look.

"I can supply you with lots of material, A.k.a. Let's see." He stroked his chin thoughtfully. "How about the time the young widow chartered me to fly her to Nantucket? Long way from here. By the time we got to the Massachusetts coast, it was a dark and stormy night. Nobody got murdered, but the lady tried her best to fuck me to death."

Bellamy flinched at the word, but refused to let him rile her, which she knew was his intention. Keeping her features schooled, and with deliberate patience, she said,

"I hired you because I wanted to learn if you'd read my book and, if you had, what your reaction to it was."

"Well, now you know. Cost you two-point-five grand plus fuel costs to find out. Was it worth it?"

"Yes."

"Good. I want my passengers to feel like they get their money's worth. The widow sure as hell did." He gave her a goading grin, which she ignored. Then his grin reversed itself and he swore under his breath. "If Gall thinks he's getting his broker's fee off this charter, he's sadly mistaken."

"Maybe he didn't tell you because—"

"Because he knew I'd say no."

"Because he thought it would be good for you to see us."

"How could it possibly have been good for me?"

"It gave us all an opportunity to mend fences."

"Mend fences."

"Yes. To put it behind us. To forget—"

"*Forget*?" He leaned forward again, this time with such angry impetus he made the table rock. "That's what I've been doing for the past eighteen years. At least it's what I've been *trying* to do. You said it happened a long time ago. Well, not long enough, lady. Not long enough for me to put it behind me. To forget it. To have everybody else forget it. And now you, *you* come along and write your freaking book about that Memorial Day—"

"Which was published as fiction. I never intended—"

"—and the whole ugly business is out there again for everybody in the world to gnaw on. If you wanted to write a story, fine. Why didn't you make one up?" He thumped his fist on the book. "Why did you have to write this story?"

She resented having to account to him and let him know it by matching his anger. "Because I want to forget it, too."

He gave a bark of humorless laughter. "Funny way of forgetting, writing it all down."

"I was twelve years old when it happened. It had a dramatic effect on me. I overcame a lot of it, but I needed to expunge it."

"Expunge?" He raised a brow. "That's a five-dollar word. Did you use it in your book?"

"I needed to write it all down so it would become something tangible, something I could then wad up and throw away."

"Now you're talking. Be my guest." He gave the book another shove closer to her. "You can start with this copy. Pitch it in the nearest trash can." He stood up and turned toward the door, saying over his shoulder, "Let's go."

"Do you see ... ? Dent? Are we okay?"

Those were the first words his passenger had uttered since she'd climbed aboard. In case she needed to talk to him during the flight, he'd instructed her on the use of the headset. "All you gotta do is plug this into here, and this into here." He demonstrated with the cords attached to the headset. "Put the mike near your mouth, like this." He moved it to where it was almost touching her lower lip. "And talk. Got it?"

She nodded, but he figured it didn't matter if she understood or not; she wouldn't have anything to say. Which was fine with him.

But now, about twenty minutes into their forty-minute flight, they had encountered some light turbulence and she was speaking to him in an anxious voice. He turned so he could see into the cabin. She was gripping the arms of her seat and staring anxiously out the window. Heat lightning was showing up on the western horizon, revealing a bank of thunderclouds. They were flying parallel to them, but she was on edge.

He was well aware of the weather system, knew from consulting the radar where it was and the direction and speed at which it was moving. He had filed his flight plan accordingly. "Nothing to worry about," he said into his mike. "Those storms are miles away and won't amount to much anyway."

"I just thought... maybe we could take another route?"

"I filed a flight plan."

"I know but... Couldn't we fly farther away from the storms?"

"We could. But I'd rather dodge a thunderstorm than have an MD80 that doesn't know I'm there fly up my ass." He turned around so she could see his face instead of the back of his head. "But that's just me."

She gave him a drop-dead look, yanked the cords from the outlets on the wall near her chair, and removed her headset. He focused his attention on the job at hand, but when the turbulence became even rougher, he looked back to check on her. Her eyes were closed and her lips were moving. She was either praying or chanting. Or maybe cursing him.

Gall, whom he'd notified of his approach, had turned on the runway lights. He set the airplane down with the ease of long practice and skill and taxied toward the hangar, where he could see Gall silhouetted in the open maw of the building.

He brought the airplane to a stop and cut the engines.

Gall came out to put chocks on the wheels. Dent squeezed himself out of the cockpit and into the cabin, opened the door, then climbed out first and turned to help Bellamy navigate the steps. She ignored the hand he extended.

Which piqued him. He reached for her hand and slapped a sales receipt into it. "You owe me for the gas I got in Houston."

"Mr. Hathaway has my credit card. Excuse me. I need the restroom."

She hurried into the building.

Gall rounded the wing and glanced into the empty cabin. "Where are her folks?"

"They stayed in Houston."

"Doesn't surprise me. The old man looked like he was on his last leg. Otherwise, how'd it go?"

"Don't make nice with me, Gall. I'm mad as hell at you."

"You're richer tonight than—"

"I want a straight answer. Did you know about her book?"

"Book?"

"A book. You know, like people read."

"Does it have pictures?"

"No."

"Then I didn't know about it."

Dent searched Gall's eyes, which were rheumy but free of deceit. "I'll kill you later. Right now, I'm ready to put up my airplane and call it a day."

While he was going about it, Bellamy and Gall conducted their business in the hangar office. But he kept an eye on them, and, as she came out of the hangar, he placed himself directly in her path.

Stiffly, she said, "Thank you."

He wasn't about to let her getaway be that easy. "I may not use words like 'expunge,' but I know how to fly. I'm a good pilot. You had no reason to be scared."

Not quite meeting his gaze, she said, "I wasn't afraid of the flying."

Chapter 3

⸺◆⸺

Together Dent and Gall got the airplane into the hangar. Dent climbed back in to retrieve his sunglasses and iPad, and spotted the copy of *Low Pressure* lying in the seat Bellamy had occupied. "Son of a bitch." He grabbed the book and, as soon as he cleared the door of his airplane, made a beeline for his Vette.

Gall turned away from the noisily humming refrigerator, a six-pack of Bud in his hand. "I thought we'd crack a couple of—Where are you going?"

"After her."

"What do you mean, after her?"

Dent got into the driver's seat and started the engine, but when he would have pulled the door closed, Gall was there, the six-pack in one hand, his other braced against the open car door. "Don't go borrowing trouble, Ace."

"Oh that's funny. You're the one who set me up with them."

"I was wrong."

"You think?" He gave the door a tug. "Let go."

"Why're you going after her?"

"She left her book behind. I'm going to return it."

He yanked hard on the door and Gall released it. "You should leave it alone."

Dent didn't acknowledge the warning. He shoved the Vette into first gear and peeled out of the hangar. He knew the road well, which was fortunate, because while he drove with one hand, he used his other to wrestle his wallet from his back pocket, fish the check from it, and, after reading the address, accessed a GPS app on his iPad. In a matter of minutes he had a map to her place.

Georgetown, not quite thirty miles north of Austin, was known for its Victorian-era architecture. Its town square and tree-lined residential streets boasted structures with gingerbread trim.

Bellamy lived in one such house. It sat in a grove of pecan trees and had a deep veranda that ran the width of the house. Dent parked at the curb and, taking the book with him, followed a flower-bordered path to the steps leading up to the porch. He took them two at a time and reached past a potted Boston fern to ring the doorbell.

Then he saw that the front door stood ajar. He knocked. "Hello?" He heard a noise, but it wasn't an acknowledgment. "Hello? Bellamy?" As fast as he'd been driving, she couldn't have been that far ahead of him. "Hello?"

She appeared in the wedge between the door frame and the door, and it looked to him like she was depending on it for support. Her eyes were wide and watery, and her face was pale, bringing into stark contrast a sprinkling of freckles across her nose and cheeks that he hadn't noticed before.

She licked her lips. "What are you doing here?"

"Are you okay?"

She gave an affirmative nod, but he didn't believe her.

"You look all..." He gestured toward her face. "Was it the flight? Did it mess you up that bad?"

"No."

"Then what's the matter?"

"Nothing."

He hesitated, wondering why he didn't just hand her the book and tell her to shove it where the sun don't shine, as he'd come here to do, then turn and walk away. For good. Forever and ever, amen.

He had a strong premonition that if he stayed for one second longer, he would live to regret it. But despite the impulse to get the hell out of there and away from her and all things Lyston, he gave the door a gentle push, which she resisted. He pushed harder until she let go and the door swung wide.

"What the hell?" he exclaimed.

The central hallway behind her looked like it had been the site of a ticker-tape parade. The glossy hardwood floor was littered with scraps of paper. Brushing past her, he went in, bent down, and picked up one of the larger pieces. It was the corner of a page; T. J. David was printed on it, along with a page number.

"You found it like this when you got home?"

"I was just a few minutes ahead of you," she replied. "This is as far as I got."

Dent's first thought was that the intruder might still be inside the house. "Alarm system?"

"The house doesn't have one. I only moved in a couple of weeks ago." She gestured toward sealed boxes stacked against the wall. "I haven't even finished unpacking."

"Your husband isn't here?"

The question seemed to confuse her at first, then she stammered, "No. I mean...I don't...I'm divorced."

Huh. He tucked that away for future consideration. "Call nine-one-one. I'll take a look around."

"Dent—"

"I'll be okay."

He set the copy of her novel on the console table, then continued down the central hallway past a dining room and a living room, which opened off of it on opposite sides. The hall led him to the back of the house, where he found the kitchen and utility room. The door to the yard was standing open. The locking mechanism dangled from a neat round hole in the door.

A striped cat curiously peered around the jamb. Upon seeing Dent, it skedaddled. Being careful not to touch anything, he stepped out onto a concrete stoop, where a bag of potting soil and a stack of terra-cotta flowerpots stood against the exterior wall of the house. One of the pots had been broken. Pieces of it lay on the steps leading down to the ground. The fenced yard was empty.

He figured the house-breaker was no longer a threat, but he wanted to check the upstairs anyway. He retraced his steps through the kitchen and back into the wide hallway. Bellamy was standing where he'd left her, cell phone in hand.

"I think he came and went through the utility room door. I'm gonna check upstairs."

He climbed them quickly. The first door on his left opened into a spare bedroom, which she obviously planned on using as an office. The computer setup on the trestle table appeared to have been left undisturbed, but, as in the entryway below, pages of her book had been made into confetti and strewn everywhere. He checked the closet, but there was nothing in it except boxes packed with basic office supplies.

Midway down the hall, a quaint pair of doors with glass panes stood open. He walked through them into Bellamy's bedroom. Here, he drew up short. The room had been vandalized, but not with confetti.

Hastily he checked the closet, where he found clothes and shoes, several unpacked boxes, and a lingering floral scent. The bathroom was likewise empty except for the cream-colored fixtures, fluffy towels, and feminine accoutrements on the dressing table.

He returned to the bedroom's double doors and called down to her. "Coast is clear, but you'd better come up."

Moments later she joined him, doing exactly as he'd done when he walked in. She stopped dead in her tracks and stared.

"I take it that's not part of the decor."

"No," she said huskily.

Scrawled in red paint on the wall was: *You'll be sorry.*

The paint had run, leaving rivulets at the bottom of each letter that looked like dripping blood. In lieu of a paintbrush, a pair of her underwear had been used to write the letters.

The significance of that escaped neither of them.

Dent motioned toward the paint-soaked wad of silk lying on the carpet. "Yours?" When she nodded, he said, "Sick bastard. Police on their way?"

She roused herself, pulled her gaze away from the message on the wall, and looked up at him. "I didn't call them."

"Why the hell not?"

"Because I don't want a big deal made of this."

He thought surely he had heard her wrong, and his expression must have conveyed that.

"It was a prank," she said. "When I moved in, a neighbor warned of things like this happening in the area. There's been a rash of it. Teenagers with not enough to do. Maybe an initiation of some kind. They scatter trash across lawns. Knock over mailboxes. I'm told they hit a whole block one night last month."

He looked at the vandalized wall, the garment on the floor, then came back to her. "Your panties were used to paint a threatening message on your bedroom wall, and you put that on par with scattered trash and banged-up mailboxes?"

"I'm not calling the police. Nothing was taken. Not that I can tell, anyway. It was just...just mischief."

She turned quickly and left the room. Dent went after her, clumping down the stairs on her heels. "When I got here you were shaking like a leaf. Now you're passing this off as a prank?"

"I'm certain that's all it was."

"I think you do."

"It's none of your business. What are you doing here, anyway?" She dragged a chair from the kitchen dining table into the utility room and pushed it against the door to keep it closed. "The neighbor's cat comes to visit uninvited."

When she turned back, Dent was there, blocking her. "I've a good mind to call the police myself."

"Don't you dare. The media would get wind of it, and then I'd have that to deal with, too."

"*Too*? In addition to what?"

"Nothing. Just…just please let it go. I'm waiting for the call that my father has died. I can't take on any more right now. Can't you understand that?"

He understood that the woman was on the verge of a meltdown. Her eyes were stark with something. Fear? Her voice was unsteady, like it was about to crack. She was holding on to the ledge by her fingernails, but she was holding on, and he had to give her credit for that.

He softened his approach. "Look, thanks to your family, I'm no fan of cops, either. But I still think you should report this."

"They'll show up with lights flashing."

"Probably."

"No thank you. I could do without the circus. I'm not calling them."

"Okay, then a neighbor."

"What for?"

"Ask if you can crash on their sofa."

"Don't be ridiculous."

"A friend? Someone who could come—"

"No."

"Then call the police."

"You want to call them, you call. You can deal with them. I won't be here." She pushed him aside and made her way back into the hall. "I'll be at my parents' house."

"That idea gets my vote. You'd be crazy to stay here alone. But wait an hour. Let the police come—"

"No. I want to make the drive before the storm gets here."

"It's not coming here."

She glanced toward the window. "It may." She leaned down to retrieve her shoulder bag from the floor, where she'd apparently dropped it when she came in. She hauled the strap onto her shoulder. "You still haven't told me why you followed me home."

"To return your lousy book." He pointed toward the console table where he'd left it. Then he moved his boot through a heap of torn pages. "Seems somebody else likes it even less than I do."

She was about to speak, but faltered and looked away from him, then turned abruptly and opened the front door.

Dent reached beyond her shoulder and pushed the door shut. She came around angrily, but he was the first to speak. "This *is* about the book. Right?"

She didn't say anything, but she didn't have to. Her expression said it all.

"You're good and truly spooked, aren't you?"

"I—"

"Because you know as well as I do that this wasn't a teenager's prank."

"I know nothing of the kind."

"What else would you have to be sorry for? You wrote that book, and it made somebody real unhappy."

"I never said—"

"Unhappy enough to threaten you, and you're taking that threat seriously. I know that because you're scared. Don't deny it. I can tell. So what's going on? What gives?"

"What do you care?"

"Call me a nice guy."

"But you're not!"

There was no arguing that. For seconds they glared at each other, then her head dropped forward and she kept it bowed for several moments. When she raised it, she brushed back a strand of hair that had shaken loose from her ponytail.

"Dent, I've had a perfectly rotten day. First I had to encounter you, when you were so obviously hostile and rejecting of any olive branch. I had to stand by, uselessly, in that cancer ward and watch my dad, whom I love more than anyone in the world, suffer untold pain and indignity.

"I didn't want to leave him, but he invented a business matter that needs to be dealt with tomorrow morning as soon as the offices open. But the real reason he sent me back was to spare me having to see him like that.

"Then, during the flight home, I had to talk myself out of having a full-blown panic attack, which was not only terrifying, but humiliating because you were there to see it. I got home to find my house wrecked, and then you showed up and started giving me grief. I've had it. I'm leaving. You can stay, or leave, or go to hell. It makes no difference to me."

On her way out she flicked a master switch that turned off every light in the house, leaving Dent in the dark.

Ray Strickland was a man better avoided, and he worked at making himself appear so.

He had come by his mean countenance naturally, but he had developed mannerisms to match his appearance. A thick, low brow formed a perpetual scowl that kept his deeply set eyes in shadow. His wide shoulders and muscled arms would have made him look top-heavy if his legs weren't equally stout.

He didn't shave his head, but buzzed it closely with an electric razor every few days. An iron cross, like the German war medal, was tattooed on his nape. Other tats decorated his arms and chest. He was especially proud of the snake, bared fangs dripping venom, that coiled around his left arm from shoulder to wrist.

The serpent hid the scars.

Attached to his belt was a leather scabbard that held a knife he kept honed and ready in case somebody didn't heed the advertising and decided to mess with him.

He gave off an aura of Leave Me the Hell Alone. Most anyone who crossed paths with him was happy to oblige. Tonight he was in a particularly fractious mood.

The bar where he had stopped for refreshment was crowded and hot, the band lousy and loud. Every new arrival that came through the opaque-glass entrance increased Ray's irritation. They encroached on his space and sucked up his air. He'd left his leather vest open for ventilation, but he still felt constricted.

He signaled the waitress for another shot of straight tequila. She was wearing a black cowboy hat with a feather band, a black leather bra, and low-rise jeans. Her navel was pierced with a silver ring, and attached to it was a chain that dangled right down to *there*.

Ray let her see that he noticed. "I like that chain."

"Thanks," she said, with a silent *Drop dead* added. After pouring his drink, she turned her back to him and sashayed to the other end of the bar, giving him an eyeful of a heart-shaped ass.

The rejection made him mad as hell. Not that he wasn't used to it. Women just didn't seem to take to him, not unless he plied them with enough cheap liquor to urge on a little friendliness and cooperation. He never inspired their lust.

He just didn't have the gift. Not like his big brother, Allen. Now there was a ladies' man for you. All Allen had to do was crook his finger at a female and she'd come running. In no time flat, Allen could sweet-talk his way past her bra and into her panties. He'd loved women and they'd loved him back.

Only one had ever turned Allen down.

Susan Lyston.

After that bitch, there had been no more women for Allen. No more *nothing*.

Ray reached for his shot glass and slammed back the throat-searing tequila.

If it hadn't been for Susan Lyston, Allen would be with him tonight, chasing tail, getting drunk, having fun like they used to. 'Course they'd been a pair of wild and crazy kids back then, but Ray had no reason to think they'd be any less fun-loving now than they had been eighteen years ago. But he would never know, would he? No. Because of Susan Lyston.

Now her little sister was continuing in that same destructive vein. She'd written a book about it, for crissake! Oh, she'd changed the names, even her own. She'd set the story in a fictitious city. But those thin disguises weren't for shit if you knew the true story. Her characters were easy to match up to the real people.

It made Ray burn every time he thought of how she'd described the character representing Allen. She'd called him "smarmy." Ray wasn't sure what that meant, but it didn't sound good. His big brother was being ridiculed and reviled all over again in the pages of that goddamn book. And to make certain of it, Susan's sister, who was all grown up now and ought to know better, was on TV talking it up, profiting off of Allen and the event that had ruined his life.

No way in hell was that right. Ray wasn't going to let her get away with it.

Soon as he heard she was back in Austin, he'd started a campaign to make her rosy life a little less so. He'd wanted her worried, nervous, afraid, like Allen had been when he was arrested. Like Ray had been when Allen was arrested.

Then, after having his fun with her, he was going to make her regret she'd ever written a single word about his brother.

Today, he'd decided to send her a warning. Even though he hated making her more money off her book, he'd bought a copy and had enjoyed shredding the pages with his knife. At an Ace Hardware store, he'd bought a can of red paint and a brush. Getting into her house had been easy and so had finding her bedroom.

And this was the best part: At the last minute, he'd gotten the idea of using a pair of her panties instead of the paintbrush. He'd found her undies folded into neat stacks in a bureau drawer. He'd taken his time to choose the pair he liked best. They hadn't absorbed the paint so good, but they'd got the job done.

When he'd finished, he moved into the kitchen, where he settled in to wait for her to come home. The afternoon wore on. The temperature rose, as did the humidity, but he didn't turn on the AC. For some reason, it seemed important that he be uncomfortable. He didn't want it to be easy. He was doing this for Allen.

Night came on, but the temperature didn't go down along with the sun. He had sweat through his jeans, and his leather vest was sticking to his torso by the time he finally heard her car wheel into the driveway. He listened as she unlocked the front door and knew the instant she saw the mess in the hallway. Her gasp of surprise made him want to laugh out loud.

He was tempted to come charging out of the kitchen giving a rebel yell and scaring the living daylights out of her. Instead, he played it smart. He waited, straining to hear where she'd go or what she'd do before deciding what his next move would be.

Then the low growl of a car motor reached him. A door slammed. Footsteps on the walk.

Shit! Ray had grabbed the plastic bag containing the paint can and gotten the hell out of there. He hadn't even paused to close the back door. He jumped over the flowerpot he'd broken while jimmying the backdoor lock. He vaulted the fence and ran through a neighbor's backyard.

Eventually he covered the few blocks to where he'd left his pickup. He was panting and leaking sweat from every pore by the time he reached the truck, but he was more angry than scared. Somebody had interfered with his plan.

He took a risk by driving past her house, but men like him were into danger and taking risks. As it turned out, this one had paid off. He had identified the motherfucker who'd spoiled his fun.

Denton Carter.

At first Ray couldn't believe his eyes when he saw him standing under the porch light at Bellamy Price's front door. But there was no mistaking him.

"Cocky flyboy," Ray muttered now as he hunched over the bar and rolled the empty shot glass between his hands. Resentment bubbled inside him. Dent Carter was one of those lucky sons o' bitches who could be dragged through shit but somehow always came up smelling like roses. Ray knew he'd suffered some hard knocks over the years. He'd gotten fired from an airline. Something about a near crash.

But, true to form, Dent had rebounded. Parked at the curb in front of Bellamy's house was a sexy red Corvette, and Ray had seen for himself Dent being welcomed inside. Why wouldn't he be, when, in her book, she'd all but labeled his character a superstud?

The whole thing made Ray spitting mad.

He signaled the waitress and pulled a wad of bills from his front pocket. Warmed up by the sight of cash, she came right over to him, bringing the bottle of Patron with her.

"Another for you, handsome?"

Oh, now he was handsome? Money sure had a way of changing people's minds. He wondered how far it would get him with her. How friendly would she be if he reached out and yanked her chain? Literally. She'd probably scream like bloody hell.

"Make it a double."

She reached for a second shot glass and filled it. "What are you celebrating?"

"I'm holding a private wake."

"Oh, sorry. Who died?"

"Nobody." He raised his glass to her. "Yet."

Chapter 4

◆─◆─◆

Dent fumbled for his ringing cell phone, squinted at the caller ID, and answered with a snarl. "Are you kidding me? Two mornings in a row?"

"Get your ass out here."

Gall hung up without saying anything more, which wasn't like him. He lived to argue. He reveled in arguing with Dent. Something was up.

Dent threw off the sheet and repeated the procedure of the day before, except that he didn't shave and substituted a chambray cowboy shirt for the white shirt and necktie. He was out the door within five minutes.

In under twenty he got to the airfield, where Gall was inside the hangar, standing beside Dent's airplane. His hands were planted on his hips and the soggy cigar was getting a workout between chomping teeth.

As Dent walked toward him, Gall motioned with disgust toward the aircraft, but Dent had seen the damage the moment he got out of his car. The cockpit windshield had been cracked. There were dents as large as softballs in the fuselage. The tires had been punctured. A blade on one of the propellers had been bent. The worst of it were the gashes cut into the top of each wing, like they'd been taken to with a giant can opener.

He made a slow circuit of the aircraft, surveying the vicious handiwork, his outrage mounting. When he rejoined Gall he had to unclench his jaw to ask, "Mechanical?"

"I haven't checked anything yet. Thought I ought to leave it as it is till the insurance man sees it. Called the sheriff's office, too. They're sending somebody out. The wings alone, or the propeller by itself, either one would ground you for a spell. But both..."

Dent looked at him.

He shrugged, saying ruefully, "A month, at least. Probably longer."

Dent swore elaborately. To him this wasn't just an airplane. Or just his livelihood. This was his *life*. If he'd been attacked with a hammer and sharp blade he couldn't have felt it any more personally. "How'd he get in?"

"Used bolt cutters on the padlock. I've been meaning to replace it with one of the newer kind, but, you know... never got around to it."

"Don't blame yourself, Gall. You didn't do this. If I ever get my hands on the person or persons who did—"

"Promise to save me a piece of the son of a bitch." He tossed his cigar into the fifty-gallon oil drum that served as a trash can. "Here comes Johnny Law."

The next hour and a half were spent with the investigating deputy, who seemed capable enough, but Dent could tell this crime wasn't going to get top priority when it came to detective work. The deputy's questioning implied that the vandalism was retaliation for which Dent was responsible.

"You have any unpaid debts, Mr. Carter?"

"No."

"I'm not talking MasterCard. A bookie, maybe? Loan—"

"No."

"Any enemies? Been in any arguments lately? Got on anybody's fighting side? Know of any grudges against you?"

"No."

He looked Dent up and down as though unconvinced of that, but, discouraged by Dent's scowl, he didn't press it. He began directing questions to Gall while Dent joined the insurance adjuster, who'd arrived shortly after the deputy.

Stiff, starched, and buttoned up, the kind of corporate team player Dent despised, the adjuster asked a lot of questions, most of which Dent thought were unnecessary or stupid. He made a lot of notes, took a lot of pictures, and filled out a lot of forms, which he snapped into his briefcase with annoying efficiency but not one word of commiseration.

"They'll cheat me," Dent said to Gall as the guy drove away. "You watch."

"Well, I'll hike up the cost of parts and repairs, so it'll even out."

Dent smiled grimly, grateful that he had at least one ally who understood how deeply this affected him, and not only financially. He didn't have a wife or kids, not even a pet. The airplane was his baby, the love of his life.

"Go over her with a fine-toothed comb. I'll check back later for the prognosis."

He headed for his car but Gall stopped him. "Hold your horses. Come into the office for a minute."

"What for?"

"You haven't had your coffee yet."

"How can you tell?"

Gall just snorted and ambled toward the cubicle, motioning with his arm for Dent to follow. He was eager to get away but knew that Gall felt bad about the flimsy padlock. He could spare him a few minutes.

He filled a chipped and stained mug with the industrial-strength brew, carried it into the office, and took a seat in the chair facing the desk, being mindful of its unreliable back leg.

"I know what you told the deputy," Gall said. "Now tell me if you have any idea who did this." He was avoiding eye contact and tugging on his long earlobe, a sure sign that he was leaving something left unsaid.

"What's on your mind?"

Gall unwrapped a fresh cigar and anchored it in the corner of his mouth. "Before I left my house this morning, I saw her on TV. Early, early show. They said it was a prerecorded interview."

Dent didn't say anything.

"The book she wrote ... *Low Pressure*?"

"Yeah."

The older man sighed heavily. "Yeah."

Dent sipped his coffee.

Gall shifted his cigar around, then said, "I didn't know anything about it, or I never would've scheduled that charter. You know that, don't you?"

"Don't beat yourself up, Gall. I would have found out about the book sooner or later. In fact she said she didn't know how I'd missed hearing about it."

"Nice of you to let me off the hook," the older man

said, "but I could kick myself into next month for not hanging up on her when she called me wanting to book a flight with you." After a pause, he asked, "You read the damn thing?"

"Most of it. Skimmed the rest."

"Does it tell the whole story?"

"Pretty close. The ending is ambiguous." Dent paused a beat. "Just like the true story."

"It wasn't ambiguous to my way of thinking," Gall grumbled.

"You know what I mean."

Gall nodded, his expression grim. "No wonder you looked ready to kill her when you tore out of here last night. Did you catch her?"

"I did, but it didn't go quite as planned." Dent described what he'd found at Bellamy's house. "The bastard had used a pair of her underwear to paint the words on the wall."

"Jesus." Gall pushed the fingers of both hands through his sparse hair. "You think that was an intentional reference?"

Dent frowned his answer and caught the look Gall darted toward his damaged airplane. "Right. Her house. My plane. Same night. It would be a real stretch to think that's a coincidence." He set his empty coffee cup on the desk and stood up.

"Where are you going?"

"To talk to her about this."

"Dent—"

"I know what you're going to say. Save your breath."

"I told you eighteen years ago to stay away from that Lyston girl. You didn't listen."

"This is a different Lyston girl."

"Who's apparently just as poisonous as her big sister."

"That's what I'm going to talk to her about."

Bellamy's heart leaped when her cell phone rang. She'd kept it within reach all night as well as this morning, dreading a call from Olivia but at the same time eager to get an update. "Hello?"

"Where are you?"

"Who is this?"

He didn't deign to respond.

"What do you want, Dent?"

"My airplane came under attack last night."

"What?"

"Where are you?"

"Daddy's office."

"I'll be there in under half an hour. I'm coming in, and I'm coming up, and don't even think about denying me entrance." He disconnected.

Lyston Electronics was housed in a glassy seven-story building that was one of a group of contemporary buildings comprising a business park off the MoPac. Their communications products were high-tech and highly coveted, so everyone who worked there wore an identification badge, and security was tight.

Bellamy called the guard in the lobby and made arrangements for Dent to be admitted. "Please direct him to my father's office."

Twenty minutes later he was ushered in by her father's receptionist, whom Bellamy dismissed with a nod of thanks. She remained seated behind the desk while Dent gave the large room a leisurely survey, his gaze stopping on the mounted elk head and on a glass cabinet in which her father's collection of priceless jade carvings was displayed. He took particular notice of the family portrait that dominated one paneled wall. He walked over to it and studied it at length.

The photograph had been taken during the last Christmas season that the family was intact. Posed in front of an enormous twinkling Christmas tree was Howard, looking every inch the proud patriarch. Olivia, gorgeous in burgundy velvet and canary diamonds, had her arm linked with his. Steven, a recalcitrant fourteen-year-old, had his hands jammed into the pockets of his gray flannel slacks. Susan was sitting on the Oriental rug in front of the others, her full skirt spread around her. She was smiling broadly, confident of her beauty and allure. Bellamy was beside her, unsmiling because of her braces, virtually hiding behind the black Scottish terrier she was holding in her lap.

Dent turned to face her. "What happened to the dog? Scooter?"

"He lived to be thirteen."

"Your brother? What's he doing now?"

"Technically Steven is my stepbrother. I was ten, he was twelve, Susan was fourteen when Daddy and Olivia married. Anyway, Steven left Austin after he graduated from high school. Went to college back east and stayed there."

All he said in response to that was an indifferent *huh*.

"What did you mean by 'my airplane came under attack'?"

He walked toward the desk, then sat—sprawled, really—in one of the chairs facing it, seemingly unaware of or not caring how out of place he looked wearing jeans and a western shirt with the tail out when the dress code for the executive offices called for a jacket and tie.

But then he'd always had a very casual regard for rules.

He linked his fingers and rested his hands on his stomach. "What part didn't you understand?"

"Cut the crap, Dent. Tell me what happened to your airplane."

"Somebody broke into the hangar last night and beat it all to hell." He described the damage. "That's what we can tell just by looking. Gall hasn't checked out the systems yet."

"I'm so sorry."

"You're sorry, but I'm grounded. Grounded means no charters. Which means no income. To you...Hell, you probably don't even understand the concept."

His scorn smarted, because the truth of it was that she had never suffered a financial setback. In her family, money had never been a problem.

"The bank isn't going to suspend my payments while the airplane is being fixed. I'll be making payments on a plane I can't fly. That is until I run out of money completely and can't make the payments anymore, and then they'll come and get it. If they repossess my airplane, I'm grounded for good. So your being sorry isn't of much help, is it?"

"I deeply regret this. I do. I know you need the work."

He focused on her sharply, then laughed drily and turned his head away. But when he looked at her again his eyes were smoky with anger. "So. You checked me out. Discovered that I'm barely scraping by. Took pity. Was that what yesterday was? You threw poor ol' Dent a bone?"

"I told you why I contacted you."

He continued to look at her in that searing way until she relented.

"All right, yes. I'd read that the airline released you after the incident."

"Wrong. I walked after the incident."

"Pension? Benefits?"

"Had to be sacrificed when I told them to shove it." He pulled in his long legs and sat forward. "But we're not going to talk about my financial woes right now. What we're going to talk about is why somebody vandalized my airplane after breaking into your house and painting a warning on your bedroom wall."

"What makes you think the two are related?"

He gave her another hard look.

"It's strange, I'll admit."

"No, A.k.a. Let me tell you what's strange. Strange is that when I got to your house last night, you were scared silly. Petrified, in fact. But you wouldn't hear of calling the police. *That's* strange. And don't give me shit about publicity, not when you admit to going on TV and hawking your book. Gall saw a prerecorded interview this morning."

"I didn't want the publicity," she exclaimed. She told him about Rocky Van Durbin and *EyeSpy*. "Ever since he printed my name and picture in that rag, and announced that my novel was based on fact, I haven't had a moment's peace. I didn't want the notoriety."

"Oh, come now," he scoffed. "It helps sell books, doesn't it?"

"I don't deny that book sales increased dramatically once I got out there and began promoting it. I've cultivated a lot of fans."

"And one enemy."

She stood up quickly and stepped from behind the desk to move to the window. For several moments, she watched the traffic zipping past on the freeway, then turned back into the room. Dent's gaze was fixed on her as she went over to the leather sofa beneath the family Christmas portrait and sat down.

His eyes narrowed, and he said softly, "You know who the bad guy is."

"No, I don't. I swear I don't. If I did, don't you think I would have done something before now to stop it?"

"Stop *it*? Stop *what*? Something happened before last night? What? When?"

"It's not your problem, Dent."

"Like hell it's not." He got up from the chair in which he'd been sitting and dragged it over to the sofa, planting it directly in front of her then solidly planting himself in the chair. He propped his forearms on his wide-spread knees and leaned toward her. "Somebody did a bad number on my airplane. That makes it my problem."

"I hate that I involved you."

"Yeah. So do I."

She sighed. "Truly. I'm sorry. I understand why you're angry. You have every right to be. If I had it to do over—"

"But you don't. I'm involved, and by God I'm gonna find out who did the deed, and when I do, I'm not going to depend on the law of the land to punish the bastard. I'm going to see to it myself. Now, tell me what's going on."

She felt trapped by him but realized he wasn't going to let it go until she gave him more information. She also realized what a relief it would be finally to tell someone what she'd been experiencing for the past several weeks.

"It started in New York." She ran her damp palms up and down the tops of her thighs, drying the moisture on the fabric of her slacks. When she noticed Dent watching, following the motion with interest, she curled her hands into fists and folded her arms across her middle.

Her body language wasn't lost on him. "Scared of me?"

"No."

He studied her face for a moment, then asked her what had happened in New York.

In stops and starts, she told him about the gift-wrapped box that had been delivered to her apartment building. "A dead rat was horrifying. But when I saw its tail move and realized it was alive…" Even now, thinking about it caused her to shudder. Dent stood up. Hands on hips, he walked a tight circle and ran his hand across the back of his neck. "What kind of sick—" He broke off and muttered a stream of profanity.

"I didn't even pack," she said. "I fled. That's the only word for it. I grabbed my handbag and rushed out of the apartment. I stopped in the lobby of my building only long enough to ask the concierge about the delivery. He hadn't noted a company name, hadn't seen a truck. Just a 'man in a uniform and a Yankees ball cap.'

"He couldn't describe him in any more detail than that. I told him he needed to get a pest exterminator for my apartment, told him I would be away indefinitely, then hailed a taxi to the airport and left on the first flight I could get on.

"I called Dexter, my agent, from the taxi, and told him to cancel all my scheduled appearances and interviews. I had to hang up with him still sputtering reasons why I was crazy to abandon the tidal wave of publicity. I haven't granted an interview since. I've dodged the local media. Eventually reporters stopped trying to contact me." She shrugged. "They gave up. Other stories came along. I don't care. I'm just glad to be out of the limelight."

Dent processed all that. "Okay, you came scuttling back to Austin. Showing up unexpectedly like you did, your dad and stepmom must've thought it was weird. Did you tell them about the rat?"

"No. And they were surprised by my decision to leave New York for a while. Even more surprised when I rented the Georgetown house my second day back. I was a bit surprised by that myself," she added thoughtfully. "I told them I was tired of the city and needed a break. They didn't ask for a further explanation, because they know the real reason. That I want to be here and close to Daddy until he dies. But it's better for all of us that I have my own place."

She got up and went to a bar built into the opposite wall. "Water?"

"Sure."

She carried a bottle to him and uncapped one for herself as she returned to her place on the sofa. Dent sat back down in the chair. "How long ago was this?"

"Three weeks, give or take. When I left New York, I thought I was leaving behind a stalker. For lack of a better word. Someone who bore a grudge, or someone I'd unintentionally slighted."

When she paused, he leaned forward again. "But?"

She chafed her arms. "But I've often got the feeling that I'm being watched. Followed. At first I passed it off. The rat incident had put all these melodramatic scenarios in my head, made me jittery, paranoid. Then, about a week ago, someone broke into my car while I was in the supermarket. Nothing was taken, but I almost wish something had been."

"Maybe the would-be thief was interrupted. He popped the door lock but got scared and ran off."

She shook her head. "He got into the car. I sensed it immediately. The interior smelled like sweat. BO." It made her nauseous to think about it even now.

Dent frowned. "He only wanted to violate your space. Spook you."

"Which is more sinister than a theft."

He sat back in the chair and took several swallows of water. As he replaced the bottle cap he asked, "No idea who this smelly creep is?"

"No. But as you said last night, it must be someone who dislikes my book. Intensely." She looked away but was unable to hide her guilty expression.

"Oh, I get it now," he said, drawing the words out. "You thought it was *me*. That's why you booked the charter. All that bullshit about wanting to see how I had fared was just that. Bullshit. You wanted to see if I was your evil prankster."

"Dent, I—"

"Save it," he said angrily, coming out of the chair. "No wonder you fold up like a daylily every time I get too close. You're afraid I'm about to pounce." He gave her a scathing look. "Just for the record, I haven't been to New York lately. I wouldn't touch a rat, dead or alive. Most days I shower and use deodorant, and I sure as hell couldn't have been in two places at once yesterday. I was in Houston with you, not back here in your bedroom. And if my hands are ever on your panties, believe me, it won't be for painting."

She felt the heat rising in her cheeks and cursed her tendency to blush.

A long silence ensued while waves of anger radiated off him. Finally she said quietly, "Are you finished?"

"More to the point, are you?"

"What do you mean?"

"Here." He gestured to encompass the room. "Are you finished with what you came to do?"

"Yes," she replied, somewhat warily. "Why?"

He reached down and encircled her biceps with his hand, pulling her up off the sofa. "The people who'd be upset over your book is a short list. I want to go back to your house, see it in daylight, see if we can pick up a clue to identify the villain."

Bellamy put up token resistance, but actually that was what she had intended to do without him, so she let herself be propelled from the office. Once they were inside the elevator, he asked if she'd had an update from Houston and when she told him no, he said that was probably good news.

The banal conversation got them through the awkward confinement and to the ground level.

Outside, the sun was so bright it momentarily blinded her, so she didn't see Rocky Van Durbin until he was standing directly in her path.

"Hello, Ms. Price. Long time no see." He smirked at her, then gave Dent a slow once-over. Hitching his head toward him, he asked her, "Who's the cowboy?"

"Who's the asshole?"

Chapter 5

There was barely a heartbeat between Van Durbin's question and Dent's comeback.

Bellamy answered neither of them and instead demanded of Van Durbin, "What are you doing here?"

"Free country." He looked beyond them at the building's glass facade. "So this is the family business's headquarters."

"Is that a question? If so, I believe you already know the answer."

He flashed his smug grin. "What gave me away?"

Her repugnance plain, she sidestepped him. "Excuse us."

But he was persistent. "I only need a moment of your time. Pretty please? It's been a few weeks. We have a lot to catch up on."

The night she'd fled New York, an international rock star had been found dead in his Manhattan hotel suite, the apparent victim of a drug overdose. Speculation over whether it had been a suicide or a tragic accident had dominated the scandal sheets like *EyeSpy* for days.

That story had shortly been followed by a supermodel's

claim that an "unnamed member" of the British royal family had fathered her twins. The allegation was exposed as a publicity stunt intended to jump-start her flagging career, but it had kept the Van Durbins of the world busily hopping between continents to hound their prey.

Bellamy had thought that while he was occupied covering these stories, his interest in her would have waned if not altogether died. His showing up here today demonstrated that he wasn't finished with her yet.

Trying not to give away just how upsetting his reappearance was, she said coldly, "We have nothing to talk about," and stalked past him.

Dent followed more slowly. He was eyeing Van Durbin with distrust and disdain, and Bellamy hoped he wouldn't do or say anything to fan the columnist's curiosity. She was relieved when he fell into step beside her without incident.

However, Van Durbin wasn't about to give up that easily, especially not after tracking her all the way to Texas.

"There's going to be an update about you and *Low Pressure* in my column tomorrow," he said. "Despite your inexplicable shunning of publicity, the book is still topping the best-seller lists. Care to comment?"

Over her shoulder, she said, "You know my policy regarding your column. No comment."

"You sure?"

The taunting note in his voice was enough to bring her around to face him. He was tapping a pencil against his notepad with an air of self-satisfaction.

"True or false?" he said. "You returned to Texas to nurse your father through his final days."

She started to lash out at him for asking such an insensitive question. But she reconsidered, believing that if she gave him something, he might be satisfied enough to leave the subject alone.

"My father is undergoing treatment for a malignancy. That's all I'm willing to say on the subject, except for this: While he's ill, I hope you'll respect my family's privacy."

"Fine, fine," he said, making a notation on his pad.

"Now beat it." Dent hooked his hand around Bellamy's elbow and steered her toward the parking lot.

"Just one more question?"

They kept walking.

"Did they send the right guy to the pen for murdering your sister?"

Bellamy came around so quickly she stumbled against Dent.

Van Durbin leered. "I'm gonna pose that question in my column tomorrow. Care to comment?"

"Olivia?"

She disconnected her phone and turned toward Howard's hospital bed. "I'm sorry. I didn't think I was talking loud enough to wake you."

"I wasn't really asleep. Just resting."

He fought sleep because he feared he would never wake up. He wanted to escape the pain and desert the body that was cannibalizing itself, but he wasn't ready to die quite yet. Before he let go, there were troubling issues he wanted settled and disturbing questions he wanted answered.

"Who were you talking to?"

"Bellamy."

"Was she at the office?"

"She'd finished there and said to tell you that everything is in order." Taking his hand, she pressed it between hers. "I'm afraid she saw through your ruse."

"I knew she would. But I also knew she would go along with it to spare me."

"You're trying to spare each other, and each of you knows it."

"I don't want her here, watching me die." He squeezed her hand with as much strength as he could muster. "I don't want to put you through that, either."

She sat on the edge of the bed and leaned down to kiss his forehead. "I'm not leaving you. Not for a second. And if I could fight this thing bare-handed, I gladly would."

"I don't doubt that."

For a moment they were quiet, gazing into each other's eyes and pretending that their tears weren't tears of despair.

He didn't doubt her absolute love and devotion. Not today, and not on the day they'd stood at the altar in the company of their children and recited their wedding vows. The day they'd united their families, their lives, had been one of the happiest of his life.

They had met a year earlier at a black-tie fund-raising event. He was a major donor who was being recognized that night for his generosity. She was a volunteer checking people in as they arrived.

As she'd passed him his table-assignment card, she'd remarked on his bow tie being askew.

He patted it awkwardly. "I don't have a wife to check these things for me before I leave the house."

"My late husband thought I was pretty good at straightening his tie. May I?" She hadn't been flirtatious or inappropriate in any way as she came around to the other side of the table and efficiently adjusted his tie. Then she'd backed away and smiled up at him. "It wouldn't do to have an honoree with a crooked bow tie."

He would have enjoyed continuing their conversation, but he was summoned into the banquet hall, where the program was about to begin. He didn't see her again that night.

It took him a week to work up the nerve to call the charity office and ask for her name. During the seven years since his wife had died, he'd dated occasionally. A few of the women he'd taken out he'd also slept with, although never at home, where Susan and Bellamy were under his roof.

But he hadn't fallen in love until the night he met Olivia Maxey, and it had been an instantaneous and hard fall.

Later, she'd confessed that it had been the same for her. Referring to her husband as "late" had been calculated to let him know she was available. "The most courageous thing I ever did in my life was step around that table to straighten your tie. But I simply had to touch you, to see if you were real."

After a year of courtship, they had married.

He didn't fear death, especially. But he couldn't bear the thought of leaving her. He had to clear his throat before he was able to speak. "What else did you and Bellamy talk about?"

"Oh, she asked if I'd managed to get any rest last night. She wanted to know—"

"Olivia." He spoke her name quietly, but in a way that chided her for attempting to keep something from him. "I'm not *that* drugged. I sensed your distress when you were talking to her. What's happened?"

She sighed a concession and looked down at their tightly clasped hands. "That horrid reporter—"

"Rocky Van Durbin? He can't be dignified with the title 'reporter.'"

"He ambushed Bellamy as she left the offices."

"He's in Austin? I thought she'd outrun him, that we were through with all that."

"Unfortunately, no. She's still on his radar screen. In his column tomorrow, he's going to pose a question to his readers. And to hers, in a sense."

"What question?"

"Was the right man punished for killing Susan? Did they get the right guy? Words to that effect."

He digested that, then sighed heavily. "God knows what kind of offshoots of discussion that will produce."

"It was bad enough when Bellamy's identity was revealed." For weeks after the disclosure they'd been plagued by telephone calls asking them for comments and interviews. Several regional reporters had even shown up outside their estate and at their business offices. They'd declined all requests and eventually had handed the responsibility of fielding them over to their attorney.

"What I hate most," she said, "is that our lives will once again be on review in that horrible tabloid."

She left the bed and, clearly too agitated to sit down, paced the narrow space in front of the window. "Lyston Electronics was touted by the secretary of commerce as a model corporation. Where was Van Durbin then? Or when you instigated the profit-sharing program for every employee? None of that made headline news."

"Because that's not scintillating subject matter."

"But the circumstances surrounding Susan's killing are."

"Tragically."

"To us, yes. To everyone else, it's entertainment. And from now on, the Lyston family will be remembered only for that salacious murder in Austin." She began to cry in earnest. "I feel like the foundation of our life together is crumbling beneath me. It's more than I can handle right now."

He patted the side of the bed and coaxed her to come back to it. She went to him and leaned down to rest her head on his shoulder. "You can handle it," he said gently. "You can handle anything. And what you'll be remembered for is having been the most loving, wonderful, beautiful wife any man could have dreamed of. Making you my wife and mother to my girls was the smartest decision I ever made." He turned his head and kissed her hair. "This will go away. I promise."

For a time they clung to one another. He said all the things he knew she wanted to hear. He told her that Van Durbin and his ilk would soon be exploiting someone else's personal tragedy, and that, until then, they would rely on each other for support as they always had.

Eventually she sat up and blotted her eyes. "There's something else. I hesitate to tell you because it's almost as upsetting as the business with Van Durbin."

"What could be that bad?"

"Bellamy is with Denton Carter."

He hadn't seen that coming. He'd been as shocked and put off as Olivia when Bellamy informed them that she had booked a flight with him. Some situations were best left alone. But, after sensing the animosity on both sides, he'd thought yesterday's flight would be the last they saw of him.

"By 'with,' what do you mean, exactly?"

"I shudder to think. She told me that Van Durbin had confronted her and *Dent* as they left our building. I think it was a slip of the tongue, because her voice skipped and then she went on talking in a rush and didn't mention him again."

He pressed her hand reassuringly. "There could be a simple explanation for why he was there. Something about payment for yesterday's charter, maybe. Don't borrow trouble."

She gave him an odd look.

"What?" he asked.

"You said those very words to me when Susan started going out with him and I wanted to put a stop to it. I didn't have to borrow trouble, Howard. He *is* trouble, and I still blame him for what happened to our daughter."

"That ought to hold her." The locksmith tested the newly installed lock on the utility room door, then moved aside and invited Dent to test it for himself.

Satisfied, he nodded. "Thanks for coming out so soon. What's the charge?"

Dent paid him in cash and tipped him ten bucks for treating the repair as an emergency. After seeing the locksmith on his way out the back door, he went into the living room, where Bellamy was in conversation with the two police officers who had responded to their summons.

She was sitting on the sofa; the officers were standing amid the boxes of knickknacks and books she still hadn't unpacked. Dent, who had an ingrained aversion to cops, didn't venture any farther into the room but propped his shoulder against the door frame, which was a good observation point.

He had followed Bellamy home from Lyston Electronics, keeping one eye on the road and the other on his rear-view mirror. He didn't believe Van Durbin had followed them, but he probably didn't need to. Surely *EyeSpy* had a battalion of underpaid Internet geeks doing research and electronic investigative work. Finding out Bellamy's new home address would have been duck soup.

When they reentered her house and saw again the evidence of last night's intruder, Dent had said, "With Van Durbin in town, you've got more to worry about than media coverage of this. Call the police."

She'd capitulated without further discussion, apparently having seen the wisdom of having the break-in on record. Two uniformed officers had arrived a few minutes later. They'd questioned both of them, walked through every room of the house as well as the backyard, poking about. They'd called in another officer to dust for fingerprints. He'd already come and gone.

The questions being put to Bellamy now were similar to those the sheriff's deputy had asked of Dent earlier at the airfield, the implication being that the vandalism was retribution for something she had done.

"Have you had any cross words with a neighbor? Maid? Yardman?"

She shook her head no.

"Co-worker?"

"I don't have co-workers."

One of the policemen looked over at Dent. "You said you followed her home last night?"

"I flew her to Houston and back yesterday. She left something in my airplane. I was returning it to her."

He nodded and, with one eyebrow eloquently arched, exchanged a meaningful look with his partner. Going back to Bellamy, he said, "We, uh, took the pair of under-wear for evidence. Using a personal garment like that to paint the words on the wall . . . Well, ma'am, it suggests the perpetrator has, uh, intimate knowledge of you."

"Or he's read my book."

One's face lit up and he snapped his fingers. "I thought you looked familiar. You're that author." To his partner, he said, "She's famous."

She passed a copy of *Low Pressure* to the one who hadn't recognized her. "It's a murder mystery. Fact based. The victim was my sister. Her underpants became a key element of the investigation."

"Any idea what was meant by the warning?"

"Isn't the meaning obvious?" Dent said impatiently. "She's in danger from this guy."

Neither officer acknowledged his remark, but one of them asked Bellamy if she'd received similar threats or warnings. She told them about the rat and the break-in of her car.

"Did you report these incidents?"

"No. They were dissimilar. Different states. I thought they were random. But after this, I believe they could all be related, and the common denominator is my book."

"Why do you think that?"

"Timing, for one thing. Nothing like this happened to me before the book was published. Besides, I can't think of anything I've done to elicit this kind of malice."

After a considerable pause, and another glance toward Dent, one of them said, "Maybe it doesn't have anything to do with your book. Could someone in your personal life bear you a grudge? An ex-husband? A boyfriend you've recently broken off with? Anybody like that?"

Dent was interested to know the answers to those questions himself.

"My ex lives in Dallas," Bellamy told them. "Our divorce was amicable. He's remarried. I just moved here from New York. I haven't been seeing anyone."

"What about up there?"

"No. Only in the most platonic sense."

The two exchanged another look and seemed to agree that they had covered everything. "We'll put your house on a drive-by list. Our patrols will keep a close eye on it. Call us immediately if anything, even the smallest thing, happens."

"Thank you, I will."

"You should look into getting an alarm system installed."

Bellamy told them she would do that, then got up to walk them out. As the officers went past Dent, they tipped their hats, but their expressions didn't leave him with a warm fuzzy. They left with a promise to report back to Bellamy if their investigation led to an arrest.

"Hell will freeze over first," Dent said after she closed the door behind them. "But at least there's a police record of the break-in, and they might've lifted his prints. Considering the mess they made, I hope something comes of it."

He ran his finger through the smudge that had been left on the newel post, then wiped it on the leg of his jeans. "The deputy also dusted my airplane. If this piece of shit is ever arrested, they'll be able to connect him to both crimes and maybe even to the delivered rat."

"Maybe we should have told them about your airplane."

"And get into all that history?" He shook his head.

"I didn't want to, either."

"Let them nail a suspect first. Then we can connect the remaining dots for them."

She folded her arms across her middle and hugged her elbows as she looked up the stairwell in the direction of her bedroom. "I was really coming to like this house. Now it's been tainted."

"It'll clean up. But what about your landlord? Should you notify him?"

"He's absentee."

"Out of town?"

"Afghanistan. When he was deployed, his wife went to stay with her folks in Arizona. I leased for a year. I see no need to worry them. I'll cover the charges."

He took a business card from his shirt pocket. "The locksmith's brother-in-law does make-ready cleaning on houses and apartments. Painting included. For a fair price and a signed copy of your book, he'll have the house looking like new. And I was told that for next to nothing he'll install an alarm system."

She took the card. "I'll call him."

"First, come into the kitchen."

"What's in there? More damage?"

"No. I'm hungry."

Five minutes later they had assembled a lunch of peanut-butter-and-jelly sandwiches and glasses of iced tea. He ripped open a bag of Fritos he'd found in the pantry, and when she declined the chips, he dug in.

Around a bite, he asked, "Any word from Houston?"

"I called Olivia on the drive here. Daddy opted for another round of chemo. They're clinging to the hope it will do some good."

"Did you tell her about your house?"

"No, I didn't want to add to her worry. I did tell her about Van Durbin, though. I hated to, but at least I prepared them. They won't be caught off guard by his column tomorrow."

"Tell her about my airplane?"

"No."

"So, as far as she knows, we parted company after we landed last night."

"Actually, when I told her about being accosted by Van Durbin, it slipped out that you were with me."

"Hmm. I wonder which upset her most, knowing that you'd been bushwhacked, or that I was at your side."

"Don't be provoking, Dent."

"I haven't provoked anything. Yesterday I was completely professional, but your stepmother has always treated me like a turd in the punch bowl, a contaminant, and yesterday was no exception. Not that I fucking care."

"That's the very attitude that's provoking."

He could've said more on the subject of Olivia, but decided against it. The woman's husband was dying, after all. Besides, he'd never lost sleep over what Olivia Lyston thought of him, and he didn't intend to. "How'd she take the news about Van Durbin's upcoming column?"

"Unhappily." She pinched off a morsel of bread crust and rolled it between her thumb and finger, studying the forming ball of dough. "I can't say that I blame her for being upset."

"If you didn't want to upset your family, you shouldn't have published a book that aired their dirty laundry."

She looked at him with asperity. "I told you why I wrote it."

"Yeah, so you could make a bad period in your life

tangible, then wad it up, throw it away, and forget it. Good therapy for you, maybe. But it sucks for everybody else involved. Why didn't you pour your heart out in a journal, then lock it up and throw away the key, or bury it in the backyard, or drop it into the ocean? Why'd you have to turn your therapy into a best seller?"

Pushing his empty plate aside, he placed his forearms on the edge of the table and leaned across it toward her. "Those of us who lived the story are a bit vexed to find ourselves in your spotlight, A.k.a."

She came out of her chair. "So you've said. I don't need to hear it again."

He stood up and rounded the table to stand toe-to-toe with her. "Yeah, you do. Because somebody has moved past vexed. He's good and truly pissed off. And he's gonna be even more pissed off when it comes out tomorrow that maybe the case wasn't as tightly sewn up as believed. Susan's murder is going to be given a good, hard second look. I've got a hunch that's not going to sit well with whoever scrawled that warning on your wall."

She was staring up at him in defiance and denial of every word.

"You think I'm wrong?" he asked.

She opened her mouth to speak, but suddenly the starch went out of her. She lowered her head and rubbed her temples with her fingertips. "I wish you were, but I don't think you are."

He backed down. "Okay," he said in a softer voice, "who's the mystery guest?"

"I don't know."

"You need to find out before his little pranks turn really ugly."

She lowered her hand from her face and looked up at him. "Brilliant idea. How do you suggest going about it?"

"We start with the people who were directly involved. Begin with the key players and work outward, eliminating them one by one, until the son of a bitch is left standing, exposed."

"*We*? What about the police?"

"Do you think Starsky and Hutch there are going to go digging into an eighteen-year-old murder case?"

"They investigate cold cases."

"Not after the culprit has already been caught and convicted."

"Convictions are overturned all the time."

"But they've got to have a compelling reason to reopen the case. Can you provide them one?"

She shook her head.

"Right. My opinion? They'll wait until you're physically assaulted and/or dead before they take the threat seriously, because they probably concluded that it had something to do with me. And you believe I'm right. If you didn't, you would have spilled the whole sordid story to them while they were here. You saved yourself the breath because you have no more faith in their getting to the bottom of this than I do. And I have none. Which leaves it up to us."

"What do you know about police work?"

"Only that I don't trust it."

"You would drop everything and—"

"I'm grounded, remember? I've got nothing else to do. Besides, I have a vested interest in finding this jerk. And when I do, for what he did to my airplane, I'm going to bash in his skull."

"Lovely. Do you expect me to be your accomplice?"

"Get this straight." He took a step, bringing them closer. "I don't play nice, Bellamy. I never have."

After a taut moment, she broke his hard stare. "All right. For the time being, at least, we'll help each other. But where do we start? Who do we start with?"

He went to the chair she'd left empty moments earlier and held it for her. "We start with you."

Chapter 6

*M*e?" Bellamy exclaimed.

"You were as close to Susan as anyone. You were with her all that day until just before she was killed. Talk me through everything that happened from your point of view."

"I did that with the lead character in my book. I wrote it from the viewpoint of a twelve-year-old girl."

"I skipped the long paragraphs and only read the dialogue."

"You still know what happened."

"Not the behind-the-scenes stuff."

"That's the stuff in the long paragraphs."

"Is there something you don't want me to know?"

"No, of course not."

"Well, then. I wasn't at the barbecue, remember? I need details."

"You could go back to the book and read the parts you skipped."

"Or you could just tell me."

She gnawed her lower lip. He cocked his head to one side, prompting her. Then she suddenly began to talk, as though fearing she might change her mind if she didn't.

"Daddy had initiated the company-wide Memorial Day barbecue two years earlier. It was the first party he and Olivia hosted as a married couple. Daddy used the occasion to establish Olivia as the new Mrs. Howard Lyston and to introduce Steven as his adopted son."

Dent held up his hand. "Detail. If your dad adopted him, why didn't he change his name to Lyston?"

"Olivia would have preferred it, I think. But Steven wanted to honor his late father by keeping his name."

"Hmm. Okay. So the barbecue became an annual event. Brisket and ribs, kegs of beer, live music, dancing. Red, white, and blue banners."

"Blue Bell ice cream. Fireworks at nine-thirty."

"Quite a shindig."

"Nevertheless, it had its detractors." With her fingertip she followed a trickle of condensation as it slid down the side of her glass of tea. "There was a row at the breakfast table that morning. Steven didn't want to go to the barbecue. He called the whole thing dumb. Olivia told him, dumb or not, he was going. Susan was acting like a bitch royale because..." She shifted her gaze up to him. "Because of the fight she'd had with you."

"I came over on my motorcycle early—"

"Waking everyone up."

"Someone inside the house had to activate the gate so I could get in."

"It was me."

"See? A detail I didn't know. Anyway, I had to come early because Susan hadn't answered her phone. I didn't want to leave a message, but I had to tell her that I'd be late to the barbecue."

"You were going flying with Gall."

"He'd been doing some repairs on this guy's plane and wanted to take it up, check things out. He asked me if I wanted to go along. I jumped at the chance. I told Susan I would hook up with her at the barbecue when we got back."

"That didn't go over well."

"To put it mildly. She blew a gasket and issued an ulti- matum. Take her to the barbecue when it started, or don't bother coming at all. I told her I was going flying with Gall. She said fine, she'd have more fun without me."

"She was in a snit. She told me . . ." She hesitated, then said, "She said she'd rather die than play second fiddle to that nasty old man."

Those portentous words silenced them for several moments, then Bellamy picked up the story. "She was determined to teach you a lesson. Over Daddy's protests, she drove her own car to the park. She left ahead of us, and I remember thinking how gorgeous she looked when she sailed out the door.

"She was wearing a new sundress, one that Olivia had bought her for the occasion. The blue color set off her eyes. Her legs were smooth and tan. Her hair was golden, shiny, and perfect. In fact, everything about her looked perfect to me." She laughed softly. "Probably because I was so imperfect."

"You improved. A lot." He teamed his drawled compli- ment with a lazy-eyed once-over that he could tell flus- tered her.

"I wasn't fishing for a compliment."

"Well, you caught one anyway."

"Thank you."

"You're welcome." He shot her a teasing grin, then returned to the serious nature of the topic. "Susan went on ahead."

"Yes, despite Daddy and Olivia's wishes that we arrive together and present a solid family unit. She insisted on having her own way. I admired her daring, because I was just the opposite. I never disobeyed, never went against what my parents wanted and expected of me. I was the Miss Goody Two-Shoes of the family."

"Cooperative by nature?"

"Or simply a coward. I was also so happy to finally have a mother, I didn't want to do anything to disrupt the new family."

"How old were you when your real mom died?"

"Three. Susan was seven. Mother left us with the housekeeper while she went to the supermarket. She collapsed in the store aisle. A brain aneurysm had burst. They said death was instantaneous." After a moment's pause, she added, "I hope so. Realizing that she was dying and leaving us without a mother would have been awful for her."

"Do you remember her?"

"Sometimes I think I do," she said wistfully, "but it might just be images formed from pictures of her and stories that Daddy told me. When I started school, being without a mother made me different from the other kids. I didn't like that. I was thrilled when Daddy and Olivia married."

"What about Susan?"

"She was more wary because she was older and could remember our mother. But to Olivia's credit, she was tactful and patient with us. With Steven, too, who was suddenly no longer an only child, but the middle child having to share his mother with two stepsisters. As an adult I can appreciate how dicey the merger could have been. But there were no major upheavals."

Dent's family background suffered by comparison. He didn't want to think about what he would have become if Gall hadn't taken him under his wing. So to speak.

He resettled in his chair and folded his arms across his chest. "Miss Goody Two-Shoes goes to the barbecue."

She winced. "Not in a new sundress, mind you, but a pair of white slacks that were too big in the seat, and a red top with straps that kept slipping off my knobby shoulders." She gave a self-deprecating laugh. "I didn't have the most graceful adolescence."

He smiled, recalling how awkward she'd been. "I remember one time Susan and I passed through the kitchen where you were sitting at the table doing homework. Susan called you a dork for being such a conscientious student. You told her to shut up. But she kept teasing you. You picked up a bag—"

"Of colored pencils. I was working on a map of Europe."

"You hauled it back to throw at her, but you knocked over your glass of milk instead. You burst into tears and ran from the room."

"I can't believe you remember that." She buried her face in her hands. "I was so humiliated."

"Why? Susan deserved to be smacked for making fun of you. I thought you showed a lot of backbone by standing up to her."

"But I flubbed it and spilled my milk instead. In front of you. That was the worst of it."

"Because of the crush you had on me."

Her face turned bright pink. "You knew?"

He raised one shoulder. "Sensed."

"Oh, God. Now I'm really embarrassed. I didn't think you knew I was alive."

He'd known. But her adolescent crush on him hadn't become noteworthy until that Memorial Day, and then it had taken on a significance that disturbed him even now.

But he wouldn't go there. Not until she did.

Instead, he smiled. "What did you like about me?"

"You were so much older. *Eighteen*. You rode a motorcycle, flew airplanes, used bad words. You broke all the rules, and my parents called you reckless, rude, and undisciplined."

"And they were right."

She laughed lightly. "You were the dangerous bad boy. Every Goody Two-Shoes's fantasy."

"Oh yeah?" He leaned toward her and lowered his voice. "What do you think of me now?"

Instantly she sobered and held his stare for several seconds, then replied quietly, "I think you're still dangerous."

Quickly she scooted back her chair and began to clear the table. He watched her as she moved about the kitchen and noticed how nicely she was filling out the seat of her pants these days. She also filled out her soft, stretchy top. Not too much. Just enough.

Today she had worn her hair down. It was dark, thick, and glossy, and, whenever she moved, the longest strands grazed those not-too-much-just-enough breasts, and every time that happened, he felt a warm, pleasant tingle below his belt.

Yesterday, once she'd ditched the sunglasses, he'd

noticed that her eyes were light blue, set off by black eye-lashes. Her skin was fair, and he was really coming to like that sprinkling of freckles across her nose and cheekbones, which was an impudent contrast to an otherwise solemn face. When the time was right, he would enjoy teasing her about those freckles, as well as her girlish blush.

He wondered what had gone wrong between her and her ex, and if their divorce had been as amicable as she'd claimed.

She returned to her chair across the table from him and, as though aware of his scrutiny and the track of his thoughts, she resumed immediately. "The barbecue was exactly as you described it. Susan was the life of the party, which wasn't anything unusual. But that day she seemed to court attention."

"She wanted to make sure I'd hear about it."

Bellamy gave a curt nod. "She laughed out loud at eve-rything and spread herself thin on the dance floor, danc-ing with every man who asked her, no matter how old or how young."

"Allen Strickland."

"Yes. But they didn't link up until later in the day, after Susan had had quite a lot to drink. She and a group of older kids had left the main pavilion and had gone down to the boathouse. They were sneaking beer down there and Susan was swilling it.

"Being curious and, I admit, a bit jealous, I went down there to spy on them. Susan saw me sneaking around and threatened to kill me if I tattled to Olivia and Daddy. I told her that I wouldn't have to tell them, that if she continued drinking like that, they would know by her behavior. She told me to get lost. So I did."

"Did you tell on her?"

"No." This time as she lapsed into thought, her finger-tip followed the rim of the tea glass. "Later I wished I had told. If she hadn't been half drunk, she never would have looked twice at a guy like Allen Strickland."

"Why do you say that?"

"He was so blue collar."

"And I wasn't?"

"Well, you... you were different."

"I rode a motorcycle and flew airplanes. He drove a company truck. Appears to me that the difference between us was the vehicles."

"In terms of boyfriends, that's huge."

"Okay. Continue."

"Where was I?"

"You were blaming yourself for Susan's actions. You shouldn't. She made her own choices that day."

"But she was my sister. I should have watched out for her."

"Was she watching out for you?"

She lowered her gaze and must have decided not to venture too far in that direction, because she moved past it. "I returned to the pavilion and tried to remain inconspicuous. Susan's group eventually began trickling back from the boathouse. I became worried when she didn't come back with the rest. I wondered if she'd drunk so much she'd gotten sick. I went back to the boathouse to check on her.

"Or..." She closed her eyes and rubbed her temple. "Or am I confusing that with later?" She gave a small shake of her head. "It was so long ago that sometimes I have trouble piecing together the sequence of events."

Watching her closely, he said, "You didn't have trouble with the sequence when you wrote the book. The girl in it didn't return to the boathouse until the tornado was on top of her."

"Right," she said vaguely. Then more definitively, "Right." Still, frowning, she paused before continuing. "Susan was among the last stragglers to return to the pavilion. She looked more vibrant and beautiful than ever. Most women don't hold up too well when they overdrink, but the alcohol had made her look ... aglow.

"Allen Strickland asked her to dance. He was a great dancer. One of those men who can really move, make the steps look fluid and effortless. In full control of himself and his partner. You know the kind?"

"Not really," he said wryly. "I usually don't watch men dance."

"Then take my word for it. He was good. Susan, too. One song segued into another, and Allen Strickland stayed her partner. The way they moved together was in-your-face sexy, and everybody noticed. His hands were all over her, and she wasn't doing anything to discourage him. The opposite, in fact."

She paused for a length of time, lost in the memory.

Then, speaking softly, she said, "Considering how the two of them had been grinding against each other on the dance floor, it wasn't at all surprising that Allen Strickland was the first man the police questioned."

"You're wrong there, A.k.a.," he said bitterly. "*I* was the first."

Several hundred miles away, former Austin PD homicide detective Dale Moody was also remembering his first interview with Denton Carter. All these years later, he remembered it like it had happened yesterday. It played like a recording inside his head.

"Son, you'd just as well tell us what we know to be the truth, 'cause we're gonna find out anyway, sooner or later. It would save you some trouble and earn our good graces if you came clean now. How 'bout it?"

"I had nothing to do with it."

"You and Susan snuck off into the woods so you could be alone, am I right? Things got hot. Then, like girls sometimes do, she called a halt to it. Hell, I understand how mad that must've made you, Dent. I myself hate when that happens."

"I'll bet you do. And I'll bet it happens to you a lot. But it doesn't happen to me. It sure as hell didn't happen at the barbecue because I wasn't even there."

"You were, Dent, you were."

"Not until after the tornado ripped through! Before that I was flying with Gall. Ask him."

"I've got an officer out there now, talking to him."

"Well, then that should be the end of it. I wasn't at the barbecue, and I didn't kill Susan. She was my girlfriend."

"Who you'd had a fight with that morning."

Silence.

"Her family has told me about that quarrel, Dent. They said the two of you really went at it. She slammed back into the house. You tore away from their place on your motorcycle in a huff. Right or wrong?"

"Right. So what?"

"What did you and Susan argue about?"

"About me not going to the barbecue with her. That's what I'm trying to tell you. I wasn't fucking there."

"Watch your language, boy. Do you know who you're talking to?"

"Oh, sorry. Let me rephrase that. I wasn't fucking there...asshole."

Dale clicked his tongue as though switching off a playback machine. He knew the dialogue by heart. Like everything else relating to the Susan Lyston case, it had stayed with him. He was cursed with total recall. But, if he was rusty on a point, all he had to do was consult his well-thumbed copy of *Low Pressure*.

Which he did now, flipping through the pages until he found the scene where the character patterned after him was trying to squeeze a confession out of the victim's boyfriend. Bellamy Lyston hadn't been in that interrogation room, but she'd come pretty damn close to telling it just like it had been.

In fact, every scene in her book was eerily accurate. The lady had a talent for telling a story in a way that kept the reader glued to the pages. Dale just wished her captivating story hadn't been this story. *His* story.

It was happenstance that he'd even learned about her book. His TV had been tuned to a morning news show. He'd been waiting for his coffee to brew and hadn't really been paying much attention to what the guest and the host were talking about. But when he realized the pretty novelist was Bellamy Lyston Price, all grown up and dressed fit to kill, he'd stopped what he was doing and gave a listen.

She was saying that her novel was about the murder of a sixteen-year-old girl at a Memorial Day barbecue. That was when Dale's stomach had begun to roil, and, by the time the interview had concluded, he was swallowing hard to keep down the whiskey he'd drunk the night before. It had come up anyway, scalding and sour, searing the back of his throat.

He pulled himself together and drove to the nearest Walmart, bought a copy of the book, and started reading it as soon as he got home. It wasn't as bad as he was afraid it would be.

It was worse.

He'd felt like his belly had been ripped open with one of those instruments of torture they'd used back in the Middle Ages and his guts were on display for anybody who wanted to dig around in them to see what they could find.

His hands shook now as he lit a cigarette, poured a glass of Jack, picked up his pistol, and carried it and the drink out onto his front porch, which wasn't a befitting name for the sad-looking, warped wood platform. It matched the rest of his cabin: old, neglected, and deteriorating a noticeable degree each day.

Which also described Dale Moody himself. It would be interesting to see which would give out first: the porch, his lungs, or his liver.

If he got lucky and the porch collapsed beneath him, the fall might break his neck and kill him instantly. If he got lung cancer, he'd let it take him without putting up a fight. Same with cirrhosis. If none of that happened soon…Well, that was why the S&W .357 was always within easy reach.

One of these days he just might work up the nerve to put the barrel in his mouth and pull the trigger. A few times, when he was really drunk, he'd played Russian roulette with it, but he'd always won. Or lost. Depending on how you looked at it.

It was a hot, breathless afternoon, the thick silence shattered only by the screech of cicadas. The shade found beneath the tin roof overhang on the porch provided little relief from the sweltering heat. Through the cypresses, the still surface of Caddo Lake looked like a brass plate.

The cabin in which he'd lived alone for fifteen years was situated on a densely wooded peninsula. The cove it formed looked dark and malevolent with its low canopy of moss-laden trees and viscous swamp waters. Few fishermen ventured into the uninviting inlet. Dale Moody liked it that way. Solitude had been what he was after when he'd bought the place, paying cash, filing the documents under a name he took off a hundred-year-old gravestone.

He sat down in his creaky rocker with the fraying cane seat, sipped the whiskey, drew on the cigarette, and enjoyed the reassuring weight of the loaded revolver resting on his thigh.

As he sat there, barely putting forth the effort to rock the chair, he asked himself, as he did most days, how his life might have been different if Susan Lyston hadn't been killed that day. Would he have distinguished himself as a homicide detective, received commendations and handshakes from the mayor, stayed on with the Austin PD until he could draw full retirement? Would he still be married and have contact with his children? Would he know what his grandkids looked like?

But Susan Lyston had been killed on that dreadful Memorial Day eighteen years ago. The date not only marked her murder, it was also meteorologically significant. The first tornado to strike Austin in almost half a century had roared through the city and torn it all to hell, leaving destruction and death in its unforgiving path.

One of the hardest-hit areas was the state park where the Lystons were hosting their annual company party.

The attendees had been having such a good time that few took notice of the threatening clouds beyond hoping that rain wouldn't cancel the fireworks display scheduled for that night. Eventually, though, people became concerned about the premature dusk, the noticeable change in the barometric pressure, the supernatural stillness, and the greenish cast of the sky.

Parents started gathering up their children, who had scattered to various areas of the park to take advantage of the games and activities organized by the Lystons. The face-painting lady packed up her pots and brushes. Band members stopped playing and loaded their instruments and speakers into their van to wait out the storm. Caterers put covers over their trays of potato salad and baked beans.

But these trifling safeguards were spitballs against a juggernaut. Even if there had been time to implement more safety precautions, experts later agreed that they would have done little or no good against a twister that was a mile wide and packed circulating winds of more than two hundred miles an hour.

Austin was located south of the geographical band known as Tornado Alley, so many who lived there weren't as attuned to the dangers as were their neighbors farther north. They'd seen pictures of devastation, sure. They'd watched films on TV and marveled at these most vicious and unpredictable offspring of Mother Nature.

But one couldn't really be prepared for the power and the fury that a funnel cloud was capable of. It was something one had to experience to really know what it was like, and many who did experience it didn't live to tell about it. Several fools ignored the warning sirens and went outside to watch the cloud. Two of those disappeared entirely. Nothing of them was ever found.

City-wide the death toll was sixty-seven. Nine of those casualties were recovered from the site of the barbecue at the state park.

Twelve hours after the storm, the city was still in a high state of emergency. All of Travis County was declared a disaster area. The entire police force was working search-and-rescue, along with the fire department, the sheriff's office, the National Guard, the Red Cross, and a multitude of volunteers.

They had their hands full trying to reunite families, search for the missing and dead, convey the injured to medical facilities, restore law and order where looters were wreaking havoc, set up shelters for survivors whose homes had been demolished, and clear debris-blocked roads so emergency vehicles and public utility trucks could get through.

Around dawn the following morning, after a night spent in the midst of pandemonium, Dale had received a summons to the morgue, which, considering the state of things, was a major pain in the ass.

But he'd heeded the call. When he arrived, he'd been met by the chief ME, who'd looked frazzled and near exhaustion himself. His staff was overwhelmed by the number of bodies still being brought in, some in pieces, making identification a challenge that strained the objectivity of even the most hardened pros.

Leaving Dale even more puzzled as to why the doc had called for a detective to drop what he was doing and rush right over.

"We're both busy, Detective, so I'll make this quick. We've got a girl here, in her teens, whose body was recovered from the state park."

"She was at the Lyston Electronics party?"

"She was a Lyston. Their daughter Susan."

"Jesus."

"I'm told her body was discovered under the branches of an uprooted tree. But the thing is, the reason I called for a detective, that's not what killed her. The injuries she sustained during the tornado were postmortem."

"Come again?"

"Cause of death was asphyxiation. She was strangled."

"Are you sure?"

He'd shown Dale the cadaver. "The bruising here on her neck indicates strangulation. Where she was scraped and cut by the falling tree, she didn't bleed. She sustained blunt trauma to several organs, which could have been fatal, but she was already dead."

It had fallen to Dale to impart that news to her parents, who were already reeling from shock and grief over what they believed was a storm-related death. He'd watched Howard and Olivia Lyston shatter. Learning that their daughter had been murdered compounded their heartache a thousandfold.

Their tragedy had landed Dale Moody a murder case.

Combing the crime scene for evidence had been an exercise in futility, a joke. The tornado had ravaged the entire area. Trees that weren't completely uprooted had been stripped bare of leaves, their naked branches ripped off and tossed to the ground like toothpicks. Investigators had to hack through the natural debris just to get to the scene of the crime. The area had also been trampled by first responders and panicked survivors searching for missing loved ones.

If the perp had planned it, he couldn't have done better than to have an F-5 tornado sweep through the place where he'd killed Susan Lyston.

Dale and other detectives had tried to question everyone who'd attended the barbecue and had been in the vicinity at the time of the slaying. They'd interviewed as many as they could locate. But both the pavilion and the boathouse had been flattened. The gravel lot where over two hundred vehicles were parked had been turned into an apocalyptic landscape of twisted steel and shattered glass.

Consequently, dozens who'd narrowly escaped death had sustained serious injuries. Many were hospitalized with internal injuries, head trauma, compound fractures, cuts and contusions, and shock. It had taken weeks to track down and question everyone.

But in the meantime, Dale had grilled Denton Carter.

As the boyfriend with whom Susan had quarreled that morning, his name had gone to the top of the list of possible suspects. Right off, Dale and his team of detectives thought they had their man. The eighteen-year-old was a surly wiseass who had issues with authority. Dale heard that from faculty members of the high school from which Dent had graduated only the week before.

"He's an intelligent kid," a school counselor had told Dale. "He finished with a three-point-two GPA and probably could have done better if he'd wanted to. But that was the problem. He didn't want to. Terrible attitude. The boy carries a big chip on his shoulder."

Dale had discovered that for himself the first time he

hauled Dent Carter in for questioning. After the vulgar language, Dale had put him in jail, thinking that a night in lockup might improve his manners. But the following day he had smirked at Dale and shot him the finger when he was released.

Dale had hated watching him saunter out, but he didn't have any evidence with which to hold him. Not then, and not days later, after conducting a thorough investigation and repeated interrogations. The boy's story never deviated from what he had initially told Dale. No one could testify to seeing him at the barbecue, and the old man from the airfield provided him with an alibi. Dale had had no choice but to let him go.

His interest had shifted to Allen Strickland.

Now, Dale hefted his pistol in his palm while mentally enumerating all the facts that had pointed to Strickland's guilt. There had been enough to charge him. But there wasn't a single, solid piece of hard evidence to prove that he'd killed that girl.

The ADA assigned to prosecute the case, Rupert Collier, an eager bloodsucker if ever there was one, had built a case out of circumstantial evidence. His summation had been delivered with the fervor of a tent revival evangelist. As though fearing hell for themselves if they didn't convict, the jury had brought in a guilty verdict in under two hours.

Allen Strickland had gone to prison.

Dale Moody had turned to drink.

Eighteen years later, Bellamy Lyston Price had written a book that underscored every doubt Dale had ever entertained about what had happened in the woods that day just before the historic tornado.

And what made him mad as hell was that that damn book might conjure up doubt in the minds of others as well. The ending left a lot open to speculation. Readers might start wondering if maybe the criminal investigation had been sloppy, if maybe the ambition of the ADA had outdazzled that of the accused's court-appointed defender, if maybe Allen Strickland hadn't been the last person to see Susan Lyston alive after all.

It was one thing for Dale to rethink the Susan Lyston case all day, every day. But he didn't want anyone else to.

It had made him feel only marginally better to learn that Bellamy Price's book had made Rupe nervous, too. Rupe Collier was a bigshot in Austin these days. He couldn't be happy over having himself portrayed in the book as a ruthless young prosecutor who would go to any lengths to get his belt notched with a felony conviction, although that was exactly what he'd been and precisely what he'd done.

And he was looking for Dale.

Donald Haymaker, a buddy from Dale's days on the force who still had ties to the Austin PD and was one of the few people among his acquaintances who knew how to reach him, had called him a few weeks ago, days after T. J. David's true identity became known.

After they'd swapped trite pleasantries, he'd said, "Uh, Dale, have you heard about this book?"

He didn't need to specify which book. Dale told him he'd read Bellamy Price's *Low Pressure*.

"Me, too," Haymaker admitted with noticeable awkwardness. "I think everybody in the country has. Rupe Collier included. He, uh, he called me, Dale. He hemhawed for ten minutes or so, then casually—way too casually—asked me if I knew where you were and how to get in touch."

"You didn't give him my number, did you?"

"Hell no! But what do you think that slippery sumbitch wants with you after all these years? It's gotta have something to do with that book, don't you think?"

That was precisely what Dale thought. The book would have caused Rupe's sphincter to pucker. He would be hating it and the hype surrounding it even more than Dale did, and Dale hated it like hell.

Bellamy Lyston Price, that homely, gawky titmouse of a girl, had stirred up a damn fucking mess. It had all the potential of becoming the crowning touch to Dale Moody's miserable life.

He finished his whiskey in one slug, dropped his cigarette butt on the porch, balanced the pistol in his hand, and wished with every decaying fiber of his being that, just once before he died, he could enjoy a moment when he would know with one hundred percent certainty that he had helped convict the right man.

Chapter 7

———◆———

I was the first," Dent said, repeating it with emphasis.

He held Bellamy's stare for several moments, then, muttering an expletive, got up and moved restlessly around the kitchen. He bumped his fist against the crate of small appliances she hadn't yet unpacked and eventually went to stand at the sink. He slid his hands, palms out, into the seat pockets of his jeans and stared through the window into her backyard.

"There's a broken flowerpot on the steps," he said. "I found it last night."

"That must've been awful for you."

"Naw, it was just a flowerpot. I got over it."

"I was talking about being considered a suspect."

He turned his head and spoke to her from over his shoulder. "I got over it."

"Did you?"

Hearing the doubt behind the question, he turned back to the window, pulled his hands from his pockets, and placed them on the edge of the sink, leaning into it. "Have you ever been questioned by the police?"

"Other than being stopped for speeding, no."

"It makes you feel guilty, even though you're not. It's the loneliest, most isolating feeling in the world."

"Your father—"

"Couldn't be bothered to go with me to the police station."

"You had Gall Hathaway in your corner."

"The police questioned us separately. He wasn't in on those initial interrogations."

"If I recall correctly, he retained a lawyer for you."

"Not right away. We didn't think a lawyer would be necessary. During those first couple of shakedowns I was all alone."

"They came down hard on you."

"You could say, yeah. He thought for sure I'd killed your sister."

"The detective, you mean?"

"Moody. You called him Monroe in your book, but his name was Dale Moody. Soon as he got my name from your folks—who also thought I was the culprit—he came to my house, woke up me and my old man, asked if he could talk to me about Susan. But he didn't exactly put it in the form of a polite request. Till then I didn't even know that she'd been murdered. I learned that from him when he started trying to strong-arm a confession out of me."

"What was that like, being pressured to make a confession?"

He left the window and went to the fridge, took out the pitcher of tea and brought it back to the table. She shook her head no when he held the pitcher above her glass, so he poured himself a refill, then resumed his seat across from her. However, instead of taking a drink, he placed the fingers of both hands against the glass and rubbed them up and down.

"Dent?"

"What?"

"I asked you a question."

"I heard you."

"Well, how did you feel?"

"How do you think? I felt like shit. Enough said."

"I don't think so."

"Why not?"

"Because I'm inviting you to vent your anger, and I think you want to."

"After all this time? It's a little late."

"Yesterday you said it hadn't been long enough."

He removed his hands from around the glass and rubbed his wet fingertips on the legs of his jeans. He frowned irritably at Bellamy, but she kept her expression calm and inquisitive.

He mouthed another curse, then said, "The girl I'd been making out with two days earlier was on a slab in the county morgue. Something like that sorta messes with your mind, wouldn't you say?"

"Yes, I would."

"I was trying to wrap my brain around Susan being killed by the tornado, when this *Law & Order* wannabe shows up and starts asking me what we'd argued about, when I'd last seen her, where was I when she was being choked to death." Noticing Bellamy's grimace, he pointed at her face. "Yeah. Like that. That's how I felt."

"I tried to capture those conflicting emotions in my book."

"You described the scene real well, even down to leaving my old man out of it."

"I omitted him because I didn't have a sense of him."

Dent barked a laugh. "Join the club. I lived with him, and I didn't have a sense of him, either. For all practical purposes, the man was a fucking ghost."

That struck her as odd phraseology. "Explain what you mean by that."

"Why? Are you plotting another book?"

She slapped the tabletop as she came quickly to her feet. "Okay, don't explain it. You're the one who proposed we take this trudge down memory lane, not me. You can see yourself out."

As she went past him, his arm shot out and encircled her waist, bringing her up short and close to him.

The contact startled her, making her breath catch. They held that pose for several moments, neither of them moving, then he relaxed his arm, dragging it away from her slowly, trailing his fingers over her rib cage. Softly he said, "Sit down."

She swallowed and resumed breathing. "Are you going to act like a jerk?"

"Probably. But you wanted to hear this." He nodded her toward the chair.

She returned to it, placed her hands primly in her lap, and looked at him expectantly. But after several seconds, he shrugged. "Well? Ask away."

"I have to pull it out of you? You're not going to volunteer anything?"

"What do you want to know?"

"What happened to your mother?"

The question caught him off guard, and she was glad it was he who seemed unbalanced for a moment. He looked away, shifted his position in the chair, rolled his shoulders in a defensive gesture. "I was told she died when I was a baby."

She continued watching him, dozens of follow-up questions implied.

Finally, he said, "I never saw a death certificate. My old man never took me to visit a grave. We never commemorated her birthday or the day she died. There were no maternal grandparents. None of that. I don't even know what she looked like because I was never shown a picture of her. It was like she'd never existed. So what I figure, she left me with him. Split. Vamoosed. He just didn't have the guts to tell me."

"Maybe he never came to terms with it himself."

"I don't know. It's an unsolved mystery. Anytime I bugged him for information about her, he would say, 'She died.' End of discussion."

"So it was just the two of you?"

"Yeah, but I wouldn't call it cozy."

"You speak of him in the past tense. He's no longer living?"

"No." Then, bitterly, "Not that you could call what he did 'living.'"

"He was a ghost," she said, using the word he'd used earlier to describe the man.

"You know, on second thought, that's not an apt description. Because he *did* take up space. He wasn't invisible. He just wasn't *there*. He provided for me. Roof over my head, food on the table, clothes on my back. He saw that I got to school every day."

His moss-colored eyes turned hard. "But he never attended a single school event. He never met a friend. Never watched me play a sport, and I played them all. I signed my own report cards. He functioned. That's all. He wasn't into sports, women, religion, gardening, stamp collecting, basket weaving. Nothing. He didn't drink, didn't smoke.

"His conversations consisted of maybe three sentences, including the ones he had with me. He went to work every day, came home, served our supper, turned on the TV for a couple of hours, then went to his bedroom and shut the door. We never took a vacation. Never went anywhere. Not to the movies, ball games, pool halls, the city dump." He stopped himself and took a deep breath. "We did nothing together.

"I'd misbehave, do something *really* bad, just to see if I could get a rise out of him or, at the very least, cause a change in his facial expression. My bad behavior didn't faze him. But nothing good I did fazed him, either. He didn't care one way or the other.

"He was a consistent SOB, I'll say that for him. He died a puzzle I never solved and had lost interest in a long time before. All I know about him is that whatever it was that shut him down permanently shut out the rest of the world."

"Including you."

He raised a shoulder. "No matter."

Bellamy didn't believe he was as indifferent to the parental neglect as he pretended, but, for the time being, she let it go. "When did you first meet Mr. Hathaway?"

"He would hate you calling him that."

"All right, when did you first meet Gall?"

"I was twelve, thirteen. Thereabout. One day after school I didn't want to go home, so I struck off on my bike. No destination. Just wanting to put miles between me and my house. When I got pretty far out, I spotted this small airplane swooping down and disappearing for a few seconds, then soaring up over the horizon again. I rode toward it and wound up out at Gall's airfield, where he was instructing a student. They were doing touch-and-goes. Man, I envied them. I wanted to be in that airplane so bad."

"Love at first sight?"

He fired a finger pistol at her. "Right on target, A.k.a. You're a writer, after all."

"You fell in love with flying that day."

"Head over freakin' heels. I stayed there watching until they landed. The guy taking the lesson left. Gall had noticed me lurking, waved me into the hangar. I figured he was going to tell me that I was trespassing and to get lost.

"Instead, he offered me a Dr Pepper. He asked if I liked airplanes, and I told him yes—although until that afternoon, I didn't know it. He motioned me out to the airplane they'd been flying and asked if I'd ever been up in a single-engine. I hadn't been up in anything, but I lied and told him I had.

"He pointed out all the parts and told me what they were called. He let me sit in the pilot's seat, and gave me a rundown on what all the gauges were for. I asked if it was hard to fly one. He looked at me and laughed. 'If it was hard, could I do it?'

"Then he asked if I wanted to go up. I nearly wet myself. He asked if my folks would care, and I told him no. Which was the truth. So we switched seats, and he took off, flying directly into the sunset. We made a wide sweep and were back on the ground in under five minutes, but it was the best time of my life up to then."

He was smiling at the memory and remained lost in thought for several moments before resuming. "Gall let me help him secure the plane. By the time we'd finished, it had grown dark. When I got on my bike, he asked me where I lived, and when I told him the general vicinity, he said, 'That far? Jesus, kid, you don't even have a light on your bike. How are you going to see to get home?' I came back with something like, 'I got out here okay, didn't I?'

"He called me a damn-fool kid and a smart-ass to boot, got in his truck, and drove along behind me so I could see my way by his headlights. That was the first time—" He broke off, leaving the thought unspoken.

"The first time what?"

He averted his gaze and mumbled, "The first time anybody had ever been worried about me."

Bellamy reasoned that he had fallen in love with more than flying that day. He had started loving Gall, who had paid attention to him, talked to him, been protective of him. But she knew the man the neglected teenage boy had become would rebuff any discussion of that, so she returned to their original topic.

"Detective Moody raked you over the coals."

Emerging from the nostalgic recollections, he frowned. "Several times. I told him over and over again that Gall and I had been test-flying a plane, that I wasn't at the barbecue, and that I didn't get to the park until after the tornado."

"Why did you come to the park at all?"

"There were thunderstorms around that forced Gall and me to return ahead of schedule, so I figured I had just as well try to smooth things over with Susan. Given a choice, though, I'd have stayed in the air. Every minute I spent in a plane was better than being on the ground."

"Better even than the time you spent with Susan?"

He grinned. "Tough choice."

"She was as good as all that? As exhilarating as flying?"

"Susan, no. Sex...hmm. It's the only thing that comes close."

"What time did you get to the state park?"

"Hold on a sec." He folded his arms on the table and leaned across it toward her. "Let's explore this some."

"Explore what?"

"Sex and flying. Sex and anything. Sex and, say... writing." He narrowed his focus on her mouth. "Given a choice right now, which would you rather be doing?"

"Are you flirting with me?"

"What do you think?"

She thought her cheeks were growing so warm he probably detected her blush. His grin was unrepentantly suggestive and made her feel twelve years old again. "It won't do you any good," she said. "Because even if I was open to comparing sex to my lifework, I wouldn't want to be compared to my late sister."

His grin faded, and his eyes reconnected with hers. "I wouldn't do that."

"Yes you would."

"No I wouldn't. In any case, I don't even remember how it was with her."

"Because there have been so many since?"

"I'm a bachelor with a basic sexual appetite. I make it clear to the women I sleep with that there are no strings attached to my bed. We fine-tune the hormone levels, then go our separate ways, nobody gets hurt."

"Are you sure? Have you ever asked?"

He gradually eased himself back into the chair. After a moment, he said, "Tell you what. I'll elaborate on my sex life after you tell me what went wrong with your marriage."

Refusing to be baited, she said, "What time did you arrive at the state park?"

He snuffled a soft laugh. "Figured." Then, "What time did I get to the park? I don't know. I never could nail down a time for Moody, either, which he saw as an implicating factor. On my way there, I saw the funnel cloud. I realized the park lay in its path. I was minutes behind it, and when I got there, all hell had broken loose.

"It looked like—well, you know what it looked like. People were screaming. A lot of them were bloody and broken. Hysteria. Panic. Shock. Next to war, it's the worst thing I've ever seen."

"You were in war?"

"Air force. Iraq. Our base took some rocket fire and the bastards got lucky with their aim. Left those of us who survived it with a…a lot to clean up." His expression turned introspective. "War looks different from several miles up than when you're scooping up red mush that used to be your wing man."

He reached for his glass of tea and took a drink. They didn't look at each other and neither said anything for a time, then she asked what else he remembered seeing in the wake of the tornado.

"Your dad. He was running around like a crazy man, his hands cupped around his mouth, calling your names. Steven appeared first, looking like a zombie, acting like one. Howard shook him, trying to snap him out of his daze. Then Olivia appeared.

"She was...well, that's the only time I've seen any real emotion from the woman. She grabbed Steven and wrapped her arms around him like she was never going to let him go. Your dad was embracing both of them. He and Olivia were crying with relief over finding each other unharmed. But the group hug didn't last long because you and Susan were still unaccounted for.

"When they saw me, Olivia ran over. Had I been with Susan? Had I seen her? Where was she? She was yelling in my face, making little sense, ranting at me for breaking my date with Susan, making it my fault that she was missing, accusing me of causing trouble as always."

"She must have been out of her mind with worry."

Dent fell silent and stared into near space for a moment, then said, "Yeah, but later, after Susan's body was discovered, I thought about what she'd said. And in a way she was right. If I'd been with Susan that day as planned, she wouldn't have been in the woods with Allen Strickland. She might have been injured or even killed by the twister, but as least she wouldn't have been choked to death."

"I suppose both of us suffer a bit of survivors' guilt."

"I guess. But I never let on to Moody about it. He would have misread it. It was bad enough that I was within thirty, forty yards of Susan's body when the fireman found it. I'd been searching the woods with them. So were a dozen other men, but none of the rest became suspects. Only me. Later, Moody said it was like I had returned to the scene of the crime, as killers do. Bullshit like that," he added in a mutter.

"Anyhow, when I realized that Susan was dead, not just unconscious, I threw up. Then I went to find your parents, but when I did, I chickened out. I couldn't tell them. I just pointed them in the direction of where she'd been found."

He stopped talking and, when it became apparent that he wasn't going to continue, Bellamy prodded him. "And then what?"

"Then nothing. I was upset that my girlfriend was dead, but I knew that your folks wouldn't welcome any condolences from me and wouldn't want me hanging around like a member of the family. So I went home, went to bed.

"The following morning, Moody came calling. You know the rest. He'd talked to your parents and had made up his mind that I'd done it. He didn't have any physical evidence against me, but I was treated like a felon. For weeks my name was the one in all the papers and on the news every night. I was the 'suspect in the Susan Lyston slaying.'

"Hell, I couldn't even go to her funeral for fear of being attacked by a lynch mob." He formed a tight fist with one hand and tapped it against the tabletop. "The hell of it is, it didn't stop, not after Allen Strickland was taken into custody, not even after he was convicted," he said with raw resentment.

"See, A.k.a., the way it works? Even if you're officially cleared of all suspicion, the taint of having been a suspect stays with you. It's like a bad odor that clings to you. People have to accept that you're innocent, but there's a lingering doubt that you're entirely clean.

"I learned that during the NTSB investigation. Somebody got hold of those old headlines, plastered them all over the damn place. After that, the airline was ashamed to claim me. It's seriously bad PR to have an alleged murderer on your payroll."

She grew uncomfortable under his glare and felt compelled to acknowledge that, sadly, he was right. "I'm sorry, Dent."

"Can you be more specific? What exactly are you sorry for? For the dung heap I had to wrestle through then, or the fresh one I'm having to wrestle through now? Are you apologizing in advance for what will happen when Van Durbin's newspaper hits the stands tomorrow and all that speculation starts whirling around me again?"

"Why should it?"

"You have to ask? Before Van Durbin files that story, you can bet he'll want to identify 'the cowboy.' He'll probably crap himself when he learns I'm none other than the 'first person of interest.'"

"Who was vindicated."

"Maybe in your book, but not in real life."

"Gall provided you with an alibi that cleared you."

"Moody figured that Gall was lying."

"He had no case against you."

"Right. The only thing that saved me was that I wasn't found with Susan's panties."

Chapter 8

———◆◆◆———

Rupe Collier checked his reflection in the full-length mirror on the back of his office door. He patted his thinning hair into place to help cover the ever-widening bald spot on the crown of his head, shot his cuffs to make certain the diamonds in his Texas-shaped gold cuff links were twinkling, smiled widely to check his capped teeth for stuck food, then, approving of what he saw, left his office.

He strode into the showroom, where strategically placed spotlights shone on the new models fresh from the factory. He didn't ordinarily work the floor, but one of his salesman had told him that a customer was insistent on dealing with the "main man," and Rupe was definitely that.

The customer, pointed out to Rupe by the salesman, was bent down, peering through the tinted glass window—an option available at extra cost—into the luxurious interior of a top-of-the-line sedan.

"Rupe Collier. Who do I have the pleasure of meeting?"

The customer straightened up and returned Rupe's smile as he shook the extended hand. Rupe was pleased to see that his cuff links didn't escape notice. The other man wasn't dressed or groomed nearly as well, and that was the way Rupe liked it. It gave him a distinct advantage when it came to bargaining. In order to be a winner, one had to look the part.

The car shopper dropped Rupe's hand and motioned toward the car. "How much would this baby set me back?"

"It's worth every penny of the sticker price, *but* I can cut you the best deal in the country."

"Thirty-day guarantee?"

"On any car on the lot. I stand behind my product."

"Continuing the customer-service policies that your daddy built the business on forty years ago."

Rupe's grin widened. "You're well informed."

"Your commercials run nonstop on TV."

"I believe in advertising, in putting yourself out there." Rupe lightly slugged the man in the shoulder.

"So do I, Mr. Collier. We think alike."

"Call me Rupe."

"Pleased to meet you, Rupe. My name's Rocky Van Durbin."

Rupe's stomach plummeted.

The tabloid columnist fished a business card from the breast pocket of his off-the-rack sport jacket and handed it over. Having recognized the man's name instantly, Rupe realized he'd been cleverly ambushed. But he decided to brazen it out and pretended to read the card.

"New York City? We don't get many shoppers from way up there. I'm honored." He pocketed the card with as much nonchalance as he could fake. "If you're seriously in the market for a new car, Mr. Van Durbin, you couldn't do better than—"

"No thanks. I'm just looking."

"Sure, sure," Rupe said expansively. "Stay for as long as you like. Bob there, who you met out on the lot, will be happy to answer your questions and help you any way he can. But you'll have to excuse me. Unfortunately, I'm late for an appointment."

Van Durbin laughed. "I get that a lot." Then he squinted his ferret eyes. "By people who're afraid to talk to me."

He'd practically called Rupe Collier a coward, and Rupe didn't take the insult lightly. He felt like taking the slimy columnist by his scrawny neck and shaking him till his brains rattled. But he didn't practice his smile in the mirror every morning for nothing. He managed to keep it intact.

"I enjoy chatting with anybody from the Big Apple. But I'm expected somewhere else soon. Let's make an appointment—"

Van Durbin cut him off. "Well, see, that's a problem, Rupe. Because, soon, I gotta be somewhere else, too. Besides…" He socked Rupe in the shoulder as Rupe had done to him. "You practically wrote the book on closing the sale. Long as I'm here? Just a few minutes of your time? How 'bout it?"

Rupe's smile was growing stiff from keeping it in place. "Why don't we talk in my office?"

"Great! Thanks."

Rupe led the way, and, although he maintained his easy-breezy gait to keep up appearances, mostly for Van Durbin himself, he was anything but relaxed.

His unwanted visitor whistled softly when he stepped

into Rupe's inner sanctum. "*Niiiiice*. The car business must be good."

"Can't complain."

"My mother, rest her soul, tried to tell me I'd chosen the wrong career path. 'You can't make money in journalism.' She must've told me that a thousand times. I reminded her that Hearst had made some serious coin. Murdoch. But"—he sighed—"Mom was right. They were exceptions."

Trying not to appear overanxious, Rupe said, "How can I help you, Mr. Van Durbin?"

Van Durbin's attention had already been snagged by the copy of *Low Pressure* lying on the desk. Rupe gritted his teeth in frustration. He should have gotten rid of the damn thing after he'd read it. At the very least, he shouldn't have left it in plain sight.

Van Durbin moseyed over to it now and picked it up, then made a production of fanning through the four-hundred-and-something pages. "Now this local gal has done all right in the writing game, hasn't she? She's making a killing off this book."

Rupe was a natural showman, and he had used those innate showmanship skills to full advantage his entire life. He hoped they didn't fail him now. He moved around the corner of his desk and sat down in his cowhide chair, motioning for Van Durbin to sit in the chair facing him.

"I have a hunch that you didn't come all the way from New York to talk cars. That book brought you here. I'll take it a step further and venture that you know I prosecuted the murder case of Susan Lyston, and that's what you want to talk to me about."

Van Durbin spread his arms away from his sides. "You

caught me red-handed. Can I ask you some questions about your case against Allen Strickland? I'm addressing that aspect of the story in my column tomorrow."

Bile filled the back of Rupe's throat, but he tried to appear unflappable. "It was a long time ago. I'll stretch my memory as best I can."

"Thanks, Rupe." Van Durbin produced a small spiral notebook and a yellow pencil dimpled with a disgusting number of teeth marks. "Don't mind this. I have to write things down or I forget."

Rupe doubted that. He doubted the bastard ever forgot anything. He was sly, and he was dangerous. Rupe considered calling the dealership's security guard and having Van Durbin removed from the premises. But then it would appear that he had something to hide. He would also lose all control over what Van Durbin wrote about him.

No, better to stick to the playacting, cooperate, and give the writer something, in the hope that Rupert Collier would be depicted favorably in his column. He began by telling Van Durbin what a fan he was of the media. "You could call me a news junkie. So I'm happy to answer any questions I can. Fire away."

"Good, good. Let's start with why you left the DA's office."

"That one's easy. Selling cars pays better. A hell of a lot better. I wouldn't have an office near this *niiiiice* at the courthouse."

Van Durbin chuckled. "You decided that you'd just as well reap the benefits of your daddy's labor."

Rupe recognized that for the well-placed dig it was, but he gave a good-natured thumbs-up. "Daddy didn't raise no stupid children."

"Right. You would have been a sap to stay in public service."

That was one of those trick questions, which wasn't really a question but a statement. Rupe was savvy enough to see the trap. "I serve my community in other ways now."

"Oh, I'm sure you do." Van Durbin flashed him an obnoxious grin. "But back then, you were committed to 'sweeping Travis County's streets free of the criminal element.' I cheated. I read that quote somewhere."

"I performed my job to the best of my ability."

Van Durbin flipped back several pages of his notepad and read some of the scribbles. "Uh, I jotted down just a coupla things I wanted to ask you about. Oh, here. Was Ms. Price's book accurate? Strickland was convicted of manslaughter? Not murder?"

"That's right."

"Why not murder?"

"I determined that his crime wasn't premeditated."

"In other words, he didn't plan on killing her. She did something that set him off and wound up dying over it."

Another carefully laid booby trap. "Mr. Van Durbin, surely you're not suggesting that she 'asked for it.'"

"No, no, I'd never even imply that." But his wicked grin belied the denial. "Strickland flew off the handle, killed her in a fit of passion, something like that?"

"If you want a clarification of the difference between the charges of murder and manslaughter, you can go online and access the Texas penal code."

"Thanks, I might do that. Just so I'm clear in my own mind." He tapped his temple with the eraser of his pencil. "You and that homicide detective…what was his name?"

"Gosh...who worked that case?" Rupe screwed up his face as though searching his memory. "I can't remember offhand. I was an ADA, working my patooty off, seventy, eighty hours a week. I was getting thrown cases right and left. A lot of felony cases. Worked with a number of cops, a slew of detectives."

Van Durbin snapped his fingers. "Moody. Dale Moody."

What Rupe was thinking was *Shitshitshit!*, but what he said was, "I think you're right. I think it was Moody."

"It was. My research assistant verified it and has been trying to run him down. She's checked with the Austin PD, but he's retired and they wouldn't give her any information on him. He doesn't have an Austin address. His name's not on the county tax rolls. You wouldn't by any chance know where I could find him, would you?"

"Until a few seconds ago, I couldn't even recall his name."

"That's a no, then?"

"That's a 'Sorry I wish I could help you, but I can't.'"

Van Durbin scratched something in his notepad. "So I guess if I wanted to ask him about his investigation and Strickland's trial, I'd be out of luck."

"I guess you would."

Van Durbin propped his ankle on his opposite knee and jiggled his foot. "Unless you wanted to open up to me about it. Talk me through it yourself."

Rupe gestured down at the book. "Ms. Price thoroughly covered it."

Van Durbin frowned. "But did it seem to you...? This just might be me, understand. But it seemed to me that she left the ending open to interpretation. Did it seem that way to you?"

Rupe forced his expression to turn thoughtful for a moment, then shook his head. "No, I can't say that it did."

"Hmm." Van Durbin skimmed over everything he'd written down before flipping the notepad closed. He replaced it along with the pencil in his shirt pocket and stood up. "Well, I guess that's everything. I can't thank you enough for giving me a few minutes of your valuable time."

"You're welcome. Although I don't feel like I contributed much." Smile in place, Rupe went to the door and pulled it open.

Van Durbin was almost across the threshold when he stopped, turned, and tapped Rupe's silk necktie with his index finger. "If I were you, Rupe, you know what would eat at me?"

It took all Rupe's self-control not to brush away that finger, with its loose cuticle and the fingernail chewed down to the quick. "What's that?"

"It would eat at me that the murder weapon never turned up. You and Moody determined that she was choked to death with her underwear, right?"

Rupe gave a noncommital nod.

"But the panties never turned up, did they? And you looked every-damn-where for them."

"Obviously the jury didn't think having them in evidence was necessary to convict."

"Obviously," Van Durbin said, frowning. "But I hate loose ends like that, don't you, Rupe?"

The topic of Susan's underpants seemed to have raised the temperature in Bellamy's kitchen. Introducing that vital element into their discussion of the crime had been inevitable, but now Dent wished he'd let Bellamy bring it up first.

Too ill at ease to sit any longer in a tense silence, he got up from the table and took another aimless tour of the kitchen until his attention was drawn to a ceramic jug on the counter that contained a variety of stainless-steel doodads.

Pulling one out, he held it up and twirled it between his fingers. "What does this do?"

"It cores apples."

"You don't just eat around the core?"

But, not to be distracted, she asked, "Was your house searched?"

He returned the apple corer to the jug. "If by *searched* you mean *turned inside out*, then yeah. It was searched. Moody and an army of cops showed up with a warrant to look specifically for a pair of Susan's underwear.

"They ransacked the place. Even confiscated my motorcycle. They took it apart piece by piece. I had it reassembled, but it was never the same, and I wound up having to get rid of it."

He looked over at Bellamy, who appeared to be hanging on every word, but she said nothing, so he continued.

"That pair of panties was the Holy Grail of Moody's investigation. His thinking was that the man who was caught with them was the deviant who'd used them to strangle her."

She stared thoughtfully into near space. "Of all the indignities, the cruelties, that Olivia and Daddy were subjected to over Susan's death, I believe that aspect of it was the hardest for them. It was certainly the most embarrassing. It implied any variety of dreadful things. Either she'd been molested or..."

"Or," he stressed, "she'd willingly let the man remove them. Or she had taken them off herself. Which I'm inclined to believe."

"Why?"

He stopped pacing and gave her a meaningful look. "The first time we went out." She dropped her gaze to the tabletop.

"Also, there wasn't any other indication of sexual assault," he continued. "She wasn't bruised or torn down there. No bite marks. No semen. Whatever took place before she was killed was consensual. Even Moody thought so."

"Nevertheless, the missing underpants added a salacious element to the crime and made it all the more horrible."

"And yet..." Placing his hands flat on the table, he leaned down close to her and said in a whispery voice, "The girl in your novel is choked to death in the same manner."

"Because that's what happened."

"But doesn't it spice things up, which equates to selling more books?"

Her eyes flashed with anger. "Go to hell."

"I've been," he fired back.

She stood up so abruptly that her chair went over backward, making a slamming sound against the floor that reverberated and shocked them both into silence.

She turned to pick up the chair, but Dent stepped around the table and set it upright before she could. He'd made her temper flare. He was intentionally goading her, and he didn't know why, but he knew he didn't like himself for it. He'd begun to notice how weary she looked.

Given her father's condition, and the state of her house upon her return from Houston, he doubted she'd slept much last night. The violet half-moons beneath her eyes indicated that she hadn't slept well for quite some time.

On impulse, he said, "Want to get some air?"

She looked at him quizzically.

"Outside. Fresh air. Let's go for a walk."

She went to the window, moved aside the curtain, and looked up at the sky. "It's overcast."

"It's hazy."

"It's muggy."

"The climate is worse in here."

He took her arm and propelled her out the back door, giving her little choice. Once on the sidewalk, they fell into step companionably. She even took a deep breath of contentment.

"See?" he said. "We needed to get out of there for a while. It was getting intense."

"We rub each other the wrong way."

Looking at her askance, he said, "We could rub each other till we get it right." He watched for her blush and wasn't disappointed. She'd needed that extra color in her cheeks. It flattered her. "I'll let you go first," he offered teasingly. "Unless you want me to. Which I'm happy to do."

She rolled her eyes. "There's a park a few blocks up."

Five minutes later, they were seated in side-by-side swings with old-fashioned wood plank seats and heavy suspension chains. They were the only people near the swings. Some distance away, a middle-aged couple played catch with their young grandson. "Throw the ball to Paw-Paw," he heard the woman say.

Farther away still, a quartet of teenaged girls in skimpy shorts and tank tops practiced cheerleading. Nearest him and Bellamy a pair of lovers lay on a blanket beneath a shade tree, lost in each other.

Dent moved his swing sideways to bump lightly into hers. "I've talked you through my experiences of that day and what came after. But you stopped at the point where Susan returned to the pavilion from the boathouse and started dirty dancing with Allen Strickland."

She gave her swing a push. "What do you want to know?"

"Did you actually see Susan leave the pavilion with him?"

"Yes."

"Did you follow them?"

"No."

"Okay..." He drew out the word in the form of a lead-in.

She continued swinging, going a little higher on each arc. "Okay, what?"

"What did you do?"

She started to speak several times before words actually formed. "I headed for the boathouse."

"Why the boathouse?"

"I... I think I went to find Steven."

"You *think* you went to find him?"

The swing made several pendulous cycles before she said, "The sky was getting darker. I'd seen Steven walking toward the lake and wanted to make certain that he was aware of the approaching storm. I thought he should come back to the pavilion."

"But neither of you made it back to the pavilion in time.

The funnel dipped out of the cloud, you both got caught at the boathouse and had to take cover there."

She nodded.

"What about Susan?"

She turned her head toward him as the swing sailed past. "What about her?"

"You weren't worried about her, too?"

"Of course I was."

"But you didn't chase after her."

"She was with Allen."

"All the more reason to check on her."

"Maybe I did. I—"

"You said you went to find Steven."

"Yes, yes, just like in the book."

"Forget the friggin' book."

He set his swing to rocking crazily when he quickly abandoned it. He stepped in front of Bellamy's swing and grabbed hold of the chains, bringing it to an abrupt halt and wedging his thigh between hers to hold the seat high off the ground.

"What are you doing?"

"More to the point, what are you?" he asked. "This makes twice today that you've stalled there. Why? How come your memory is so detailed about what you wore and shoulder straps that kept slipping down, but you go all vague and sputtery when recounting what you did and where you were between the time you saw Susan return from her drinking binge at the boathouse, to when they dragged you from beneath the collapsed roof of it?"

She gazed back at him, wide-eyed and apprehensive. "I testified at Allen Strickland's trial that I went in search of Steven. I was in the boathouse when the tornado struck.

I wasn't that badly hurt, but I was traumatized by fear, in shock. That's why I was one of the last people to be accounted for, hours after the storm, even after Susan's body had been recovered. I heard people—my own parents—frantically calling my name, but I couldn't respond. I was literally frozen from fear."

"That follows what you wrote in your book."

She bobbed her head once.

"So why don't I believe you?"

Her chin went up a fraction. "Believe me or not, that's your problem."

"You're damn right it is. I've got somebody trashing my airplane all because of you and the can of worms you opened. And this is a big, fat, juicy, squiggly one. You falter every time I ask whether or not you followed Susan and Allen Strickland."

"I didn't."

"You're sure?"

"No. I mean—Yes, I'm sure. No I didn't follow them. You confused me before and you're trying to now. When I left the pavilion I ran toward the boathouse."

"Okay, so why did you choose to warn Steven of the storm, and not your sister?"

"I didn't make any such choice," she exclaimed.

"But you did, Bellamy. You just said so. You went toward the boathouse because you'd seen Steven going in that direction."

"That's right."

"Is it?"

She wiggled forward on the seat of the swing, trying to reach the ground with her toes. "Let me down."

Instead, he moved in closer, using his body to hold her in

the swing and the swing off the ground. "Did you find Steven? Were you able to warn him to seek shelter?"

"No."

"You're sure of that?"

"Of course I'm sure. That's why I was alone when they found me in the rubble."

"You didn't go after Susan? You didn't see her after she left the pavilion?"

"No and no."

"Did you also testify to that under oath?"

"I didn't have to."

"Because?"

"Because no one ever asked me. Until *now*," she said with vexation.

"So if you didn't swear otherwise, you might've followed her and Allen into the woods."

"But I didn't."

"No?"

She set her chin stubbornly and refused to answer.

He joggled the chains of the swing. "A.k.a?" he said in a singsong voice. "Cat got your tongue?"

"Why are you bullying me about this?"

"I'm only trying to get to the absolute truth."

"I've told you the absolute truth."

"You didn't chase after Susan."

"No."

"I'm not convinced."

"Too bad."

"Why does this point trip you up?"

"It doesn't."

"Yeah. It does. How come? There's gotta be a reason."

"Let me down, Dent."

"Did you run after Susan?"

"No."

"You didn't?"

"No!"

"Bellamy?"

"*I don't know!*"

She gasped in stunned surprise at her own admission, and for several seconds they stayed frozen, their faces inches apart, staring into each other's eyes. Then her head dropped forward and she repeated miserably, "I don't know. And that's the absolute truth."

He'd pressured her for clarification, but hadn't really expected it to be this consequential. If he had it to do over again, he might have relented sooner. As it was, he needed to get a grasp of the worrisome implications.

He pried his fingers from around the chain and, with that hand, tipped her head up. Tears were sliding over the freckles on her cheekbones. Her eyes were wet, deeply troubled, haunted.

"I can't remember," she said hoarsely. "I've tried, God knows. For eighteen years I've tried to bridge the gap. But that span of time is blocked out in my memory."

"Specifically, what *do* you remember?"

"Specifically? I remember going down to the boathouse and seeing Susan drinking with her friends. Specifically, I remember her coming back, dancing with Allen Strickland, and making a spectacle of herself. I remember watching them leave the pavilion together."

She looked at him and said helplessly, "But it's like… like the broken center line on the highway. Sections of time are missing where I don't remember what I did, or what I saw."

She hiccuped a soft sob. "Yesterday I told you that I wrote the book so I'd be able to throw it away and forget it. But that was a lie. I wrote it in the hope of *remembering*.

"And what I think... what I'm afraid of... is that someone read the book, and knows what I left out. He knows whatever it is that I can't remember. And he doesn't want me to."

Chapter 9

Dent wished he could dismiss her fear, but he'd come to the same unsettling conclusion. Someone was afraid that the constant retelling of the story would unlock a memory that had been sealed deep inside her subconscious for almost two decades.

Bellamy the child with a faulty memory hadn't represented much of a threat to that individual. But Bellamy the woman with a best-selling book definitely did. *You'll be sorry* now seemed less of a warning than a vow.

Also Dent feared that this elusive memory she so desperately wanted restored was one better left in the vault of her subconscious. Her psyche had blocked it for a reason. She might later regret learning why she'd been protected from it.

But he had selfish reasons for wanting her to recapture it, primarily his own vindication. So for the time being, he would keep his concerns to himself and continue to help her.

With the pad of his thumb, he wiped the tears off her

cheek, then, using his thigh to hold the swing steady, cupped his hands in her armpits, lifted her off the seat, and lowered her to the ground. Even then, he withdrew his hands with reluctance.

He took a cautious look around. It had been five minutes since the lovers had come up for air. Paw-Paw and his wife had given up on the ball toss and had packed their grandson into their van and left. A forty-something man in shirtsleeves and slacks had parked his dusty sedan, gotten out, and walked straight to a picnic table, where he sat down and immediately opened up both his collar and his cell phone. While talking into his phone, he ogled the cheerleaders, who were doing flips. Dent figured the guy had timed his visit to the park when he knew they'd be there.

No one was interested in him and Bellamy.

Coming back to her, he asked, "Who all knows about your memory block?"

She looked at him with an expression that spoke volumes.

When he realized what she was telling him, his jaw dropped. "You're shittin' me."

"No," she said softly. "You're it. I never told anyone. My parents were so upset over losing Susan, over everything, I didn't want to add to their anxiety. When Moody talked to me, I told him the version that I ultimately wrote in the book, and for all I knew that was true.

"I tried to remember. I swear I did. But then Strickland was arrested. Moody and Rupe Collier were confident that they'd solved the mystery, so it seemed less important that I recall everything.

"During Strickland's trial, all I was required to testify to was how suggestively he and Susan had been dancing, and I could truthfully answer those questions. I couldn't point the finger at Strickland and positively identify him as Susan's killer. Nor could I deny that he was. But neither could anyone else in that courtroom."

"He was convicted with only circumstantial evidence."

"A preponderance of it."

"But no physical evidence."

"They matched his DNA," she argued.

"A couple strands of his hair. Susan's clothing also had traces of Mr. So-and-So's dandruff and Mr. What's-His-Name's skin cells. She'd danced with a lot of men. She was crawling with DNA from a dozen or more people."

"But Strickland's saliva—"

"He admitted to kissing her open-mouthed and that his mouth had also been on her breasts."

"What you're saying is that you think Allen Strickland killed her."

"No. I'm only saying that he was Moody's best guess. But if Allen Strickland *was* the guilty party and sent to Huntsville to contemplate his sin for twenty long years, justice was served, right? Why, then, is somebody terrifying the hell out of you for bringing the world's attention to it? And speaking of . . ." He placed his arm over her shoulder and brought her close to his side as he turned around and started walking away from the swing set. "I wonder who the guy in the pickup is."

"What guy? Where?"

"Don't look." He hugged her tighter to keep her facing forward. "Just keep walking."

"Someone is watching us?"

"Can't be sure. But the same truck has driven by twice in the last few minutes. I wouldn't have thought much about it except that he's now coming by for a third pass. This is a pretty park, but I don't think he's admiring the duck pond or the gazebo. He doesn't look the type."

"What type does he look like?"

"I can't make out his facial features, but his truck screams bad-ass bubba. Lots of bumper stickers, skull and crossbones on the mud flaps, get-the-blank-out-of-my-way tires. I'd bet money there's a gun rack in the cab."

"You noticed all that?"

"I'm used to searching the horizon for aircraft I must avoid, which usually look like a moving speck. One pickup roughly the size of my apartment is easy to spot. Do you know anyone who drives a truck like that?"

She shot him a look.

"I didn't think so." He stopped and bent down as though to pick a dandelion, and in the process glanced down the street in time to see the pickup round a corner a few blocks away. "Gone."

Bellamy looked in that direction, but was too late to catch a glimpse of the pickup. "It could have been anybody."

"It could have been, but I've come down with a bad case of paranoia."

"I think we're both being paranoid."

"Don't try to bullshit a bullshitter, A.k.a. You had a meltdown a few minutes ago. You're scared, with reason. You said yourself that our guy doesn't want you to remember what really went down."

"I said that, yes, because I know about my memory loss. He doesn't."

"Which makes him even more desperate to learn what you're up to, why you've stayed silent till now."

"If I'd known something crucial to the case, I would have come forward with it during the investigation. I would have told everything I saw."

"Not if what you saw scared you senseless." He looked deeply into her eyes and said what she probably knew but hadn't had the courage to acknowledge, even to herself. "Like witnessing your sister's murder."

She recoiled. "But I didn't."

"Someone thinks you might have. *I* think you might have."

"Well, you're wrong. I would remember that."

"Okay," he said, not wanting to add to her distress. "But we need verification of everything you do remember, or think you do. We need someone who was there to fill in the gaps that you and I can't." He hesitated. "We need to talk to your parents."

"About this? Absolutely not, Dent."

"They need to know."

"I won't resurrect the worst time in their lives."

"You already did."

"Well, thank you for reminding me of that," she snapped. "When I began writing *Low Pressure*, I didn't know that it would be published when Daddy was fighting for his life."

"You may soon be fighting for *yours,* and they would want to know that."

"You saw a redneck in a souped-up truck, like that's a rarity in Texas. But suddenly my life is in danger? You're blowing this way out of proportion."

"Oh, denial now. That's healthy."

She had the grace to look away in concession.

"Your parents need to know about the potential danger."

Adamantly, she shook her head.

"Howard's got money. He could hire a bodyguard for you."

"Have you lost your mind? I'm not going to have a bodyguard."

He backed down from that. "Tell them, Bellamy."

"No."

"Talking about it with them could shake something loose."

"I said no! And that's final. Drop it."

He hadn't counted on getting her to agree, but her insistence was aggravating. He placed his hands on his hips and exhaled. "Okay then, Steven. And before you butt in with all the reasons why not, hear me out. You and he were at least in the same general vicinity when the tornado struck, which coincides with the time your memory goes kaput. He's the next logical choice of who we should talk to."

Reluctantly, she mumbled, "Probably."

"Did he help supply you with missing facts when you were writing the book?"

"We met once in New York for lunch."

He waited expectantly to hear more, but when she offered nothing, he said, "I'm not interested in what you ate."

"Steven wasn't very forthcoming with his impressions of that Memorial Day."

"Why not?"

"He wasn't very forthcoming about that, either."

Dent frowned.

"Don't read anything into it," she said. "That was a terrible time for him, too. It's in his past. Over. Buried. I don't really blame him for not wanting to talk about it."

"You said he went back east when he left Austin. Where?"

"He's in Atlanta now."

"Atlanta." He checked his wristwatch, then resumed walking, but at a brisker pace. "If we hurry, we can make the four-thirty nonstop flight."

"How do you know there's a—"

"I used to fly it."

Ray Strickland drove away from the park and out of Bellamy Price's neighborhood. He didn't believe he'd drawn her and Denton Carter's notice, but he didn't want to. He wanted to wait until he was ready to make his move. Then they'd notice him, all right.

Heeding his growling stomach, he stopped at a 7-Eleven on the access road off the interstate and bought a burrito and a Big Gulp. He returned to his truck and, as he ate seated behind the steering wheel, he ruminated on what he'd witnessed and what his next course of action should be.

The bitch was no longer hawking her book on his TV every time he turned the damn thing on. But did that matter? Not really. To Ray's way of thinking, the damage had been done the day the book went on sale. It was still out there, being read by thousands of people every day.

Viciously, he tore off another bite of the burrito.

She'd made his big brother look like a patsy at best, and a killer at worst. She had to die for that. But, not wanting to make it too easy on her, he'd planned on playing with her for a while before he killed her.

He'd especially enjoyed getting into her car and rubbing his hands over the leather seat still warm from her ass. That had almost been as good as sifting through the panties in her bureau drawer.

But while these small violations had been fun, he was ready to get on with it. He could practically hear Allen whispering in his ear, "Strike while the iron is hot," and Ray always heeded Allen's advice.

That strutting pilot was another reason to move things along. Ray would have given one of his tattoos—except for the snake—to see Dent Carter's face when he saw what had been done to his airplane. He would have gone ballistic. Ray wasn't afraid of him. Hell, no. But he was an additional complication that must be taken into account.

Ray had been keeping an eye on her house all morning, and sure enough, when she returned, Dent had been with her. Police had come and gone, but Ray wasn't too worried on that score. While inside her house, he'd been very careful. Besides, he didn't have a police record. He'd never been fingerprinted.

In fact, outside of his workplace, few people even knew he was alive. It wasn't like he had a large circle of friends. He went to work. He came home. He worked out there with his own set of weights. If he went out, to a diner, to the movies, he went alone. If he felt like talking to someone, he pretended Allen was there, listening, laughing, giving him advice.

He'd continued to watch Bellamy's house while the hours ticked by. Ray wondered what they were doing in there. Cleaning up the mess he'd made, or something more fun? Dent-the-superstud was probably after a piece of baby sister's snatch, wanted to see how she compared to the other one.

What really had gotten to him, though, was their little

stroll to the park. They'd looked so carefree, when they should have felt his threat, sensed his lurking, even if they hadn't seen him.

Swinging, for godsake. Like a couple of kids without a worry in the world. Heads together. What had they been whispering about? What a sucker Allen Strickland had been? It made Ray's blood boil.

He wanted vengeance for Allen, and he wanted it now. No more pussyfooting around. He was a man of action. Jean-Claude Van Damme wouldn't wait around. Vin Diesel wouldn't put off till tomorrow what should be done today.

He stuffed the remainder of the burrito into his mouth, balled up the wrapper and tossed it to the floorboard of his truck, then sucked half his Big Gulp through the plastic straw.

He was about to start his truck when his cell phone rang. His boss, calling again. This made about the tenth time today he'd tried to reach him, but Ray had ignored the calls because he knew why the guy was calling. He wanted to know why Ray hadn't been on the job for the third day in a row.

Because Ray Strickland had more important things to do, that was why. He didn't have to answer to anybody. He made his own decisions.

He picked up the phone, said, "Fuck you," to the caller ID, then switched it over to vibrate so it wouldn't bug him anymore.

He cranked on the truck, peeled out of the 7-Eleven parking lot, and headed back toward the neighborhood he'd recently left. He made two circuits around the park. They were no longer there. He drove toward her house, propelled by blood lust, no particular plan in mind except to stop Bellamy Price from breathing. Getting that asshole Denton Carter at the same time would be a bonus. Extra points. Allen would be tickled pink.

But as Ray turned onto Bellamy's block, the Vette streaked past him in a blur of crimson.

All Ray had time to note was that there were two people inside it.

He gunned his truck and made a U-turn at his earliest opportunity. But his pickup couldn't match the Vette for speed and maneuverability. By the time Ray was headed in the right direction, the Vette had vanished.

As soon as the flight went airborne, Bellamy said to Dent, "I can't believe I let you talk me into this."

"First class?"

"The trip."

"We'll get there in time to have some dinner, get a good night's sleep, see your brother first thing tomorrow, come back. Less than twenty-four hours."

"During which I'll be out of pocket. I'm afraid Daddy will take a turn."

"If you get a call, we'll charter a jet back."

"Easy for you to say."

"You can afford it. You're rich and getting richer."

She said nothing to that. "But not telling them that we're going feels devious."

She had called Olivia en route to the Austin airport and had spoken to her father as well. Both had assured her that he was comfortable, that the drugs were working to curb the side effects of the most recent chemotherapy, and that for the time being he was holding his own. Even so, his oncologist had urged him to remain hospitalized so he could be closely monitored.

"I agree that's best," Bellamy had told her dad. "But I miss you."

"Miss you, too, sweetheart. I've become accustomed to seeing you nearly every day."

Although he had put up a brave front, he'd sounded feeble, which had only intensified her guilty feelings for leaving Austin without notifying them of her trip to go and see Steven.

With Dent setting the pace, they had practically jogged from the park back to her house, where he'd allotted her only five minutes to toss a change of clothing and some toiletries into a bag before hustling her out to his car.

He wove through Austin's insane traffic at seventy miles an hour, which would have left her breathless with fright had she not been navigating the airline's equally maddening telephone reservation lines.

The security check line had never been so long or slow moving. They made it to the boarding gate with only minutes to spare. Bellamy insisted on sitting on the aisle, telling Dent she didn't like the window. He'd said God forbid that she look out and spot a cloud.

They'd been bickering ever since. Now she said, "You didn't even give me time to think about it."

"If you'd thought about it, you wouldn't have come." He looked around the first-class cabin. "Where's the flight attendant?"

"The seat belt sign hasn't been turned off yet." She spoke absently because her mind was elsewhere. "The man in the pickup—"

"I didn't get a good look."

"Neither did I. You were driving too fast. All I caught was a glimpse of his tattooed arm, which was propped in the open driver's window." She paused, then said, "It could have been a coincidence that he was going in the direction of my house."

"It could have been."

"But you don't think it was."

"Put that truck in some areas around Austin, and it would fit right in. In your neighborhood, in the municipal park..." He shook his head. "Uh-uh. What was a guy like that doing cruising the streets of white-bread suburbia? Looking for his lost pit bull?"

Anything else they said would've been speculative, so there was no point in discussing it further. Besides, Dent's fidgeting had become annoying. "What's the matter with you?" she asked.

"Nothing."

"Do you need the bathroom?"

"No."

"Then...Oh." Suddenly she realized why he was so restless. "You dislike being a passenger. You want to be piloting the plane."

"Damn right."

"Are you still qualified?"

"Qualified, yes. But no longer licensed for this size jet. I'd have to be retyped."

"But you could fly it."

"In a heartbeat."

"You sound confident."

"You don't want to fly with a pilot who isn't."

"I don't want to fly with one who's overconfident, either."

He held her gaze for several beats. "Something on your mind, A.k.a.?"

She wanted to ask him about the incident that had cost him his career in commercial flying, but his hard expression caused her to shy away. "The attendant is up now."

"About freaking time."

When she reached their aisle, she smiled down at Bellamy. "It's a pleasure to have you on board, Ms. Price. I loved your book."

"Thank you."

"Are you on a book tour?"

"No, I'm taking some time off."

"Don't make us wait too long for the next book. Something to drink?"

"Diet Coke, please."

The attendant reached across her to set two cocktail napkins on the armrest between her and Dent. "And for you, sir? Something stronger?"

"You read my mind."

"I'm good at that."

"I'll bet you are," he said, giving her a slow grin. "Bourbon on the rocks."

"That would have been my first guess."

"Make it a double."

"That would've been my second guess," she said with cheekiness, then pulled back and started up the aisle toward the galley.

Bellamy gave him an arch look.

He said, "If I can't work the kite strings, I'd just as well drink."

"It's not that. It's..." She looked after the shapely

attendant as she made her way forward toward the galley. "It's always been easy for you, hasn't it?"

Catching her drift, he said, "Flirting? It would be easy for you, too, if you'd let it be."

"Never. I'm not equipped."

He slid a glance over her. "Your equipment is fine. Better than fine. But you've got this TFR posted—"

"TFR?"

"Temporary flight restriction posted around yourself that defies anyone to breach your airspace." He turned slightly in his seat to study her better. "Why the barrier?"

"Just my nature, I suppose."

"Try again."

"Okay, blame the gene pool."

"Meaning?"

"Susan inherited all the 'it factor' genes. When I came along, there were no more left."

"You're full of crap. Want to know what I think?"

"Actually, no."

"I think your ex is to blame."

The flight attendant returned with their drinks before Bellamy had a chance to respond. Dent absently thanked her for the drinks, but his attention stayed fixed on Bellamy, who was made uneasy by his scrutiny. She poured her cola into the glass of ice and took a sip. Finally, because he didn't relent, she turned to face him. "You're dying to know?"

"Hmm."

"He was an up-and-coming electronics engineer in our company. Brilliant. Innovative. Hardworking. Handsome in his own way."

"Otherwise known as ugly."

"Average good looks."

"If you say so."

"We began going out together after business meetings, first with a group, then by ourselves, and that evolved into actual dating. Olivia and Daddy approved of him one hundred percent. He was pleasant company, he was a gentleman, he was easygoing in any given situation. We got along beautifully. We became engaged at Christmas and were married in June. Lovely wedding with all the trimmings." She glanced down at the armrest. "Your ice is melting."

He hadn't seemed to notice until she'd called his attention to it. Picking up both the small bottles of bourbon, she emptied them into his glass.

"Thanks."

"You're welcome." She sipped her Coke. He sipped his drink.

Eventually he said, "If that's the end of the story, then you're still married to this pleasant, hardworking, brilliant electronics engineer who sounds as boring as hell to me. So does your marriage."

She took a deep breath before continuing. "Things rocked along nicely for a couple of years. We were compatible. We never fought." She smiled wanly. "In hindsight, maybe we should have. We weren't *un*happy."

"Just?"

"Just that there seemed nothing much to look forward to except years of sameness."

"Monotony."

"I thought a child might help to—"

"Break up the boredom."

"Create a newer, stronger bond between us. He agreed.

In fact, he loved the idea of a child. We worked on it, and two months later were rewarded by a dual pink stripe on the home pregnancy test."

She picked up her glass and rattled the ice, but didn't drink from it. "Olivia and Daddy were over the moon. They wanted a grandchild so badly. Everyone was excited. We were discussing motifs for the nursery, considering names. Then—" After a significant pause, she said, "In the tenth week, I miscarried."

She was staring into her glass of cola but could feel Dent staring at her. Finally she looked up at him and shrugged. "That was the end of it. I got a D and C. My husband got a girlfriend."

Chapter 10

————❖————

Dale Moody glowered suspiciously at his ringing cell phone and debated whether he could be bothered to answer it. After three rings he checked the caller ID. Haymaker. Who had recently warned him that Rupe Collier was on his tail.

Ordinarily it was months between his and Haymaker's telephone visits. It didn't bode well that he was calling again so soon.

He answered. "What's up, Hay?"

"Rupe Collier came sniffing again."

"When?"

"This afternoon. And this time he didn't phone. He pulled up into my driveway while I was out watering the yard. No way I could avoid him. His hair's thinning. You can't tell it on TV."

"What did he want?"

"Same as before. You. Says it's real important—*vital* was the word he used—that he talks to you before tomorrow."

"What happens tomorrow?"

"You ever hear of *EyeSpy*?"

"The kids' game?"

"The tabloid."

Dale listened with increasing despair as his old buddy recounted Rupe's story about a shifty columnist for a widely read tabloid newspaper. It seemed that Dale Moody was the only English-speaking person on the planet who didn't read Van Durbin's column or wasn't at least familiar with his byline.

"According to Rupe, this Van Durbin's column tomorrow is about *Low Pressure* and the true story it's based on. He's going to bring into question whether or not the guy who got the time did the crime. This has got Rupe's tighty-whities in a wad. He called the columnist pond scum, which is funny, coming from someone as slippery as Rupe."

Dale failed to see the humor in any of this. In fact, if he was a lesser man, he'd break down and bawl.

"Anyhow," Haymaker continued, "he's all hot and bothered to talk to you before this writer from New York gets to you."

"Gets to *me*?"

"I haven't told you that part yet. Rupe says Van Durbin was asking about you. Asked if Rupe knew where you were, how to get in touch with you. He's got research people checking every avenue they can think of."

"Shit."

"Suddenly you're a real popular guy, Dale. Seemed to me that Rupe was more interested in keeping you from talking to this Van Durbin than he was in talking to you his own self."

Rupe's worst nightmare would be him talking to any media about the Susan Lyston case and Allen Strickland's trial.

"Hay, did you tell him—"

"Not a damn thing. I wouldn't." After a slight hesitation, he added, "Only thing is...See, Dale..."

"What?"

The former policeman made a sound of disgust. "Rupe's carrying the note on a used car I bought from him last year. The wife wanted the mother-lovin' thing. I hate it, but she had to have it. The bank wouldn't loan us enough to buy it, but Rupe made it easy for us to drive it straight off the lot with no money down. Interest rate out the wazoo, but the wife... You know how it is. Then two months after we became the proud owners of the car, she got laid off out at the quarry. I can't sell—"

"You're behind on the payments, and Rupe is using that as leverage for you to give me up."

Haymaker's silence was as good as a confirmation. Dale uncapped the bottle of Jack Daniel's on his TV tray and took a swig straight from it. "How much time did he give you?"

"Till eight o'clock in the a.m."

"Jesus. Rupe must be real scared of this Van Durbin character."

"Right down to the shine on his Luccheses. He's afraid that guy will tree you before he can."

"How much do you owe him?"

"Look, Dale, don't worry about that. I wouldn't sell out a cop buddy to that asshole. I only told you so you'd know how jumpy Rupe is to find you. I won't tell him squat, but you gotta believe that I'm not his only resource.

"I'm figuring he'll call in every favor and marker he's holding on personnel inside the Austin PD and city hall. Some of our former colleagues didn't think as kindly of you as I did. *Do.* So consider this a heads-up.

"And, Dale, Rupe may not stop at arm-twisting, either. While he was in the DA's office, he cut a lot of deals with felonious types. I know of one who works for him now as a repo man. Guy carries a chain saw as his persuader, and I kid you not."

Dale took Haymaker's implied warning to heart. He would put nothing past the former prosecutor. "I appreciate you telling me, Hay."

"You covered my back more than once, and I don't forget stuff like that."

"Are you gonna be okay?"

"You mean about the car? No sweat. My son will give me the money."

"You sure?"

"The little prick is always happy to oblige. Gives him an opportunity to remind me of what a lousy provider I am and always have been."

Before they hung up, Haymaker promised to call him with updates as they happened. Dale tossed his cell phone onto the metal TV tray, lit a cigarette, and drew hard on it as he stared thoughtfully into the half-empty bottle of whiskey.

Rupe Collier was afraid his life was about to be derailed. Well, good. It was about time the son of a bitch realized the consequences of the deal he'd made with the devil. Dale had been living with them for eighteen years.

The loaded pistol was a lure he could barely resist.

But for one more night, he did.

*   *   *

"Come again?"

"Atlanta."

"Texas or GA?"

"Georgia."

Dent might just as well have told Gall he'd gone to Timbuktu. He was sitting on the edge of the hotel room bed, his elbows on his thighs, staring down at the toes of his boots. Realizing it was the posture of a child preparing for a parental lecture, he straightened up. "We thought—"

"We? Who's the second party? Or don't I already know?"

"Are you going to keep interrupting? Because if you are, I'm going to hang up."

Dent could imagine his mentor clamping down hard on his cigar and scowling.

"Thank you," Dent said politely, then with emphasis, "*Bellamy and I* are trying to reconstruct that Memorial Day. Who did what, and when."

"What brought this on?"

Dent told him about Van Durbin's accosting them and what the subject of tomorrow's column was going to be. "It doesn't matter whether or not there's any substance to the question. Just posing it implies that something ran afoul. He's a weasel. Has this nasty little grin that suggests he's seen your mother nekkid. I could break him in half. *You* could break him in half. But his column is famous nationwide, and, with just a little finessing of the facts, he can do a body either a lot of good or a lot of harm."

"This situation just gets better and better."

"Tell me." Dent sighed.

"So why did you sign on for more crap? Get away from her."

"I told you, we're trying—"

"Yeah, yeah, but didn't she cover the details of that day in her book?"

"There's a problem with that."

Gall harrumphed. "I can hardly wait. Lay it on me."

"There are gaps in her memory of that day. She's lost segments of time." He gave Gall an abridged version of everything Bellamy had told him.

When he finished Gall said, "So what she *thinks* she remembers, and what she *believes*, aren't necessarily what actually *happened*."

"Right."

"And what she disremembers—"

"Is apparently a threat to somebody who's kept a secret for eighteen years and doesn't want it revealed now. Which places Bellamy in danger."

Gall released a long stream of air, running out of breath before he ran out of expletives. "Which once again puts you up to your neck in the Lystons' shit."

"It's my shit, too, Gall."

The old man didn't refute it. How could he? The Lyston case had factored significantly into how the airline regarded Dent following the accident.

"Okay, so why Atlanta?"

Dent explained why they were there. "Bellamy wanted to call and give Steven advance notice of our visit, but I thought a surprise attack would ensure a more honest reaction from him. I didn't want to give him time to think about it."

"Well, that makes one smart thing you've said since we started this conversation. When is this ambush going to take place?"

"Tomorrow."

"Uh-huh. And what will the two of you be doing to pass the time between now and then?"

"None of your goddamn business."

Gall snorted. "That's what I figured."

"You figured wrong."

"Separate beds?"

"Separate rooms. Happy now?" Gall made a sound that could have been interpreted any number of ways. Since Dent didn't want that topic explored, he left it alone. "What about my airplane?"

"I wondered when you'd get around to remembering that you've got a real problem of your own."

With a few more minutes of give-and-take in a similar vein, Dent had been given a complete assessment of the damage and an estimate on the time it would take to repair it.

"In the meantime I'll go bankrupt."

"Don't go jumping off a building yet," Gall said. "I've already talked to a guy."

Dent was instantly suspicious. "What kind of guy?"

"One with lots of discretionary funds. He called me a while back looking for a private pilot."

"No way."

"Hear me out, Ace."

"I don't need to. My answer is no."

"He's got an incredible plane. Brand-spankin'-new King Air 350i. All the bells and whistles money can buy. Pretty as a picture. You'd fuck it if you could."

"How come he doesn't already have a pilot?"

"He did. He didn't like him."

"Why not?"

"He didn't say."

"Bad sign."

"Or a lucky break for you."

"You know my golden rule, Gall. Never again will I fly for anybody except *me*. I for damn sure won't be a rich guy's chauffeur. He'd probably want to put me in some dumb cap and uniform."

"You don't have to sign on for the rest of your miserable life. Just till your airplane is fixed. And you haven't even heard the best part."

"What's the best part?"

"In the interim, for a reasonable percentage of every charter, he'll let you use his King Air. What do you think of that?"

Dent gnawed the inside of his cheek. "How reasonable a percentage?"

"I took a stab at twelve. He said okay. Prob'ly could have got him to agree to ten. The money doesn't matter to him. He wants his plane 'broken in' by a good pilot."

The deal was better than reasonable, especially considering how much Dent could charge per hour to charter an airplane of that caliber. But he resisted the temptation. "I'd be at his beck and call. And at the whim of his wife and bratty kids. I'd probably have to fly a yapping lap dog, too."

"I didn't say it'd be perfect," Gall grumbled. "But you could keep eating."

Dent loathed the prospect of having a boss, of taking orders, of having his time, his life, governed by somebody else. But Bellamy's two-point-five grand wouldn't last long. He could tighten his belt, literally, and skip a few meals, but he had to keep making payments on his loan or he'd lose his airplane to the bank.

"We'll talk about it when I get back," he said. "Soon as we set down at Austin-Bergstrom, I'll come straight out."

"I'll be here. Unlike some people I know, I don't go winging off without telling anybody."

Dent ignored that, and, at any other time, he would simply have hung up. But he had more to talk to Gall about. "This columnist, Rocky Van Durbin, he's a snake. He didn't know who I was this morning, but he will by now, and he'll be all over that. If he comes nosing around—"

"I'll kick his Yankee ass."

Dent actually grinned, not doubting for a moment that Gall would, and that he would enjoy it. But his grin was short-lived because he needed to stress the importance of his next warning. "Listen to me, Gall. Are you listening? This is serious." He described the pickup truck he'd seen earlier. "I got a bad vibe. Could be nothing. But—"

"But you trust your instincts, and so do I."

"You haven't seen a truck like that around your place or near the airfield, have you?"

"No."

"You swear?"

"Why would I lie?"

"Mule-headedness. Misplaced pride. Sheer meanness. Shall I go on?"

"I haven't seen a truck like that. Swear."

"Okay, but keep your eyes peeled. Promise?"

"I'll promise, if you'll tell me something."

"What?"

"What are you doing with her?"

"For crying out loud, Gall, how many times do I have to say it?"

"I heard what you *said*. But if you're telling me the

truth, and you're not even getting laid in the bargain, then what's in it for you?"

"Exoneration."

After a considerable pause, Gall said, "Fair enough, Ace."

Responding to the soft knock, Bellamy went to the door connecting her room to Dent's and pressed her palms as well as her forehead against the cool wood. "What, Dent?"

"I need to ask you something."

"You can ask me through the door."

It had been somewhat surprising to her that he hadn't pestered her for details on her marital split, but, after she'd told him about the dissolution of her marriage, they had both lapsed into a brooding silence, exchanging only desultory conversation for the remainder of their flight.

The busy, noisy restaurant where they'd eaten dinner hadn't been conducive to intimate conversation, so they'd kept theirs impersonal and as light as possible given the circumstances.

When they'd checked into the chain hotel, he'd remarked on the economic reasonableness of sharing a room, but she'd ignored the remark, and when they reached their neighboring rooms, they'd parted company.

It would be best to leave it that way.

But he knocked again and said, "I have to be looking you in the eye when I ask what I need to ask."

She counted to ten silently.

"Come on, A.k.a. You can always scream and knee me in the balls if I get out of line. But I won't."

She hesitated a moment longer, then, with exasperation, flipped the latch and pulled open the door. "What?"

He took in the haphazard, scraggly topknot of hair and her squeaky-clean face. She wore a shapeless T-shirt and plaid flannel pajama bottoms that pooled over her bare feet, one of which she folded over the other in a parody of modesty.

He snuffled a laugh. "That's how you go to bed?"

"That's your question?"

He grinned. "Not that it isn't sexy."

"I wasn't going for sexy. I was going for comfort."

He'd made himself comfortable, too. He stood in stocking feet, bringing her eye level with his chin rather than his clavicle. Several of the pearl snaps on his shirt had been undone. She tried to keep from looking at his chest in the open wedge.

"Your question?"

Reaching behind him, he pulled a toothbrush from the back pocket of his jeans. "Can I borrow some toothpaste?"

"Why didn't you buy toothpaste when you bought the brush?"

"Have you got some, or not?"

She turned away, went into the bathroom long enough to get the tube from her toiletry bag, and returned with it, noticing that he'd stepped across the threshold into her room. Staying at arm's length, she extended the toothpaste to him. He took it from her, but instead of uncapping it, squeezing some paste onto his brush, and leaving, he pocketed both and stayed.

"I do need the toothpaste, but that wasn't what I was going to ask."

She folded her arms across her middle and waited for him to continue.

"What's the plan for tomorrow?"

"Oh." For a moment the simplicity of the question took her aback. She hadn't expected a practical one. "Maxey's is a ten-minute drive from here. It opens for lunch at eleven-thirty. I thought we should arrive about then."

"Giving Steven no time to become too busy to see us or to duck out the back door."

"Something like that."

He bobbed his chin. "Good plan. Want to meet for breakfast first?"

"I'll just have coffee here in my room."

"You don't eat breakfast?"

"Sometimes."

"But not tomorrow."

"Dent."

"Okay. Fine. No breakfast for you. So...we'll meet around, what? Eleven-fifteen?"

"Perfect."

"Up here or in the lobby?"

"Are you always this detail oriented?"

"Absolutely. Pilots usually don't get do-overs. The airplane can be on autopilot, but you don't want the pilot to be, do you?"

She knew he was baiting her, but she went along. "Lobby."

"Roger that."

"Is that all? If so, it's late." She gestured toward the open door behind him, but he didn't take the hint.

"Did you talk to Olivia?"

"No change."

"That's good."

"I suppose. Did you speak to Gall about your airplane?"

"He tacked at least another two weeks on to how long the repairs will take."

"I'm sorry."

"Yeah, me, too."

Then for the next several moments, neither of them spoke or moved. She swallowed, hearing the gulp herself and knowing that he probably had, too. "I'm going to say good night now, Dent." Again she gestured toward the gaping doorway.

"I haven't asked my question yet."

"You've asked several."

"But not the main one."

"I'm exhausted. Can't it wait until tomorrow?"

"Was your heart broken?"

Of course she knew what he was referring to, and she figured he wasn't going to give up and go away until she answered him. "Over losing the baby, yes. Very much so. Over losing him, no. The breakup was an inevitability. Long before the documents were filed, he and I were already separated emotionally.

"His plans to remarry were announced even before our divorce became final. He and his intended relocated to Dallas. I moved to New York and started outlining my book. There were no blowups, no fireworks. It was all very civilized." As an afterthought, she added, "Just like the marriage had been."

At some point during the telling, he'd shortened the distance between them. She had retreated from the intensity of his eyes by lowering hers, and now found herself talking to that enticing triangle that provided a view of soft brown chest hair.

His voice low, he said, "A shame about your kid."

She only nodded.

In her peripheral vision she saw him raise his arm, and a second later the clip holding up her hair was released. He caught the tumbling strands and combed his fingers through them.

"Dent? What are you doing?"

"Getting out of line."

Then his arm curved around her waist and he lowered his head. His lips caught the startled breath that escaped hers, and the shock of the contact brought back the vivid memory of the first time she'd ever seen him.

She and Susan were at a Sonic drive-in. He'd pulled up beside their car on his motorcycle and had looked past Bellamy in the passenger seat to Susan, who was behind the wheel.

The lazy smile he'd sent her sister caused curls of sensation deep inside Bellamy's twelve-year-old body. It was an awakening that, even from her inexperienced point of view, she had understood was sexual. The stirrings had intrigued and thrilled her, but the mind-stealing strength of them had frightened her.

It still did.

She put her hands against his chest and tried to push away.

"You didn't scream," he whispered against her lips as his brushed back and forth across them, barely glancing them on each pass. At first. But when she still didn't scream, or even murmur a protest, he cradled the back of her head in his palm, his mouth claimed hers, and the kiss became deep.

As a virginal preteen, and as a woman who'd taken lovers, she had daydreamed about kissing Denton Carter.

While writing her book, specifically the sex scenes between him and Susan, it hadn't been her sister he was kissing, caressing, and taking with adolescent fervor. It had been her. The fantasies had left her aroused, but irritated with herself. Surely her imagination embellished how good lovemaking with him would be.

But now she realized that her daydreams had actually been tepid. His kiss was delicious and darkly erotic. It delivered. It promised more. And the substance of what it promised made her wet, feverish, and needy.

His hand moved over her hip and into the loose waistband of her pajamas, where it applied pressure to her ass, drawing her forward, lifting and securing her against him.

"Damn," he groaned. "I knew you'd feel good."

His mouth scaled down her throat, then lower, leaving her T-shirt damp where he planted kisses as he moved toward her breasts, which were so tight and tender she realized she had to stop this now.

"Dent, no."

She gave his chest a forceful push. His hand snapped free of her pajama bottoms and he fell back, cursing when his spine came up hard against the edge of the open door. "What the hell?"

"I don't want to."

"No?" He looked down at her nipples so obviously peaked against the thin fabric of her T-shirt. "Then want to explain—"

"I don't owe you an explanation."

"Well, you kinda do. One minute you're kissing me back like there's no tomorrow and whimpering make-me-come noises. The next, you're shoving me into doors. Forgive my confusion."

"Well, we can't have you confused, can we? I don't want to have sex with you. Is that clear enough?"

His body was rocking slightly, like he was furious, on the brink of losing his temper. She actually flinched when he whipped the tube of toothpaste from his pocket and pitched it onto the bed. "I lied. I don't need anything from you."

Then he backed into his room and slammed the connecting door closed.

Chapter 11

When Bellamy stepped off the elevator and into the hotel lobby a few minutes before the appointed time, she saw Dent seated in an easy chair reading the sports section of the newspaper. He stood up as she approached. "Braves lost last night."

"I don't follow baseball until the World Series."

"And then there's this." He passed her the day's edition of *EyeSpy*. "The headline speaks for itself. In the article, I'm the 'ruggedly handsome stranger later identified as Denton Carter,' boyfriend of your slain sister."

With a sinking stomach, Bellamy scanned the front page, which was dominated by Van Durbin's column. The text was accompanied by a snapshot of her and Dent. She realized the shot had been taken yesterday outside Lyston Electronics. "His photographer was hiding and used a telephoto lens."

"Not my best side," Dent said, scrutinizing the grainy photograph. "Pretty good of you, though."

She stuffed the newspaper into her shoulder bag. "I can't read this now or I'll throw up."

Traffic along Peachtree Street was at a crawl due to construction. They got stuck at an intersection where they sat through three cycles of the traffic light. Dent swore under his breath and played an impatient tattoo on the steering wheel with his fingertips. Yesterday's chambray shirt had been replaced by an oxford cloth, the color of it close to the mossy green of his eyes. It was tucked in. His jeans were belted.

"Where did you get the shirt and belt?" she asked.

"Ralph Lauren store in the mall across the street from the hotel. I was there when it opened. Dammit! If that moron would pull forward into the intersection to make his left turn..." He finished on a string of oaths, then once again the light turned red before they could get through the intersection.

"You're not mad at the traffic or other drivers. You're mad at me."

He looked over at her.

"This visit with Steven could be awkward. It won't help if you're pouting over what happened, or didn't happen, last night. There. It's out. Let's not make it an unsightly wart that's *there* but no one acknowledges."

"Don't sweat it, A.k.a. I asked, you—"

"Funny. I don't recall you asking."

"Maybe not in so many words, but, just FYI, in a crotch-grinding embrace, when a man's got his tongue in your mouth and his hand on your ass, it's a pretty safe bet on what he has in mind. I *asked*, you said no." He shrugged with supreme indifference and returned his attention to the traffic. He lifted his foot off the brake. The car rolled forward only a few yards before he had to brake again.

"You should have known better than to try," she said. "You're the one who remarked on my TFR. Except that it's not temporary. I don't relate well to men in that way. I never have."

"Well, that creates a communication problem for us."

"Why should it?"

"Because 'that way' is the *only* way I relate to women."

They sat through another cycle of the traffic light in teeming silence. Then he said in a low voice, "One thing, though. About your kid, your baby…it being a shame that you lost it?"

She turned to look at him.

"I meant that. I don't want you thinking that I said it just to soften you up." He shot her a one-second glance. "I can be a bastard, but not that much of one."

Maxey's was already bustling when they arrived. The hostess, dressed in a short black dress and four-inch heels, was a rail-thin, platinum-blond beauty. Bellamy could have been invisible, because the young woman's baby blues homed in on Dent. In a drawl practically dripping honey, she asked if he had a reservation.

"We're just having drinks," he told her.

Once they were seated on stools that looked too insubstantial to support an adult, they ordered glasses of mint-sprigged iced tea. When they were served, Dent said, "Sip slow. That's an eight-dollar glass of tea. God knows what they charge for a cheeseburger." Then he looked around the dining room, with its cloth-draped tables and creamy pale orchids in the center of each, and added, "If they even make a cheeseburger."

"There he is."

Bellamy had spotted her stepbrother, who was leaning across a table to shake hands with two diners. Steven had been a sullen but good-looking boy. He'd grown
into an incredibly attractive man. His dark hair was swept
back from his high forehead and left to fall in soft waves
almost to his shoulders in a fashion that was distinctly
continental. He wore a black suit with a white silk T-shirt
that seemed color-coordinated with the smile he flashed
as he moved from table to table to greet his patrons.

"Excuse me? Aren't you Bellamy, Steven's stepsister?"

She turned toward the man who had addressed her
from behind the bar. He had salt-and-pepper hair and a
pleasant smile.

"I thought it was you," he said. "I recognize you from
television." He extended his hand. "I'm William Stroud,
co-owner of the restaurant."

"Pleased to meet you." She introduced Dent. The two
men shook hands.

"Does Steven know you're here?" he asked.

"I wanted it to be a surprise."

His smile remained in place, but she noted a flicker
of misgiving in his eyes. "He'd want you to have the best
table. Leave your drinks. I'll bring them over."

He rounded the end of the bar and escorted them to a
corner booth on the far side of the dining room. "Steven
sometimes sits here because you can see the whole room.
I'll get him."

She watched as William Stroud wended his way
through the tables and sidled up to Steven. He spoke only
a few words to him before Steven quickly looked their
way. His gaze lit momentarily on Dent, then focused on
Bellamy and maintained eye contact with her as he said

something to William, who nodded and returned to the bar. Steven started walking toward the booth.

"He doesn't seem all that surprised to see us," Dent murmured. "Or happy about it."

Bellamy, by contrast, was overjoyed to see Steven. She slipped out of the booth and was waiting to embrace him when he reached her. She hugged him tightly and held on even as she felt him easing away.

She had loved him from the day Olivia had introduced him to his soon-to-be stepsisters. She and Steven had bonded instantly and had remained close friends until the event that had shattered all their lives. Their friendship, as strong as it had been prior to Susan's death, couldn't withstand the strain of the tragedy. The pall cast over the family, and over each of them singly, had remained through Allen Strickland's trial and beyond.

By then, Steven was making plans to go away as soon as he graduated.

When he left for university, Bellamy had been disconsolate, sensing that his leaving would be permanent and that their separation would entail more than geography. Sadly, her foreboding had come about.

She clasped both his hands. "It's so good to see you. I've missed you."

"Howard . . . ?"

"No, no, that's not why we're here," she said, quickly alleviating his concern. "His prognosis isn't good, but he's still with us."

"He's defied the odds by living this long."

"He doesn't want to leave Olivia," she said, and Steven nodded solemnly in agreement. She motioned toward Dent. "You remember Denton Carter."

"Of course."

With apparent reluctance on both parts, the two men shook hands. "Swanky place," Dent said.

"Thank you."

Bellamy tugged on Steven's sleeve. "Can you sit with us for a while?"

He glanced over his shoulder as though searching for a valid reason to excuse himself, or perhaps for rescue, but when he came back around, he said, "I can spare a few minutes."

He slid into the booth next to Bellamy and across from Dent, placed his clasped hands on the table, and divided a look between them. "Let me guess. You're here because of today's column in that gossip rag. I thought—hoped— we were old news by now."

"I'd hoped so, too," she said. Steven had gone straight to the heart of the matter, no chitchat, no catching up, which saddened her immeasurably, but she had to address his consternation. "I tried to hide behind the pen name, Steven. I wanted to remain anonymous and never wanted anyone to know that the book was based on Susan's murder."

"For days after you were exposed, I had to dodge the press. Van Durbin sent a stringer here to interview me. I refused, of course. Things calmed down when you returned to Texas. Then this morning..."

"I know. I'm sorry."

"Well," he said, smoothing out his frown, "all that aside, I congratulate you on your success. I'm happy for you on that score. Truly."

"You just wish I hadn't become successful at your expense."

"I won't deny it, Bellamy. I'd rather not have been a character in your story or had our connection revealed."

She looked out over the busy dining room. "It doesn't seem to have hurt your business."

"No, I must say that hasn't suffered."

"Your success is to be congratulated, too. Three restaurants now, and all of them sweethearts of every food critic."

"It's a good partnership. William manages the kitchen and bar. I handle the business and service training."

"A division of labor that's working well." Bellamy smiled at William as he approached the booth with a tray of drinks.

He set a glass of tea in front of each of them. "I can bring you something else if you'd like. Bloody Mary? Wine? An appetizer?"

"This is fine, thank you," Bellamy replied. "Thank you also for loaning us Steven for a while."

"You're welcome."

He placed his hand on Steven's shoulder and spoke directly to him. "If you need anything, I'll be at the bar." He gave the shoulder a squeeze before moving away.

Steven watched Bellamy watch William as he withdrew and made his way back to the bar. When her enlightened gaze came back to him, he said, "Yes, in answer to the question you're either too polite or too offended to ask. William and I are more than business partners."

"How long have you been together?"

"Last New Year's Eve we celebrated our tenth anniversary."

"Ten *years*?" She was incredulous. "I'm not offended by anything except being excluded from knowing. Why didn't you tell me?"

"What would it matter?"

His harshness wounded her deeply. Had all the times they'd laughed and talked together, all the times he'd taken her side against Susan's and vice versa—had all those shared experiences meant nothing to him?

When she was on the brink of flunking an algebra exam, it was Steven who'd convinced her that the test wouldn't define the rest of her life, but then had coached her to a passing grade. It was he who had insisted that her braces were barely noticeable and that her pimples would eventually go away. Whenever her self-esteem was at a low ebb, he'd forecasted that one day she would be beautiful and that her future would be bright. Brighter even than Susan's.

She had considered him more brother than stepbrother, and she had thought he felt the same about her. Yet he had shut her out of his life effectively and entirely. She had been dispensable to him, and realizing that was acutely painful.

"*You* mattered, Steven," she said, her voice husky with emotion. "You, your life, your loves mattered to me."

He looked somewhat chastened. "Try to understand. When I left Austin, I had to abandon everything. That was the only way I could survive. I had to make a life for myself that was free of that one. If I'd taken any aspect of it with me, even you, I would have stayed shackled to it all. I had to make a clean break. No attachments. Except for Mother, and I keep her at a distance that's safe to my well-being."

"That's why you made an excuse anytime I tried to get together with you in New York."

"You were a reminder of the worst years of my life. You still are."

"And you're still a shit."

Steven looked sharply at Dent, who'd spoken for the first time since their lukewarm handshake.

"You were a sniveling, selfish kid, and so far I've seen no improvement."

"Dent!" Bellamy exclaimed in a whisper.

But he wasn't finished. "She went to a lot of trouble to come here. You could at least *pretend* to be glad to see her."

When she was about to speak again, Steven held up his hand. "It's okay, Bellamy. He's right. I am a shit. It's a survival tactic. Not meant to hurt you." He smiled ruefully as he reached out and stroked her smooth cheek, and, as though reading her thoughts of several moments earlier, murmured, "Just as I predicted. The duckling has turned into a swan."

Then he lowered his hand, and the glimmer of affection she'd seen in his eyes flickered out. "It took time, therapy, and diligence, but I reinvented myself. I was content with the life I'd made. But now your book and the ballyhoo it's created has brought back everything I ran from. Once again, I'm that skinny, frightened kid being grilled by the police."

"Dale Moody?" she asked.

"Big guy. Barrel chest. Gravelly voice. He questioned me several times. The interrogations didn't come to anything, but being a suspect, even for a short time, scarred me for life."

"Dent said as much."

Steven looked over at him, taking him in fully. "Pardon my curiosity. There was no love lost between you and our family, but here you are in Atlanta with Bellamy. Why?"

Bellamy spoke before he could. "I chartered a flight with Dent in the hope of mending fences."

"It didn't work. In fact, Mother was terribly upset over seeing him."

"Yes, I know."

"So why is he here with you now?"

After a lengthy hesitation, she said, "Someone has been menacing me for weeks. I need to know who and why."

She recapped for Steven everything that had happened and ended by saying, "I haven't told Olivia or Daddy. Please don't mention it, because they don't need another worry. But we—Dent and I—don't think the acts of vandalism done to my house and his airplane were random or coincidental. Whoever committed them is somehow connected to that Memorial Day."

He frowned skeptically. "That's an awfully broad leap, isn't it?"

"Dent and I have nothing else in common."

Steven gave each of them a long look. "I'm connected to that day. Did you come to accuse me of painting a threat on your bedroom wall?"

"Of course not." She reached for his hand. "I'm hoping you'll share some of your recollections and impressions of that day."

"To what end? You've already written the book on it."

Dent snickered at the wry remark. She didn't acknowledge it. She had decided that, for the time being, she would tell no one else about her lost frames of time. But it was important that Steven fill in some of the gaps. "Will you answer a few questions?"

He looked annoyed. "What purpose will be served by talking about it?"

"Humor me. Please."

He considered it for a moment, then gave her a brusque nod.

She wasted no time. "Shortly before the tornado, you left the pavilion and went down to the boathouse."

Another curt nod.

"Why? Why were you going to the boathouse?"

"For beer."

"Beer? You hated beer. You told me that you had tried it at a party and hated the taste."

He shrugged. "I wanted to give it another try. Word had got around that some guys had smuggled beer to the boathouse. I went to check it out, but no one was there. Only a bunch of cans. I was on my way back to the pavilion when somebody spotted the funnel and everybody started screaming. I was nearer the boathouse, so I ran back and took cover there."

She nodded absently. "When I came after you—"

"When you came after me?"

"To warn you of the approaching storm."

"You did?"

His reaction mystified her. "Why does that surprise you? It was in the book. If you read it—"

"I did. But I thought you were only capsulizing for narrative clarity."

"That's not the way you remember it?"

"After I left the pavilion, I didn't see you again until you were rescued from the wreckage of the boathouse."

"You didn't see me there earlier?"

He shook his head. "I have no idea how you got there."

Bellamy glanced over at Dent. He was looking at her, his eyebrow eloquently arched. Turning back to Steven, she said, "After the tornado, you managed to get out from under the debris."

"It was sheer luck that I wasn't crushed by the collapsing walls. But that section of the boathouse fell outward instead of in. I was scratched up and dazed, but nothing serious. I managed to wiggle my way out of the rubble and wandered back toward the pavilion. Howard and Mom practically smothered me with hugs. But of course they were frantic to find Susan and you."

Steven's recollections of the storm's aftermath coincided with Dent's, so Bellamy didn't linger on them. "Why did Detective Moody question you?"

"Because of the sexual overtones of the crime. He interrogated every man past puberty, especially those close to her. The boyfriend," he said, tipping his head toward Dent. "I was her stepbrother, but that didn't exclude me. Even Howard was questioned."

Bellamy was stunned. "Daddy was questioned? You can't be serious."

"I'm sure that Mother and Howard protected you from knowing about it because of the disturbing implication."

"It's not disturbing, it's disgusting."

Steven looked down and traced the white tablecloth's weave pattern with the tip of his finger. "Moody wasn't so far off base."

His softly spoken words had the effect of falling bricks. Bellamy was shocked dumb. Dent said nothing, either, but placed his elbow on the table and cupped his mouth and chin with his hand. Steven must have felt the pressure of his solemn stare, because when he gave up his study of the tablecloth, it was Dent he addressed.

"I don't need to tell you what she was like, do I? You

know firsthand that Susan was sexually supercharged. Which must have been great for you. But for her younger stepbrother who was grappling with his sexual identity, she was a nightmare with a malicious streak."

Bellamy swallowed with difficulty and said gruffly, "Are you telling us that you and Susan..."

"No," he said with a firm shake of his head. "Never the grand finale. But not for her lack of trying. As it was, she got off by torturing me."

"Doing what?"

"Are you sure you want to hear this, Bellamy? It's ugly."

"I think I have to hear it."

"All right." He took a breath. "Susan made a practice of sneaking into my room at night. Two, three times a week. Sometimes more often."

"When did it start?"

"On Mother and Howard's wedding day."

Bellamy gasped in disbelief.

"She would lie down beside me, rub up against me, talk dirty, describe to me all the things we could be doing if only I wasn't so afraid of getting caught. She would take off her clothes and dare me to touch her."

He snorted a sound of self-deprecation. "God knows, sometimes I wanted to, because I was struggling with the realization that I was gay. At that point in my life, I was desperate to disprove it. But, in truth, the harder she tried to lure me, the more repulsed I became."

"Did she know you were gay?"

"Maybe. Probably. Which would have made the torment even more delightful to her. It got to where I couldn't stand the sight or smell of her and made no secret of it. She only became more aggressive and daring.

"Once, she got into the shower with me and told me that Mother was just across the hall. She said that if I made a sound, and Mother caught us, she would tell her and Howard that I was forcing her to go down on me every night. I knew that she could cry on demand and was capable of convincing them of anything."

He looked hard at Bellamy. "I'm sorry to be the one to destroy your delusions of our perfect family, but perhaps it's time you knew the truth about our dearly departed sister."

"You should have told me."

"So you could have put it in your book, made it more salacious?"

She flinched as though he'd slapped her. "I don't deserve that, Steven."

He seemed to agree, because he exhaled deeply. "I'm sorry. Uncalled for."

"Why didn't you tell me at the time? I would have stood by you during the fallout."

"I didn't want there to be any fallout. I didn't want anyone to know, but especially not you. You were so different from her. Innocent. Sweet. The peacemaker. And you were my pal. I was afraid that would change if you knew about me and Susan."

"It wouldn't have."

"Maybe," he said, still doubtful. "But in any case, I was ashamed."

"You weren't doing anything wrong."

"There were times when my body responded to her in spite of myself, when I couldn't control getting an erection. I didn't desire her in the least, but I was an adolescent boy with raging hormones and no other outlet for them.

She'd touch me, and I would explode, and she would mock my humiliation. Actually," he added thoughtfully, "I'm surprised that she never gloated to you about what was going on. She was jealous of you. Did you know that?"

"Impossible."

"It's true. She was jealous of the special relationship you and Howard had. He favored you, and she knew it. It also miffed her that when I came into the family, you and I forged a sibling bond that I never had with her, or even wanted. Not that she craved my friendship, but she didn't want to be second on anyone's list."

He looked across at Dent again. "You weren't her one and only. She told me about all the boys she 'did' behind your back. She was a slut who gave away free samples. It was befitting that she was strangled with her own underpants."

"Steven, please," Bellamy whispered.

"You wanted to hear this; you're going to hear all of it," he said testily. "One Sunday at family dinner, Susan passed a pair of her panties to me under the table. Here I was, seated between her and Howard, and she reaches for my hand and presses her underwear into it. I became so hot with fear and mortification I thought I'd pass out. And all through the meal, she was smiling that sly, triumphant smile that was uniquely hers.

"That was the kind of demeaning joke she liked to pull. There were many more times when she did some-thing similar. I could go on and on, but it would serve no purpose. She can no longer make my life hell. She's dead. And I'm glad."

He fell silent for several moments, then roused himself as though coming awake after a bad dream. He looked out over the dining room and said, "I need to get back to work. Besides, I've said everything I plan to. Except this." Before continuing, he made certain of their full attention.

"Moody questioned me extensively, but my story never changed. Not one word of it. He didn't have any evidence to place me where her body was discovered. Nor could he cite an opportunity for me to have killed her. But what he never asked me, what he didn't know, was that I sure as hell had a motive."

Chapter 12

The fist came out of nowhere and crashed into Rupe's face like a wrecking ball.

He landed hard on his butt. Lightning bolts of pain pierced his skull and ricocheted off the inner walls of his cranium. His ears rang, and he was momentarily blinded.

Before he could even cry out, he was grabbed by his shirt collar and jerked to his feet with teeth-jarring, bone-shaking velocity. The planet teetered, then spun out of its orbit, making him sickeningly dizzy. He gagged on the nausea that filled his throat. His head wobbled on his neck uncontrollably. Blood streamed from his broken nose into his slack lips.

"Hey, Rupe, long time no see."

Being shaken like a rag doll, Rupe blinked against the skyrockets of pain still exploding from within his skull. The earth righted itself and, finally, the multiple blurred images wavering inches from him coalesced into one of an older, heavier, uglier Dale Moody.

"How're you doing, Rupe?"

Dale knew the extent of the other man's pain, because Dale had had it described to him before. He'd landed a blow just like the one he'd delivered to Rupe on a fellow cop, who'd later waxed poetic about the various levels of excruciating pain to be found on the receiving end of Dale's right fist.

In answer to Dale's question, Rupe mumbled unintelligibly.

"Sorry? I didn't catch that."

Dale, still gripping a fistful of expensive, imported silk/cotton blend, hauled Rupe by his shirt collar over to his rattletrap Dodge and propped him against the rusty, dented rear quarter panel. "Would you take this heap for a trade-in?"

"Fgnuckyoo." With his rubbery lips and swelling nose, that was the closest Rupe could come to correct pronunciation.

Dale grinned, but it was a nasty expression. "I'll take that as a no." Keeping his grip on Rupe with one hand, he used the other to open the back door of his car, knock the top off a white foam cooler, and take from it a bag of frozen peas he'd brought for the occasion.

"Maybe this will help." He crammed the bag over Rupe's brutalized nose.

Rupe cried out in fresh pain, but he reached up and snatched the bag of peas from Dale's hand. He applied it more gently and glared at the former detective from behind the smiling Green Giant. "I'm filing charges of assault."

"Will that be before or after your eyes swell shut? I hope you don't have any TV commercials to do this week. You're gonna look like shit for a while. Maybe you can buy shirts that'll match your bruises."

"You're a..."

"I know what I am," Dale said brusquely, all traces of humor vanishing. "And I know even better what you are. Now, we can stand here all night swapping insults. I've got nothing else to do. But you're a busy man. You're also the one who's bleeding and hurting like hell. Your better option is to talk to me like you've been itching to do. I drove halfway across the state to get here. So talk, you son of a bitch."

Rupe continued to glower at him, but Dale knew better than anyone that the former ADA was good at thinking on his feet. Even in a tight spot like this, he would be searching for an angle that would turn the situation to his advantage. Knowing this about his nemesis, Dale wasn't surprised when Rupe cut to the chase.

"The Lystons' younger daughter. Remember her? Bellamy? She's written a book."

"Old news, Rupe. *Low Pressure*. I know all about it. I also know about the tabloid writer who's exploiting it. I stopped on my way here to gas up and saw today's issue in a rack by the register. Bet the cashier would've been blown away if she'd known she was selling a copy to one of the featured personalities.

"I fared better than you, Rupe," Dale continued conversationally. "I was only mentioned as the 'former lead investigator, unavailable for comment.' But Van Durbin went on at some length about you. Reading between the lines, I'd say he wasn't all that impressed with your public service to Travis County. He said you couldn't give him a 'definitive' answer when he asked you about hard evidence, which in this case was a pair of lacy underwear. Van Durbin relished that."

"I read it." Rupe lifted the makeshift ice pack from his nose, looked with disgust at the imprint his blood had made on it, then tossed it aside. It landed on the pavement near his feet with a loud splat. Rupe looked down at it and used that opportunity to take in the parking lot at a glance.

"Nobody's around," Dale told him. "Nobody to rush to your rescue. Which is your own fault for parking way out here at the edge of the lot. What? Are you scared somebody will notice you coming and going out of that young lady's apartment up there?

"You really should choose another place for your shabby rendezvous, Rupe, or you're liable to get caught with your pants down. How old is she, anyhow? Eighteen? Nineteen at a stretch? Is she even legal? Shame on you, diddlin' a girl too young to buy beer. You being a church deacon and all."

If looks could kill, Dale would be dead. "Your pal Haymaker?" Rupe spat. "Is he your snitch?"

Ignoring that, Dale continued taunting him just for the hell of it, just because it felt good. "Does your wife know you're banging a hot young thing? Come to think of it, your missus might not be all that upset about it. She might be glad to learn you can still get it up." Dale leaned in and whispered, "But you'd better hope Van Durbin doesn't get wind of it."

Rupe scoffed. "He has a column in a cheap rag that people line their birdcages with. So what? What harm can he really do me?"

"Austin's King of Cars?" Dale mocked.

Rupe wiped dripping blood from the end of his nose and shook it off his fingers. "That was the ad man's suggestion."

"Whatever, Rupe. Whatever. You've done real good for yourself. But it could all go away like that." He snapped his fingers half an inch from Rupe's brutalized face.

"You think I'm scared of Van Durbin?"

"No, but you're scared shitless of me." Dale crowded in on him. "First the book, and now Van Durbin, have stirred up the dust, but I'm the one who could choke you on it."

"You'd choke, too."

"But I don't have anything to lose."

With both hands, Rupe pushed against Dale's broad chest. Dale fell back a step, and Rupe gave him and his car a scornful once-over. "That's readily apparent."

Dale ignored the insult. "You, on the other hand, have made a large target of yourself. You're easy pickin's for a media crucifixion."

"Save your threats. If you tried to destroy me, you'd fail."

"I don't think so."

"You're already beat, you just don't know it," Rupe said. "That's why I've been trying to reach you, to tell you that if you get to feeling sentimental about Allen Strickland, law, justice, and the American way, you'll be digging your own grave and yours alone."

"If the Susan Lyston case was reopened—"

"See, that's what I'm talking about. Beat before you start." He looked at Dale and shook his head sorrowfully. "Do you think I'd let that case file just languish there in the PD like a ticking time bomb?" He barked a laugh, which caused him to wince with pain. "Hell, no, Dale. That file was adiosed weeks after Strickland's conviction."

Dale balled his hands into fists and gritted his teeth. "That file contained all my notes on the case."

"And you were awfully cooperative to hand everything over to me when requested, Dale. I really do appreciate that."

Dale closed the space between them. "Where is it?"

"I didn't just have it sneaked out of the PD, Dale. I lit the match, watched it burn, then scattered the ashes to the four fucking winds. So if anybody tried to find it now, they would be SOL."

Again, he looked Dale up and down and laughed. "You came out of hiding and got all dressed up for nothing. Sorry, Dale." He raised his hands and shrugged elaborately, assuming the smug air that made Dale despise him.

But Dale waited, knowing it was coming. He waited. Waited.

And when the King of Cars smiled his billboard smile, Dale slammed his fist into the grillwork of dentistry, destroying it with knuckles of iron and almost two decades of pent-up wrath.

Rupe howled, covered his mouth with both hands, and slid down the side of the car.

Using the toe of his boot, Dale pushed him away from the wheel so he wouldn't impede him when he drove away. Then, standing over him, he said, "You put the squeeze on Haymaker again, I'm gonna come back and hack off your sagging balls with a dull pair of pinking shears. I had a case once, a guy did that to his poker-playing buddy. He got three years for it. But it taught the other guy a lesson on cheating that he never forgot."

During the flight back to Austin, neither Bellamy or Dent was very talkative. Parting with Steven had made her terribly sad, because now she knew he had deliberately excised her from his life, whereas before, she'd deluded herself into believing that circumstances were responsible for the rift.

But her somber mood was largely attributed to what he had revealed about himself and Susan. "How could I have lived in the same house with them and not have known?"

She didn't even realize she'd posed the question out loud until Dent replied. "You were a kid. Maybe you sensed something between them but didn't recognize it for what it was."

"I just thought they didn't like each other much."

After a moment, Dent said, "He could be making it up."

"He wouldn't invent a lie like that. It's too painful and embarrassing for him."

"Would he lie about something else?"

She looked at him, her question implied.

He said, "Steven didn't see you at the boathouse just before the storm. But you didn't see him there, either, did you?"

"I might have. I can't remember."

"Okay. But he told us that he went to the boathouse to get contraband beer when he didn't even like beer. Kinda struck me as strange."

"You think he's lying about where he was when Susan was killed?"

He raised his shoulders. "It's something to think about, that's all. He admitted to having motive."

"So you believe that part, that Susan came on to him sexually."

"Yeah, I believe it."

They lapsed into silence. Eventually she said, "She was

selfish and vain. But I had no idea that she could be that cruel-hearted."

"Didn't you?" Speaking with quiet intensity, he said, "Your quest for the truth could turn up more ugly surprises, Bellamy. Are you sure you want to continue?"

"I have to."

"No you don't."

"I won't stop now, Dent."

"Maybe you should. Why keep going when there may be other land mines out there?"

"Nothing could be as bad as the secret we uncovered today."

He looked at her for a long moment, then, without saying anything more, faced forward.

"The other boys," she said haltingly. "The ones she boasted having been with..."

"What about them?"

"You didn't know?"

"Sure I knew." He leaned his head back and closed his eyes. "I didn't care."

They spent the remainder of the flight in pensive silence and didn't speak again until they exited the Austin-Bergstrom terminal for the parking garage where he had left his Corvette.

Bellamy offered to call a car service to take her home. "If you'd rather not drive me all the way to Georgetown."

"I'll drive you. But Gall's airfield is between here and there. I'd like to stop on the way."

Gall's pickup was the only vehicle around. The wind sock hung limply on its pole in the late evening heat. Dent drove his car into the hangar, and, as he and Bellamy limbed out, Gall walked toward them, wiping his greasy hands on a faded shop rag.

"How is she?" Dent asked, referring to his airplane.

"Coming along. Want to take a look?"

Dent peeled off in that direction. Gall looked at Bellamy and angled his head toward the office. "It's cooler in there. Air's on. Watch the back leg of the chair when you sit."

"Thank you."

She went into the office and gingerly lowered herself onto the seat of the chair with the unreliable leg. As she watched Dent and Gall discussing the airplane, she took her cell phone from her shoulder bag.

It had logged three missed calls from her agent, two from the publicist. She could only imagine the tizzy the new edition of *EyeSpy* had caused. They were probably celebrating the boost in publicity.

She hadn't yet read the copy Dent had given her that morning. She admitted to a morbid curiosity about what Van Durbin had written, and only if she knew the content of his column could she prepare a rebuttal against any untruths, but she couldn't bring herself to read it now. After the visit with Steven, she felt emotionally whipped.

Disinclined to return the professional calls, she punched in Olivia's number. An automated voice mail answered. She left a message. It still seemed underhanded that she'd gone to see Steven without his mother's knowledge. Olivia made no secret of missing him terribly and often lamented that she didn't see enough of him.

Bellamy wondered—well, she wondered many things. But there were questions she couldn't put to Olivia without breaching Steven's confidence. As curious as she

was to know what Olivia knew about his private life, she
would abide by the pact they'd made as preteens to keep
each other's secrets.

Gall and Dent were now looking at another airplane
that was parked inside the hangar. Gall motioned Dent
toward it. He seemed to hesitate, then walked over to it.

Gall stood with him for several seconds, then turned
and, leaving Dent, came into the office. He was chuck-
ling to himself as he moved behind the desk and sat down.
"Knew he couldn't resist."

"Is that a new airplane?" Bellamy asked.

"Less than fifty hours on it."

"Who does it belong to?"

He told her, and she recognized the name. "He's a state
senator, isn't he?"

"Yep. Plus he owns about a third of the land between
Fredericksburg and the Rio Grande. Beef cattle."

"Oil and gas, too, if I'm not mistaken."

Gall nodded. "He's offered Dent a job as his private
pilot, but he's too stubborn and too proud to take it."

She looked out into the hangar, where Dent was running his hand along the wing of the airplane, following its
curvature. Rather like he had run his hand over the shape
of her hip last night, outside and inside her pajamas. His
hand had been as unshy as his kiss, both taking what they
wanted.

The recollection made her face feel hot. Caught in a
fog of erotic memory, she missed Gall's question the first
time and had to ask him to repeat it.

"I asked what you thought of him."

She tried to regard Dent objectively, which was impossible. "I'm still forming my opinion."

"Your folks didn't like him."

"I'm not my folks."

He didn't remark on that.

"You've known him for a long time."

"Sure have." He tossed the soggy remnants of his cigar into the trash can and unwrapped a fresh one.

"Do you ever light those?"

He frowned cantankerously. "Haven't you heard? Smokin' is bad for your health. God knows he drummed that into my ears till I either had to quit or kill him just to shut him up about it."

"Dent lectured you on smoking, when he's so reckless in his own right?"

Gall fixed his rheumy gaze on her. "Reckless? I guess in some areas of his life he could exercise more caution."

"He drives way too fast."

"Yeah, he likes speed. And on occasion he drinks too much and wakes up in a bed he ought not to be in. But I'll tell you one damn thing." He held the cigar between two fingers as he wagged them at her. "He's the best damn pilot I've ever run across."

When she didn't comment, he took it as an invitation to expand.

"Some pilots are taught to fly, and they learn good enough to keep the airplane from crashing. If the machine is in working order, and the pilot doesn't fuck up, the thing will fly. You gotta use your hands and your feet and you gotta have a pretty good head on your shoulders and at least a little common sense, so you don't make a stupid mistake or take a gamble that gets you killed. But even the smartest of men can be the lousiest pilots. You know why? They make it mental. They don't do it from their gut."

He gave his belly a loud smack. "The good pilots do it from here. They feel it. They know how to do it before they ever take a lesson. Sure, you gotta learn about the weather, how to read instruments. There's a lot that can be taught to improve natural skill, but, in my book, that skill—something you're just born with—is essential. I don't have it. But I know it when I see it."

He removed his cigar from his mouth and studied the end of it as he rolled it between his fingers. "I got to shake hands with Chuck Yeager once, out at an air base in New Mexico. I was just a kid, a grease monkey, but in my work I got to rub elbows with lots of flyboys who later became astronauts and such. Damn good pilots. The kind I'm talking about. The ones who do it by instinct."

He tipped his chin down and looked at Bellamy from beneath the shaggy line of his eyebrows. "But I wouldn't trade ten of them for one Denton Carter." As though to underscore the statement, he jammed the cigar back into the corner of his mouth and anchored it there with his teeth.

Amused, she said, "I don't intend to dispute you."

"Well," he grumbled, "just in case you were of a mind to." He looked beyond her. She turned so that she, too, could see into the hangar where Dent was still inspecting the airplane. "Only a nekkid woman would hold that much fascination for him," the old man remarked with a cackle.

"When he first started coming out here, he was a moody little bastard, full of piss and vinegar and lots to prove, ready to take offense at the drop of a hat. But when he got around the airplanes, I saw the look that came over his face. There's an expression for it. Uh...What's the word?" he asked, rapidly snapping his fingers.

"Rapture?"

"Yeah. Rapture. Like somebody that ought to have sunlight shining on him through a stained-glass window. That's the way Dent got whenever he looked at an airplane in flight."

"He told me about the first time you took him up. He said he fell head over heels in love with flying."

Gall shifted his eyes off Dent and back to her. "He told you that?"

"In those words."

"You don't say? Huh." He tilted his head and studied her for a moment. "I've never known him to talk about it before."

She weighed the advisability of asking her next question, but decided she would never know the answer if she didn't ask. "What happened in the cockpit during that flight that nearly went down? I don't think either the media or the public got the full story."

"What has Dent told you about it?"

"Nothing. He changes the subject."

"Well, then, you won't hear it from me. If he wants you to know, he'll tell you his own self."

Her cell phone rang and when she saw the calling number on the LED, she answered before it could ring a second time. "Olivia? You got my message? How's Daddy?"

To give her privacy, Gall left the office and rejoined Dent in the hangar.

"Admit it, Ace, it's a sweet puppy."

"It's a nice airplane."

Gall scoffed at the understatement. "Yeah and Marilyn *Mon*-roe was a blonde." He continued to admire the airplane as he said, "The senator wants you bad. He thinks you got a raw deal from the airline."

"What does he know about—"

"He wants to give you a chance to reinstate—"

"I don't need to prove—"

"Just shut up a minute and hear me out, okay? He's now willing to take only ten percent of your charters, *and* he's upped the offer on your salary. Upped it a lot. It's a cream puff of a deal. The guy's bending over backward to get you to say yes, and you'd be crazy—Are you listening?"

He had been, but he'd become distracted when Bellamy emerged from the office. He had only to look at her face to know that something was dreadfully wrong.

She walked quickly toward them. "It's Daddy. I've got to go to Houston. Can you drive me home right away so I can get my car?"

Dent responded immediately by taking her arm and ushering her toward the Vette. "We'll get there faster if I drive you."

"I have a better idea. Fly this down there." Gall motioned toward the new airplane. "He urged me to put you in the cockpit, give you a taste of it."

"I'm not insured."

"He insured you."

"Without ever flying with me? Or even meeting me?"

"Shows how confident he is. He left it here for you to fly. Says it'll get rusty otherwise. And the lady here has an emergency."

Dent turned to Bellamy and took her shoulders between his hands. "Depends on you. I'm type-rated to fly an airplane this size, but I've never been in that cockpit."

She shook her head in apparent confusion.

"It's like the first time behind the wheel of a new car," he said. "You gotta familiarize yourself."

"How long does that take?"

"Coupla hours."

"I can't wait that long."

"Or a coupla minutes." He gripped her shoulders tighter and said without equivocation. "I can fly it, but it's your call."

In under two hours they arrived at the ICU waiting room, where Olivia was sitting alone, hugging her elbows, staring into space. She shot to her feet when she saw Bellamy, but made no move toward her when Dent appeared behind her.

Bellamy asked, "Are we too late?"

"No." Olivia sat back down as though her legs had given out from under her. "He's drifting in and out of consciousness. They're afraid he'll lapse into a coma. That's why I called you when I did. This may be your last chance to speak to him."

Bellamy crossed the room and put her arms around her stepmother. They clung to each other for several minutes, crying together. Eventually Bellamy pulled away and blotted her face with a tissue. "When can I see him?"

"The doctor is with him now. He's trying to determine if there's anything viable they can do. The nurse promised to come and get me when we can go in."

She looked past Bellamy toward Dent, who had come no farther than the doorway. "Dent flew me here," Bellamy explained. "Fortunately we were able to leave almost immediately after I spoke with you."

Olivia thanked him with cool politeness.

He acknowledged her thanks with a nod, then said, "I need coffee. Can I get some for either of you?"

They shook their heads in unison. Then, as soon as he was out of sight, Olivia looked at Bellamy with a mix of bewilderment and annoyance.

Bellamy took a deep breath, reasoning that she had just as well be straightforward. "He and I have spent time together and have become better acquainted over the last couple of days. I don't expect you to understand."

"Well, thank you for that, because I don't understand. Not at all."

"Then at least give me credit for being a grown-up who can make up my own mind about people."

She hadn't meant the rebuke to sound as stern as it did. Contritely, she reached for Olivia's hand and pressed it between hers. "I can see why you and Daddy didn't consider him an ideal boyfriend for Susan. He wasn't like the sons of people in your circle. He was unpolished and disrespectful."

"Our dislike extends beyond his lack of manners, Bellamy. We hold him partially responsible for what happened to Susan."

The blame was misplaced and grossly unfair, but rather than dwell on that, Bellamy countered more diplomatically. "He didn't come away unscathed. He's never gotten over being a suspect." She paused, then said, "Neither has Steven."

Chapter 13

——◆◆◆——

Olivia flinched. "Steven?"

"Dent and I went to see him."

"In Atlanta?"

"We flew there last night and saw him today."

"How was he?"

"He looked wonderful. He's definitely in his element. The restaurant is gorgeous, and it was packed for lunch."

Olivia searched her eyes for a moment, then looked down at their clasped hands. "Did you meet William?"

"Olivia." Bellamy waited until the other woman was looking her in the eye. "Why am I the last to know that Steven is in a seemingly solid and very happy relationship?"

"Did you ask him that?"

"He told me that he cut all ties to his former life, including me."

"Then you have your answer."

"It hurts," Bellamy whispered.

Olivia stroked the back of her hand. "Don't be too hurt.

Even I wasn't introduced to William until after they'd been together for more than a year."

"It didn't wound you to be shut out?"

"Of course it did, but I was given no other choice except to honor Steven's wishes for privacy. Years ago, he asked for distance from the family." She smiled sadly. "I granted it because I love him, and I understood where he was coming from."

Her expression turned reflective. "He didn't have a very happy childhood. He watched his father die slowly of ALS. He'd barely reached adolescence when I married Howard. Who couldn't have been a better stepfather," she was quick to add. "But Steven's transition into the new family was difficult."

Olivia had no idea how difficult.

"He was fine with you," she said. "You two took to each other right away. But he and Susan had personality clashes. Steven was introverted, Susan the polar opposite." If Olivia believed personality issues were the only problem that had existed between Steven and Susan, then clearly Steven had kept Susan's abuse hidden from her and Howard. If he had wanted them to know, he would have told them, so his secret would remain safe with Bellamy.

"Sometimes I think…" Olivia hesitated, but when Bellamy prompted her with an inquisitive tip of her head, she continued. "I think Steven must have felt a bit abandoned when Howard and I married. He'd had me all to himself for years, then suddenly had to share me with another man. And my love for Howard was so passionate, so consuming, that Steven might have felt slighted."

She dabbed at fresh tears and spoke in a voice made

husky by emotion. "Howard is my Prince Charming, you know. My knight in shining armor. I loved my first husband dearly, but what I felt for him was like a spark to a bonfire when compared to the way I feel about your father. When we met, Howard seemed larger than life to me. Can you appreciate that?" She looked into Bellamy's eyes, seeking understanding on a woman-to-woman basis.

Bellamy nodded. To her twelve-year-old self, Dent had been larger than life. He'd been that way in her daydreams as well. "Yes. I know exactly what you mean."

"My first husband's prolonged illness had been a financial drain. There wasn't much left in the coffer after he died, so I was lucky to have my job at the accounting firm. I wasn't a charity case, but I was on a budget.

"So here I was, a working single mom. And there was Howard, a man of wealth, importance, and position. He excited and terrified me all at once."

"Why terrified you?"

"I knew from the start that he had fallen in love with me, knew he wanted me in his life. He told me so on our second date. And, Lord knows, I wanted him. But I was afraid of failing to live up to his expectations. What if he thought that I'd married him only for the security and benefits that came with him? I would have loved him no matter what, and wanted so badly to make him happy, to make his life as full and complete as he'd made mine."

Bellamy squeezed her hand. "You have. There's absolutely no doubt of that, Olivia. You've been his lifeblood. As his only surviving child, it almost pains me to say this, but when he draws his last breath, it will be your name on his lips."

With a sob, Olivia leaned forward and rested her forehead against Bellamy's shoulder. For a time, Bellamy stroked her back, giving her what small comfort she could when her Prince Charming was about to leave her.

Eventually she sat up straight and wiped the tears from her eyes. "Okay, I've had my cry. We got off the subject. Why did you go see Steven at this particular time?"

"Even when I was researching my book, he was reluctant to talk to me about that Memorial Day. We'd never discussed it as adults. I wanted to hear his point of view."

The warmth she'd shared with Olivia just moments earlier cooled significantly. Olivia bowed her head and stroked her furrowed forehead with the pads of her fingers.

"Bellamy, Howard and I held our peace when you were writing the book. We didn't like the idea, but it wasn't our place to interfere. But this...this obsession of yours is puzzling and upsetting. *Terribly* upsetting if I'm being honest. We don't understand it." Raising her head, she met Bellamy eye to eye. "Don't you want to put the incident behind you, forget it?"

"I can't," Bellamy whispered earnestly. But she refrained from telling her stepmother that she couldn't forget what she couldn't remember.

She was spared having to say anything more when a nurse entered the room. "Mrs. Lyston, the doctor will be available shortly to speak with you. In the meantime, Mr. Lyston is conscious if you want to go in."

Olivia gave Bellamy a nudge. "You go. He'll want to see you." Then, clutching Bellamy's hand, she added, "But promise me you won't upset him with talk of Susan's death."

* * *

Bellamy was shocked by how much her father had declined over the two days since she'd seen him. His cheeks and eye sockets were deeply sunken, making his face look skeletal. He breathed through colorless, partially open lips even though he was getting supplemental oxygen through a cannula. Beneath the light blanket, his form looked pathetically unsubstantial.

She moved to the bedside and took his frail hand in hers. At her touch, his eyes fluttered open. "Hi," she whispered.

"Hey, good-lookin'. Whacha got cookin'?"

It was their special greeting, one that had made her giggle as a girl, especially if it was accompanied by a gentle poke to her ribs. Now, she smiled through her tears.

"Forgive me for not standing," he said.

"You're forgiven." She leaned down and kissed his cheek. "Sit."

Mindful of all the tubes and lines snaking from beneath the covers to various machines, she carefully lowered herself onto the edge of the bed.

"Where's Olivia?" he asked.

"Waiting to talk to the doctor."

"He's going to tell her she needs to give up and let go." His voice was creaky with emotion and his eyes shone with unshed tears. "Help her through this, Bellamy."

"You know I will."

He clasped her hand more tightly. "There's something else I need you to do for me."

"Don't worry about the business. It's a well-oiled machine that practically runs itself. But I'm willing to do whatever you need me to."

"This isn't about the company. It's about Susan."

Bellamy glanced over her shoulder, almost expecting Olivia to be there admonishing her to remember her promise. "Let's not talk about her, Daddy. It pains you too much."

"Your book—"

"Upset you. I know. I'm sorry. I never meant—"

"You raised questions."

Unsure of what he was getting at, she said nothing.

"Was that intentional?"

"No," she replied, releasing her breath slowly. "But as the story unfolded, implied questions emerged. I suppose they've been buried in my subconscious."

"In mine, too."

"What?"

"I've harbored questions, too."

She was stunned. "Such as?"

"Primarily, I question the same thing that tabloid columnist did. Allen Strickland went to prison for killing Susan. But did he do it? I don't want to die with uncertainty, Bellamy."

"What makes you think it wasn't him?"

"Maybe it was. But I don't want to spend eternity with *maybe*. I need to *know*."

Her visit with Steven had left her feeling that the preteen Bellamy had been better off not knowing everything that was happening around her. She also came away realizing that *Low Pressure* had been written from a very naive perspective.

On that Memorial Day, there had been strong undercurrents at play, nuances that, as a twelve-year-old, she hadn't perceived. Even if she had sensed them, she wouldn't have had the maturity to identify and understand them.

Dent had cautioned her that any truths uncovered might be terribly ugly, possibly explosive, worse even than the one she'd learned about Steven and Susan. She had come close to believing that the course safest to her peace of mind would be to leave the past alone.

But now, her father was asking her to dig deeper. How could she refuse to grant—or at least attempt to grant—his dying wish? His asking this of her renewed her resolve to continue turning over stones regardless of the ugliness she might find beneath.

"I want to know with certainty, too, Daddy. Since I wrote the book, very recently in fact, some things have come to light that I didn't know."

"For instance?"

"Susan was seeing other boys, not just Dent Carter."

"You've been talking to him?"

"Among others."

"Do you trust him?"

"He's given me no reason to distrust him."

"He wouldn't, though, would he? Has he romanced you yet?"

She cast her eyes down.

Knowing what that signified, he grimaced. "Ask yourself why he's latched on to you, Bellamy."

"Why do you think he has?"

"He wants to trump all of us. What better way to get the last laugh than by taking you to bed?" As though the thought of that caused him grief, he sighed and closed his eyes. Several moments ticked by before he reopened them. "Talk to the detective."

"Dale Moody?"

"Start with him. I watched him during Strickland's trial. He was a troubled man. Find out why." He squeezed her hand again. "Will you do this for me?"

She made him the only promise she could. "I'll do my best."

"You always have." He reached up and touched her cheek with fingers the color and texture of parchment. "You always strived to please. You wanted everyone to be happy. I think you even married a man you didn't love only because you knew Olivia and I approved of him."

"Water under the bridge, Daddy."

"Don't let me off the hook so easily. I didn't consider your happiness nearly as often as you considered mine. You sort of got obscured by the tragedy of Susan, which preoccupied Olivia and me through Strickland's trial. Then we became so wrapped up in rebuilding our lives, I fear we viewed the big picture, and didn't pay enough attention to what was right in front of us."

"Daddy, I *never* felt obscured or overlooked. I swear. I was shy. I didn't want to draw attention to myself." She patted his hand. "You were there anytime I needed you, and I always knew you loved me."

She wanted to throw herself over him, to hold on tight, and beg him not to leave her. When he was gone, she wouldn't have any blood relatives left, and knowing that filled her with despair and a terrifying sense of finality.

But she wouldn't add a display of childish fears and sorrow to his own suffering. He wasn't choosing to die. He didn't want to leave Olivia, or her, or life itself. The best demonstration of her love would be to make his passing as peaceful as possible.

"If I do this," she said softly, "I can't stay here with you."

"I want you here. But it's more important to me that you find out if they punished the right man, and you haven't got much time."

By way of a pledge, she kissed his forehead again. "I understand, Daddy. You want peace. You need to know."

He held her near him for a moment longer and whispered, "So do you."

Dent took a bite of his jalapeño and Jack cheese omelet and washed it down with a sip of coffee. "Do you plan on telling me, or what?"

Seated across from him, Bellamy situated the paper napkin in her lap and used her fork to rearrange the food on her plate, which he noticed she'd barely touched. Throughout the meal, she'd avoided making eye contact with him, and the tension in the IHOP booth was palpable. He'd decided to address it.

"Tell you what?" she asked.

"Why you're giving me the silent treatment. On the flight home, you said no more than three words."

"The headset was uncomfortable."

"It didn't seem to bother you on the flight down."

"Well, it was hurting my ears on the flight back. Besides, I didn't want to distract you. It was an unfamiliar cockpit, remember?"

"Thanks. I appreciate the safety precaution. But since we landed, in fact since we left the hospital in Houston, you've been noticeably incommunicado. Of course, I'm merely your chauffeur." The remark finally earned him eye contact.

"What's that supposed to mean?"

"Figure it out."

"You volunteered to fly me down there, Dent."

"No I didn't. Gall volunteered me."

"You didn't have to agree to it."

"But I did. Gladly. Which begs the question of why you treated me like a leper once we got there."

Her face turned bright pink, indicating to him that she knew exactly why he was a bit hacked. She'd emerged from the ICU looking wounded and miserable, and, when he'd pushed himself away from the wall of the corridor where he'd been waiting, she'd walked straight to him.

By instinct, his arms had closed around her to provide a comforting hug, but when he touched her, she'd gone as rigid as a two-by-four. He'd dropped his arms, and she'd left him to join Olivia, who was standing nearby quietly weeping into a tissue. Since leaving that ICU, Bellamy had kept her distance.

Not that he cared. But it pissed him off all the same, especially after the way she'd cozied up to him last night and then had left him wanting. And because he still was. Wanting.

"If I didn't fawn over you," she said snidely, "it could be because my mind is on something else. Like, that may be the last time I see my dad alive. Something preoccupying like that."

Shit. Now he felt like a heel for deliberately provoking her. Being a nice guy was work, and he obviously had a long way to go before he got it right. "Considering the way of things, my complaining was selfish. I'm sorry."

She made a dismissive motion with her shoulder.

"Did you two have an emotional parting?"

She nodded.

"Then why'd you part?"

"What?"

"If he's that near death, why'd you leave? I figured I would be flying back alone, that you would stay in Houston so you could be there with him when he died. Why were you in such a hurry to get back to Austin tonight?"

She picked up a french fry, but returned it to her plate without eating it. "We had a sobering conversation."

He gave her a pointed look.

"About matters that are private."

"Hmm." But he continued to hold her gaze.

Finally she said, "He advised me not to trust you."

So much for trying to be a nice guy. He speared a sausage link, taking his anger out on it. "Howard Lyston's dying words, and they're about me. I'm flattered."

"It wasn't only about you. He asked me to do something for him."

"Pick out his burial suit?"

She glared at him.

"It's gotta be something that urgent or you'd still be down there."

She fumed for several more seconds, then turned her head away and looked through the window out across the parking lot of the restaurant. When she came back to him, she said, "Before he dies, Daddy wants to know for certain that Allen Strickland was the man who killed Susan."

Reading his startled expression, she said, "Yes, you heard right." She then recounted the conversation with her father.

When she finished, Dent frowned. "He's had doubts about Strickland's guilt all these years?"

"It seems so."

"And he raises the question now? *Now.* When he's on his deathbed? Jesus!" Frankly, he thought laying this burden on Bellamy at this particular time was a shitty thing for her father to do, but he edited the way he expressed his opinion. "He's given you an awfully tall order. Does he realize that?"

"He said I needed to know the truth, too. Basically, when you think about it, he's only asked me to do what I was already doing."

Yes, but failing herself was one thing. Failing her dying father was quite another. Dent didn't express that opinion at all, because he was certain Bellamy had already thought of it. That would explain why she looked like she'd been beaten with the chain that she was now using to tow the weight of the world.

He tried to wash down his resentment toward Howard Lyston with a sip of ice water. "Okay, what's your next move?"

With a weary gesture, she pushed back a strand of hair. "Daddy suggested I talk with Dale Moody."

"I can't believe I'm agreeing with him about anything, but Moody's a good choice."

"I have to find him first. I wanted to interview him for my book. He couldn't be found."

"I'll help."

She looked at him uneasily. "Dent, I can't keep asking you to—"

"You didn't ask." His gaze narrowed on her. "Oh, wait. I'm untrustworthy."

"I don't think that."

"No? Then why are you looking at me like you're trying to see past a disguise?"

"I know you want to clear your name."

He waited for more, and when she didn't proceed, he leaned forward. "But?"

"But is that your only motive for sticking around?"

"What does Daddy think? You listen to him and respect his opinion. Why does he think I'm hanging around?"

"He didn't say."

"Liar. What did he tell you?"

"Nothing."

"Yeah, right." He continued to try to stare the answer out of her, but her lips stayed stubbornly compressed. "Fine," he said. "Truth is, I don't give a damn what your daddy thinks about me. But I'll be perfectly candid with you as to why I'd like a tête-à-tête with Moody: Payback."

"Is that supposed to relieve my concern? You can't—"

"Relax. I won't do anything physical." After a beat, he added, "Probably." He gestured to her plate. "Finished?" When she nodded, he slid out of the booth.

She excused herself to go to the ladies' room. He told her he'd settle the bill and bring the car around.

The night air was thick and cloying, which didn't improve his mood. Contrary to what he'd told her, he *did* care what her old man had said about him. Not that he gave a shit about his opinion, but he did care about Bellamy's. It was directly after her visit with her father that she'd become aloof and untouchable, so he'd said or done something that had raised red flags of caution against Dent Carter.

Feeling truculent, he made his way across the parking lot, which, at this time of night, was only about a quarter full. He pulled his keys from his jeans pocket and had nearly reached his car when he sensed a shift in the sultry air, a sudden motion behind him.

Even before he fully registered these sensations, he was propelled against the side of his Vette, where he landed hard. A strong hand clamped the back of his head, banging his face down onto the roof of the car with enough force to split skin.

Hot breath filled his ear. "She's some high-toned pussy, isn't she, flyboy? Too bad she's gonna die."

Dent tried to raise his head, tried to dislodge his attacker, but he was as solid as a bale of hay. And even as Dent assessed the situation and realized that he was in real trouble, he felt the prick of a sharp blade at the base of his spine. He ceased struggling.

"Good thinking. That's eight inches of double-edged, razor-sharp steel. You might hear the pop when it punctures your spine. Probably be the last thing you hear."

"What do you want?" Dent asked, trying to buy time while he figured out a way to break the man's hold.

"Is she good? Slippery and tight?" Leaning forward, he licked the side of Dent's face from chin to eyebrow. "Never can tell about these rich girls, can you? One thing I know, she's gonna die bloody."

Dent, fueled by rage and disgust, kicked backward and caught the guy's kneecap with the heel of his boot. He grunted and fell back, but only a step. Dent took advantage. He spun around and jabbed his elbow into the guy's face, then landed a blow to his gut. But it was like hitting a slab of beef and only served to enrage the man, who swiped at him with the blade.

Dent saved himself from being eviscerated by spinning around at the last possible second. The knife cut a wide arc across the small of his back. Instinctually, he reached back. The knife bit into the back of his hand and sliced into his knuckles.

"Dent!"

He heard Bellamy's shout, heard her footsteps as she ran toward them. "No!" he shouted. "Stay away."

But she kept coming and, when she reached him, he pushed her hard to the ground. "He's got a knife."

"He's gone." She came quickly to her feet and closed the distance between them. "You're bleeding!"

"Hey! What's going on?"

"I saw him. That asshole shoved the woman to the ground."

Diners, having noticed the commotion from inside, were pouring out of the exit and rushing toward them. Dent looked around, but his attacker had vanished. "Get us the hell out of here," he said to Bellamy, straining the words through gritted teeth.

God bless her. She didn't do that female thing. She didn't ask questions, didn't demand an explanation, didn't scream or screech or upbraid him for putting her in this situation. No, she just placed her arm around his bloody waist and half carried him to the passenger side of the Vette. She opened the door and helped him into the seat.

Then she grabbed the ignition key from him, slammed the door, and ran around the hood. She called out to the well-meaning bystanders. "I'm okay. A misunderstanding. That's all." Then she got into the driver's seat and started the motor.

"Can you drive a six-speed?"

By way of answer, she wheeled out of the parking lot

and by the time she fishtailed into traffic, she was already in third gear.

"Did you see him?" Dent asked.

"Only a blur as he ran away. Was he robbing you?"

"No." He craned his neck around to look out the back window. "Do you see a pickup in the rearview mirror?"

She glanced into it. "I can't tell. Only headlights. Would he be following us?"

"I don't know. Drive in circles."

"I'll take you to the hospital."

"No."

She whipped her head around and looked at him. "But you're bleeding. All over."

"Yeah, onto my leather upholstery. What about you?"

"I'm fine."

"I pushed you down. I was—"

"I know. You wanted me out of the way of him. Scraped palms, but otherwise I'm okay. Better than you."

Unleashing a stream of profanity, Dent popped all the buttons on his shirt and used the tail of it to scrub the side of his face, which was still damp with saliva.

"Where should we go?" Bellamy asked.

"For now, just drive."

She did, with concentration and surprising skill, weaving in and out of traffic adroitly but not recklessly enough to attract the notice of a traffic cop. After ten minutes and a switch from one freeway to another, she whipped across two lanes of traffic to make an exit, and when she brought the car to a jarring stop at the bottom of the ramp, they were the only car in sight.

With her hands keeping a white-knuckle grip on the

steering wheel, she turned her head and looked at him, her question clear although unspoken.

"I think I was introduced to our redneck friend with the souped-up truck."

Ray was furious.

His ears echoed with a sound as irritating as a buzz saw. Maybe he was hearing his blood as it surged through his veins. His heart was pumping hard and fast with fury and frustration.

He'd come this close to opening up Dent Carter's belly. *This close.* The charmed bastard had narrowly escaped, thanks to her and her cry of alarm, which had drawn the attention of people inside the restaurant.

Carter had been bleeding, but not enough to kill him. Ray could've finished him off. But he hadn't waited this long to get revenge for his brother only to mess up in the final moments.

So he'd run before anyone could get a good look at him. He'd run the two blocks to where he'd left his truck, then he'd gotten the hell out of the vicinity. Not out of cowardice, mind you, but from caution.

"Know when to fish and when to cut bait," Allen had told him.

But the night's efforts weren't entirely wasted. He'd drawn blood. He'd left the pair of them with a lot to think about, and that was satisfying. They'd be worried now, wouldn't they? He liked imagining them puzzling over who he was and living in dread of when he would strike again.

For weeks, he'd been trailing her like a glorified bloodhound. Sick of that, he'd decided earlier today to attack at the very next opportunity. But he'd lost track of them. All day he'd driven back and forth between her place and Carter's, but they hadn't surfaced.

But sooner or later, Carter always wound up at that crappy airfield, so, around dark, Ray had positioned his truck where it couldn't be seen from the highway and had watched the road leading off it to the airstrip.

Was he smart or what? Because, sure enough, around ten o'clock, the red Corvette had come speeding up to the highway. Keeping a safe distance from it, Ray had followed it to the IHOP. Through the windows he'd watched them eat. And, forty minutes later, when Dent came out alone, Ray, disbelieving his good luck, had seized the opportunity.

No, Carter wasn't dead. But Ray had gotten his message across. As of tonight, he hadn't just changed the rules of play. He'd changed the whole fucking game.

Chapter 14

I t's a dump."

Dent went into his apartment ahead of Bellamy, switched on the overhead light, then moved immediately to the bed and pulled the bedspread up over the rumpled sheets and pillows.

Two pillows, she noted. Each bearing the imprint of a head.

"I'm going to shower off the blood so we can see what's what. Make yourself at home." He grabbed a pair of shorts from a chest of drawers, then went into the bathroom and closed the door.

On the way here, they had stopped at a convenience store. Its stock of first-aid items had been limited, but she'd bought one of everything, not knowing what she would need to tend his wounds.

Now she placed the sack of purchases on the dining table in the kitchen alcove and sat down in one of the two chairs, then took a look around. He hadn't exaggerated. The apartment was a dump. Being one large room, the areas of it were distinguished only by the flooring. The sleeping area had a different color carpet from the living area. The patch of kitchen was covered in vinyl tiles. Only the bathroom was separated by a door.

Except for the unmade bed, it was basically neat. But the meager furnishings looked like cheap rental pieces with chipped veneers and stringy upholstery. The faucet in the kitchen sink dripped with loud and regular *ploinks*, and the fabric panels that passed for draperies hung limply on crooked rods. There were no pictures on the walls. No books, or even shelves in which to place books or keepsakes.

It was a sad place, indicative of a solitary life.

Even sadder was that the only difference between this place and her condo in New York was the quality of the furnishings. Hers had been purchased through a decorator and had been costly. They were tasteful and pleasing to the eye.

But they held no memories or sentiment for her. Anyone could have owned them. They didn't represent a home. They were as lacking in personality as the chair in which she sat here in Dent's dismal kitchen.

The comparison made her feel even more despondent than she already was.

He came out of the bathroom wearing only the boxers he'd taken in with him. He was drying his wet hair with one towel and pressing another to the small of his back. There were two places on his face where the skin was split. Those cuts had been left to bleed. He'd wrapped a washcloth around his injured hand.

"How long have you lived here?" she asked.

"Two years, give or take. Since I had to sell my house.

When I left the airline, I could no longer sustain the lifestyle to which I had become accustomed. Housing market was crap. I took a beating on the sale, but I had no choice."

"Savings?"

"Everything went into the down payment on my plane."

With the towel he'd used on his hair, he dabbed at the bleeding gash on his cheekbone just below his right eye. "I hope you don't faint at the sight of blood. The son of a bitch made me a goddamn sieve."

"We should have called the police."

"We'd have made the front page of tomorrow's *Statesman*. The witnesses saw me push you to the ground. I'd have probably been arrested, held while questioned, and by the time it was sorted out, we'd be news just because of who we are."

He was right, of course, which is why she'd let him talk her out of seeking emergency treatment for him. Her father lay dying; Olivia was hanging on to her fortitude by a thread. They didn't need to open the newspaper tomorrow and read about their daughter's involvement in an assault-and-battery in the parking lot of a twenty-four-hour pancake house.

"Would you know him if you saw him again?" she asked.

"Heavy bastard. Solid. Left arm is covered in a tattoo. A snake with fangs dripping venom. You said the guy in the pickup had a heavily tattooed left arm that was propped in the open window. Putting one and one together..." He left her to do the math.

During the drive here, he had related to her the details of the attack. "Except I'm skipping the dirty parts."

"Dirty parts?"

"Nasty things he said about you."

Most alarming, he'd told her what his attacker had threatened to do. Now she said, "He wants to kill us."

"That's what the man said."

"But why? Who could he be?"

"I'm thinking. I'm also still leaking."

"Oh, sorry." She motioned him over to the table, where she remained seated. "Turn around."

He presented her with his back. The shorts were riding low on his hips, revealing an oozing red line like a wide smile across the small of his back.

"Dent, you should go to an emergency room."

He peered over his shoulder, trying to assess the damage himself. "I doubt they'd believe I cut myself shaving."

"You could claim it was an accident."

"Like what?"

"I don't know," she said throwing up her hands, her voice breaking with frustration.

He turned around to face her and tipped her chin up. "Hey, you reacted with nerves of steel, then drove like Mario Andretti. You're not going to crack under pressure now, are you?"

She lifted her chin off the perch of his fingertips and, placing her hands on his hip bones, turned him around none too gently. She emptied the contents of the sack onto the table and uncapped an ominous-looking brown glass bottle. "I hope this antiseptic burns like hell."

It must have because he hissed and cursed as she applied it. To distract him, she passed a cotton ball doused with the liquid up to him. "Dab that on your face and hand. How is it?"

He unwound the washcloth and took a look. "The cuts

aren't deep. Fingers will probably be stiff in the morning, but he could have cut them off."

She shivered. "That's the least of it. But why give you warning? In the time he took to issue those threats, he could have killed you."

"Disappointed?"

"I'm serious," she said, speaking up to him when he looked down at her from over his shoulder.

"Maybe he was afraid that somebody was watching from inside the restaurant. Or he's more bluff than bite. Or he's a psycho who's lost his powers of reason. It's anybody's guess until we know who he is and why he has it in for us." He checked her progress. "About finished?"

"It's not bleeding as much."

"Because you damn near cauterized it with that stuff."

She unrolled a length of gauze and gently tapped it into place over the wound. "Turn," she said. He made three revolutions while she wound the gauze around his middle, then placed vertical strips of adhesive tape at intervals to secure it.

"You're getting hair caught in that tape."

"I'm trying not to, but I can't see what I'm doing if you don't move your hands." He did, and she pressed a final strip inches away from the silky stripe of hair that bisected his abdomen and disappeared into the waistband of his shorts. With affected detachment, she said briskly, "There. Done."

But when she tipped her head back and looked into his face, the intensity with which he was looking down at her stopped her breath. In a voice that was low and husky and suggestive, he said, "As long as you're in that neighborhood, anything else you want to do..."

Moving slowly, he reached out and traced the shape of her lower lip with the pad of his thumb, then brushed aside her hair and gently rubbed her earlobe between his fingers. Desire blossomed in her lower body and brought a whimper to her throat that she was powerless to contain.

While working on his back, she'd tried to remain indifferent to the shape of his buttocks beneath the thin cloth of his shorts, but now the temptation to put her arms around him and test the firmness of those taut muscles against her palms was almost too powerful to withstand.

She wanted to say *To hell with everything* and lean forward, nuzzle that enticing ribbon of hair, then follow it with her lips down to his sex that was so seductively close it made her weak with yearning. To take Dent into her mouth, to taste him...

Another sound issued from her, but when she moved, it wasn't to put her hands on him, or to kiss the skin that smelled of soap and man, of Dent. Instead she pushed his caressing hand aside, stood up, and edged round him.

"Don't be cute, Dent. This is hardly the time—"

Whatever else she was going to say—and later she couldn't remember—was left unspoken. He reached for her as she made to go past him, pulled her to him, and closed his hand around her jaw to tilt her face up. "You grew up to be a hell of a woman, Bellamy. The way you worked that gear shift was a major turn-on."

If last night's kiss had been a flirtatious invitation to misbehave, this one was a lesson in mastery. It was possessive, carnal, and dominating to a degree that alarmed her. Not that she feared him. She feared her susceptibility to him, feared the forbidden wish that he would do to her at least some of what his kisses portended.

But she resisted being completely drawn in, and, sensing that, he raised his head and released his hold on her face, but only in order to slide his hand down over her breast. He plumped it and tugged gently on her nipple with his fingertips as he nudged the vee of her thighs with his erection.

"Let yourself think about something else for a little while," he coaxed, whisking his lips across hers. "Relax and have some fun for a change."

Then he captured her mouth again. Relax? Impossible. Not when her body was urging her to draw him in, to partner with his tongue. She wanted to drive her fingers up into his hair and hold his head steady while she lost herself in his intoxicating kiss.

Instead, she forced herself to do nothing, to respond with neither ardor nor aversion. She willed herself to go perfectly still and react to nothing.

Quick to realize that he was the only one engaged, he angled his head back and searched her face.

"Daddy said you would try to get the last laugh on us by sleeping with me."

He let go of her immediately. "Oh, *that's* what Daddy said. That explains the deep-freeze treatment."

The gashes on his face had reopened and were bleeding, making him appear even more dangerously angry when he stalked to the closet and reached inside to yank a pair of jeans off a hanger. He pulled them on with abrupt, jerky motions, but when he tried to button them, he helplessly raised his hands to his sides. "This could take a while."

Bellamy flushed hotly, but not from embarrassment. She gestured toward the rumpled bed. "Did you really expect me to get into bed with you when you haven't even changed the sheets from the last one?"

He plowed his fingers through his damp hair. "Look, I left her here the morning I flew you to Houston. I hadn't thought about her till we came through the door and I saw the bed. I don't even know her name."

"You didn't care to ask?"

"No."

"Just like you didn't care that Susan had others while she was dating you?"

"Why should I have cared?"

"You didn't love her? Even a little?"

"*Love her?*" He laughed. "Hell, no. I was a horny teenager, and she put out."

"And that's all my sister mattered to you?"

He put his hands on his hips. "How much do you think I mattered to *her?*"

"You mattered enough to make her furious when you showed up at the barbecue late. I think she would rather you not have come at all than to—"

All the blood seemed suddenly to drain from her head. She fell back on a wave of dizziness, but the image in her mind's eye was crystal clear: Dent, astride his motorcycle, gesturing angrily at Susan, who was splendidly, gorgeously in a rage that matched his.

The memory had popped open like a three-dimensional greeting card, gaudy and stark in detail. Bellamy's breathing became as rapid and choppy as her heartbeat. "You were there. At the boathouse. With Susan. Before the tornado."

He swore and took a step toward her. "Bellamy—"

"No!" She stuck both hands in front of her, palms

out, then clasped them to the sides of her head as she put words to the tumbling recollections. "Susan didn't come back from the boathouse with the beer-drinking group. I got worried, thinking she might be sick from drinking too much. It was such a hot, muggy day, and I thought..."

"Listen. Let me explain."

"I went to look for her, didn't I?"

He said nothing.

"You know I did. Because...because you saw me watching the two of you, didn't you? *Didn't you*?"

"Bellamy—"

"All this time," she cried, "you could have told me! Why didn't you tell me that I was remembering wrong? Why didn't you—" The answer became obvious in a lightning bolt of clarity. "You weren't flying with Gall. You didn't have an alibi. You were in the state park, and you were fighting with Susan."

For several moments, neither moved, then she lunged for the door and pulled it open.

"*Fuck*! Bellamy!"

She bolted through the doorway with such impetus that the only thing to break her fall from the second-story breezeway was the metal guardrail. She landed against it hard, banging her pelvic bone painfully. She gave a cry of pain, then another of fear as Dent's hands closed around her upper arms.

Her sharp cry caused the two men on the parking lot below to look up. They'd been lounging against the hood of a car, but Rocky Van Durbin came instantly to life. He shouted, "There!" and pointed her out to his photographer, who was at the ready. The flash on his camera exploded in bursts of blinding light.

Dent wrenched Bellamy's gripping hands off the guardrail and hauled her back into the apartment, then kicked the door shut.

He vented his frustration on the door, beating his fist against it to emphasize each eruptive, foul word. His impulse was to tear down the stairs and make Van Durbin sorry he had ever heard of Denton Carter, then go to work on the photographer and destroy his camera.

But when he'd suffered similar ambushes following Susan's death, and again during the NTSB's investigation into the near crash, Gall had been there like a flea in his ear, warning him against impetuous reprisals. "Reporters thrive on angry reactions. You want to beat 'em at their game? Ignore 'em."

The gash on his cheekbone was throbbing like a son of a bitch, and when he wiped his face the back of his hand, already bleeding from the cuts on his knuckles, came away streaked with brighter, fresher blood. He figured the cut on his back had reopened as well.

When he turned into the room, Bellamy flinched, which made him all the madder. "If you're more scared of me than you are of them, you know the way out."

He left the path to the door clear for her as he retrieved his blood-soaked jeans from the bathroom floor and fished his cell phone from a pocket. He then strode into the kitchen and consulted the telephone number for the complex manager, which a previous tenant had penciled onto the faded wallpaper.

Viciously he punched in the number, and the call was answered almost immediately. "Yeah, that notice you put in everyone's mailbox last week? About the guy who exposed himself to a woman in the North Unit? Uh-huh. Well there are two guys in the parking lot of South. They're taking pictures through people's windows with a telephoto lens. I'm almost sure it's the same two I saw talking to some little girls on the playground this afternoon. You'd better call the police. Okay. Bye."

He disconnected and looked over at Bellamy, who hadn't moved or taken her wide gaze off him. "That ought to keep Van Durbin and his sidekick busy for a while." He buttoned up his jeans and ripped off a length of gauze, which he folded and used to stanch the bleeding on his cheek. "I'm going to have a beer. Want one?"

She didn't respond.

He took a can of beer from the refrigerator, opened it and sucked up the suds that spilled over the top, then took a deep swallow. He sprawled in the only easy chair in the apartment and calmly sipped at his beer, while Bellamy stared at him as though he was an exotic and potentially dangerous animal that should be caged.

The rings around her eyes were so dark they looked like they'd been put there by punching fists. Her face had been leached of color, but that might have been caused by the glare of his unforgiving overhead light. She looked completely done in, but his ire was such that he didn't go easy on her.

"Well?" he said.

"What?" Her voice sounded rusty from disuse.

"You're not going to ask?"

"Wouldn't you just deny it?"

"Yes. But think what a great plot twist this would make for *Low Pressure: The Sequel*. You could shock your readers right out of their socks. The boyfriend was the killer after all. He, a sexual deviant if ever there was one, got away with murder.

"Flash forward eighteen years. He puts the moves on the baby sister, who's all grown up now. Filled out real good. Makes his mouth water. She kisses like a bad girl till he acts on the invitation, then she shuts down like a maiden missionary. When she says 'No!' to him, he wigs out, takes her sweet body, and..." He gave an exaggerated shudder. "Grisly stuff. A page-turner for sure."

She gave him a withering look, then went to the window, where colored lights were flashing on the slats of the uneven blinds. "The police are here. Three squad cars."

"Why don't you race down there and tell them that you've finally nabbed your sister's killer?"

"Because I don't believe you are. You are, however, a jerk."

He scoffed. "You're a writer and that's the worst insult you can come up with? Baby sister also has the vocabulary of a maiden missionary. If you want me to, I can help you with some bad words."

"I won't buy into this asinine conversation, Dent."

He finished his beer and set the empty can on the wobbly coffee table.

After a time, she said, "Van Durbin will tell them it's a false charge."

"Of course he will. But he'll have to explain what he was doing down there with a photographer, which will amount to him admitting that he's stalking you. He'll have to do some fancy footwork."

"They'll trace the call to your phone."

"They can't. It's a burner. The number doesn't show up on caller ID. Eventually they'll realize it was a hoax and let them go, but in the meantime that bloodsucker will be in the hot seat. If there's a god, he'll attract a boyfriend in lockup."

She turned away from the window. "You're clever. You respond quickly to a crisis situation."

"A skill that makes me a good pilot." He pursed his lips thoughtfully. "I guess it would also make me a good murderer, wouldn't it?"

She sat down on the matching love seat facing his chair, perching on the edge of the cushion as though she might have to make a quick getaway. "Why did you lie to the police?"

"I don't think it would have gone too well for me if I'd told them that I'd intercepted Susan at the boathouse and that we'd had a lovers' quarrel. And don't read anything into the word 'lovers.' I don't mean it literally."

"How did you know she would be at the boathouse?"

"I was driving up that lane—you know the one, that led to the pavilion?" She nodded. "Susan flagged me down. She was alone."

"What was she doing?"

"Primping."

"Primping?"

"She was looking at herself in the mirror of a compact, putting on lipstick, fluffing her hair. Things girls do."

"I described to you how pretty she looked when she returned to the pavilion."

"Oh, so now you think I'm making that up so that it fits with your recollection?"

Wearily, she said, "Go on."

"I said something to the effect of 'Here I am, better late than never.' But she didn't think so. She told me that she'd made other plans that didn't include me. At first I tried to placate her. I apologized for choosing a ride in an airplane over her. I promised to make it up to her, promised it wouldn't happen again. Bullshit stuff that guys say when they—".

"Don't really mean them."

He shrugged. "She was having none of it. I could see that what was left of my Memorial Day was rapidly turning to crap, so I got mad, told her…" He stopped, and when Bellamy raised her eyebrows, he said, "More bullshit stuff that guys say when a sure thing is no longer sure. Unlike you, I have an…*earthy*…vocabulary. I called her some rather descriptive and ugly names."

She stared into space for a moment and when she refocused on him, she said, "In my mind's eye, I can see the two of you quarreling. But I don't remember anything after that."

"I rode off into the sunset."

"There was no sunset. The sky was stormy."

"Another figure of speech."

A thoughtful frown creased her forehead as she sank back into the cushions of the love seat, which made him embarrassed over the god-awful thing. It was a piece of junk, just like everything else in the place. When he'd sold his house, with its swimming pool and heavily wooded backyard on a bluff that overlooked downtown, he'd assumed a necessary indifference to his living conditions.

He'd rented this place because it was all he could afford. He slept here. Sometimes screwed here. Showered and kept his clothes here. He ate carry-out and hadn't used the cookstove more than once or twice. The fridge was virtually empty.

He hadn't given any thought to his lifestyle until he looked at his shabby habitat through Bellamy's eyes. And now he realized that what he did within these walls you couldn't call living.

Which was exactly what he'd said of his dad.

The similarity jolted Dent, and he angrily rejected it.

He was glad Bellamy diverted him by asking another question. "After you left the park, where did you go?"

"Everywhere. Nowhere. Gall had locked up the hangar and left when I did, so there was no point in going back to it. I didn't want to go home and watch my dad watch TV. So I just drove around, blowing off steam, and looking for fun in some other place."

"Who could corroborate that?"

"Not a damn soul. But that's what I did. The weather turned really bad, really fast. The lightning was fierce. When it started hailing, I took cover under an overpass. The sky turned that greenish-black color. I was several miles from the funnel, but I saw it when it dipped down out of the clouds and realized that it was right on top of the state park, so I got on my bike and went back." He spread his hands. "You know the rest."

Bellamy lapsed into another thoughtful silence.

Dent left his chair, went to the window, and peered through the blinds. The parking lot below was clear of all activity; the only vehicles in it were those belonging to residents. He smiled at the thought of Van Durbin being at the mercy of cops who thought they'd captured a pervert.

But his smile faded when a twinge of pain reminded him of the man who'd attacked him. He wanted to retch whenever he thought of the man's tongue sliding down his cheek and the crude references to Bellamy. Before Dent even realized his hands were forming fists, they were drumming the outside of his thighs.

"One thing puzzles me."

He turned back to her. "Just one?"

"It's a big one. I could have corroborated that you'd left the park. I watched you ride away. Why didn't you tell Moody that I'd seen you leave the park while Susan was still alive and well?"

"It wouldn't have done any good. You'd lost your memory."

"You didn't know that until yesterday, and it came as a surprise to you."

Too late, Dent realized he'd trapped himself.

Bellamy sat forward. "Instead of lying to Moody and inventing an alibi with Gall, why didn't you simply tell Moody that I could vouch for you?" When he still didn't say anything, she pressed him for an answer. "Dent? Why?"

"I figured it was better that Moody didn't know I'd been there at all." Suddenly he got up from his chair, went over to the bed, and began stripping it.

She followed him. "There's more to it than that. I know there is."

"What makes you think so?"

"Because you won't look me in the eye."

Abruptly he turned. "Okay, now I am."

"What am I missing?"

He shook his head. "I'm not going to talk about it any more tonight. My brain needs a break and so does yours." He went back to pulling the sheets off the mattress.

"I need to know."

"Not tonight, you don't."

"Yes. Tonight."

"Why tonight?"

"Because my dad might die at any time."

"And you'd be unable to fulfill his dying wish."

"Yes."

"Too bad. I'm not talking about it any more tonight."

He rolled the sheets into a ball, which he crammed into a wicker hamper in the bathroom, then moved to the closet and began rummaging through the items jammed onto the shelves above the rod. "There are some clean sheets around here somewhere."

"Why won't you fill in this one gap for me?"

He stepped around her carrying a set of sheets to the bed.

"What don't you want me to remember?"

"Nothing."

"I don't believe you."

"Grab that corner, will you?"

Absently she fit the contour sheet over the corner of the mattress, then straightened and looked down at the bed. "What are you doing?"

"Changing the sheets so you won't be offended when you come to bed."

She watched him tug the top sheet into place. He held a pillow with his chin and pulled the case over it. "You think that fresh sheets will change my mind about us sleeping together?"

"I don't know what you have in mind, A.k.a., but all I plan to do is sleep. I'm exhausted and, honestly, no longer in the mood." He gave her a critical once-over. "Besides, you look like something out of the *Thriller* video. No offense."

He patted the button fly of his jeans. "It stays done up for the rest of the night, so don't even think about trying to cop a feel while my eyes are closed. In fact, thanks to the shithead with the snake tattoo, I'll probably have to sleep on my stomach." He motioned toward the far wall. "Catch the lights."

He lay down on his stomach and socked the pillow until he got it the way he wanted it, then laid his head on it and closed his eyes.

Feeling helpless to do anything else, Bellamy walked over to the wall switch and killed the overhead light, then felt her way back to the bed. She toed off her shoes but lay down on her back fully clothed and tense, aware of him next to her, and mistrustful of his pledge to sleep and nothing more.

After several minutes, he mumbled, "You can relax. I'm not going to choke you with your panties while you sleep."

"If you'd wanted to kill me, you would have done so by now."

"Gee, thanks for the vote of confidence."

She'd caught only a glimmer of the memory, but it had been an important one. Dent was withholding the rest of it from her, and she needed to know why. She longed to free all of it from her subconscious, to watch the scene at the boathouse in its entirety, to hear the argument between him and Susan to its conclusion.

She sensed that the quarrel between them was pivotal to the events that had come afterward, and that if she could remember it, she would remember much more.

Speaking quietly into the darkness, she said, "If it was insignificant, you would tell me what I saw or overheard."

He lay silently.

"Which means that my memory is blocking something important."

He didn't say anything.

"You didn't love Susan."

Silence.

"Did you even like her?"

"Bellamy?"

"Yes?"

"Go to sleep."

Chapter 15

———◆———

Bellamy awakened to the smell of freshly brewed coffee. When she pried open her puffy eyes, she saw Dent sitting at his dining table, fully dressed, sipping from a steaming mug as he flipped through the pages of a telephone directory. Sensing that she was awake, he looked toward the bed.

"Surprise! You're still alive."

Ignoring that, she sat up and arched her back to work out a kink. "What time is it?"

"Going on nine."

"I didn't mean to sleep so late. I need to call Olivia."

"Mugs are in the cabinet to the right of the sink."

She found the mugs, filled one with coffee, and placed her call, then left a message when it went straight to voice mail. "I suppose if there was any change I would have heard from her." She joined Dent at the table.

"There's nothing for breakfast. Sorry."

"Coffee's fine." But it wasn't. Her first sip caused her to grimace.

"Gall's recipe," he explained. "It would knock a mule on its ass."

"Milk?"

"I checked. It's curdled."

"Doesn't matter," she said, bravely taking another sip. "This morning I could use the jolt."

"Sleep okay?"

"Like a log. You?"

"I did all right. I stayed awake for a while wishing you'd try to cop that feel." Then, "Ah, the blush is back. I was getting worried for a while there. Last night you went pale at the thought of sleeping with a killer."

"Dent."

"Did you wake up convinced I'm innocent?"

"Not guilty. But far from innocent."

"There's a difference?"

"In my mind. How's your back?"

"I think the cut closed up overnight. There's no fresh blood on the bandage."

He still looked like the survivor of a long battle. The cuts on his face had begun to scab, but they were puffy and surrounded by dark bruises.

Motioning at the telephone directory, which, judging from the looks of it, was several generations old, she asked who he was looking up.

Sidestepping the question, he stretched out his long legs beneath the table. "Go with me for a minute here."

"All right. I'm listening."

"Assume that all this—the rat delivery through last night's parking lot adventure—is reprisal."

"For the book?"

"For that and/or the incident that inspired it. In your

kitchen yesterday, one of us remarked that it would be a short list of people who would harbor that kind of grudge and go to those lengths to settle it."

"You said that, or near enough. You asked me who I thought the mystery guest was."

"Okay, let's name the possibilities." He raised his finger as though to count them off. "Me."

"You didn't fake the knifing."

"So I'm eliminated? Thanks," he said drily. A second finger joined the first. "Your parents."

"We can strike them, too. Cancer is a solid alibi."

He held up a third finger. "Steven. He has some serious issues and grievances."

"But it wasn't he who jumped you last night. Besides, he wouldn't harm me, no matter how angry he is over the book."

"I guess," he said, but dubiously. "Those are the principals. If it's not one of us, it's gotta be someone more removed."

"Tangential."

"Back to the big words. But, yeah."

"Dale Moody?"

"Possibly. But what's his beef? Besides coming across as not too bright or competent in your book."

"Daddy said he looked like a troubled man during the trial. He should have been pleased with the conviction. What was the problem?"

Of course Dent didn't have the answer, but thoughtfully he added, "Moody's a big guy, or was, like the lummox who jumped me. Let's put a check mark next to his name. Who else?"

"What about Rupe Collier?"

"Definitely wasn't him at the IHOP."

"No. So who does that leave?"

"Strickland."

She reacted with a start.

"Not Allen," he said. "But maybe his brother. Roy."

"Ray," she corrected.

He motioned at the directory. "That's who I was looking up."

"What made you think of him?"

"Process of elimination. Of this group of people involved, even tangentially—did I say it right?—he and Allen were by far the most redneck." He looked down at the cut across his knuckles. "He'd be royally pissed by how his big brother was portrayed in your book."

"It was a fair portrayal."

"Of a killer. But what if he wasn't? An excellent reason for a vendetta is your brother getting sent to prison for a crime that he didn't commit."

"And then dying there."

"Allen didn't *die*, Bellamy. He was *murdered*."

She flinched at the word, and it reverberated there between them for several ponderous moments. Less than two years into his twenty-year sentence for manslaughter, Allen Strickland had been fatally stabbed in the Huntsville prison yard by a fellow inmate.

After a prolonged silence, Dent pulled in his legs and leaned upon the table. "We've talked about every aspect of this business, but you've never mentioned Strickland's ultimate fate. Why's that?"

"Habit, I suppose," she said quietly.

"Habit?"

"I remember the day we found out he'd been killed. I

was a freshman in high school. Rupe Collier called my parents just as I was about to leave for class."

"How did they react to the news?"

"They didn't receive it cheerfully, which would have been distasteful and insensitive. But they weren't so hypocritical that they expressed deep sorrow, either. Daddy just looked... very somber. I remember him saying, 'That's an end to it, then.'

"And the way he said it was like... like a mandate that it never be spoken of. Then he got up and left the room. Olivia followed him. To my knowledge, no one in our household ever mentioned Allen Strickland's death again."

Steven hadn't referred to it yesterday. Nor had her father, who had referenced Strickland's imprisonment but not how he'd died. Perhaps the question posed by Van Durbin in his column yesterday had made them all too uneasy to talk over the possibility that not only had he been unjustly incarcerated, but that he'd also died needlessly.

"I ran across Ray Strickland's name when I was researching the book," she said to Dent. "He was quoted in numerous newspaper write-ups of the trial, always professing his brother's innocence. But if he was the man at IHOP, I wouldn't have recognized him. The man I remember from the photographs had bushy hair and a mustache that grew down over his jaw."

"A razor would have taken care of both in five minutes."

"Did you find a telephone listing for him?"

"No. But I don't believe we'll have to search for him. He'll find us."

That was an unnerving thought. "Maybe we should get the police involved, after all. We could report last night's assault on you, give them his name, and—"

"And if Ray Strickland, brother of the late Allen, turns out to be a law-abiding, tax-paying, churchgoing man living in the suburbs with a wife and adoring children, you'll have made another enemy. It would make news, and Van Durbin, assuming he survived his night in lockup, would—"

She waved her hands to cut him off. "I see where you're going." As she organized her thoughts, she pulled her lower lip through her teeth. "We don't *know* that Strickland is our pickup driver, but it *feels* right."

"It does to me, too. *Low Pressure* ends with Allen receiving his sentence. You didn't cover his death in prison. Ray might've seen that as a slight. He might consider it unfair. In his mind, you exploited his personal tragedy, but you didn't tell the whole story."

She placed her elbows on the table and held her head. "Lord. I would happily apologize."

"I don't think that's gonna do it for the guy I met last night." He exhaled heavily. "On the other hand, I could be way off track. The hell of it is, we don't know who we're dealing with."

She dropped her hands back onto the table. "There's still Moody."

He thumbed the curled pages of the phone book. "I also tried to look him up."

"Good luck with that."

"When you were trying to locate him before, did you contact the Austin PD?"

"I started there. I was told that he'd retired, but that's all I learned. Human Resources claimed not to have an address for him, no contact information whatsoever."

"He must draw a pension."

"It's automatically deposited into a checking account.

The bank is headquartered in North Carolina, and they hung up on me when I asked for privileged information about their customer. I ran a Google search and tried to obtain his social security number, but gave up when I came under suspicion of identity theft."

"Family?"

"An ex-wife who said she didn't know where he was, but that she hoped he was in a cemetery."

"He may be. Did you check death records?"

"Along with tax rolls, voters registration, the DMV." She shook her head. "Believe me, I looked. And not just in Texas."

"He was a cop. He would know how to disappear."

"He's not the only thing that went missing," she said, her tone gaining Dent's full attention. "With the bribe of a few beers, I talked a detective into letting me review the Susan Lyston case file. I could have saved my bar bill. He reported back that the file was missing."

"Did you believe him? Maybe he was holding out for a sweeter bribe. I would have."

She responded to his insinuating smile with an eye roll. "He seemed genuinely perplexed, upset, and embarrassed by his and the police department's failure to produce the file. I think he genuinely wanted to help."

"Or he genuinely wanted to get laid and then get an acknowledgment in your book."

"Not every man thinks like you."

"Sure they do." It was a rote response because he appeared to be already concentrating on something else. He was gazing into space and tapping his thumbnail against his front teeth. "I have an idea of who may know where Moody is."

He stood up and took the telephone book with him. Pointing to her half-empty mug of coffee, he said, "Bring that with you. You can finish it on the way."

"I can't go anywhere without first stopping by my house. I'm a mess."

He looked her over. "Right. Okay. Good, in fact. I'd like to leave my Vette in your garage."

"Why?"

"It's too easy for that knife-wielding son of a bitch to spot."

He pulled into the driveway behind her car. "I'll switch cars while you're making the overhaul."

"I look that bad?"

"Allow yourself at least fifteen minutes." He was ragging on her, but his rascally smile suddenly reversed itself. "What's that?"

Propped against her front door was a large manila envelope.

"When I spoke with the house painter yesterday, I asked him to leave an estimate in the mailbox, but I guess the envelope was too large."

However, when she picked it up and read the bold label stuck to the front of it, her stomach sank. "Van Durbin."

She worked open the sealing adhesive and removed several eight-by-ten photographs. All of them were of her and Dent. Sorting through them quickly, she said, "These were taken—"

"Yesterday. At the Austin airport."

Clearly recognizable in the background was the ticketing area where they had stopped at an automated kiosk to pick up their boarding passes for the flight to Atlanta.

There was another photograph of them hurrying toward the security check line and one of them in line waiting their turn.

The fourth picture, obviously taken from a distance with a telephoto lens, had been snapped after they'd cleared security and were rushing toward the gate. Their backs were to the camera.

And Dent's hand was planted solidly on the small of her back.

She went through the photos a second time, now noting that in each shot he was touching her. She didn't remember there being that much physical contact between them, but the evidence was there.

The most startling picture had been taken while they were waiting in the security check line. He was pulling a small piece of leaf—a holdover from their trip to the neighborhood park—from her hair. It had seemed like nothing at the time. The gesture had lasted no more than a second or two, but the camera had caught them with their faces close, his fingers in her hair. They were smiling into each other's eyes in a way that was indicative of much more than his teasing remark about being unable to take her anywhere without dusting her off first.

The photos implied an intimacy between them that now made her feel hot, self-conscious, and glad that her back was to him. She cleared her throat. "Van Durbin must have left them here yesterday before tracking us to your apartment last night."

"Busy guy." He sounded distracted, and she wondered if he, too, was surprised to find himself caught in such telling tableaus.

"Why did he bother to hand-deliver them?" she asked.

"To let us know that we can run but we can't hide. I hope the bastard had a rough night in jail." She sensed his leaning in to get a closer look at the photographs from over her shoulder. Speaking in a low voice, he said, "You know, to look at these, you'd think—"

"Oh!" she exclaimed suddenly. "That's Jerry."

"Huh?"

"Jerry." She pointed out a face in the airport crowd in the background. The man was looking at her and Dent, not at the camera, but it had a clear angle on his face.

"Who the hell is *Jerry*?"

She laughed. "He's...he's nobody. An ardent fan." Shaking her head with dismay, she said, "What a bizarre coincidence."

Tucking the photos under her arm, she unlocked her front door and the two of them went inside. "Let me go first." Dent moved her aside as he reached beneath his loose shirttail and produced a pistol.

Bellamy gasped. "Where did that come from?"

"Pepe's Pawn Shop, I think it was called. It's a tamale stand now."

"Dent! I want nothing to do with guns."

"*Gun*. Only one. And you never have to touch it."

"What are you doing with it?"

"Discouraging anything our tattooed friend has in mind for us. Now stay put till I check things out."

After a swift walk-through he returned and reported that the house was as they'd left it the day before. She was relieved to see that he'd tucked the pistol away.

"I checked the mailbox and found this." She held up the letter envelope with the painter's estimate inside. "Seems fair. And I like the idea of his being the locksmith's brother-in-law. Saves me from having to give a house key to someone else."

She reached for her cell phone, but Dent said, "Call him later. I want to hear about Jerry, your ardent fan."

"He calls himself my number-one fan." She picked out the photograph with him in it. "The focus is soft, but I'm almost certain that's him."

Dent studied the man in the picture.

His deep frown caused Bellamy to ask, "What?"

"I don't know. Something. Tell me about him."

"There's not much to tell. I don't know him, not even his last name. He came to one of my first book signings and thereafter kept popping up at personal appearances and lectures in New York, always bringing several copies of the book for me to autograph."

"New York? So what was he doing at the Austin airport yesterday?"

"I have no idea."

"You told me that your sense of being watched started when you got to Austin. Ever get that feeling in New York?"

"Sometimes. But I thought it was claustrophobia, being surrounded by a crowd."

"You're always surrounded by a crowd in New York."

"Yes, but—"

"This was different? And it started when you began publicizing your book?"

She nodded. "The first time it happened, I was signing copies at a mystery bookstore. I thought the spooky atmosphere, all the people waiting in line, caused me to get flustered and panicky. I felt...airless."

"Was Jerry there?"

"I think so."

"When was the last time you saw him?"

"The day—" She stopped suddenly.

He cupped his ear with his hand. "The day . . . what?"

"I left the city."

"Same day the rat was delivered. Where'd you see Jerry that day?"

"Outside the network studio. But I'm positive that one has nothing to do with the other."

"Well, I'm not. Positive, that is. Maybe Jerry's stalking you."

"With evil intent? Absolutely not. He's harmless."

Dent raised an eyebrow as though questioning that assertion.

"I swear to you, Dent, he's about as sinister as a glass of milk. Bookish. Mild-mannered. Ordinary looking. He blends into the woodwork."

"I'm scared already. Just the type you gotta watch out for. A creep."

She looked at him with asperity. "You've never seen him. How do you know?"

"How do you know he isn't? How do you know he hasn't got the bodies of authors past buried in his basement?"

"Please."

"Okay, then explain why he followed you to Texas."

"Who said he followed me? I'm sure yesterday was a coincidence."

"He's your number-one fan. He sees you *coincidentally* in an airport like fifteen, twenty states away from where you're both supposed to be, and he doesn't come rushing over to speak to you, make his presence known? He doesn't say, 'Oh my God! I can't believe this! My favorite author out here on the frontier!'"

"Put that way..."

"Right." He took the photograph from her and carried it over to the window, where the light was better. He studied it for several long moments, then his chin went up suddenly and he looked over at her.

"Yesterday. In the park. Two lovers lying on a blanket, getting it on. A pair of grandparents playing ball with their grandson. A group of cheerleaders practicing. And a late arrival. An ordinary-looking guy. Kept his back to us while he appeared to be talking into his cell phone." He tapped the photograph. "It was your Jerry."

Rupe had been in the dental chair until midnight last night. He'd called his dentist even before driving himself to the hospital following his violent encounter with Dale Moody.

Fortunately he and the dentist played golf together, so Rupe had his cell-phone number. "No, it can't wait till regular business hours tomorrow," he'd said when the dentist balked. "It's an emergency. I'll be there by eight."

At the hospital, the ER doctor recognized him despite the damage done to his face. "Say, aren't you the King of Cars? What happened? You sell somebody a lemon?"

"I ran into a door." He'd had to speak carefully to prevent his loosened caps from falling off. He'd already lost one, creating a significant gap in his top row of pearly whites.

"Yeah, that happened to me once," the doctor said, adding archly, "When I owed a guy money."

Ha-ha. I get it. The doctor turned out to be an intern, and once he'd stopped with the wisecracks, which Rupe had borne with false good humor, he confirmed that Rupe's nose had indeed been "busted all to hell and back."

With Rupe gnashing his teeth despite the loose caps, the doctor had repositioned his nose the best he could, taped it, and then told Rupe that plastic surgery would probably be required to make it cosmetically pleasing again.

"But nothing can be done until the swelling goes down."

"How long with that take?"

"Several weeks. Six, eight maybe." The prospect of a long, slow healing process seemed to delight him. He ripped a prescription for painkillers off a pad, and as he handed it to Rupe, he said, tongue in cheek, "Don't be a stranger."

Cute. That was the tag line with which Rupe signed off all his television commercials.

He had stopped at his house long enough to wash down two of the pain pills with neat scotch and to change his clothes, which still bore the heel marks of Moody's boots. Fortunately, his wife and kids were spending two weeks in Galveston with his in-laws, so he hadn't had to make explanations. By the time they returned, he wouldn't look quite so bad, and he would have thought of something plausible to explain his altered appearance.

At eight o'clock, the dentist had met him at the back door of his office, and then Rupe had spent four grueling hours with a blinding light in his eyes and sharp instruments in his mouth.

When he awoke this morning, his nose was throbbing, his eyes were swollen practically shut, and, although his caps had been re-cemented to last for a thousand years, his gums were too tender even to sip coffee.

Looking at himself in his bathroom vanity mirror, he muttered, "Fucking Moody," and pledged to find the former cop and kill him.

Toward that end, he called Haymaker.

"Hey, Rupe," he answered cheerfully, "how's it hanging?"

"You son of a bitch, you turned him on to me, didn't you?"

"Who? Turned who on to you? What are you talking about?" Haymaker's voice was so ridiculously innocent it was taunting.

"I'm going to ruin you."

"If you could've, you would've. Know what I think, Rupe? I think you've lost your touch. That edge you once had just ain't what it used to be."

"I'm giving you one last chance, Haymaker."

"To do what? My car note is current. I even paid a month ahead. So don't send one of your goons after that sorry tin can you sold my wife, or I'll have to report it stolen."

"Tell me where Moody is."

"Oh," he said, dragging out the word. "So that's what this is about. Moody. You haven't found him yet?"

Rupe could swear Haymaker smothered a laugh. "If you don't tell me—"

"I swear, Rupe. Dale hasn't shared his current address with me. Waterboarding wouldn't get it for you."

"Find out where he is. You have until this time tomorrow. If you don't come through, you're going to have me as an enemy for the rest of your life. And, Haymaker, you don't want that."

"Uh, Rupe. I don't think you ought to be worrying about Moody."

"I'm not worried. I can shut him up forever. I can shut

you up forever. And I don't even have to get my hands dirty. I don't even have to leave my office. I can—"

"What I mean is," Haymaker said, interrupting. "I don't think having Dale and me killed is gonna solve your problem. Because, see, I'm looking out my front window as we speak, and guess who's coming to call?"

Chapter 16

———◆———

While Bellamy was showering and dressing, Dent swapped out their cars, then made toast and scrambled eggs, which she ate hungrily when she rejoined him in the kitchen. More casually dressed than he'd ever seen her, she had on a pair of snug jeans and a white shirt. She looked good and smelled great.

Once they were on I-35, driving back to Austin in her car, she asked him where they were going. "Haymaker. He partnered with Moody during the investigation."

"I vaguely remember him."

"I saw them more than you did and got the impression they were pals off the job. Maybe he can tell us where Moody is." Then he reintroduced the subject of Jerry. "What do you make of your number-one fan being in the Georgetown park yesterday and then apparently following us to the airport?"

"I admit that it smacks of stalking. If I ever come face-to-face with him again, I'll tell him that his behavior is making me uncomfortable."

"Oh, that should put the fear of God into him."

She shot him a dirty look and the conversation died there.

Donald Haymaker lived in one of Austin's older neighborhoods, which hadn't yet had an influx of younger people looking for homes to redo and modernize. As they approached the small porch of his house, Bellamy asked, "How do you think we'll be received?"

Dent didn't have time to venture a guess. The former police officer opened his door even before they rang the bell. He regarded them as curiously as they assessed him.

He'd developed a pot belly, which looked comical in contrast to his hairless, bandy legs and knobby knees. His eyes were small and squinty, his nose upturned and sharp at the end. Put a silly cap on his head, and he'd look like one of the Rice Krispies elves.

He made a point of appraising the cuts and bruises on Dent's face. "Still finding trouble, I see."

"I guess no introductions are necessary."

Haymaker snorted. "You I would've recognized anywhere. Even with your face messed up." Then he shifted his gaze to Bellamy. "You? I wouldn't have known, except that I've been seeing you on TV."

"May we come in?" she asked politely.

He hesitated for only a moment, then stood aside. Beyond a small foyer was a cluttered living room that boasted a large flat-screen TV. Family pictures were lined up on the mantel. A mutt lay sleeping in the corner of the sofa. Taking up a lot of the floor space was a faux leather recliner with an oil stain matching the size and general shape of Haymaker's head.

He motioned them toward the sofa, where Bellamy

crowded in between Dent and the dog, who wasn't instructed to vacate his spot in order to make room for them. Haymaker took the recliner and adjusted it to a comfortable angle with the footrest up. The bottoms of his white socks were gray.

He grinned puckishly. "What can I do for you folks?"

Dent got straight to the point. "Produce your buddy Dale Moody."

The former cop laughed a little too loudly and loosely for it not to sound forced. "Old Dale," he said, shaking his head and smiling fondly. "Wonder what became of him?"

"Well, for one thing he got drummed out of the Austin PD."

Haymaker lunged upright in his lounger and stabbed the air with his index finger. "That's a damn lie. Where'd you hear that? Dale left the department by choice. He wasn't fired. He wasn't even suspended."

"So no one ever found out about what he did to me?"

Beside him Bellamy twitched with surprise, but she didn't say anything. He'd asked her to let him loosen up Haymaker. He hadn't told her how he intended to go about it.

Haymaker's tongue darted out to wet his lips. "Okay, yeah, Dale was a tough cop. He wasn't always politically correct. Sometimes he got a little carried away, especially with punks like you who thought they were smarter than him."

"I *was* smarter than him. I called his bluff and didn't confess, and he didn't follow through on his threat. I still have both eyes in perfect working condition."

He turned to Bellamy. "Moody showed up at my house when my dad was at work. He bent me backward over our kitchen table and pressed a Phillips screwdriver to my eyelid. He said if I didn't confess to choking Susan, he was going to puncture my eyeball and destroy forever any chance I had of flying an airplane.

"I was alone. I didn't have a lawyer. For over an hour, Moody tried to get a confession out of me by threatening to blind me." He turned back to Haymaker. "And this son of a bitch held me down while he did it."

Haymaker rolled his narrow shoulders. "No harm was done, was it? You made out okay."

"Allen Strickland didn't."

Bellamy's softly spoken words had a noticeable impact on Haymaker, who began fidgeting even more, making the faux leather beneath him squeak. "You can't lay it at Dale's door that Strickland was killed in prison. The boy was tried in a court of law. He was found guilty by a jury of his peers—"

"On nothing but circumstantial evidence."

"I don't know anything about that," he said quickly. "I was present only a few of the times that Dale questioned him, then I was assigned to another case."

"You didn't help Moody and Rupe Collier cook up the case against Strickland?"

"No." Then, realizing he'd walked into a trap, Haymaker began backpedaling. "What I mean is, they didn't cook up anything. They had a solid enough case to get a conviction. The jury thought so."

"What did Detective Moody think?"

In response to Dent's question, his beady eyes blinked nervously. "What do you mean?"

"Was it sheer coincidence that Moody left the police department shortly after Allen Strickland died in Huntsville?"

Haymaker squirmed some more. "Dale didn't confide in me why he quit. He...he had some problems with the bottle. Lots of cops do, you know," he said defensively.

"Why did he?"

"Trouble at home. He was married to a real harpy. My wife wouldn't win any prizes, but that one of Dale's—"

"We're not here to talk about his marital woes or his drinking habits." Dent sat forward, propping his forearms on his thighs as he moved closer to the former detective and lowered his voice to a confidential pitch. "Bellamy and I think that maybe the reason Dale Moody quit being a cop, and seemingly dropped off the face of the earth, is because he couldn't live with his guilty conscience."

Haymaker was finding it hard to look either of them in the eye. "I wasn't his priest or his shrink."

"You were his friend, though. His one and only." Dent gave Haymaker several moments to wonder how he knew that before enlightening him. "After that screwdriver incident, I wanted my pound of Moody's flesh, so I started following him. You were the only person that he met after hours. You were his only drinking buddy. I trailed the two of you for weeks, night after night, from bar to bar.

"Then Gall, who I never could pull anything over on, demanded to know what I was up to. When I told him, he called me a numbskull and told me that if I wanted to assault a cop and ruin my life, fine, but that he wasn't going to be a party to my ruination. He ordered me off his property and told me not to come back."

He spread his hands. "I loved flying more than I hated Moody. I gave up my revenge plot, and the only thing that came from my amateur surveillance was the knowledge that Detective Moody had only one friend." He tipped his head toward Haymaker. "If anybody knows where he is, it's you."

The man rubbed his palms up and down the legs of his baggy plaid shorts. "What do you want him for?" Looking at Bellamy, he said, "You already did a number on him in your book. You looking to drive the nails in his hands a little deeper?"

"I wanted to interview him for my book but couldn't find him," she said. "I was as accurate as I could be, based on the impressions of a preteen girl. It wasn't my intention to cast aspersions on Detective Moody. Why would I? He captured and helped convict the man who killed my sister."

"So there you have it," Haymaker said, slapping the padded arms of his chair. "The end."

"No, not the end," she said. "Not if you think I 'did a number on him.' Is that how he perceives it, too?"

"I don't know what he perceives."

"You're lying," Dent said.

Bellamy placed a cautionary hand on his knee. In a gentler, less combative voice, she asked, "Does Moody see it that way, too, Mr. Haymaker? If so, wouldn't he welcome the chance to set me straight?"

"Uh-uh. No way. He won't talk to you." Haymaker gave a decisive shake of his head.

"How do you know?"

"Because he won't even talk to me about it, and I'm his best...only...friend. As wiseass here has pointed out." He cast a sour glance at Dent. Dent didn't respond. Bellamy was making headway where he hadn't, so he yielded the floor to her.

She asked Haymaker, "Have you tried to get him to talk about it?"

"For eighteen friggin' years. I don't know what-all went on. But what I do know, Dale wasn't ever the same after that boy got killed in prison. After it happened, he stayed drunk for a month, then just up and announced to me that he was leaving the department, leaving his family, leaving Austin, and that was that."

"But you're still in contact?"

He shifted his weight, scratched his head, and seemed to consider how much he should impart. When he looked at Dent, it was with hostility, but he responded to Bellamy's calm gaze.

Releasing a long sigh, he mumbled, "We talk by phone. Off and on. Not regular. Half the time, he doesn't answer or call me back if I leave a message. I worry about him. He's not a well man. Chest wheezes like a bagpipe."

"That's too bad," Dent deadpanned. "Where does he live?"

"I don't know."

Dent looked around the room. "Got a Phillips screwdriver handy?"

"I'm telling you, I don't know where he lives!" Haymaker exclaimed. "Swear to God I don't. You could put my eye out and I still couldn't tell you." Then he raised his pointed chin defiantly. "Even if I could, even if he lived next door to me here, I wouldn't tell y'all, 'cause Dale would want nothing to do with talking to you. You've wasted your time coming here."

Dent and Bellamy exchanged a look, each conceding that they believed him but were at a loss as to where to go from there.

Then, moving suddenly, Dent reached across the space separating him from the small table at their host's elbow and picked up a cell phone.

Haymaker's recliner sprang upright. "Hey!" He tried to snatch the phone from Dent's hand.

He held it just out of the other man's reach. "Moody's number is in here, right? Call him. Tell him we want to talk to him. Tell him you think it would be a good idea. It would give him a chance to validate the outcome of his investigation."

"He doesn't have to validate shit."

"Then that's what he can make clear to us." Acting on a hunch, Dent added, "At the very least, he can explain how he and Rupe Collier built their case against Allen Strickland."

Haymaker's elfin eyes darted back and forth between them. "You've got nothing on them."

"So there were some machinations?" Bellamy said.

"That's not what I said," he sputtered. "Don't put words in my mouth, missy."

"We're not really interested in what you have to say, Haymaker. We want to talk to Moody." Dent grinned with malice. "If he bent some rules, we'll be giving him a chance to cleanse his soul. When he dies, he'll go to heaven instead of hell. Good for everybody."

"Call him, Mr. Haymaker," Bellamy softly urged.

He silently debated it for several moments, then held up his hands in surrender. "Okay. Fine. I'll think about it."

Dent said, "You've got five seconds."

"Look, come back tomorrow—"

Dent made a honking sound like a quiz-show buzzer. "Can't wait till tomorrow."

"How come?" Haymaker looked at Bellamy. "What's your all-fired hurry?"

"I have my reasons for needing to see him as soon as possible. Call him."

The former cop continued to fidget, continued to stew.

"Time's up." Dent slid his thumb across the bottom of the screen, engaging the phone. "If you call him, you're his concerned friend offering advice. If I call him, you're the buddy who betrayed him. You choose."

When Steven saw the name on his phone's caller ID, he signaled William to take over for him at the hostess stand and quickly made his way into the relative quiet of the office behind Maxey's busy kitchen. His phone had stopped vibrating by the time he closed himself in, so he redialed. Olivia answered on the first ring.

"Sorry I couldn't answer in time, Mother. Is it Howard?"

"He's holding on by a thread."

Steven could tell by the hoarseness in her voice that she'd been crying.

"So am I," she added shakily. "A very slender thread. He'll have minutes of perfect clarity, and then periods when he lapses into a semiconscious state that terrifies me. I'm afraid he'll never come out of it. He looks so old and feeble I can barely believe it's my Howard."

"Jesus. I know how hard this must be for you." If William were dying, he would feel like his world was collapsing and he was powerless to stop it. "I'm sorry you're there dealing with this alone."

"Bellamy was here last night." When he didn't say anything, she softly added, "I know she came to see you,

Steven. She told me. I was surprised she went all that way, given Howard's condition. He was desperate to talk to her last night."

"I'm sure he fears that each time he sees her will be the last."

"Exactly. Which makes me wonder why he sent her away."

"He did?"

"She was here barely an hour. She saw Howard alone for ten, maybe fifteen minutes, then she and Dent left."

"Dent was still with her?"

"He flew her down."

"They seem to be fairly chummy."

"Much to our dismay. I can't imagine what she's thinking."

"She probably thinking he's a superstud. Just like Susan did."

Olivia said nothing in response to that, probably because she was offended by the very idea and couldn't bear to consider the implications.

"They flew back to Austin late last night," she continued. "I don't know what her hurry was, why she didn't stay over until this morning at least."

"Did you ask her?"

"She told me that Howard had sent her back to do something for him, but when I pressed her on it, she was evasive. When I asked Howard about it, he brushed it off as being unimportant."

"Well, then—"

"But I think they're keeping something from me, and I'm afraid." She began to cry.

"Mother, don't do this to yourself. You're reading

something into nothing. You're exhausted and over-wrought, and in your present circumstances, who wouldn't be?"

"Everyone's dancing around the issue."

"What issue?"

"I don't know!" she exclaimed raggedly. "That's just it. I feel like I'm the only one not in on the joke. I hated that you and Bellamy had drifted apart. I'm thrilled that you got together. But what was so urgent that she left her dying father and went to see you *now*? What did you talk about?"

"We caught up on each other's lives. She met William. I told her about the restaurants, congratulated her on her book's success. It was like that."

"Why are you lying to me, Steven? Bellamy herself told me that she went to see you to talk—as adults—about that Memorial Day."

He lowered his head and closed his eyes, pinching the bridge of his nose until it hurt. "All right, yes. Bellamy wanted to hear my perspective of events because apparently there are things she doesn't know."

"I don't understand her preoccupation. Truly I don't. It's ancient history."

"Not to her it isn't. It's very much in the present."

"Do you think that's healthy? For any of us?"

"No."

"So what did you tell her? Did you tell her—"

"That I had pimped for Susan that day?"

"That's a horrible thing to say! About your stepsister and yourself."

"How would you put it?"

"Not nearly as crudely."

"Well, I didn't tell Bellamy about it in any terms."

"There's no reason why you should have. Boys and girls have been using go-betweens since there were boys and girls. Susan wanted to dance with Allen Strickland, and she asked you to deliver the message to him. It had tragic consequences, but, at the time, it was an innocent action, something that any typical teenage girl would have done."

Except that Susan wasn't typical and was by no means innocent.

He'd never shared with his mother or Howard the horrible secret of what was happening in his bedroom most nights, but he had admitted to them what had happened at the barbecue.

"If it was all that harmless, Mother, why did you and Howard want me to keep it from the police?"

"All we said was that if Allen Strickland didn't make a point of it when they questioned him, you shouldn't volunteer it. It wasn't germane."

"Detective Moody might have disagreed."

Surely he would have wanted to know how manipulative Susan was and that it was she who had initiated the encounter with Strickland.

"Over there, in the blue shirt, standing next to the oaf with the long mustache. I think they're brothers. Be sure you tell the right one. God forbid that drooling cretin comes over here instead."

"I'm not going to tell them anything."

"Steven…"

"If you're so hot to dance with him, go ask him yourself and leave me the fuck alone."

"Steven sa-id fu-uck. Steven sa-id fu-uck."

Her taunting singsong had made him feverish with anger. But she knew that, and she used it.

"Of course you only say the word, you don't do the deed. Because you're scared." Leaning close and putting *her lips directly to his ear, she whispered, "But I know you want to. I know you want to with me. I know you want to right now."*

When he tried to move away, she blocked his path. "You go tell that guy I want to dance with him, or I'll tell Olivia and Daddy that you got jealous of Dent and came into my room while I was naked and tried to rape me."

"Rape you? That's a laugh."

"Who do you think they'll believe?" She gave him a *look that said she was capable of finessing it any way she wanted, and he knew she could.*

Burning with hatred of her, he had approached Allen Strickland on her behalf.

As though reading his mind, his mother said gently, "That boy had been ogling her all day, Steven. He and that brother of his. Sooner or later Allen would have worked up his courage and asked her to dance without any help from you."

"Possibly. But the fact remains that he did have my help."

"Please don't dwell on it and upset yourself. Although I know it's difficult to put that day out of your mind when you can't get away from Bellamy's book. It's everywhere. Even here in the hospital's gift shop."

"The horse has left the barn, Mother."

"Yes, but I thought that when she stopped the publicity, things would die down. Instead we're on the front page of that wretched tabloid again. Dent Carter has insinuated himself back into our lives, Bellamy is like a woman obsessed, and I can't help but feel that this mysterious mission she's on for Howard has something to do with it."

Steven jumped in before she could work herself into another crying jag. "Mother, the only times in your marriage that Howard has done something behind your back was when he was shopping for a fabulous gift or planning an extravagant trip. If he sent Bellamy on a secret mission, it's to do something that will spare you further heartache."

"My heart already aches, Steven."

"Cancer is cruel."

"So is the irony."

"Irony?"

"Howard and I have had a near-perfect life together. It was marred by a single tragic event. Yet now, when our time together is about to end and we should be reliving blissful times, it's Susan's murder that's at the forefront of everyone's mind." Her voice cracked. "And why?"

Quietly Steven said, *"Low Pressure."*

Chapter 17

The state senator's plane was already on the tarmac when Dent and Bellamy arrived at the airfield.

Gall took one look at Dent's battered face and scowled. "Who the hell did that?"

"It doesn't hurt."

"Not what I asked."

"I'm going to call Olivia. Excuse me." Bellamy went into the hangar and took out her cell phone.

Dent motioned toward the airplane. "Decent of him to make it available to us. Last night and today."

"I told you, he wants you to get used to it. He called early this morning, wanting to know how you liked her. Says he hopes you'll become so enamored with flying it you'll go to work for him." He clamped down on his cigar. "'Course if he could see you now, he might change his mind."

"Not now, Gall."

Dent bypassed him as he made his way into the hangar and went over to his own airplane. "How're the repairs coming?"

"Replacement parts are ordered. Some were promised by the end of the week. Others will take longer to get."

Dent gave the wing of his airplane a pat, then went over to the computer table and sat down. "Have you checked out the airport in Marshall?"

"Its got two runways. One's five thousand feet. Plenty long enough."

As he and Bellamy left Haymaker's house, Dent had placed a call to Gall, asking him if the senator's airplane was still available and, if so, to get it ready for flight. He'd also asked him to look into the county-owned airport in east Texas, three hundred miles from Austin.

While he methodically went through his preflight routine, Bellamy was pacing the concrete floor of the hangar, her cell phone to her ear. He wondered who she was talking to. Her conversations with Olivia never lasted that long.

After filing his flight plan, he signaled to Bellamy that they were good to go. She ended her call and went into the hangar's restroom, although the head on the two-million-dollar airplane was much nicer. She'd probably be too modest to use it during flight, though.

Dent, hoping to smooth things over with Gall after being so brusque with him earlier, approached the workbench where the older man was tinkering with a piece of machinery. "Thanks for helping out on such short notice."

Gall just looked at him, waiting for an explanation for the sudden trip, which Dent felt he deserved.

"From Marshall, we're driving on to Caddo Lake. It's near—"

"I know where it's at." Gall gave his cigar an agitated workout. "Going fishing?"

"In a manner of speaking. Detective Moody, now retired, lives on the lake. He's agreed to see us. And I don't want any flack from you about it."

Gall stopped chomping his cigar, removed it from his mouth, and pitched it toward a trash can, which he missed by a foot. "Flack," he said with disgust. "How 'bout me giving you some common sense? Something you seem to have a shortage of these days. In fact, you haven't acted like you have a lick of it since you got attached to that lady, who belongs to a family that damn near ruined your life. You show up this morning looking like Rocky. You're on your way to see a man who you once vowed to kill. You're packing. And I'm not supposed to give you flack?"

"How'd you know I was carrying a piece?"

"I didn't. Till now. *Jesus!* You're taking a pistol to a meeting with Moody?"

"Will you calm down? I'm not going to shoot him. We're just going to talk to the man. He's no threat to me anymore. He's old, in bad health, reportedly on his last leg."

"How do you know all this?"

"I have my sources."

"He's got his sources," he muttered. He hitched his chin toward the wounds on Dent's face. "Who beat you up?"

"The redneck I warned you about." He gave Gall an abbreviated account of the attack.

"Did he cut you bad?"

"It's okay."

"You see a doctor?"

"Bellamy took care of it."

"Oh, and she's qualified to do that, I guess."

"It wasn't that bad, Gall. I swear."

"You report it to the police?"

Dent shook his head. "We were afraid it would make the news. Bad enough that Van Durbin staked out my apartment last night, and he didn't even know about the knife fight."

"Van Durbin see her there with you?"

"He got pictures."

If Gall's scowl was any indication, nothing Dent told him had won his approval. "Back to the redneck—he have a name?"

"I think it might be Ray Strickland, Allen's brother. But that's only a guess."

"Why would he come after you?"

"Retribution, maybe." Dent raised one shoulder in a shrug. "That's the best Bellamy and I could come up with."

"Bellamy and you." He snorted an expletive that Dent hadn't heard since leaving the military. "Dent, why are you doing this?"

"I told you why."

"Exoneration. Once and for all. Okay, I get it. But what? The shit your life is in isn't deep enough? You need this to top it off?" He gave Dent no time to defend his actions. "You could get yourself killed. What good will vindication do you if you're dead? As for her, do you think she'd want to partner with you if she knew—"

"She knows."

Gall, shocked silent by Bellamy's declaration, turned quickly to find her standing behind him.

"I know he was in the state park, quarreling with Susan shortly before she was killed. I saw them. My memory of it came back last night during a heated argument."

Gall swallowed noisily and for once seemed at a loss for words. "Well..."

She smiled and even reached out and laid her hand on the sleeve of his coveralls. "I know you lied in order to protect Dent. Your secret is safe."

"You're not going to tell Moody?"

"I'm more interested in hearing what he has to tell us."

"Speaking of which," Dent said, "if we don't get there soon, he may change his mind and refuse to see us."

They went outside, but before they boarded, Dent drew Gall aside. "This redneck guy, whoever he is, means business, Gall. Watch your back."

"Don't worry about me, Ace."

"I'm not. I'm worried about me."

"How so?"

"I plan to hurt him for what he's done to Bellamy and me. But if he hurts you, I'll have to kill him."

"Who were you talking to for so long?"

Bellamy had accepted Dent's invitation to sit in the cockpit, and, despite her complaint about the discomfort of the headphones, she'd put them on and plugged in so they could communicate.

Staring at the horizon, she released a weary sigh. "Dexter. My agent. He had left twenty or more voice-mail messages, the last one threatening to jump off the Brooklyn Bridge if I didn't return his call. So I did."

"And?"

"He'd seen Van Durbin's column yesterday. It's created renewed hype. He thinks I should reenter the arena and ramp up the publicity. I said no. The book has already climbed two spots on the best-seller list without my having to do anything. Dexter says that with just a little media coverage, it could go higher, stay longer. The movie deal would get sweeter. Et cetera. I said no. Again. Emphatically."

"Will they be dragging the East River for his body?"

She laughed. "When I left New York, he threatened to jump from the Empire State Building. He hasn't yet."

He exchanged several transmissions with air-traffic controllers when they were passed from one's airspace to another. The cockpit controls were as alien to her as the surface of Neptune.

When he was free again to talk to her, she asked, "How did you ever learn what everything is for?"

"I learned it because I have a very healthy respect for gravity. The ground is always there, trying to pull you down. It's the most important thing to keep in mind."

"Why are crashes usually attributed to pilot error?"

"Because they make the last mistake, and it's hard for them to defend themselves or explain their actions if they're dead."

"That's terribly unfair, isn't it?"

"Can be, yeah. Pilots aren't infallible. They screw up. But typically a crash is caused by a series of mistakes or mishaps. They stack up, and that's what the cockpit crew is left to deal with. Have you ever heard of the Swiss cheese model?"

"I think so, but refresh me."

"In order for a catastrophic event, such as a plane crash, to occur, a sequence of events precedes it. Think of these separate factors as slices of Swiss cheese lined up one behind the other. If any one of the holes in them doesn't align with the others, the series of events is changed or curtailed, and a catastrophe is prevented."

"But if all the holes line up—"

"The door is open for disaster."

"The pilot's mistake is the hole in the last slice of cheese."

He nodded. "Say an airplane mechanic has a fight with his nagging wife, goes out and gets drunk, and is hungover at work the following day. During a preflight check, the first officer—co-pilot—spills his coffee over an electronic panel, which could result in its shorting out.

"He reports it, this mechanic is called to come and replace it. He doesn't feel good to start with, now he's working under pressure, knowing that the clock is ticking, and that everyone on board is disgruntled over the holdup. To make matters worse, the weather is deteriorating, and they want to get this bird out of there before the worst of it moves in, stranding passengers and crew for hours longer.

"The panel is replaced. The mechanic signs off on it. The captain and co-pilot are aware of the storms, but, between them, they've threaded a needle like that many times. They taxi, the tower clears them for takeoff, they check the radar one last time, and off they go.

"At about a thousand feet, they encounter some heavy turbulence. In an effort to get them out of it, the ATC instructs them to turn left. The captain responds. But as the plane goes into the turn, it gets struck by lightning, which in reality doesn't cause an accident, but it can make things hairy.

"So now, the plane is in a steep left bank, flying in turbulence, trying to climb out of heavy rain and hail, at night, because the flight was delayed on account of the panel replacement. When…" He paused for dramatic effect and glanced over at her.

"When the fire warning for the left engine sounds and lights up red. The captain reacts immediately and does exactly what he's been trained and conditioned to do for years on a 727. He pulls the fire warning lever, instantly shutting down that engine.

"What he *doesn't know* is that he's responded to a false warning. It sounded because it had grounded out after the coffee was spilled on it, which went unnoticed by both pilots and the mechanic. The turbulence, or the lightning strike, something, caused it to go off at that critical moment. The captain's quick action to correct an emergency, which didn't exist, actually created one.

"Remember, the plane was already in a left turn. Well, you *never* turn into a dead engine because the opposite one accelerates the plane into an even steeper turn. Wings quickly go vertical. Nose goes down. The airplane is doomed. Everyone onboard dies.

"But who do you blame for the crash? The captain made the last mistake. But you could also blame the clumsy first officer who spilled his coffee, or the mechanic who failed to notice that the fire warning had been damaged along with the panel he'd replaced. You could blame his wife for being a nag and driving him to drink the night before, making him feel like dog shit and not nearly as sharp as he normally would have been. You could take the blame all the way up to God for the crappy weather and that particular bolt of lightning.

"The sequence of events proved disastrous, but if only one of the contributing factors had been taken out of the equation, it might never have happened." He paused and gave a shrug. "That's a simplistic, layman's explanation, but you get the gist of it."

Bellamy hesitated, then asked, "What happened on Flight 343?"

He turned his head and looked at her for several beats. "I just told you."

The gravel road wound through the thick grove of cypress trees and dead-ended in front of Dale's cabin. He heard their car approaching long before it appeared.

He couldn't explain, even to himself, why he had listened to Haymaker's earnest pitch that he agree to see them. He should have hung up on him, should never have answered his call in the first place. But he found himself listening, and there was some logic to what his friend had said.

When Haymaker finished his spiel, which ended with his telling Dale that an interview might do his mind and body good, Dale surprised himself by asking Haymaker to hand the phone over to Bellamy.

They wasted no time on an exchange of phony pleasantries. She asked him the name of the nearest regional airport, and when he told her, she asked if he'd be there to meet her.

"No. Rent a car. Got a pencil?" After giving her directions from the airport to his place, he said, "Come alone."

"Dent Carter will be with me."

"I'll only talk to you."

"Dent will be with me."

She was unbending, and he could have used that condition to scotch the whole thing. But he figured that if Dent meant to kill him, as he'd once threatened to, he wouldn't do it with her as a witness.

As of this moment, they were the only two people on the

planet who knew his whereabouts, and that in itself filled him with misgiving. But it was too late now to change his mind. With a crunch of gravel, the car rolled to a stop.

Moody watched from his sagging porch as they alighted, she with more alacrity and eagerness than Dent, who'd been driving. Dale figured that behind his Ray-Bans the boy's—the man's—eyes were cutting like razors. Hostility radiated off him like mist off a bog.

Bellamy was less guarded. She came up the steps as though not noticing how dilapidated they were and extended her hand to him without a qualm. He shook hands.

"Thank you for agreeing to see us."

He bobbed his chin once but kept an alert watch on Dent, who took the steps up onto the porch in a measured tread. They eyed each other like the adversaries they were.

Bellamy brushed a mosquito off her arm. "Maybe we should go inside," she said. Dale turned and opened the screened door, whose squeak seemed abnormally loud. In fact all Dale's senses had grown more acute since their arrival. He realized how lazy he'd become now that he no longer had to depend on his wits and constant awareness of his surroundings, which, while a cop, had been second nature to him.

Dale gauged the gashes and bruises on Dent's face to be no older than a day, if that. It spoke to Dent's character that he was unselfconscious of them. He'd been a tough bastard at eighteen. Maturity hadn't softened him one iota. Which made Dale all the more cautious. Being that he was soft and inflated where Dent was hard and honed, he would lose in a fight. In a clean fight, anyway.

Bellamy was prettier in person than on television. Her eyes had more depth, her skin a softness that studio cameras couldn't capture. She also smelled good, like flowers. Dale felt a pang of yearning to touch a woman, which he hadn't had the pleasure of doing for several months now. It had been years since he'd had the pleasure without having to pay for it.

Loneliness, even if self-imposed, tasted metallic. Like the blue steel barrel of a pistol.

Once inside, Dent peeled off his aviator sunglasses and slid them into his shirt pocket. Dale said, "You can relieve yourself of the handgun, too. Just set it there on the table."

Dent didn't ask how he knew he was carrying. Dale supposed he realized the pointlessness of the question. A former cop would know. Dent reached behind his back and pulled the pistol from the holster attached to his belt.

"After you, Moody." He motioned down at Dale's left hand in which he'd kept the .357 palmed and held against his thigh.

When he hesitated, Bellamy said, "Please."

He looked down into her large, expressive eyes, which were perhaps the only feature reminiscent of the girl she'd been, then he met Dent's level stare. Neither relented, exactly, but they moved simultaneously and set their weapons on the TV tray already crowded with Dale's bottle of whiskey, his pack of cigarettes, lighter, and ashtray.

Since he didn't have an extra chair, he said, "You can sit on the bed, I guess."

He could have saved himself the trouble of making it up in advance of their arrival. The bedspread was something he'd found in a garage sale. It didn't quite cover the stained top sheet. Beneath its ragged hem, the exposed springs screeched when his guests sat down on the foot of the bed.

Dale held up the bottle of Jack by its neck. "Drink?" They shook their heads. "Mind if I do?" But he didn't wait for their go-ahead before pouring himself three fingers' worth. He took a swig, then set the glass down so he could light a cigarette, and after taking a long pull on it, he sat down in his armchair—another castoff—and gave them his undivided attention.

Bellamy glanced at Dent, and when he said nothing, she nodded toward the copy of her book that Dale had left on the top of his television set. "Did you read it?"

"Yeah."

"What did you think of it?"

"You want a review? You're a good writer."

"Did I accurately capture the events as you remember them?"

"More or less."

Dent shifted his position, making the bed rock. "That's no answer. We didn't come all this way for you to be cute."

Dale took a shot of whiskey. "What did you come here for?"

Bellamy leaned toward him. "I want you to tell me that you believe with all your heart that Allen Strickland was guilty."

He held her pleading gaze for as long as he could stand it, then looked down and studied the burning tip of his cigarette.

"Maybe he still thinks I killed her."

Dale, knowing Dent had said that just to goad him, fired back. "I thought, and still think, that you were capable of it."

"You could always apply a screwdriver to my eye again, see if I confess this time."

The girl admonished him just by softly speaking his name.

But being reminded of the strong-arm, illegal tactics he'd used to interrogate Dent caused Dale's gut to clench. "I didn't believe for a single minute the alibi you and your sidekick came up with."

"We went flying that day."

"I'm sure you did. What I couldn't prove was what time you came back."

"It was in Gall's log."

"Log, my ass. He could've written any damn time in his log. Do you think I'm stupid?"

"No, I think you're clever. Clever enough to tell Rupe Collier that he couldn't build a solid case against me. That's when you two decided that Allen Strickland might be the surer bet on getting a conviction."

Dale shot to his feet so quickly he nearly upset the TV tray. He saved the bottle of whiskey first, grabbing it before it could topple over. Then he crushed out his cigarette in the overflowing ashtray. He could feel their eyes like red-hot pokers on his back as he moved to the screened door and stared sightlessly at what had been his unchanging view for far too long.

And suddenly he realized how very tired he was, and not only of the view. He was so damn weary, body and soul. Sick to death, literally, of it all. Just—as kids these days said—*over it*. He was almost a score of years too late to try to make things right. But he had one last shot at redemption and decided then and there to take it.

"I was eating lunch at one of those good Mex'can

places on the east side of town. Haymaker called to tell me that Allen Strickland had been killed in the prison yard that morning. Stabbed in the back three times before he hit the ground. Each stab had punctured an organ. He was dead in under a minute. Seems he'd gotten in with a bad group—"

He paused and looked over his shoulder at them. "You gotta admit he was a slick, hustling type. In the pen, he affiliated with a gang of like minds." He faced forward again. "The murder was blamed on gang warfare within the prison, although no one was ever brought up on charges.

"Anyway, I left my plate of food on the table, went outside, and threw up. Hard. Till I was completely empty, and then I kept on retching. Because the last I saw of Allen Strickland, he was being escorted from the courtroom after his sentencing. He turned to where I was seated in the gallery, looked me straight in the eye, and said, 'I didn't kill her. God is my witness.'

"Now, I've heard hundreds of guilty men and women swear on God and all the angels that they're innocent. But I believed Allen Strickland. So, no, Ms. Price, I don't believe with all my heart that he was guilty of killing your sister. I never did."

He remained as he was for as long as it took him to take a deep breath and release it slowly. Surprisingly, he didn't feel as washed clean, as sanctified, as he thought he might after making that admission, and realized that he'd been naive to think it would be that easy.

He turned back into the room and, resuming his seat, picked up the glass and drained it of the liquor. The two people sitting shoulder to shoulder on the bed were watchful.

She was the first to speak. "If you didn't believe in his guilt, how ... why ..."

"How and why did I get the grand jury to indict, and a jury to convict? I could reel off a dozen good reasons, but the main one? We had to get the egg off our faces."

"We?" Dent said.

"Rupe and me."

"So he's tarnished, too?"

Dale chuckled over Bellamy's quaint term for *corrupt*. "You could say. Anyhow, we'd gone public with one prime suspect." He looked at Dent. "But you had an alibi. We didn't believe it, but we couldn't crack it. That's when Allen Strickland started looking like a winning prospect.

"We were desperate to make good our promise to the Lystons, the PD, everybody, that we'd produce the culprit and bring him to justice. We couldn't let this big, juicy case get away from us.

"Here we had us a prominent family's daughter slain at the company barbecue, during the worst storm in half a century. The girl was pretty, she was rich, she'd been found stripped of her panties. And you gotta hand it to Rupe, he's a showman. He baited the sex hook every time he gave the media a sound bite.

"You know," he continued thoughtfully, "I think he was actually glad we never found her underwear, because that kept the public dwelling on it. Had her panties been the murder weapon? Where were they now? Would they be found? It was like a damn soap opera. Tune in tomorrow for the next episode."

He dragged his hands down his face. "At one point, Rupe even suggested we plant a pair of underwear to be 'found' by a rookie cop, someone unassuming, so it would look convincing. We'd have to show them to your parents for identification. They would deny they were Susan's, of course, but it still wouldn't look good for the guy who'd been found with them. It would make him look like a collector."

"You were actually going to plant false evidence on Allen Strickland's property?" Bellamy asked.

Dale's gaze slid involuntarily toward Dent. "This was early in the investigation."

Dent stared at him for several beats, and when the implication sank in, he shook his head with disbelief. "Christ."

He stood up and began to prowl the room as though looking for something or someone to hit. Dale thought he might be the target, but Dent moved to a window, where he propped his shoulder on the frame and stared out over the desultory waters of the lake. Dale noted that there was a spot of dried blood on his shirt about waist level.

Before he could ask about it, Bellamy said, "I didn't like him."

"Who?"

"Rupe Collier. I didn't like him when he talked to my parents during the trial, assuring them that he was going to send Susan's killer to jail for a long time. Then, when I was researching my book, I called him and asked for an interview. I made several appointments with him, all of which he canceled at the last minute. I suppose he ran out of excuses because I was finally allowed ten minutes of his time. He was—"

"You don't have to tell me how he was," Dale said. "I know all too well." He flexed the fingers of his right hand. The knuckles were bruised and sore from their contact with Rupe's teeth, but he enjoyed the discomfort and only wished he'd struck the grinning son of a bitch even harder. "He told you squat, right?"

"He was wishy-washy and vague," she said. "Finally he told me that he'd forgotten the details of the case, and that instead of talking to him, I might try coaxing the police department into showing me the case file."

Dale tipped his chin, his question implicit.

"I tried," she said. "Unfortunately, the file had gone missing."

"That's right."

"You knew?"

"Rupe's too ambitious and too good at covering his ass to have let that file survive," he said. Then he pulled himself up out of his chair. "And I'm too good at covering my own ass not to have made a copy of everything."

Chapter 18

———◆>◆<◆———

Startled, Bellamy and Dent glanced at each other, then watched as Moody went into the kitchen area of his cabin, which was demarcated by a short bar with a chipped Formica top. He opened the oven beneath the greasy range and took from it an accordion file folder that was expanded beyond capacity. The original elastic cord had been replaced by a thick rubber band.

"I've been afraid I'd get really drunk one night, forget it was in there, and turn on the oven." He carried the folder over to Bellamy and handed it to her, then returned to his chair, lit a fresh cigarette, and poured himself another drink.

Dent rejoined her on the bed as she removed the rubber band and folded back the flap. The file contained a daunting amount of material. Thumbing through the well-worn edges of paper, she saw copies of various things: official forms and documents, lined notebook sheets filled with handwriting, transcriptions of recorded interviews, and countless scraps of paper with only one or two words scribbled on them. It would take weeks to sort through.

"I took lots of notes," Moody said, "and confiscated the notes of other detectives. Took me several days to get everything copied on the sly while Rupe was breathing down my neck to turn the file over to him. There's stuff in there from Haymaker, notes he took until he asked to be taken off the case and reassigned."

Dent raised his head and looked over at him.

"The screwdriver thing made him squeamish," Moody said.

"How did you feel about his abdication?"

"It might have pissed me off, but I didn't have time to think about it." He indicated the file. "I was kinda busy."

"Busy trying to crack me," Dent said.

Moody shrugged his massive shoulders. "It's usually the boyfriend. Or someone equally close to the victim."

"My father and stepbrother?" she asked.

"Anybody who fell into the category of close male associate."

"But my *father*?"

"Look, I'm not going to apologize to you for doing my job."

Because she didn't want to antagonize him into silence, she backed off that. "I don't understand why Allen Strickland didn't come under suspicion immediately. Even according to your own notes...At least I assume this is your handwriting." She held up the top sheet.

He nodded.

It was a copy of what appeared to be a page torn from a spiral notebook, covered with boldly scrawled annotations. Most had been written in a cryptic shorthand that only Moody would be able to decipher, but some of it was legible. A red pen had been used to underscore one of the notations: a name with a star beside it.

She scanned the page. "You wrote down the names of witnesses who mentioned Allen Strickland when you interviewed them?"

Moody nodded.

"At least some of them must've remembered seeing the way he and Susan were dancing together," she said. "Why wasn't he the prime suspect from the beginning?"

Obviously the question made Moody uneasy. Beneath his heavy, crinkled eyelids, his eyes shifted to several points in the room, including Dent, before returning to Bellamy. "He might've been, except that your folks were the first people I talked to. They gave me Dent's name and told me about the argument he'd had with Susan that morning."

"So I shot straight to the top of your list."

"Yeah. I didn't go back to Allen Strickland till you'd been eliminated."

"Allen was another likely choice. But even then you didn't think he'd committed the crime, did you?" Bellamy said. "Why not?"

He took a sip of his drink.

"Why not?" she repeated.

"First time I questioned him, he told me that Susan had turned him down flat and had made fun of him for trying."

"And you believed that?" she asked.

"Usually a guy, especially a ladies' man like him, doesn't admit to being turned down, so I figured he was telling the truth. At least partially. Then there was his brother."

She and Dent exchanged a look.

"What?" Moody asked.

"We'd like to hear this first," she said. "Go on, please."

He took a draw on his cigarette and blew the smoke toward the ceiling. "I questioned them separately. Allen's brother—Ray was his name—told me that he knew what Allen had in mind when he left the pavilion with Susan. Wink, wink. Ray stayed behind, drank some more beer, flirted and tried to get lucky himself. But when the weather turned bad, he got worried. He was reluctant to interrupt anything that Allen had going, but..."

"Being his brother's keeper," Dent said.

Moody raised his glass as though saluting him. "Ray told us detectives that he went into the woods, but met Allen on the hiking path, making his way back." He gestured to the file. "Notes on several interviews with him are in there. But in one, he told me that Allen was 'fuckin' furious.'"

"He admitted that?"

"He did. But he also said he didn't blame his brother for being angry, because he could hear your sister's laughter. She even called out, 'Don't go away mad, Allen.' And then she told him to go home and jack off while thinking about her. Words to that effect."

Bellamy felt Dent's eyes on her, watching to see how she would respond. She tried to keep her expression schooled.

"Anyhow, both the brothers, during individual interviews, told me the same thing. That Allen had left Susan in the woods, laughing at him."

"Why didn't this testimony come out during the trial?" she asked. "Since the case was built on circumstantial evidence, it would have provided strong reasonable doubt."

"It would have, yes. Allen's court-appointed attorney was relying heavily on Ray's testimony," Dale said. "That's why he was fit to be tied when Ray didn't show up the morning he was scheduled to be on the stand. The lawyer couldn't account for his witness's whereabouts or provide a reason for his failure to appear.

"He threw himself on the mercy of the court and asked for a postponement in the proceedings, just until after lunch, so he could track down his witness. Rupe hit the ceiling. He put on a dog-and-pony show about the defense attorney's attempt to annoy the jury into an acquittal." Moody made a sound of derision. "It was one of his best performances."

"I must not have been in court that day," Bellamy said. "I don't remember that scene."

Dent said, "Let me guess. The judge denied the request."

Moody nodded. "And Ray never got to testify."

"Why wasn't he in court that day?"

"Because he was in the hospital. He'd been seriously injured in a car wreck on his way to the courthouse. It was several days before he was stable enough to be deposed, and his deposition was read aloud in court, but it didn't have quite the same punch as a live testimony would have had. By the time Ray was well enough to leave the hospital, it was too late. Allen had been convicted and transferred to Huntsville."

"Jesus," Dent whispered. "No wonder he's gone mental."

Moody sat forward. "What?"

"Ray Strickland hasn't forgiven or forgotten."

Moody was quick to catch his drift. He motioned toward Dent's face. "He did that?"

"Show him your back," Bellamy said.

Dent stood and raised his shirt. They told Moody about the events of the past few days that had led up to last night's attack. "He doesn't have the mustache anymore," Dent said. "He looks like your basic skinhead."

"Then how do you know it's Ray?"

"We don't. But whoever he is, he's got a death wish for Bellamy and me, and the only thing she and I have in common is that Memorial Day."

"And her book," Moody said, not kindly.

"If it is Ray, maybe his grievance began when he was unable to testify at Allen's trial," she said. "He let his brother down. To this day, he must be haunted by that auto accident."

"Wasn't an accident."

Moody spoke in such a low rumble that at first she wasn't sure if she'd heard him correctly. She looked at Dent, but his focus was on the former detective and what he'd just said.

Moody lifted his bloodshot gaze to them and cleared his throat. "It wasn't an accident. Rupe arranged for a guy to T-bone Ray at an intersection. This guy took his job seriously and rammed into him at a high rate of speed. I recall Rupe saying that it was not only a miracle that the crash hadn't killed them both...it was also a damn shame."

Ray spat a pulverized, half-masticated sunflower-seed shell out the open driver's window of his pickup. On the seat beside him was a pair of binoculars, through which he'd watched Dent and Bellamy climb into the shiny blue and white plane with the unfurled Texas flag painted on its nose, and take off into the wild blue yonder.

He hated like heck that he hadn't killed Dent when he'd had the chance last night. Not only was he still an obstacle to getting to Bellamy, but without her personal pilot, she couldn't be flying off to God knew where, leaving Ray to wonder when they'd be back and he'd get another run at them.

But if he'd taken the time to finish Dent off last night, there was a good chance he'd have been caught, and that would have meant no vengeance for Allen. He needed to keep reminding himself of that and stop second-guessing his snap decision to run.

He'd gone home, gotten some shut-eye, and, over his morning cereal, had decided to keep watch on the airfield, where Dent eventually came to roost. He'd been staking it out for less than an hour, when, sure enough, they'd shown up. In her car, he noted.

Even viewed through the binoculars, last night's handiwork on Dent had shown up bright and bloody. It did his heart good to see the damage he'd inflicted on the flyboy's pretty face. He chuckled at the thought of how much that slice across his back must hurt.

But neither the injury or the scare he'd given them was enough. They had to die like Allen had.

He tossed the bag of sunflower seeds onto the dash and got out of the truck to stretch his legs and get the blood flowing again into his butt, which had gone numb hours ago. But he was gonna stick it out and stay here till they came back, no matter how boring it got.

Since they'd left, smaller planes had come and gone from the airfield. Through the binoculars, Ray had watched the old man going about his work, filling fuel tanks, situating chocks when a plane taxied in, chewing the fat with

the pilots before waving them off. Then he would disappear
into the hangar. Ray figured he was repairing the damage
done to Dent's plane, and the thought of that never failed to
make him smile.

His boss continued to call periodically. His voice-mail
messages had gotten nastier. *Screw him*, Ray thought. He
was beyond answering to somebody, to anybody. He was
a man with a mission, a man to be reckoned with, like the
heroes in his favorite movies.

His hand absently strayed to his left biceps, where he
kneaded the tissue that still caused him occasional pain.
Beneath the dripping fangs of the tattooed snake the skin
was ropy with scars. His whole left side, from shoulder to
ankle, had been severely injured in the car wreck.

The worst of the damage had been done to his left arm.
It had been pulverized in the accident, and then further
disfigured by all the surgeries required to make it useable.
It probably would have been cut off if not for a vascular
surgeon who'd wanted to use Ray as a guinea pig.

As soon as the last skin graft had healed well enough
to endure the tattooing needle, Ray had covered the scars
with the snake. It had taken several sessions because the
scarring was extensive and the snake was an elaborate
and intricate pattern, each detailed scale a thing of beauty
unto itself.

But the agony he'd suffered in the hospital, and during
all the months of physical therapy, and the pain of getting the tattoo, had been nothing compared to the mental
anguish he'd suffered over missing his brother's trial. He
hadn't been there for Allen when Allen had needed him
most.

His older brother had been the only person in his life

Ray had ever loved, because, remarkably, Allen had loved him. Ray was ugly, and he didn't have a very winning personality, but Allen had seen past his faults.

They hadn't known their father. Their mother had been meaner than sin, and when she died, the two brothers had stayed drunk for a week, not out of grief, but in celebration. After putting her in the ground, it was just the two of them, but Allen hadn't seemed to mind taking over the parental role.

He'd been a constant source of encouragement, telling Ray that he was okay, that there were a lot of people uglier than him, that he might not be book smart, but he was street smart, and that, in Allen's estimation, was the better kind of smarts to have.

Allen made him feel good about himself.

After repeating twelfth grade, Ray finally earned a high school diploma, and Allen helped him get a job doing the same thing he did: driving a delivery truck for Lyston Electronics. Things had been going great for them. They had actually looked forward to the Memorial Day barbecue.

It had started out being the blowout party they'd anticipated and had only turned tragic when Allen began messing around with that Lyston skank. Her pansy of a stepbrother had delivered her invitation to dance, and fatefully Allen had accepted. Up to that point in her book, Bellamy Price had described the day to a T.

But she'd made out like Allen had approached Susan first, not the other way around. She'd led thousands of readers to believe that he'd taken her into the woods, tried to rape her, and then killed her when she resisted.

But Allen had told him he'd left her very much alive

and laughing at him, and if Allen had said it, then that
was what had happened.

If it hadn't been for the car wreck, Ray would have testified in court that he'd met Allen as he was making his
way through the woods back to the pavilion. He would
have sworn it on the Bible. But it would've been a lie.

It wasn't until after the tornado had ripped through
the state park that the two of them had reunited. Ray
had staggered back to their car and had fallen to his
knees in relief when he saw that Allen, too, had survived
by taking cover under the Mustang they'd worked on
together to restore. Other vehicles had been sucked up
into the funnel and dropped great distances away. Others had been twisted and mangled so they'd looked like
wads of tinfoil. But their car had survived, and so had
Allen.

He'd had tears on his face when he pulled Ray into a
hug tight enough to squeeze the breath out of him. He was
so glad to see him alive and whole he'd pounded him on
the back till it hurt. Ray hadn't minded.

"Where the hell have you been, little brother?"

"L-looking for you."

That's the way it had gone down, but when Moody
showed up and alleged that Ray had killed that girl,
Ray told him, steadfastly, that when they left the woods,
together, they'd left with her laughter ringing in their
ears.

The jury never heard that from him. Allen was convicted.

No one had cared when he got killed except for Ray,
who'd blubbered like a baby when he was told. At his
brother's grave, he'd sworn vengeance. Not, however,
on the unidentified prisoner who'd shoved that shiv into

Allen's back, but on the people who'd put Allen in that place.

However, Ray soon learned that vengeance wasn't that easily achieved.

The Lystons were seemingly untouchable. They were wealthy and well protected, and after a few clumsy attempts to get close to them, Ray got scared off.

He had the same problem with Rupe Collier. The guy was a media magnet, always standing in the spotlight.

Dale Moody disappeared.

Over time, as years went by, to Ray's everlasting shame, his resolve had weakened.

Then Susan's sister had written that book, and Ray's hatred had crystallized, becoming pure and diamond-hard again. He focused it on her. She was the worst of the lot. She hadn't even had the decency to include in her book how badly and unjustly Allen had died.

Ray wouldn't stand for it. An eye for an eye. She had to die.

He was up to the task of taking her life. He'd been making himself ready since the day he got word of Allen's death. Defying the odds the doctors had given him, he'd done everything humanly possible to restore his arm to full capacity. Ignoring the pain, he'd worked long hours with weights and stretching bands, doing everything and anything that would recondition and strengthen the muscles and tendons. And, by God, those years of training and patience had paid off. He was older, smarter, and better conditioned than he'd been before that car wreck.

He glanced at the western horizon. It would be sunset soon. Then dark. The airstrip was an isolated place, where something terrible could befall a person alone after the sun went down.

Bellamy and Dent were skipping off anytime they took a mind to, making it hard for Ray to plan.

No problem. He had come up with an idea that would get them to stay put for a coupla days. Which would be more than enough time.

Bellamy was astonished to learn the extent of Rupert Collier's treachery. "He arranged for a car wreck that almost killed two people? I thought he was nothing except an egotistical buffoon, a laughable caricature of the used-car salesman."

"That's what he wants everybody to think," Moody said. "He's so obnoxious he's disarming."

"It won't work with me," Dent said. "I can't wait to talk to this asshole who wanted to plant a pair of panties in my house."

"You won't get anywhere," Moody said. "He's laid his groundwork. Underground work, more like it. For every one of his schemes, he's got a steel safety net. He's protected himself so well the CIA couldn't get to him."

Reluctantly Bellamy acknowledged that the man wielded some kind of power. "How does he get people to go along with him?"

"He finds where a person is vulnerable and pushes that button."

Dent nodded toward the bottle of whiskey. "Was that your button?"

"Ambition," Moody mumbled into his glass as he raised it to his mouth.

Bellamy didn't believe him, and she could tell Dent

didn't, either. An ambitious detective would have distinguished himself by exposing a crooked prosecutor, not covering for him.

Moody lowered his glass and divided a look between them, then expelled a gurgling sigh. "I was having a thing with a woman who worked in the department. I was married. She was young. She got pregnant. Rupe promised to make the mess go away. She resigned, and I never saw her again."

"What did he do to her?" Dent asked.

"I don't know. I didn't want to."

Under his breath Dent muttered deprecations.

Bellamy refocused on the file and asked Moody, "If I read every single thing in here, would I know who killed Susan? Do *you* know?"

"No. And I *have* read every single word in there many times over. I've memorized most of it, and the person who killed her is as much a mystery as he was when I left the morgue and took my first drive to the crime scene."

"So for all you really know," Dent said, "it could've been Allen. Ray could have been lying to protect his brother when he told you about Susan's laughter, all that."

"Could have been, I suppose. Everybody lies," he said, looking hard at Dent. Then his gaze moved back to Bellamy. "Except maybe you. You didn't have much to say about anything."

"I didn't remember anything."

Moody squinted at her. "What do you mean?"

Beneath his breath, Dent said, "Bellamy."

But she ignored the subtle warning. "I lost time," she said to Moody.

He didn't take a drink or a draw on his cigarette the

whole while she was explaining her memory loss. When she finished, he ground out the cigarette, which had burned down to the filter, and lit another.

"You testified at trial."

"Answering truthfully all the questions put to me. I testified to seeing Susan and Allen leaving the pavilion together. Rupe Collier asked if that was the last time I saw my sister alive, and I told him yes, because it was. The defense attorney didn't cross-examine. He must have thought I had nothing else to contribute, and I didn't."

Moody aimed another plume of smoke toward the ceiling, which was so thick with cobwebs they formed a ghostly canopy. "That's an awfully convenient time period to be erased."

"It's not convenient to me. I want to remember."

"Maybe you don't," he said.

"I do." She left the bed and walked over to an aged map of the state that was tacked to the cheaply paneled wall. With her index finger, she touched the circled star representing Austin, then moved her finger over to the darker green patch denoting the state park. "For eighteen years, this has been the epicenter of my life. I want to move out of it."

Coming back around, she said, "Maybe I would have moved past it if Daddy and Olivia had permitted me to go to the spot where Susan was found. I begged them to take me. They refused. They said it would only upset me. So I never saw the place where my sister died.

"It wasn't like I wanted to consecrate the ground or anything. She wasn't a very admirable person." Homing in on Moody, she said, "I'm sure you deduced that from what people told you about her. I looked up to her because she was pretty and popular and self-confident. All the things I wasn't. But I can't honestly tell you that I loved her."

She glanced at Dent, who was biting the inside of his cheek and looking as tightly wound as a spring. Obviously he wished she hadn't told Moody about her memory loss. His fuming gaze telegraphed a warning that she should shut up.

But she wasn't finished. "I want to know who killed her, Mr. Moody. Because, regardless of her personality or promiscuity, she didn't deserve to die that way, with her skirt bunched up around her waist, her bottom bared, lying facedown on the ground, holding on to that dainty little purse she carried that day." She lowered her head and took a deep, shuddering breath. "She was robbed of all dignity and grace."

She stared at a spot on the grimy vinyl floor, her head coming up only when Moody said, "Well you're wrong about one thing." He sloshed the last of the whiskey into his glass and swirled it as he talked. "That dainty little purse was found the following day in the top of a tree, fifty yards from where her body was discovered. It had her name stitched inside, so it was brought to me. I took prints off it, but there were only hers. So I returned it to your parents, and they cried, happy to get it back."

He paused and let that sink in. "If you saw her lying there facedown holding on to it, you were at the scene of where she died. And you were there ahead of the tornado."

Chapter 19

The silence inside the cabin was so prolonged and absolute that Dent imagined he could hear the dust motes spinning in the stifling air.

Bellamy stood frozen, her gaze fixed on Moody as he hauled himself up out of his chair, wove his way over to the screened door, pushed it open, and stepped out onto his sorry excuse for a porch.

Tilting his face skyward, he remarked, "Looks like we finally may get some rain."

Dent glanced out the nearest window and noticed that clouds had gathered in the west, blocking out the setting sun. The atmosphere inside the cabin was gloomy, but due less to the weather than to Moody's disturbing disclosure.

When he came back inside, the screened door shut behind him with a loud clap that caused Bellamy to jump. As though there had been no suspension of conversation, she asked gruffly, "You think I killed her?"

Moody halted and, swaying on his feet, eyed her up and down. "You? No."

"But you said . . . you said . . ."

"I said that if you saw her with her purse in her hand, you had to have seen her before the tornado struck."

"Maybe you got it wrong," Dent said. "Maybe the purse was found at the scene, and you're too drunk now to remember where you got it and when."

Moody glowered at him. "My crime scene was compromised, but I know when I came by the fucking purse. It's in my notes," he said, gesturing to the file lying on the bed. "Dated."

Bellamy returned to the bed and sat down beside Dent. In a haunted, breathy voice, she asked, "I had to have seen her purse there, in her hand. Why else would I have said that?"

"You only imagined it because you'd seen her carrying the purse," Dent said. "Within days, everyone knew the position her body was in when she was found. It was all over the news."

She looked deeply into his eyes as though desperate to believe his explanation. But he didn't think she did.

Moody settled back into his chair. "The bruise on the front of her neck was a band." He ran his finger across his throat in an even line. "The ME's opinion—which I shared—was that she'd been strangled by a garrote of some kind. Typically that happens from behind. She was overpowered and didn't put up a struggle."

Dent felt a slight tremor go through Bellamy. "Are you sure?" she asked.

"We didn't get any skin or blood from beneath her fingernails." Addressing Dent, he said, "First thing I looked for when I questioned you was scratch marks on your hands and arms."

"I didn't have any. Did Strickland?"

"None that couldn't be explained by him crawling under his Mustang to escape the tornado."

"That should've eliminated us as suspects."

"Not necessarily. She also had a knot on the back of her head, which she'd got before she died. What we figured is that she was struck from behind. By what, we were never able to determine. She fell facedown and was rendered unconscious, or at least too stunned to defend herself while the perp finished her off."

"With her panties," Bellamy said quietly.

"According to you, your stepmother, and the housekeeper who did the family laundry, she wore only one kind. Made of stretchy lace. Strong enough to choke someone to death. Rupe demonstrated in court how it could have been done. That was another of his shining moments."

"Didn't his courtroom shenanigans irk Strickland's defense attorney?" Dent asked. "Did he ever file an appeal?"

"Right away, but before the appellate court had time to consider his case and make a ruling, Strickland was killed."

"How did the lawyer react to his client's murder?" Dent asked.

Moody snorted a mirthless laugh. "He moved over to the DA's office. At Rupe's urging. He's still there, far as I know."

Bellamy said, "Allen died for nothing."

"Far as I know."

Later, when he thought back on it, Dent figured it was Moody's smirk that had set him off. He saw it, and the next thing he knew, he had closed the distance between the bed and Moody's chair, and he was bearing down on the former detective.

"You and Rupe made quite a team. He was the brains and you were his bitch boy. It was working so well, why'd you quit?"

"Back off."

"Not till I hear from you what I want to hear. You've admitted you knew Strickland was innocent from the get-go. How did you know?"

"I told you. He said that Susan had laughed at him. Guys don't—"

"Give me a break, Moody. Guys don't admit it and then whine about it. If she turned him down, he would have been steamed. He would have been cursing her, calling her names. Which would have been implicating, not exonerating. So sell that rationale somewhere else, because to me it smells like bullshit."

"His brother—"

"Who you said could have been lying. You had to have had something else that cleared Allen. What was it, Moody?"

The former detective looked at Bellamy where she still sat on the end of the bed. When his bleary gaze came back to Dent he said, "When I'm ready."

"When you're ready? What the hell does that mean?"

"It means, I've said all I'm gonna say to you."

"You lousy sot. She needs to know what you know," Dent shouted. "Like fucking now."

"Watch yourself, boy." Moody struggled to stand up, but when he stood face-to-face with Dent, Dent didn't back down, not even when Moody picked up his pistol from off the TV tray.

"What?" Dent scoffed. "You're going to shoot me?"

"Just keep pushing me and see."

"I don't think so. You're too chicken-livered." Dent leaned closer until the barrel of the pistol was touching his shirt.

Bellamy gave a strangled cry.

"It's all right," Dent said. Holding Moody's hostile stare, he said, "He's not going to pull the trigger."

"Don't be so goddamn sure."

"The only thing I'm sure about is what a coward you are. You didn't have the guts to stand up to Rupe Collier, and you don't have the guts to blow your own brains out now."

"Dent!"

Bellamy sounded anguished and frightened, but neither he nor Moody heeded her.

Moody's face was congested with anger. He was breathing hard. Dent felt the barrel of the pistol wavering as though the hand holding it was trembling.

"At least only one man died on account of me," he snarled. "I gotta live with that. You gotta live with nearly killing a whole airplane full of people."

Dent hit him. Hard. Moody took the blow on the chin and it sent him reeling backward, arms windmilling, until he broke his fall against the kitchen bar. He sank to the floor and landed in a heap.

Dent walked over to him, took a handful of his hair, and forced his head up. Moody looked at him through glazed and bloodshot eyes. "Don't measure me by your yardstick, you miserable turd." He bent down close. "You would've framed me for murder if you could've. You've had almost twenty years to set the record straight about your dirty dealings with Rupe Collier. You haven't. Instead, you've been skulking in this hellhole, trying to drown your guilt in whiskey. Bellamy and I gave you a chance to atone, and you still can't own up to what you did. You're a goddamn coward."

Making his disgust plain, he released Moody's hair, went back to the bed, took Bellamy by the hand, and pulled her up. On their way to the door, he paused. "You know, Moody, Rupe Collier is so dazzled by his own image, so far up his own ass, he no longer knows right from wrong. What makes you worse than him, you do."

"I can't fly in this."

Neither Dent or Bellamy had said a word since Dent had retrieved his pistol from the wobbly TV tray, shoved open the screened door, then stood aside and brusquely motioned her through it.

She had left the case file on the bed. As Dent dragged her past Moody, she'd paused, feeling she should say something. But the truth of it was, her revulsion matched Dent's. Her eyes met the detective's briefly before his head dropped forward. Without another word, she and Dent had left the dreary cabin.

For twenty minutes, he'd been speeding down the state highway in the direction of Marshall, pushing the rented sedan as though expecting it to respond with the velocity of his Corvette and cursing when it didn't.

The sky had grown increasingly dark. Raindrops had begun to land hard on the windshield. Without music from the radio, or conversation between them, each splat sounded loud and ominous.

A jagged fork of lightning and the sequential crack

of thunder emboldened her enough to speak. "I can't fly in this," she repeated, since Dent hadn't responded the first time.

Now, he jerked his head around toward her. "Do you think I would?"

"Then..." She gestured at the airport signpost as they whizzed past it.

"I've got to secure that airplane. Anything happens to it, it's my ass." Snidely, he added, "Unless you're good for it. You've got a lot of money. Maybe your daddy would buy it for you."

"Shut up, Dent. You're only mad at yourself."

"Myself?"

"For being so hard on Moody."

"Wrong. If I'd been as hard on him as I wanted to be, I would have killed him."

When they reached the airport, he whipped into a parking space, his motions conveying his short temper as he shut down the car, got out, and slammed the door. Braving the elements, he ran toward the entrance to the airport terminal.

Bellamy cringed when another drumroll of thunder vibrated through the car. She didn't want to be stranded inside it with nothing to protect her from the storm except for the window glass and a few panels of thin metal. But leaving the car and exposing herself to lightning and thunder was out of the question, even for the short time it would take her to run into the terminal.

Talking herself through her rising panic, she reached for her cell phone and placed a call to Olivia, who answered immediately. "Where are you? What's that racket?"

"It's thunder." But she didn't say where she was. "How's Daddy?"

"Doing better, actually." Judging by the unnatural brightness in Olivia's voice, Bellamy suspected that she was at his bedside and putting up a false front. "He's eager to talk to you."

"I'd like that. But first, tell me how you're holding up."

"Hanging in there. I talked to Steven earlier today. That helped."

"I'm glad to hear it."

"And, in spite of everything, he was happy to see you yesterday."

"I'm glad to hear that, too."

"I'll hand the phone to Howard now."

Through the phone, Bellamy could hear her father urging Olivia to use this time to get something to eat. Seconds later, his weak voice whispered, "Hey, good-lookin'."

"Whacha got cookin'?"

"Olivia won't be gone long. She knows something's up, and it's scaring her."

"Maybe you should tell her."

"It would only cause her to fret, and she's got more than enough to worry about. I tried to talk to her today about my funeral service. She wept so hard I didn't have the heart to continue."

Bellamy made a murmur of regret. "Is there anything I can do?"

"I told you what you could do for me. Any progress?"

It wasn't exactly progress that Dent had been attacked with a knife. Or that Van Durbin and his photographer had captured compromising pictures of them at the airport and outside Dent's apartment. But the tabloid exploitation

of her circumstances now seemed of little or no impor
tance compared to the seriousness of the circumstance
themselves.

"Do you remember Allen Strickland's brother, Ray?"

"Yes," her father replied. "He was mouthy with us
the trial, and after Allen was killed, he came to the co
porate offices and tried to bluster his way past the guard
He was subdued and escorted off the property. That's th
last I've heard of him. Why?"

"He was mentioned in a conversation I had today wit
Dale Moody."

"So you saw him? So soon?"

She didn't waste her father's time explaining ho
the meeting with the former detective had come abou
"He's a chain-smoking alcoholic living alone in squalo
He admitted that he never thought Allen Strickland wa
guilty, but he stopped short of confessing exactly how h
and Rupe Collier engineered his conviction."

"I'm surprised he would admit even that much."

"He's a broken man. This case ruined his career and hi
life. He claims still not to know who killed Susan." Sh
hesitated to tell him more, but then remembered the impo
tance this held for him. "There's something else, Daddy
She told him how she'd come to describe the crime scene.

"But you were never at the crime scene," he said.

"It seems I was. I just don't remember being there."

There was much to explain and only a brief time i
which to cover it. Cringing each time lightning struck, sh
talked her father through it as quickly as possible.

"When I mentioned Susan's purse, Moody jumped o
it immediately. Is it true that he brought it to you day
later?"

"Yes," he said hoarsely. "We were told it had been found in a tree."

She sighed. "Then it seems certain that I either witnessed the crime or came upon Susan's body soon after she was killed. In any case, I saw it before the tornado ravaged the area."

"Jesus, Bellamy. Oh, Jesus."

She'd expected a swift and firm denial that she'd been anywhere near the crime scene. Instead, he sounded as though his worst fear had been realized.

"Daddy, what?" When he said nothing, she pressed him, "Do you think that I intentionally withheld information?"

"No, of course not."

"Then did it ever occur to you that I had memory lapses?"

"No. I would have gotten help for you."

"Would you?"

Instead of answering, he said, "Ah, Olivia's back and she's brought with her... What is that? Vegetable beef soup. I'd better go now, sweetheart, and make sure she eats all of it. Thank you for calling."

Then he was gone, and his sudden disconnect left her stunned.

The entire conversation seemed surreal. She needed to think it through and determine what it meant. But just then Dent returned. He got in and quickly pulled the door shut against the gusting wind.

"Damn, it's blowing."

"What about the airplane?"

"The hangar manager figured it must belong to somebody important, so he'd already moved it inside. I tipped him twenty bucks." He took a longer look at her. "You okay?"

Lying, she nodded.

"I also checked the weather radar," he continued. "This is only the leading edge of a wide band of storms that isn't predicted to move out until after midnight or better, so I stopped by the rental office and told them we'd be keeping the car overnight." He turned the ignition key. "I made note of a hotel a few miles back."

It was a short drive, but by the time he pulled the car under the hotel's porte cochere, he could tell that Bellamy was holding herself together by sheer force of will. She'd kept her eyes closed and hadn't uttered a sound. She was drawn up as taut as a bowstring, and her lips were so tightly compressed they were rimmed with white.

He parked the car where it wouldn't block the through lane, got out, and went around to open Bellamy's door. With a hand beneath her right elbow, he gently eased her out and placed his arm around her shoulders as he guided her through the entrance.

It was a moderately priced chain hotel, having a typical lobby with a navy and burgundy color scheme, polished brass lamps, and silk plants. Since Bellamy seemed incapable of moving, he secured a room with his own credit card, which he was reasonably sure would clear.

Within minutes of entering the lobby, he was unlocking the door to a room on the third floor and shepherding Bellamy inside. He went straight to the wide windows and closed the drapes, then used the remote on the nightstand to turn on the TV, which would help to muffle the noise of the storm. He switched on all the lamps.

Bellamy hadn't moved from the spot where he'd left her. He went to her and chafed her upper arms. "Do you get like this every time it storms?"

"Since the tornado."

"Have you seen somebody about it?"

Through chattering teeth, she laughed, but not because what he'd said was funny. "Thousands of dollars' worth of somebodies. I've tried every form of therapy imaginable. None has helped."

"Do you have something to take?"

"I stopped getting the prescription filled."

"How come?"

"The medication didn't help, either. It only made me woozy in addition to being petrified."

"Maybe you should try the Dr. Denton Carter remedy." His arms went around her and pulled her close.

But when he bent his head down to nuzzle the side of her neck, she pushed him away. "That's your remedy for everything."

"It works for everything."

Although she'd squirmed out of his embrace, it hadn't been altogether unsuccessful. A smile was tugging at the corner of her lips, which had regained some of their color.

"I've got to go move the car," he said. "Are you going to be all right if I leave you alone?"

"I'm usually alone when this happens. I've learned to panic quite well in private."

He bent his knees to bring himself eye level with her and tilted his head. "Will you be all right?"

"Yes. Inside, with the drapes drawn and the lights on, it's better. I'll take a hot shower. That's calming, too."

"Okay then." He walked toward the door, but she

stopped him. When he turned back to her, she said, "You didn't get yourself a room."

He held up the key card. "Yes, I did. Don't use all the hot water."

He found a parking spot not too far away from the building. On his race back, he had to lean into the strong wind. Small hail stones pelleted him and bounced on the pavement. The lightning was ferocious. But it wasn't raining all that hard, so when he reentered the lobby, he was relatively dry. And starving.

From the lobby phone, he called their room. When Bellamy answered, he asked if she wanted to join him in the restaurant. "Or would you rather me have them box up something and eat in the room?"

"I'd prefer that."

"Need me to come up and wash your back?"

She hung up on him.

He had his hands full when she opened the door to him twenty minutes later, fully clothed, but her hair still damp and smelling of shampoo. "What's all this?"

"Vending machine toothbrushes. And paste," he added with emphasis. "Two cheeseburgers, two fries, two beers for me, one split of white wine for you. We'll toss for the peach cobbler. That was the last of it."

While she spread their dinner on the round table, he took a quick shower, returning to the main room dressed but without his damp boots.

Bellamy seemed to be as hungry as he was, and they ate quickly, deciding to save the cobbler for later. He carried his second beer over to the bed, rolled the pillow into a ball, and supported his head on it as he stretched out on his back.

"This is cozy." He patted the space beside him. "It could get cozier."

"Cut it out, Dent. I'm not going to sleep with you."

"Sleeping was last night's agenda. Not what I had in mind for tonight."

With a decisive punch, she muted the TV. Then, curling up in the easy chair, she put her hands palm to palm and slid them between her knees as though to warm them. But it was also a slightly protective gesture, which should have alerted him to what was coming.

"What Moody said—"

He interrupted her with a long, drawn-out groan. "Talk about a mood kill."

"What he said about you living with what nearly happened."

"But didn't."

"Still, it can't be easy to know how close you came to—"

"Taking out a hundred and thirty-seven people?" Watching her down the length of the bottle, he took another drink of beer, then set it on the nightstand and came off the bed, all in one motion. "Thanks a lot. I've now officially lost my buzz." He moved to the dresser and leaned into the mirror above it to inspect the cuts on his face.

"Why did you voluntarily leave the airline after the incident?"

"Too bad it's not Halloween. I could trick-or-treat."

"Why won't you talk about it?"

"I wouldn't even need a mask."

"It might help if you opened up about it."

"Bad as these bruises look, I may still have them come Halloween."

"Dent?"

"*What?*" He came around so quickly she actually recoiled.

But she didn't give up and go away. "Why won't you talk about it?"

"Why are you so damn curious? Morbid fascination? Are you one of those people who goes online to watch videos of plane crashes, people jumping off buildings, multi-car pile-ups?"

"Don't do that."

"What am I doing?"

"Slamming the door. Getting defensive. Is that how you were with the investigators?"

"No, we all became chums. Christmas cards. Birthday greetings. They name their babies after me."

She frowned. "You told me that the only way you can relate to a woman is sexually."

"All evidence to the contrary."

"This is your chance to relate to one, to me, in another way."

"That way is no fun. No *fucking* fun."

He returned to the bedside table, picked up the bottle of beer, and took a swallow from it. As far as he was concerned the conversation was over. But Bellamy continued to watch him with those damn soulful eyes that pulled him in and under, and, before he'd even planned it, he asked, "What do you want to know?"

"You were the co-pilot?"

"Yes."

"You spilled your coffee?"

"Isn't that what I told you?"

"The mechanic, replacing the electrical panel—"

"All true."

"The weather?"

"Also a factor, but not severe enough to ground us."

"But when you were on takeoff—"

"The most critical time of any flight."

"—you were instructed to turn left to avoid a thunderstorm."

"Which was the right call."

"Lightning struck the plane."

"Popping several circuit breakers, including one that controlled the CVR. Cockpit voice recorder. Which wasn't relevant until later."

"A fire warning came on for the left engine, but there wasn't a fire."

"Just like I told you. False warning."

"But the captain shut down the left engine."

"Correct."

"That's what *he* did."

"Yes."

"What did *you* do?"

"I flew the frigging airplane!"

His shout was followed by an abrupt, charged silence. Bellamy sat upright. He cursed himself and moved back to the bed, where he sat down on the end of it and pressed his thumbs into his eye sockets. He kept them there for a minute or more, then slowly lowered his hands and looked over at her.

"The captain didn't like me, and the feeling was mutual. He was a totally by-the-book kind of guy, and that kind of pilot. He regarded me as a misfit who didn't fit the image and didn't deserve to wear the uniform. In a best-case scenario, we wouldn't have been scheduled to fly together. But we were. That was the hole in the first slice of Swiss cheese."

He stopped to collect his thoughts, to relive that instant in time when he realized that the captain had made an egregious error. "I told you earlier that he reacted as he'd been trained to do on a 727. The thing was, that's not what we were flying. We were flying an MD80. He'd been trained on the 80, of course, but his upgrade had been recent. When the event occurred, an older reflex kicked in. He reacted to the fire warning without checking the instruments for secondary indications of a fire. Oil temp. Oil pressure. EGT. Exhaust gas temperature.

"I instantly checked the gauges. Nothing said fire or damage. I realized the goddamn warning was false. By now we're in a steep left bank, and our airspeed is decreasing. The right engine is pushing the airplane further to the left. The nose is dropping, right wing is tipping up. The airplane wants to roll over."

"That's what you reacted to."

"Yeah. I jammed the right rudder to try to bring it out of the turn. I pulled back on the yoke to try to bring the nose up and get the craft level, while bringing it back to the right to straighten it up. And it all had to be done immediately and simultaneously. There wasn't time to think about it or talk it over. There were no options.

"Now this took seconds. *Seconds.* During that time, he and I are yelling at each other. He was shouting at me that it was his aircraft, and I was telling him that what I was doing had to be done. We're shouting over each other. It was a damned good thing that CVR circuit breaker had popped. That saved us both some embarrassment later on.

"Anyway, I managed to pull us out of it. He stopped yelling. In eight, no more than ten, seconds, he'd pieced it together, realized his error and how close it had brought us to a catastrophe. He even thanked me, I think. At that point, we were both awfully busy.

"Passengers were screaming. The flight attendants were trying to restore calm. We had no way of knowing the extent of the injuries or damage to the cabins. We were still flying in moderate to severe turbulence on one engine.

"I asked him if he wanted to restart that left engine, since apparently nothing was wrong with it. He opted to leave it off. He took control again and we returned to the airport. Disaster averted."

He stared at the pattern in the carpet between his feet. "No one died, but a lot of people were injured when we pitched. One was a baby that was in his mother's lap, not strapped in. Lawsuits were filed, and the airline paid out millions to settle." He looked over at Bellamy and said with a bitterness that went bone deep, "You know the rest. It made big news."

He got up and walked over to the window. Parting the drapes, he looked out. "Stopped lightning."

"Your actions saved them."

"I got lucky."

"You know better. Why weren't you hailed a hero?"

He sighed. "Because you can't have a first officer taking over for a captain who's flying the airplane. He had twenty years' experience on me. He was an airline golden boy. Give him another few seconds, he would have realized what had happened and what needed to be done to fix it. He would have done exactly what I did."

"But you didn't have those seconds to spare."

He shook his head. "We were going in, and it's a miracle that we didn't in spite of what I did."

"Did the captain own up to his mistake?"

"Yes, but he also took some of the credit for reversing it and saving everyone."

"You didn't tell them otherwise?"

"No, we covered for each other. There was no voice recording to disprove us."

"So why did you leave the airline?"

"While the NTSB was still investigating the event, a reporter for one of the networks went digging into my past and discovered that, in my youth, when my girlfriend turned up dead, I was named a suspect by the police. 'He was later cleared of all suspicion,'" he quoted, sneering.

"Like hell I was. The implication was that, despite the spiffy uniform, I was still a shady character. The story didn't sit well with the airline. Even after the accident report had been completed, I was urged to extend my leave. That was as good as telling me to get lost. So I got lost."

"Letting them and everyone else think—"

"Whatever the hell they wanted to," he snapped.

"You didn't care?"

"No." He crossed to the night table, picked up the bottle of beer, and drained it.

"It didn't bother you to walk away from it?"

"No."

"I don't believe you on either count."

He turned to her, poised for a fight, ready to argue, but her expression was soft and misty, and it instantly deflated him. He sat down on the side of the bed, bending his head low, and, for a moment, said nothing.

Then, "The airlines have rules and regulations for a reason. From the crew members' socks to how they fly the airplanes, there are standards that everyone's gotta adhere to. They're responsible for the lives of thousands of people every day. To be good at moving all those people, to do it efficiently and safely, everything has to be done uniformly.

"But that word crawls all over me. I tolerated it while I was in the air force. We were at war. I got it. Orders had to be followed. But in the corporate world? Regulation *socks*?" He shook his head. "The captain was right: I wasn't a good fit. So I didn't mind leaving the structure." Looking over at her, he said, "But to walk away from the flying was tough. That was bad."

"You still fly."

"And I love my airplane. But I miss the big ones. I miss jet propulsion."

"You could always go back."

"No. Even if an airline would consider hiring me, which is highly unlikely, I took a position. I gotta stick to it."

"You could fly corporate jets."

He waited for a moment, then, acting on impulse, reached across the distance separating them. He slipped his hand beneath her shirt and curled his fingers inside the waistband of her jeans. Pulling her out of the chair and toward him, he said, "Buy one. I'll fly you."

Positioning her between his thighs, he pushed up the hem of her shirt, undid the button on her jeans, and spread open the two ends of the waistband with his thumbs.

"Dent…"

"We related on your level, Bellamy. It's time we came down to mine."

Then he pressed his open mouth against that wedge of pale, smooth skin.

Chapter 20

At the touch of Dent's mouth, Bellamy's bones seemed to liquify. Reflexively she reached for something with which to support herself and wound up clutching handfuls of his hair.

"Does this hurt?"

Hurt? He was tenderly kissing the dark bruise on her pelvic bone, made last night when she banged into the iron railing outside his apartment. "No."

"Good."

He kissed the spot again then eased down the zipper of her jeans, his mouth moving into the widening gap, doing wonderful things that caused her insides to quicken.

"Dent," she murmured. "We can't."

"We are." His breath was warm on her skin as he rubbed his face against her. "You taste good." A gentle suction of his lips pulled her skin against his teeth; he nipped her lightly, making her breath catch.

He angled back and looked up into her eyes, then gave his full attention to each button on her shirt as he pushed it through the hole. He worked his way up from the bottom and, when all were undone, opened her shirt and kissed the slight indentation between her ribs just under her bra.

Using the fingers of both hands, he caressed the loose strands of hair that brushed across her nipples. "That's been driving me nuts." Pushing her hair aside and leaning in, he replaced his fingertips with his mouth, first on one breast, then on the other, biting her gently through the lace cups of her bra.

He bracketed her hips with his strong hands, turned her, and pulled her down onto the bed, then leaned above her and claimed her mouth in a kiss so deeply passionate, so uniquely Dent, that she banished her resolve never, ever, to let this happen.

They kissed long and hungrily. While his hands moved over her, he took her mouth boldly, sweetly, teasingly, and continued to kiss her until they were breathless. When they broke apart, he buried his face in the crook of her neck and whispered, "I think you have a talent for this."

He worked his hand into the opening of her jeans, into her panties, and barely paused to cup her mound before easing her thighs apart, separating and caressing, and finding her ready. Instinctually she raised her knees and angled her hips. With a growl of satisfaction, he slid his fingers deep into her.

Oh, God! This was Dent. The Dent of her most innocent adolescent daydreams and her most erotic adult fantasies, making her whimper with each intimate stroke of his fingers, every breath-grabbing brush of his thumb.

His hair was soft against her breasts, now freed from the lace cups of her bra. Gently and avidly he loved them with his mouth, his tongue, while from low in his throat came sounds of arousal that were altogether masculine.

He wanted her, and for these moments, he was hers. Exclusively hers.

She closed her arms around his head, and arched up to meet the thrusts of his fingers and beg the exquisite pressure of his thumb. She called his name as the first ripple of ecstasy washed through her.

Then came the tide.

Ray had watched the sun go down, and then had given his eyes hours to grow accustomed to the dark. He now felt that his night vision was as keen as that of the coyote he could hear yipping in the hills to the west of the airfield.

A single-engine plane had landed at twilight, but had stayed only long enough to refuel and then had taken off. Shortly after that, the landing-strip lights had been extinguished, leaving only a pale glow coming from inside the hangar.

Ray got out of his truck and jiggled his legs to restore circulation. He did a few deep knee bends, then some curls with his left arm. He caressed the scabbard attached to his belt and kept his hand there as he headed toward the hangar.

The ground was uneven, rocky, and strewn with patches of wild grass and occasional cacti. Fearing a mishap, he didn't walk fast, but he moved as quickly and quietly as he could.

When he got to within fifty yards of the hangar, he slowed his pace and bent almost double to decrease the size of the target he made. He didn't think the old man would detect him, but he wasn't taking any chances. He'd looked forward to this. He was pumped. He wanted nothing to prevent him from doing what he'd come to do.

After tonight Denton Carter and Bellamy Price would know that Ray Strickland was a fearsome son of a bitch. The attack in the IHOP parking lot had been chicken feed compared to the blow he was about to strike. This would shatter them, rattle them, make plain the threat he posed, and intensify their fear.

Twenty yards from the building, he dropped to the ground and lay there, imagining himself to be as invisible as the special forces guys. He loved watching movies about camouflaged sniper types who could lie in one position for hours, days if necessary, waiting for the perfect shot.

He thought of himself like that now: lethal, invisible, and invincible. His weapon of choice wasn't a high-powered rifle but a double-edged blade. He'd passed the long hours of the afternoon and evening stropping it to razor sharpness. He now slid it from the scabbard, loving the hiss it made against the leather, which sounded both sexual and sinister.

He gripped the bone handle in one hand as he belly-crawled to the exterior wall of the hangar. Pressing his ear to the corrugated metal, he heard the twang of a guitar picking out the melody of a Hank Williams song.

Ray hated hick music like that, but he was glad the old man liked it. It would screen any sounds he made. Emboldened, he slid up the washboard metal until he was on his feet, then crept along the wall, following it toward the front of the building and the half-moon of concrete onto which the hangar opened.

By the time he reached the corner, his heart was

pounding and his breathing was fast and shallow. He took several moments to slow them down, then counted to three and poked his head around the wall and peered into the hangar.

He took in everything at a glance that lasted no more than a second or two. The old man was lying on his back beneath Dent's airplane, his legs and feet sticking out from under it. An extension cord that snaked across the concrete floor was supplying power to the radio, which was sitting on the wing, as well as to a work light that lay beside the old man beneath the fuselage. In addition to the light were an open toolbox and a greasy rag.

This was going to be easier than he'd thought.

"This is for you, Allen," he mouthed. Then, exultant, Ray charged into the hangar. Before the old man had time even to realize he was there, he plunged the blade of his knife, hilt-deep, into his belly.

Even as orgasmic aftershocks were causing Bellamy to gasp, Dent levered himself above her and hastily unbuttoned his fly, then sank down into another of those kisses of hers that felt like fucking. As his tongue plundered her mouth, the eroticism of it compounded his urgency.

He positioned himself between her thighs and rubbed the tip of his erection against her dampness, cursing the barrier of clothes that he would have to work around. At some point, they would need to stop and take a breather. That would be when they'd get naked. He really wanted to be skin-to-skin with her, lying lengthwise on the bed, and doing this thing right. But he couldn't be bothered now. He had to get inside her, where she was silky and hot and wet. Surprisingly so.

She didn't give off the vibe of a woman who would ignite that quickly and burn that fiercely. Who would have guessed that she, of the reserved manner and solemn eyes, would be so damned sensitive where it counted?

And, man, was she. Barely a glancing touch to that sweet spot, and her body was electrified. Made him feel like all the great lovers in history rolled into one, made him crazy to claim her, made him desperate to feel those contracting responses again. Except around his penis, from inside her. Now.

He reached between them to move aside her panties.

"No!"

At once, her head began thrashing from side to side and all four limbs started flailing. She shoved him away and scrambled off the bed. By the time he realized what had happened, she had her back to him and was hiking up her jeans.

"What the hell?"

"I can't. I can't. I told you."

Disbelief held him back for a few seconds, then he launched himself off the bed and reached for her. At his touch, she jumped like she'd been shot. She whipped around. "Don't touch me. Don't say anything. Just..." Frantically, she motioned for him to back up and give her space.

He somehow—miraculously, he thought later—managed to tamp down his surging rage. That had been his first reaction. But he was quick to realize that she wasn't being coy. Or a tease. Or just plain cruel.

Instead, she was a woman in full freak-out mode, and, unless he wanted her screaming the hotel down and bringing on the house detective, he'd better do as she said.

Clumsily she replaced the cups of her brassiere and buttoned up her blouse. Maybe she remembered what he'd said about where her hair fell and how that drove him nuts, because she pushed it back off her face and hooked it behind her ears. She took deep breaths and shook her hands at her sides like somebody literally trying to get a grip. Finally, a little bit restored, she looked at him.

"I know it's unfair." She glanced down at his open fly, blinked rapidly, gulped air. "Terribly unfair. I'm sorry."

He said the only thing that immediately came to mind. "You buttoned your shirt wrong."

She stared at him for several seconds as though trying to make sense of that. Then she looked down at her shirt and saw the mess she'd made of aligning the buttons with the right holes. She didn't fix it, only ran her hand over the placket to smooth out the bunched fabric.

"I never meant to...I shouldn't have let you..." She glanced past him at the bed, then raised her hands to her cheeks, which were flaming. "You must think I'm awful. I apologize for not stopping sooner. Before...I should have stopped you before...But I didn't, and I'm sorry. I just... can't."

He ran his fingers through his hair, which minutes ago she'd been about to rip from his scalp. He blew out a gust of air. "Yeah, I kinda got that."

"This was a bad idea. I'll move to another room." She started toward the dresser where she'd left her large shoulder bag.

"Leave it," he said. "You're staying here."

"Haven't you heard—"

"Yeah I heard. About a dozen times. You can't. What do you think I am? It's hands off. I get it. Okay? *Okay?*"

Still wary, she hesitated, then, after a moment, bobbed her head.

"Okay. But I'm not going to let you be by yourself when you're one degree away from a total meltdown."

"I'll be fine. I'm not going to—"

"Bellamy, we are sharing this room, this bed, for the rest of the night, and that's all there is to it."

"Like you have a say in what I do."

"Tonight I do," he said with heat. "And if you ask what gave me that right, I just might tell you in language so graphic it would cause you to blush like you've never blushed before. So ask at your own risk."

She didn't say anything.

"All right, then." He motioned toward the bed behind him. "Which side do you want?"

It took him a long time to go to sleep. Despite her flipping out, which should have doused any and all amorous inclinations better than a cold shower, he didn't immediately recover from his throbbing lust. Because, although he'd given his word not to touch her, he was aware of her being within touching distance, aware of everything about her.

He knew the instant she fell asleep. Her body, which had been as unyielding as an I-beam, eventually relaxed. Her breathing became steady and deep and—*What the hell was wrong with him?*—sexy.

In order to get even halfway comfortable, he had to unbutton his fly again.

Which wasn't such a good idea, because when he came out of a sound sleep hours later, he was masturbating. But then he realized it wasn't his hand, but Bellamy's, that was feeling around his alert cock.

He moaned pleasurably and turned onto his side, laying his arm across her waist, his leg over her hip, and pulling her against him.

"Dent."

"Good morning," he mumbled, smiling lazily, eyes closed.

She planted her other hand firmly against his chest. Now the woman couldn't take her hands off him. How great was that?

"Dent."

He took her groping hand, drew it to his straining erection, closed her fingers around it, and released a long, low sigh. "Tighter. Yeah. Like that."

"Dent!" She wrested her hand away. "It's your phone."

"Hmm?"

"Your *phone*."

He jerked his head up and back, eyes springing open. "What?"

"I was trying to get to your phone. It could be important."

The jingle penetrated the passion that had fogged his mind and muffled his ears. He flopped over onto his back and lay gasping for breath and cursing liberally. Feeling blindly, he angrily yanked his cell phone from where it was clipped to the waistband of his jeans and blinked the calling number into focus.

He didn't recognize it, but he had words for the person on the other end. "Who the fuck is this?"

"Who the fuck you think?"

"Goddammit, Gall! I'm gonna kill you!"

"Get in line."

Dent, struggling to cap his arousal, covered his eyes with his forearm. "What's that mean?"

"Your pickup-driving redneck?"

"Yeah?"

"He came calling. He's out for blood, all right."

Dent sat up, swung his feet to the floor, and drew his shirttail over his lap. Bellamy had also sat up, her eyes watchful and worried, correctly gauging the seriousness of his expression.

"Tell me," Dent said into the phone.

"He was parked several hundred yards from the field a good part of the day."

"How'd you spot him?"

"Didn't. Guy from Tulsa on his way down to South Padre stopped here to refuel. He'd spotted the truck on his approach. Since it was out in the middle of nowhere, he thought it might've been somebody lost or broken down, needing help. I told him I'd check it out.

"Which I did. After he took off, I got some binoculars. The moron thought he was well hidden in the brush, but his truck was facing south. The sun was reflecting off his windshield like a spotlight all afternoon."

"Could've been somebody hunting rabbits, taking in the scenery. How can you be sure it was my guy?"

"I got more than one good look at him. Big guy. Solid. Black leather vest. Tattooed left arm. Ugly son of a bitch, too."

"Did he see you?"

"Anytime I checked on him, I did it from inside. And he had his own binocs. He was watching me. I went about my business, acted like I didn't know he was out there. Night came on. He was still there, and I figured he'd been waiting for dark to pay me a visit. I was ready for him."

"What did you do?"

Gall described the stage he'd set for the man they believed to be Ray Strickland. "He fell for it. He barreled into the hangar, screaming like a banshee, and shoved his knife into what he believed to be my gut. Was actually a piece of a blown-out tire. Looked pretty natural, though, when it was zipped up inside my coveralls. Same curvature as my belly." He chuckled.

"Gall, this is nothing to laugh at."

"No, I guess not."

"What did he do when he realized he'd been tricked?"

"I'm not rightly sure. Messed hisself maybe. 'Cause I tripped the breaker switch and all the lights went out, the radio went off, and he was left in total darkness and silence, not knowing what the hell had happened.

"I could hear him cussing a blue streak as he tried to dislodge his knife from that tire, but in the end, he took it with him, my coveralls included. Just scooped it all up and ran like hell. Left my shoes, and I'm glad. I just now got them worked in."

"Did he return to his truck?"

"Yep. Made it okay, I guess, 'cause I saw the headlights when he drove off. One good thing, before it got dark, I got his license plate number."

"Did you call this in?"

"To that sheriff's deputy who came out after your plane was trashed. I told him I thought it was probably the same guy. Gave him a description of Strickland. He said they'd lifted dozens of partial prints off your airplane, which they're 'sorting through.'"

"They've got missing kids to find and meth labs to shut down. I doubt my damaged airplane has priority."

"Yeah, and if they stopped Strickland today, all they

could hold him on is theft of a pair of coveralls. He's probably disposed of them by now. Bastard. They were my favorite pair."

Although Gall was making light of it, Dent could tell the older man had been shaken. Dent sure as hell was. Attacking him was one thing. Attacking Gall was a clear indication of just how vindictive this individual was.

Worried for Gall's safety, Dent asked if he was still at the hangar.

"No, I got the place locked up good and tight, then left. Short night, but, you know."

"This guy won't appreciate being made a fool of. You're probably not safe at home, either."

"I didn't go home."

"My place?"

"No safer than mine."

Dent remembered the strange phone number. "Whose number is this?"

"A lady I know."

"*Lady?*"

"She'll put me up for a day or two."

"You know a lady?"

"What? You think you got a monopoly?"

"Not lately," Dent grumbled, cutting a glance toward Bellamy. She'd returned to the armchair that she'd been sitting in the night before. She was listening intently to his side of the conversation and could probably hear Gall, too.

"Sorry to call you at this hour of the morning," Gall was saying. "But I just got settled in here. Thought you should know right away."

Dent agreed, he just didn't know what to do with the information. He rested his forehead in his hand, weakened by the thought of what could have happened to Gall if that pickup had been parked facing north instead of south. "Sorry I yelled at you when I answered."

"I'm used to it."

"I'm still sorry."

There was an extended moment of silence, which was full of understanding but no unnecessary sloppiness. Finally Gall asked about their meeting with Moody, and Dent gave him a rundown. "He and I had no kind words for each other."

"You didn't shoot him?"

"No, but I hit him."

"Overdue. Got to give him some credit, though."

"For what? Plotting to frame me for murder?"

"For admitting it."

Dent didn't say anything.

"What are you going to do now, Ace?"

"Hold on." He covered the receiver and said to Bellamy, "Are you speaking to me this morning?"

"You kept your word."

"Yeah, I'm a regular choirboy. One who's desperate for coffee. The help-yourself bar in the lobby opens at six. I noticed the sign. Would you fetch me a cup?"

"What don't you want me to hear?"

"Nothing."

"You're not that much of a choirboy. You couldn't look innocent if you tried, especially when you're lying. But"—she stood up and got her bag—"I'm desperate for coffee, too. Besides, I need to check in with Olivia."

Dent stared at the door for several seconds after it closed behind her, then raised the phone to his ear again. "Gall?"

He snorted. "No more separate rooms?"

"Shut up and listen. I sent her on an errand, but she'll be back soon. I didn't want her to hear this. I won't go into the details now, but Moody told us yesterday that it's almost certain Bellamy witnessed her sister's death."

"Jesus Christ."

"It shook her up. I don't know all the psychological whys and wherefores, but that would be traumatic enough to cause a memory shutdown, wouldn't you say?"

"Damn straight."

"This guy, Ray Strickland, has reason—and a solid one—to want vengeance for his brother. But I'm afraid he's not the only one who's stalking Bellamy." He told Gall about her fan Jerry. "She dismissed him as a harmless, bookish type, an admirer who's gone a little overboard."

"She's probably right."

"Probably. Maybe. But in the park, he pretended not to notice us. At the Austin airport he was near enough to touch her. Close enough to address her, at least. If he's gushy over his favorite writer, why didn't he gush?"

"Maybe he was intimidated. She's got big bad you at her side now."

"Yeah, okay, maybe. But factor Jerry into everything else, and his unlikely presence in Texas doesn't seem quite so innocent or coincidental."

"But you said this Jerry is a fan."

"*Appears* to be a fan. But say he's only pretending to be and is actually someone with an axe to grind."

"Say he is. He's been close to her on several occasions, right? Even while she was still in New York. Why hasn't he struck?"

Dent had no answer to that. And when Gall asked him

what so-called Jerry's connection to Susan's death could be, Dent didn't have an answer to that, either.

He threw a glance toward the door. "She's back. I'm going to pretend that we've been talking about something else." He grabbed the pen and small tablet on the nightstand. "Give me that license plate number for the pickup."

He was jotting it down when she came through the door carrying a cardboard tray with two tall paper cups of coffee. When he saw the doughnuts she had also brought, he blew her a kiss.

"Don't go back to the hangar, Gall. Until you know we're on our way back, stay in bed with your lady. You'll be safer there."

He laughed. "You don't know my lady."

"Soon as the weather clears and we can take off, I'll call you with our ETA."

"You'll have to call this number."

"Where's your phone?"

The old man wheezed a sound of disgust aimed at himself. "In the pocket of my coveralls. The ones Strickland took with him when he hightailed it out of here."

Chapter 21

Bellamy could tell that Dent was worried and preoccupied as he bit into the glazed doughnut and took a sip of coffee.

"I heard most of it," she said. "He meant to kill him."

"A knife in the belly? I'd say so."

"And it's my fault."

"No it isn't. It's this creep's fault. He'd better hope the police catch him before I do."

She went over to the window and opened the drapes. It was no longer stormy, but the sky was overcast, making for a dreary-looking day. Which was appropriate, because not only did she feel the weight of responsibility for the attack on Gall, but in addition to that, the latest report from Houston was dismal.

When she'd called Olivia from the hotel lobby, she reported that Howard's condition had sharply declined overnight. His lapses into semiconsciousness were becoming increasingly longer. His lungs were filling with fluid, and he could no longer swallow.

As her husband's systems began shutting down, Olivia was emotionally unraveling.

"Do you want me to come right away?" Bellamy extended the offer sincerely, although it was in direct opposition to her father's request.

Olivia underscored it. "If Howard wanted you here, he wouldn't have sent you away. As much as I would like having you here to lean on, I must go along with his wishes. But it means a lot to me that you offered. Thank you."

Bellamy wondered if her stepmother would be quite so grateful if she knew that her husband's decline could be the result of his disturbing conversation with Bellamy yesterday afternoon.

Rather than relieve him of his lingering doubts and anxiety regarding Susan's death, she had contributed to them by passing along what Moody had told her. She still didn't know what to make of her father's anguished response to the possibility that she'd witnessed the crime, and it seemed doubtful that she would have an opportunity to ask him.

Beyond her concern for all that, she was disconsolate over losing him. For months she'd been trying to brace herself for this inevitable outcome. But now that his death seemed imminent, she realized the futility of trying to prepare for it. One couldn't. *She* couldn't. Death was unacceptable. Even now, when it seemed likely that she would never see her father again, she wanted to reject the finality and permanence of his departure.

But it was a reality that she must face. Quietly she said, "Daddy's going to die soon."

Dent moved up behind her and placed his hands on her shoulders. "Do you want me to fly you down there?"

"I offered to go. Olivia said no. And she's right. As

much as I want to be there and see him one last time, I can't go back on the promise I made him."

"Which was a bitch of a promise to ask of you."

She tended to agree. The more she learned about that horrible day, the more confounding the facts became. And this quest for the truth had placed her and the people around her in danger. She wanted to fulfill the promise she'd made her father, but she feared the cost of doing so.

She said, "We can't just stand by and let Ray Strickland continue his personal vendetta."

"The police have his license plate number. Hopefully he'll be apprehended soon."

"But until he is—"

"We gotta keep looking over our shoulders."

"We're not the only ones."

He turned her around to face him. "You're frowning. What are you thinking?"

"You're not going to like it."

"Try me."

"We need to warn Moody."

"You're right, I don't like it."

"He sent Ray's innocent brother—"

"*Presumed* innocent brother. Even Moody's not sure."

"Okay, but if Allen Strickland was innocent, Moody is a target for Ray's retribution."

"He's had years to get retribution on Moody. He hasn't."

"My book set all this into motion." When he was about to counter that, she placed her fingertips against his lips. "Don't bother. You know it. I know it. First you, now Gall, were nearly killed because of it. I don't want anyone else to be hurt, Dent. I feel guilty enough already."

He released her and turned away.

"You think I'm wrong?" she asked.

"No, dammit, I think you're *right*. I just hate having to do that guy a favor."

"I understand why you feel that way."

"Thanks for that. What's the 'but'?"

"*But* he owned up to the injustices he did."

"Some of them. He didn't play his ace."

"He might have, if—"

"What?"

"If you hadn't badgered him. I think he withheld it out of stubbornness. He didn't—"

"He didn't want to lose a pissing contest with me."

She just looked at him.

He conceded with a sigh. "Okay, maybe I shouldn't have hit him, but we'd given him plenty of chances to confess his sins before the cigarettes and booze launch him to the Pearly Gates."

"The cigarettes, the booze, or the pistol."

"He did seem to have a love affair going with that thing. Couldn't keep his hands off it." He thought about it for a moment longer, then said grudgingly, "You'd better call Haymaker. Tell him to call Moody and—Why not?" he asked when she shook her head.

"We can use Ray Strickland's attack on Gall as a bargaining chip. Out of the goodness of our hearts—"

She ignored his snort.

"—we'll tell him what happened last night and warn him to beware of Strickland. In exchange, he'll tell us whatever it is he's holding back."

"And you think he'll go for that." Clearly, he was doubtful.

"It's worth a try. We need to know what he knows, Dent."

"Okay, okay. Call the son of a bitch. Lay out your terms."

"I can't call him. I don't know his number. Haymaker used his phone to call him, and took it back as soon as I'd finished talking to Moody."

"Get his number from Haymaker."

"Talking to Moody on the phone won't be as persuasive as being face-to-face with him. We have to go back to his place."

"No. We don't."

"We do. You know we do."

"Bellamy, if he blows his brains out today or tomorrow, or if he waits too long to do it and Strickland gets to him first, I really don't care."

"I don't believe that."

"Believe it."

"Even if you don't care about Moody's fate, you can't get vindication for yourself until you know everything, and you won't know everything unless we convince Moody to give it up."

He held her stare for several moments, and she knew she'd won when he muttered a litany of curses. "All right, we go back," he said. "But one thing, and I mean it."

"What?"

"I'm eating the peach cobbler before we go."

The overcast day made Dale Moody's property look even more forlorn. Cypress tree branches weighted down by the humidity drooped low enough to brush the roof of the sedan as it passed beneath them. The murky lake waters were still and sullen looking.

The cabin itself was empty.

As the car rolled to a stop, Dent had such a bad feeling about it that he made Bellamy wait while he went up the steps, onto the rickety porch, and through the screened door, halfway expecting to find only the remains of the former detective.

But there was no sign of Moody, dead or alive.

"He's not here," he called to Bellamy, who joined him inside the sad dwelling that stank of stale tobacco smoke, mildew, and mice.

"I'm a bit relieved that we didn't find him slumped in that chair with his pistol in his hand," she said.

"Me, too," he admitted.

She glanced behind her through the screened door. "The lake?"

"If he drowned himself, he drove his car into the water. It's not here."

"I hadn't noticed, but you're right."

On the metal TV tray, which seemed to be the focal point of the room and of Moody's life, were the overflowing ashtray and an empty whiskey bottle. "Conspicuously missing is the .357," Dent remarked.

Bellamy went into the kitchen and checked the oven. "Also conspicuously missing is the case file. What do you make of that?"

"That he took his evidence with him and isn't coming back."

The idea came to Rupe as he was trying to eat a bowl of Cream of Wheat, which was about as solid a food as he could manage.

The second morning after taking the beating from Dale Moody, his gums were still puffy and red and hurt like hell from the extensive dental work. His nose was so grotesquely swollen it spread practically from ear to ear and made slits of his eyes. His own kids would have run screaming at the sight of him.

He'd cooked the Cream of Wheat himself, having called the maid the night of the attack and told her to take a few days off. He didn't want anybody to see him like this, not even the person who cleaned his commode.

Making up an excuse that stretched plausibility, he'd had his assistant cancel everything on his calendar, including a day's worth of filming TV commercials and a luncheon for leading businessmen at the governor's mansion. He'd encouraged his wife to stay another week or two at the beach.

Rupe Collier had gone underground.

But as he gingerly masticated the warm cereal, he rethought his position. He could be a victim who crawled into his lair and hid until he was once again presentable, which, according to the cheeky ER doctor, could be as long as two months.

Or he could milk this for all it was worth.

Which, after a day of self-imposed solitude, was an option Rupe found much more appealing.

He looked like a monster, but that was why the drastic change in his appearance would be so effective. Customers and TV viewers who were used to seeing him immaculately dressed and groomed would be outraged over what he'd suffered. Victims of violent crime won sympathy, right? They deserved and often got a soapbox, and when they spoke, people listened. Rather than hide his disfigurement, he would grandstand it. He would make his brutalized face a *cause celebre*.

Excited by the prospects, he fed the remainder of his breakfast to the garbage disposal and went in search of a business card he had planned to throw away, if not shred. Fortunately, he'd done neither. He found it in the satin-lined pocket of his suit jacket. He called the cell-phone number, and it was answered on the second ring.

"Talk to me."

"Mr. Van Durbin? Rupe Collier."

The columnist's disgruntled tone changed, becoming instantly chipper. "I'm still not in the market to buy a car."

"I could make you a good deal on one, but that's not why I'm calling."

"What's on your mind?"

"I've been thinking about our conversation."

"Is that so?"

"Our chat called to mind some *ambiguities* regarding the Susan Lyston case. Elements of it, that I'd rather not have been reminded of, have resurfaced, and I can't stop thinking about them. Especially in light of...." Rupe let that dangle like the carrot it was intended to be.

"In light of what?"

"You'll know when you see me. Are you free?"

Twenty minutes later the *EyeSpy* columnist rang his doorbell, and when he saw Rupe, he exclaimed, "Christ on a crutch!"

It was the astonished reaction Rupe had hoped for. If he got that kind of response from a jaded writer for a sleazy tabloid, think how an average decent person—and potential customer of Collier Motors—would react.

He ushered Van Durbin and his photographer inside, promising the latter that he could take pictures of him after he'd had his talk with Van Durbin. He left the scruffy young man in the den with a cold can of Coke and ESPN on the flat screen, then led Van Durbin into his home study, which was furnished even more lavishly in Texas chic than his office at the dealership.

The writer picked up a silver frame that held a place of honor on the corner of Rupe's desk. "Your wife?"

"A former Miss Texas."

Van Durbin gave an appreciative whistle and returned the frame to its spot as he sat down in a chair facing the desk. He removed his pencil and notepad from the breast pocket of his jacket and quipped, "So, how does the other guy look?"

Rupe formed a reasonable facsimile of a smile, wondering if it looked as distorted as it felt, and figuring that if it did, all the better. "I didn't land a single punch."

"You sold the guy a lemon?"

He and the ER doctor must have attended the same school of comedy. Rupe formed the expected grin, then turned serious. "I wish that was all it amounted to." Leaning back in his chair, he made a steeple of his fingertips and studied his manicure. "I wasn't quite truthful with you before, Mr. Van Durbin."

"Your wife was only first runner-up?"

If Rupe's gums weren't already throbbing, he would have been grinding his teeth. He wanted to squash Van Durbin beneath his boot heel like a cockroach. It was taking a huge amount of self-control to appear contrite.

"When we spoke a few days ago, I was trying to protect the integrity of the Austin Police Department and the honest officers who serve this community."

"Implying that there are some *dishonest* officers serving it as well?" Van Durbin winked. "Let me guess. Dale Moody."

"As you are already aware, he and I worked closely together to indict and convict Allen Strickland. However—"

"I thrive on howevers."

"—there were some...tactics...used during that police investigation which I found off-putting. I turned a blind eye to them. I'm not proud of it, but I was young and ambitious, and I was assured that these, uh..."

"Tactics?"

"Yes. I was assured that they were commonplace and accepted as a part of police work. An unpleasant aspect of the job, perhaps, but excusable because, after all, officers deal with lawless individuals. Often, violence is the only language that violent offenders understand. I was told—"

"By Moody? He's the one telling you all this?"

"That's right. Anytime I asked Dale how he had come by a piece of information during an interrogation, or how he'd obtained an article of evidence, he would dismiss my concerns. The more outspoken I became about his methods, the more truculent he got.

"So," Rupe said, raising his hands in the sign of surrender, "I took the high road. I backed off. I let him conduct his investigation as he saw fit. I concentrated on what I could control, which was preparing the case for trial and representing the state in the courtroom."

Van Durbin squinted at him. "Having second thoughts about Strickland's conviction?"

"Not at all. I did my job. His fate was up to the twelve jurors, not me."

"Then what's this little mea culpa chat about, Rupe?"

"I believe Bellamy Price shares the misgivings I had about Dale Moody's investigation. In her book, the detective's competence and integrity are brought into question."

"So are the prosecutor's."

"She did that for dramatic effect, to create tension and conflict between those two characters. I didn't take it personally. But apparently Dale Moody took offense at the way his character was portrayed, because since you and I spoke the other day, he's come out of hiding."

Van Durbin swiftly added two and two together. "Holy shit! Dale Moody did that to you?"

"Night before last. He jumped me and attacked so viciously I was powerless to defend myself."

"You didn't write *Low Pressure*. Why'd he attack you?"

"Your column. He saw me quoted in it."

"You didn't say anything derogatory about him."

"No, but—"

"He knows you could have."

Rupe didn't respond but made a face that strongly hinted that the writer had guessed correctly. He reached up and touched his bandaged nose. "I think this demonstrates how afraid Moody is that you'll turn up something that could prove to be embarrassing. Possibly criminal," he added in an undertone.

Van Durbin gnawed on the eraser of his pencil as though weighing a decision, then hiked up his hip and withdrew a sheet of paper from his rear pants pocket. He unfolded the square and pushed it across the desk toward Rupe. "Recognize them?"

It was a grainy black-and-white photograph of Bellamy Price leaning over a balcony railing, looking terribly distressed. Behind her was a bare-chested Denton Carter. "Where was this taken? When?"

"Outside Carter's apartment, night before last."

"What was going on between them?"

"Don't I wish I knew," Van Durbin said, bobbing his eyebrows. "But that looks like a bandage around his waist to me. And get a load of his face. Doesn't look as bad as yours, but he'd taken a pounding, too."

When Rupe raised his eyebrow quizzically, Van Durbin shrugged.

"I don't know who, what, when, where, or why." He frowned with malice. "Never got a chance to ask him, either. He sicced the police on me and my photographer."

He relayed what had happened and Rupe laughed in spite of the pain it caused.

Van Durbin scowled. "Funny now. Wasn't then. Took me hours to get my editor on the phone so he could tell them I wasn't a weenie-wagger. The point is, Denton Carter got crosswise with somebody."

"You think it was Moody?"

Van Durbin turned his question around. "What do you think?"

Rupe thoughtfully settled against the back of his chair. "I don't know. If one of them is bearing a grudge against the other, it should be Dent. Moody came down hard on him, and, if not for Dent's alibi, he would have been tried for the crime."

"Wait," Van Durbin said, sitting forward. "Are you saying it could have gone either way? Dent Carter or Strickland?"

Rupe didn't answer, letting the writer draw his own conclusions and hoping to Christ he would catch Rupe's drift without being so smart as to see through the manipulation.

Lowering his voice to a confidential pitch, Van Durbin said, "Doesn't that kinda contradict what you said earlier about second-guessing Strickland's conviction?"

"I said Strickland's fate was in the hands of the jurors."

"But their verdict was based on what you told them, and you told them he was guilty."

"My arguments to that effect were founded on what came from Moody's investigation. Was everything factual? At the time, I accepted it as such."

"Maybe it was."

"Maybe."

"But you're not one hundred percent sure?"

"Moody was under a lot of pressure from his superiors to nail that girl's killer. He'd already put forth one suspect that fizzled. He'd've been made to look like a bumbling fool if his case against Strickland had fallen apart, too. The man was determined to see Strickland convicted."

"By whatever means necessary?"

Again Rupe avoided giving a straight answer. "All I'm saying is that Dale felt the squeeze from city hall, the PD, the almighty Lystons, and Joe Q. Public."

"So he bent rules to produce a culprit."

"I didn't say that."

"But if he's got nothing to hide, why did he attack you?"

Rupe looked pained. "My thought exactly. It's hardly the action of a man who is entirely innocent of wrongdoing. He also threatened me against speaking about this. To you. To anyone. But saying nothing smacks of a cover-up, and I want no part of it."

Van Durbin's ferret nose was practically twitching. As though composing the opening sentence of his next column, he said, "Moody nailed the wrong man, and that innocent young man died bloody in prison."

"You've put words in my mouth that I didn't say, Mr. Van Durbin. If you print that, I'll demand a retraction and sue your newspaper. I hope to God that justice was served," he added piously. "However—"

"There's that word again. It gives me a hard-on."

"If you want an exclusive quote from me, here it is. And this is all I will ever say on the subject: I swear on the heads of my beautiful wife and children that I did my job as prosecutor to the best of my ability, with integrity and a burning desire to see that Susan Lyston got the justice she deserved. I can't speak to the motives or actions of former detective Dale Moody."

"You would have been disappointed."

Dent looked over at Bellamy where she sat in the right-hand co-pilot's seat. She had been quiet throughout most of the flight, and he'd left her to her own thoughts. He figured she was reflecting on her dad's declining condition and how his death would impact her.

But obviously he'd somehow factored into her thoughts, and they were compelling enough for her to have put on the headphones so she could share them with him now.

"Disappointed?"

"If we'd gone through with it last night, you would have been in for a letdown."

"I *was* let down."

"Yes, but not like you would have been if we'd continued." She faced forward again, but he knew that her mind wasn't on the view through the cockpit window. "When I described my marriage to you, you remarked on how boring it sounded."

"I was being a smart-ass."

"Of course you were. But you were right. Except for one thing. My husband wasn't to blame, I was. Through no fault of his own, he became bored with me."

"Okay, I'll bite. Why did he get bored with you?"

"I have issues with intimacy."

"With fucking."

She winced. "That's an aspect of it."

"What's the other aspect?"

She didn't answer, leading him to believe there was no other aspect, but even if there was, this was the one that had caused her marriage to fail, the one that had caused her to freak out on him last night, so this was the aspect that interested him.

"What kind of issues?" he asked. "Other than the use of the word. You don't like it. A lot of people find it offensive, but they still do the deed. So what sent you into orbit last night? I had bad breath? My feet stank?"

"It wasn't anything you did or didn't do. I'm to blame. Let's just leave it at that."

"No, let's not."

"I don't want to talk about it."

"Then why'd you bring it up?"

"To tell you again that I'm sorry it happened."

"Apology accepted. Now tell me why I would have been disappointed. Which I think is total bull crap, by the way. But what makes you think I would have been?"

"Now's not the time to talk about it."

"It's the perfect time. I've got to fly the airplane. So no matter what my reaction is, I can't act on it. You're safe to say anything."

She wrestled with indecision for nearly half a minute, then said, "When Susan—"

"Aw, jeez. I had a feeling this was going to come back to her."

"Everything comes back to her."

"Only because you let it."

"We're discussing this at your insistence. Do you want to continue or not?"

He motioned for her to continue.

"The manner in which Susan died left a lot of people thinking that she had it coming. Even if they didn't say so out loud, it was implied. By the media. The same with close friends. Condolences were sometimes tinged with a reap-what-you-sow undertone. We all sensed it. Daddy, Olivia, Steven, and me.

"One day during the trial, Allen Strickland's defense lawyer came right out and stated that if Susan hadn't been sexually promiscuous, she would still be alive. Rupe Collier objected. He and the defense lawyer got into a shouting match. The judge sternly reprimanded the lawyer, ordered that the comment be stricken from the record, and instructed the jury to disregard it. But the damage had been done.

"Up till then it had only been an insinuation which we—the family—had publicly ignored. But once it was put into actual words, we could no longer pretend that each of us hadn't entertained similar thoughts.

"And owning up to such disloyalty toward Susan was painful for all of us. Olivia broke down and sobbed for hours. Daddy drank heavily that night, and that's the only time I've ever seen him overindulge. Steven withdrew to his room without saying a word to anyone.

"And I..." She paused and took a deep breath. "I also locked myself in my room where, after hours of tearful contemplation, I concluded that the source of all this grief was Susan's sexuality.

"She didn't deserve to die because of it, but none of us would be suffering as we were if she hadn't given in to sexual impulses. Ergo, they had to be bad. Dirty. Destructive. That's the conclusion I reached."

She smiled wryly. "This at a time when I was going through puberty and beginning to experience the kinds of mysterious and uncontrollable yearnings that had cost Susan her life. I thought I would be destined to end like her if I surrendered to them. Instead I resolved to deny them. I pledged not to become like my sister."

A dozen different responses instantly came to his mind, but all were crude, inappropriate, and insulting to Susan. He chose the safer option and kept them to himself.

"During high school, I developed mad crushes on a few boys and did my fair share of dating, but—to counter Susan and her reputation—I kept my virginity. Through college and young adulthood, I slept with the occasional guy, but I didn't let myself have fun in bed, so my partners rarely did. As I got older, I got better at the pretense, but men must sense when a woman isn't really into it."

She glanced at him, but, again, he prudently said nothing.

"My husband never questioned my reserve, before or after we married, although he felt it. I never turned him down, but I wasn't, hmm, adventurous. Maybe he hoped he could eventually overcome whatever hang-ups were keeping me from enjoying him as I should. But it never happened, and I suppose he tired of trying to force it. Losing our baby was just the last of his disappointments in me."

A few seconds elapsed, then she looked over at him. "There. Now that you know, you should feel better about last night. It had nothing to do with you or your technique."

He waited until he was certain that she was finished, then he said, "Let me get this straight. At twelve years old, you made this stupid pledge to deny your own sexuality, and you've spent the past eighteen years trying to uphold that vow?"

"No, Dent," she said sadly. "I've spent eighteen years trying to break it."

Chapter 22

By turns, Ray was enraged and nervous.

The man at the airfield had made a fool of him.

He must've looked real stupid to the old codger, when
he'd thought he was being so clever.

He was aware of his limitations. In high school, he'
been told he read below a second-grade level. That wa
okay. He could live with that. But it stung deep to b
exposed as a complete imbecile.

By now Dent and Bellamy would have heard the stor
of how he'd walked—charged—right into the carefull
laid trap. Ray imagined the old man wiping tears from hi
eyes, slapping his knee with hilarity as he told them, "H
came running in here and stabbed a slab of rubber. Wha
a jackass."

They would have had a good laugh at his expense
Instead of being scared of him, they'd regard him a
a clumsy buffoon. The thought of that infuriated him
Mostly, though, he was mad at himself. He hadn't don
Allen proud.

He needed to fix that.

And that was what made him nervous, because he wasn't sure what he should do next.

Once he'd put some distance between him and the airfield, he'd switched his truck's license plates with those of another pickup he found at a twenty-four-hour Walmart. He'd put on a straw cowboy hat so that his near-bald head wouldn't be so noticeable. He'd swapped out his leather vest for a shirt with long sleeves that would cover up his snake tattoo. The old man couldn't have seen it because it had been too dark inside the hangar, but Dent Carter might have noticed it when he jumped him at the IHOP. It made Ray easily identifiable.

He hated having to cover it. Like some people felt about wearing a cross on a chain around their neck, or carrying a rabbit's foot for good luck, Ray believed that his snake tattoo gave him special powers. He felt stronger and smarter every time he looked at it or touched it.

Afraid to stay in his apartment in case the police came looking for him there, he'd driven around all day, no destination in mind, never stopping for long, just keeping on the move. All the same, he felt trapped, like things were closing in on him.

But by damn, he couldn't get caught until Bellamy Price was dead. So anything he did now had to count, and it had to count big. He must be bold.

"Take the bull by the horns." That was what Allen would advise.

With his brother's words of wisdom echoing inside his head, he took the next exit off I-35 and made a U-turn beneath the overpass, reentering the freeway in the northbound lanes.

He knew what he had to do, and it didn't have to be fancy.

Feeling much more confident now, he rolled up his shirt-sleeve and placed his exposed left arm in the open window of his truck, practically daring anyone to mess with him.

Right off, Gall sensed the tension between Dent and Bellamy.

No sooner had her toe touched the tarmac than she excused herself to call her stepmother. Gall watched her enter the hangar, then turned to Dent, who was coming down the steps of the airplane.

"How was your flight?"

"Fine."

Gall patted the side of the airplane. "This puppy practically flies herself, doesn't she?"

"No airplane flies itself."

"Just saying."

"You've said it. I'd be crazy not to hire on with this guy."

"As I said, I'm just saying." Gall motioned toward the hangar. "What's with her?"

"Bellamy?"

"No, the Queen of Sheba. Who do you think?"

Dent glanced in her direction. "The news from Houston isn't good."

"That explains it." After a beat, he asked, "What's with *you*?"

"With me? Nothing."

"Something."

Dent took off his sunglasses and rubbed his eyes with the back of his hand. "I'm tired, is all."

"Pull my other leg."

"All right." He folded down the stems of his glasses and slipped them into his shirt pocket. "I'm tired of your questions." He started for the hangar. "Got any coffee?"

"Don't I always?"

"Yeah, and it always sucks."

"You've never complained before."

"I'm too nice."

Gall harrumphed. "Nice you ain't."

Dent muttered, "So I've recently been told."

"She's not making it with you, is she?"

Dent stopped and came around, his eyes throwing daggers.

Gall took his cigar from his mouth and shook his head with bafflement. "This ain't like you, Ace."

"Don't go thinking I've lost my touch. She says no, it's her problem."

"Not what I meant."

"Then what did you mean?"

"A woman says no, it ain't like you to give a flip."

Dent opened his mouth, but closed it before saying anything. Then he started toward the hangar again.

Gall said, "I'll brew you a fresh pot."

Dent called back, "I'll brew it myself."

By the time Gall had secured the senator's airplane and rejoined them, Dent was foisting a mug of steaming coffee onto Bellamy. Using both hands, she took the over-sized mug, looked into it, but didn't drink from it.

"How's your daddy?" Gall asked.

"No change. Still not good."

"Sorry."

She gave him a bleak smile. "I appreciate your asking."

Dent, sipping his coffee, motioned toward his airplane. "Where'd you lay out the dummy?"

"Behind the left wheel. But the real dummy was that idiot."

"You don't have to be smart to be dangerous," Dent said. "The man who attacked me has a lot of rage inside him. I felt it. Heard back from the sheriff's deputy?"

"He left a voice mail on the hangar phone. It was Ray Strickland, all right. They ran the plates on the pickup. But when a state trooper stopped a small pickup with those plates, it wasn't Strickland driving. It was a young black woman, college student, dean's list, works part time at Walmart. No police record, nary a blemish on her good name, and she'd never heard of Strickland."

"Ray switched the plates."

"Seems like. So they're looking for a truck with this college kid's plates now."

"Is Ray employed?"

"At a glass works of some kind out on the east side. According to the deputy, they checked there, and Ray's foreman said he hasn't reported to work for several days. Not answering his cell phone. He's not at his house, either."

"Whereabouts unknown," Dent said.

"You got it."

"No sign of . . . the other?"

Gall, realizing that Dent was referring to Bellamy's fan Jerry, cast a look in her direction, but she seemed to be lost in her own thoughts. They must've been troubling. Her brow was furrowed, her eyes staring vacantly.

"Naw," Gall said to Dent. "All the same, you two gotta be careful."

"Planning on it."

"What else are you planning?"

"Moody was pretty straightforward with us, but he fell short of making a full confession. He didn't tell us *the* thing that might have made a difference in the outcome of the case. We need to talk to Rupe Collier."

Gall spat a chunk of cigar to the floor. "It might not mean doodle-dee-squat, but Rupe was on TV today. Caught his show while I was still at my lady's place."

"His show?"

"He wasn't hawking cars, but conducting a press conference."

"What?" Dent exclaimed.

Bellamy suddenly came to life. "Talking about what?"

"About how his face got fucked up. Not in those words, of course. But Ace here can't hold a candle to how bad Rupe looked." He gave them a description. "He claimed not to have got a good look at his attacker and was vague about where the assault had taken place, but he played the victim angle up big. You ask me, the timing of this is fishy."

"It stinks to high heaven." Dent turned to Bellamy. "We need to have a heart-to-heart with the former ADA. Do you know where his office is?"

"His flagship dealership. That's where I met with him."

"He whipped the media into a frenzy during that press conference," Gall told them. "That car lot is surrounded by reporters hoping to grab another sound bite or two, which Rupe is good at. You couldn't get anywhere close without them swamping you, too."

"That leaves his house," Bellamy said quietly. When he and Dent turned to her, she added, "I know where he lives."

*   *   *

"No wonder you know his address," Dent said as he turned onto the street. "You hail from the same ritzy neighborhood."

The Lystons' estate where she'd grown up was several streets over. "Don't hold that against me."

"You ever been inside Rupe's place?"

She shook her head. "After Strickland's conviction, my parents were invited to his Christmas open house three years in a row. They declined each time, and I guess he and his wife finally got the message, because the invitations stopped coming."

Rupert Collier's limestone house sat on a rise of sprawling lawn with well-tended grass, centuries-old live oak trees, and lush flower beds. Parked at the curb in front of it was an Austin PD squad car.

Dent asked, "What do you think?"

"They're probably here to discourage the media from storming the castle." She gave it a moment's thought, then said, "I have an idea. Pull up and get out like we're expected."

He parked at the curb directly behind the police car. As soon as he cut his engine, two officers alighted and approached their car from each side.

"Your idea doesn't include jail time, does it?" he asked.

"I hope not." She pushed open her car door and got out, smiling brightly at the policemen. "Hello. We're here to see Mr. Collier."

One of the officers said, "Sorry, ma'am. His house is off limits to visitors."

"But we have an appointment."

"You media?"

"Hardly," she said around a light laugh. "We're personal acquaintances."

One officer squinted at her, looking more closely. "Aren't you the lady who wrote the book?"

"That's right. Mr. Collier helped me when I was researching the legal aspects of it."

The two officers exchanged a look across the hood of her sedan. The one standing nearer to Dent stared into his face as though trying to see past the dark lenses of his sunglasses so he could determine the reason for the bruises. Dent acted supremely unfazed by the scrutiny.

Turning back to address her, the cop said, "Mr. Collier didn't mention to us that he expected anybody this evening."

"Well in light of his getting beat up, our appointment might have slipped his mind. Wasn't that just awful?" She flattened her hand against her chest. "I hope y'all catch the person who assaulted him."

"You can bet we will, ma'am."

"Oh, I have no doubt of it. In any case, I'm sure Rupe... uh, Mr. Collier... will want to see us. In fact, he asked for the meeting. I have some vital information for him about Dale Moody and Jim Postlewhite."

Dent, who was standing in the open wedge of the driver's door, jerked his head in her direction, but his surprised reaction went unnoticed by the two police officers, who were fixated on her.

One gave his partner an inquisitive look, and when his partner said, "Better let him know," the first said, "Wait here," and started up the walk toward the house.

Bellamy smiled up at the other, the one who'd recognized her. "Have you read *Low Pressure*?"

"My wife bought it when she read that it was based on a true crime that occurred here. Must be good. She hasn't put it down since she started it."

Bellamy smiled. "I'm glad to hear that."

While engaged in this conversation, she was also well aware of the one taking place at the front door of Rupe's house. After a brief exchange, the officer made a gesture as though tipping his hat to Rupe, then he turned away from the door and motioned them forward. "He says it's okay."

After thanking the officer with whom she'd been chatting, Bellamy went around the hood of the car, and she and Dent started up the walk. Under his breath, he asked, "When did you become an eyelash-batting, breathless Texas belle?"

"When I needed to."

"Why haven't you ever tried it on me?"

"Because I didn't need to."

"And who the hell is Jim Postlewhite?"

"Trust me."

That was all she had time to say. They were now within earshot of the front door, where Rupe Collier stood waiting. The damage done to his face was so extensive that if he hadn't peeled back his swollen lips and smiled, he would have been unrecognizable. The teeth were unmistakable even rooted in red, puffy gums.

"Well, well, look who the cat dragged in!" The false bonhomie was for the benefit of the police officer, who stood aside for Bellamy and Dent so they could proceed across the threshold and into the two-story vestibule. "Thank you, Officer."

Rupe waved him off and closed the front door, then turned to them, his smile still in place. "You thought I'd be angry, didn't you? Fit to be tied that you finagled your way in here?" Laughing, he shook his head. "Actually, I'm tickled to see you. Come in."

He walked past them and motioned that they follow. The hallway was wide and long and dotted with area rugs of marginal quality. From the vaulted ceiling hung three massive chandeliers better suited to a Spanish castle. The rooms they walked past were ostentatiously decorated.

Finally they arrived at a den that was more tastefully furnished and actually looked like it was lived in rather than there just for show. It had a wall of windows overlooking a limestone terrace and a sparkling swimming pool with a fountain in its center.

Rupe motioned them toward a sofa. "Have a seat."

They sat down side by side. On the coffee table in front of them lay today's issue of *EyeSpy*. The picture of them taken on the apartment-building balcony comprised one-third of the front page.

"Worth a thousand words. At least," Rupe said.

Bellamy tried to appear unaffected by both the photo and his remark, which was difficult to do when he was wearing a hyena's grin and bobbing his eyebrows suggestively.

"My wife is out of town, and I gave the housekeeper time off, so I can't offer you anything except a cold drink."

"No, thank you."

Dent, whose jaw looked carved of granite, shook his head.

Rupe sat in an easy chair adjacent to the sofa. He said to Bellamy, "Congratulations on your best seller."

"I doubt that you're that happy about it."

"Why wouldn't I be?"

She stared him down, saying nothing.

Eventually his smile turned sheepish. "Okay, I was a little put off that you didn't portray the ADA as a more dashing figure, especially since I'd granted you an interview while you were writing the book. The prosecutor should've been the hero. He brought the criminal to justice."

Speaking for the first time, Dent said, "Did he?"

Rupe's sly gaze slid over to him. "I thought I did." He leaned forward slightly. "Or are you ready to confess? Did you come here today to bring me Susan's panties?" Dent was off the sofa like a shot, but Bellamy grabbed a handful of his shirttail and pulled him back down.

The car dealer laughed. "I see you're still a hothead with a short fuse. Not that I'm surprised. Leopards don't change their spots. What'd you do, lose your temper in the cockpit? Is that why you almost crashed that airliner?"

Bellamy jumped in before Dent could respond. "That you even asked Dent if he wants to confess is an indication that you weren't convinced of Allen Strickland's guilt."

Rupe leaned back in his chair and placed his hands on the padded armrests, as relaxed and confident as a potentate on his throne. "Sure I was."

"Was Detective Moody?"

Rupe snuffled with disgust. "He might've been if he'd been thinking with a clear head." Looking at Dent, he said, "You should know better than me what a drunken brute he was. The screwdriver? He told me about that. And not with remorse." Shaking his head sadly, he said, "The man was a blight on our fine police force."

"Which makes one wonder why he was assigned to be the lead investigator of my sister's case."

"I wondered that myself. Because, from the beginning, Moody botched the investigation. Several times I requested that he be replaced by someone more competent. Sober, at least. My requests were denied."

"Were you given a reason?"

"Bureaucratic politics. That's what I was told, anyway."

Bellamy knew with certainty that he was lying. He wasn't as good at it as he probably thought himself to be. She didn't counter any of his statements, figuring that if she gave him enough rope he would hang himself. On the other hand, they could dance this dance all night. His smugness was beginning to grate.

"Dent and I met with Dale Moody yesterday."

He blinked several times but quickly recovered. "Here in Austin?"

Ignoring the question, she said, "He's a troubled man."

"Shocker."

"He had quite a bit to say about you."

"I'm surprised that he was sober enough to talk."

"He made himself understood. He owned up to some unethical behavior."

"Did he now? Did he also own up to this?" He pointed to his face.

Bellamy was taken aback, although, given the rancor with which Moody had spoken of his former cohort, she shouldn't have been. What surprised her was that Moody hadn't told them himself.

"Surprise attack," Rupe continued. "He came at me from out of nowhere. I hadn't had any contact with him since he quit the department and left Austin. All of a sudden, *Bam!* He's trying to send my nose out the back of my skull."

"What provoked him to do it?"

"Your book. Didn't he tell you? He didn't take kindly to it. He didn't like how the investigating officer in your story came across. He also didn't like that I'd granted an interview to Rocky Van Durbin. But why shouldn't I? I've got nothing to hide," he said, spreading his arms wide.

"Apparently Dale Moody does. When he read Van Durbin's interview with me, he got incensed. Crawled out from whatever rock he's been hiding under, sought me out, beat me up, and left me with a warning."

"Which was?"

"To keep my mouth shut about the Susan Lyston case and everything associated with it. You probably received the same warning."

"Actually I didn't," Bellamy said.

"Hmm. Well, I guess he thought you said all you had to say about it in your book." He looked at Dent. "Were you in on the meeting between them?"

"Yeah, I was there."

"Huh. Judging by the looks of you, Moody didn't roll out the welcome mat."

"Oh, you mean this?" Dent lightly ran his finger over one of the gashes on his face. "Moody didn't do this. Ray Strickland did."

Rupe's head went back several inches. "*Ray* Strickland? Allen's brother? No shit? Pardon the French, Ms. Price." Back to Dent. "Last I heard, he'd been in a terrible car wreck. Almost killed him."

"He's very much alive."

"Where did you connect with him?"

"In the parking lot of an IHOP."

"No, seriously."

"In the parking lot of an IHOP," Dent repeated, dead-pan. "He's holding a grudge."

"Against you?"

"Against everybody, is my guess. I'd watch my back if I were you, Rupe."

"What'd I do?"

"You sent his brother to prison, and he died there. The man's mad, and he's mean."

"He's mad." Rupe looked at Bellamy and smirked. "Well *that* doesn't surprise me. Your book got a lot of people riled, didn't it? If you had it to do over again, would you write about your sister's murder?"

She didn't deign to answer. "Tell me about Jim Postlewhite."

"You mentioned that name to the cop outside. Who is he?"

"He *was* a Lyston Electronics employee. Head of the trucking fleet. He was Allen Strickland's boss."

"You said 'was.'"

"He's deceased."

Rupe shrugged. "The name doesn't ring a bell, and remembering names is one of my strengths."

"Search your memory."

"Sorry, the name means nothing to me."

"It meant something to Dale Moody."

"Then you should be asking him."

"I intend to." She tilted her head to one side. "What was it that convinced Moody of Allen Strickland's innocence?"

"If he was convinced of Strickland's innocence, that's news to me."

"Is it?"

"If Moody was convinced otherwise, why did he give me everything I needed to win a conviction?"

"You didn't apply any pressure?" Dent asked. "No arm-twisting involved?"

"Not everyone has your hoodlum mentality."

"What about Ray Strickland's auto accident?" Bellamy asked.

"What about it?"

"Moody says you staged it to keep him from testifying in his brother's defense."

Rupe sputtered a laugh. Then he leaned forward from the waist and said, "Moody has drunk a lot of whiskey. He's delusional." Then his eyes narrowed on them. "What is this, anyway? Why the third degree? Surely you're not taking the word of that burned-out cop over mine. If you are, you're making fools of yourselves. My slate is clean. I only did my duty and carried out the law of the land."

"Try selling that to Ray Strickland before he guts you."

Rupe shot Dent a fulminating look, then came back to Bellamy. "Turning the tables here, mind if I ask you something?"

She gave a small nod of consent.

"You took license with every character in your book, including your sister. No offense, but Moody and I learned things about her that'd make a sailor blush. She was a little more...*worldly*...than you made her out to be in the novel." He looked at Dent and winked. "Am I right?"

"Go fuck yourself."

Rupe only laughed. Going back to Bellamy, he said, "I just wondered, by painting her purer than she was, were you being respectful of the dead, or just naive?"

"I portrayed her the way I remember her."

"Really?"

"Yes."

"Come on, now, you can tell me. Just between us," he said, winking again, "did you love her all that much? Or even like her? Weren't you just an itsy-bitsy bit jealous of her?"

"Where are you going with this?" she asked coolly.

"Nowhere. Just thinking out loud." He thoughtfully tapped his fingertips against his lips. "If you'd been a little older at the time, I'd have wanted to know exactly where you were when she was killed."

Bellamy realized he was only baiting her, but it was working. Her palms were damp when she slid the strap of her bag onto her shoulder and stood up. Dent stood up with her and placed his hand on her elbow as though sensing her unsteadiness.

She said to Rupe, "We won't take up any more of your time."

"Not a problem." Looking very pleased with himself for having derailed them, he slapped the armrests of his chair as he pulled himself out of it.

He followed them from the room and down the hallway. He opened the front door and, with a flourish, motioned them through it. "Don't be a stranger."

Bellamy stepped over the threshold, then turned back. "Moody has drunk a lot of whiskey, but when he was more sober, he took extensive notes, especially during his investigation into my sister's death."

"That's right, he did," Rupe said. "He was known for his note-taking. But, along with all the documents and such, Moody's notes went into the case file, which—"

"He copied. Before you had the original destroyed."

Chapter 23

"**W**here did you come up with this Postlewhite?"

Dent had been itching to ask her, but he'd waited until they were in her car. Per usual, he had insisted on driving.

"Yesterday, when I scanned that page in Moody's file, the name registered with me because it was starred on the original and underscored in red on the copy. I meant to ask what that signified but got distracted by everything else he was telling us and never went back to it. It occurred to me that if it was noteworthy to Moody, it might be to Rupe."

"Good move, A.k.a. You said 'Postlewhite' and Rupe looked ready to hurl."

"He definitely paled beneath his bruises."

"I only glanced at that sheet in Moody's file, but there were all kinds of scribbles on it. Notes. Names. How did you remember Postlewhite's?"

"Well, beyond it being starred and underlined, I remember him. One day when I was visiting Daddy at work, he came into the office to leave some paperwork. After being introduced, he told me to call him Mr. P. and made a big deal of my being there, treated me like an honored guest, talked to me about school, asked me what my favorite subject was. Like that."

"He took notice of you."

"At a time in my life when few people did. I never forgot his kindness. I saw him from a distance at the barbecue. He waved at me. He was a nice man."

"I doubt that's why Moody put a star next to his name. Any idea?"

"None. But I think Rupe knows."

"I'd bet money on it." Coming to a stop sign at the intersection, he asked if she wanted to stop at her parents' house. "While we're in the neighborhood."

"Would you mind? When I moved into my house, I left some dress clothes behind to be packed up later." Looking sorrowful, she added, "I'll need them soon."

When they pulled up to the gate, she gave him the code and he punched it in. As he followed the driveway up to the house, he said, "Place hasn't changed much. Still makes me feel like I need to pull around to the rear, so if it's all the same to you I'll wait in the car."

"I won't be long."

She rang the bell and was greeted by a uniformed housekeeper, who peered around Bellamy to curiously scope him out. She asked something, Bellamy replied, then the two went inside. In under ten minutes, Bellamy came out carrying a suitcase. He got out and helped her place it in the backseat.

"Different housekeeper from the one I remember," he said.

"Helena has been working for my parents for about ten years. She's very concerned about Daddy. Olivia's keeping her updated, but I also promised to call her as soon as I heard anything."

"Where to now?"

"Haymaker."

"I agree. We need to get Moody's cell-phone number out of him."

"He'll be reluctant to give it to us."

"My hoodlum mentality may come in handy."

She smiled. "I'm going to depend on it."

"Long drive from here to his place. Call first, see if he's there."

"That would warn him that we're on the way."

"Not if you hang up when he answers." He passed his phone to her. "Use mine. No name shows up."

Before leaving Haymaker the day before, they had obtained his land-line number as well as that of his cell phone. Bellamy called each of them twice but got voice mail on both. "So now what?" she asked, visibly frustrated.

"We fall back and regroup."

Ray complimented himself on his stamina and self-discipline.

He'd been inside Bellamy Price's closet for going on five hours, patiently waiting for her to come home. He didn't know when that might be, but she had to return eventually. Whenever that was, he would be ready, physically and mentally.

Getting into her house had been easy, the only challenge being to kick a curious cat out of the way as he'd slipped in through an unlocked window partially concealed by a tall shrub. The house was silent and empty and smelled of cleaners and fresh paint.

The message he'd left on her wall had been painted over, which didn't bother him much. That had been a dumb idea. This time he had something better in store. Her walls may get streaked with red, but it wouldn't be paint.

Before taking up his post in her closet, he'd opened her bureau drawers and played with some of her underthings. Just for the heck of it, just because he could, just because it gave him a naughty thrill that would have shocked a snooty rich girl like her.

He wasn't around women much, and none he'd ever been with had worn stuff this nice. He'd liked the feel of her silky, lacy things against his face, his snake tattoo, his belly. But after a time, he'd reluctantly refolded everything he'd handled, put the articles back as they'd been, and closed the drawers.

He'd considered hiding beneath the bed, then opted for the walk-in closet. He would have better mobility. She would open the double louvered doors and there he would be.

"Surprise!" Saying it in a stage whisper, he'd practiced his lunge several times.

Her closet smelled even better than the sachets he'd found in her chest of drawers. It smelled like perfume. He held one of her blouses to his face and breathed deeply. But he hadn't wasted a lot of time on that indulgence, knowing that he must psyche himself up for what he had to do.

To prep himself, he'd flexed and extended his fingers. He'd done some curls with his left arm and made wide circles with it to loosen his rotator cuff. He'd cracked his neck, stretched his spine, and rolled his shoulders. He'd gone through these exercises every twenty minutes to keep himself limber and alert.

He'd left the closet only once when he'd had to pee. He'd gotten a kick out of unzipping and exposing himself in her bathroom. He'd watched himself in her mirror as he stroked and squeezed. "How do you like that monster, missy?" He thrust his hips toward the mirror. But as fun as it had been to imagine her reaction to such aggressiveness, he'd done the smart thing by zipping up and returning to his hiding place.

Night had fallen, but his eyes had adjusted gradually to the deepening darkness, so he hadn't minded staying in the closet with the door closed. Patiently he'd waited. Another hour passed. Then two. He'd routinely done his exercises to keep his body revved and his mind as sharp as the blade of his knife.

He'd waited.

And now, he heard a key turning in the front door latch.

"The painter must have been here," Bellamy said as she pushed open her front door and stepped inside. "I can smell the fumes."

Dent followed her in, carrying her suitcase, which he set just inside the front door. "Will the odor bother you?"

"As tired as I am, nothing could keep me up tonight. But I do want to make a run at Haymaker first thing in the morning."

"I'll check upstairs."

He started up, but she stopped him. "The painter's been here. The locksmith secured the house. I'm sure it's okay. Don't bother. Thank you for seeing me in."

"I didn't just see you in. With that knife freak on the loose, no way am I leaving you here alone tonight."

"I'll be fine."

He studied her for several seconds, then came down the steps slowly. "You throwing me out?"

"Spare me the wounded-puppy eyes."

"What kind of eyes would you prefer?"

"Spare me that, too."

"What?"

"The flirting. Sexy smile. Smoky eyes. Tone of voice." She sighed. "Didn't you understand what I was telling you today?"

"Be more specific."

"What I told you on the flight back."

"You're not having sex with me."

"That's right. So you should just say good night and leave."

"You really want me to go?"

"Yes, I do."

"I can't."

"Can't?"

"My car is locked inside your garage."

Chagrined, she tipped her head forward and let several moments elapse. Then, "Follow me."

She led him into the kitchen, where she unlocked the door that opened into the garage. Reaching around the jamb, she hit the button on the wall, and the motor for the overhead door engaged.

When it was up, she turned back to him. "There. You're free to go." But he didn't move. He waited her out until she stopped glancing about at anything and everything else before finally garnering the courage to look him in the eye. "We've already talked about this, Dent."

"We didn't finish the talk."

"I did."

"Without giving me a chance to counter."

"You don't get to counter, because it's not an argument. I told you from the start that you and I...that it wasn't going to happen. Ever."

"Using Susan as your excuse."

"Susan wasn't an excuse, she—"

"Was a slut. And out of some backward sense of obligation or balance or whatever, you're denying your own sexual inclinations."

She placed her hands on her hips. "And you believe that my *inclinations* will just naturally lead me to you."

"They did last night."

She dropped her arms back to her sides. "That was—"

"I know what it was, and it was too wet to have been faked."

She wished her blush wouldn't give away her embarrassment. But she didn't mind revealing her anger. "Are you waiting to be thanked? Congratulated? What? Is your ego—"

"Don't turn this around and make it about me," he said, raising his voice to match hers. "My ego's fine."

"How well I know. I'm sure your other women—"

"This isn't about them, either. This is about you. About why you have this sad and lonely thing going when—"

"I?" she exclaimed. "*I'm* sad and lonely? Have you looked at *your* life lately? You have one friend. *One*," she emphasized, holding up her index finger. "You sleep with women whose names you don't know. You live in a shabby rathole. And you dare to describe my life as sad and lonely?"

His head went back as though she'd struck him. "Oh, that's good. Play that card."

"Card?"

"That Lyston card. That rich-people card. That you're-shit-on-my-shoes card. Maybe I should've driven around to the delivery entrance of your mansion."

She pushed him out of her way as she stormed past. "I'll close the garage door later. Right now, I'm going upstairs. I want you out of here by the time I come back down."

She made it as far as the staircase before he overtook her and planted himself between her and the first step. He said, "Nice try, but it's not going to work."

"I don't know what you're talking about."

"Yeah, you do. You're trying to piss me off so I'll go away mad and we won't continue talking about what we need to talk about."

"We don't *need* to talk about anything. We're *not* going to talk about anything. Will you please just *go*?"

"Uh-uh. No soap. The subject is still you and your hang-ups."

"You don't care about my hang-ups. You just want a warm body to sleep with tonight."

"Okay. I admit it. I want to sleep with *your* warm body. But whether or not you go to bed with me, this still needs to be said."

She folded her arms across her middle. "All right, what? The abridged version, please, so you can get out of here." She hoped her stance, her tone, would either discourage or anger him enough to leave.

Instead he stayed, moved a step closer in fact, and spoke softly. "Take it from a man who's touched you inside and out, there's nothing wrong with you, except that you won't believe there isn't."

She swallowed, but said nothing.

"I don't know what went on the mind of the twelve-year-old Bellamy Lyston, but you, the woman, need to scrub all that crap about not following the same path to destruction that Susan took.

"If your marriage was boring and the sex needed CPR, your unimaginative husband has to bear at least fifty percent of the responsibility, because if he'd got you to respond the way you responded to me last night, he wouldn't have been bored. Because it was a turn-on just to watch. To feel. And, frankly, I think he's an asshole for allowing you to assume all the blame for the failure of the marriage."

She found enough voice to speak. "He didn't know that I did."

"Don't kid yourself. He knew. And in his mind, you're also to blame for his affair."

"Why do you think that?"

"I don't *think*, I *know*. And the reason I know is because I'm a guy. And when we go out and do whatever we damn well please with our dick, we justify it by telling ourselves and anybody else who'll listen that 'She has only herself to blame. If only she'd done this, if only she'd done that. But she didn't, so she left me with no choice except to get my jollies between another pair of thighs.' A lot of women buy into that. Don't. Because it's total horseshit. But that's getting us off the track."

"There is no track."

"There's a track. And it's this: You buttoned yourself up at the age of twelve, and that's a shame. Because the fact is that you're beautiful, talented, and so damn smart it's scary sometimes. You are also sexy as all get-out."

"Thank you for the outpouring of compliments, but

I'm still not sleeping with you." She turned her back on him. Or tried to. He kept her where she was by placing a gentle hand on her shoulder.

"You're sexy, mostly because you're unaware of it. That thing you do with your teeth and lower lip?"

"I don't do anything—"

"You do it all the time. You bite it. Right here." He placed the pad of his thumb in the center of her lower lip, and it caused a tingle down low.

"Oh, yeah, A.k.a. Sexy as hell. You never see it, but your ass turns heads. In those jeans, it's practically given me whiplash. Don't even get me started on your freckles."

"You can't see them. I use concealer."

"And I like you."

The wooing didn't surprise her. This was Dent Carter, after all. But that declaration stunned her, and, seeing her reaction, he laughed lightly.

"Shocks the hell out of me, too. I didn't expect to like you, because you're a Lyston. But…" He paused as his gaze roved over her face, taking in the features of her face one at a time. "You're okay," he said in a low, throaty voice.

For only a moment, she was susceptible to those eyes, his words, his face, which was never far from her mind and hadn't been for years. Then she drew herself together and remembered why they were engaged in this conversation.

"You're just talking pretty to get me into bed."

"Well, sure." He flashed his dirtiest grin, then sobered. "But I also happen to mean everything I said. I'm saying it more for your good than mine, and I rarely do anything unselfishly."

Maybe it was that admission that kept her there, still

and expectant, when she should have moved away. But she didn't. So he put his arms around her and drew her close, and, oh my God, it felt good.

It felt even better when he slid his hands down over her bottom and applied enough pressure to mold her to him. The way their bodies meshed made her knees weak.

"This is purely unselfish on your part?" she murmured.

Laughing softly, he nuzzled her ear. "Not this, no. Feel how well we fit? Damn. No way in hell could you be a letdown."

He felt it immediately. She'd been molding herself to him, making adjustments that put his control in jeopardy.

And in the next instant she went as rigid as a flagpole. Her hands pushed against his chest to break the embrace, and when she backed away, her eyes were as wide as saucers.

"What did you say?" she asked in a hoarse voice.

Dent couldn't account for her sudden withdrawal, or for the way she was looking at him. At a loss, he held his arms out to his sides. "What?"

"You said ... you said ... I couldn't be a *letdown*. That's what you said. Specifically. A letdown. Why did you use that particular word?"

"Because that's the word you used earlier today. I was merely repeating—"

"No, wait!" She pressed the heels of her hands to her temples as though trying to squeeze out a thought. Or perhaps to keep an unwelcome one inside, and the possibility of that made him slightly queasy.

"Bellamy ..." He took a step toward her, but she stuck out her hand to halt him.

"You used that word because Susan used it." Her eyes were on him, but they were seeing something else, someone else. "She said it at the barbecue. At the boathouse. During your argument."

He hadn't remembered the exact terminology Susan had used, but the memory that had just worked itself free of Bellamy's subconscious was a bad one, one that he'd hoped she would never regain. His heartbeat spiked, but he played it calmly and coolly, played it dumb. "I don't remember what she said."

"Yes you do!" she cried shrilly. "You remember. That's why you refused to talk about it night before last at your apartment. I knew you were holding something back." She covered her mouth with her hands and closed her eyes. "I remember. Oh God, I remember now what you wanted to keep from me."

Her breaths started coming in harsh gasps. "You and Susan were in the throes of your argument. You were trying to placate her, to kiss and make up, but Susan was furious. She said...she said that if you wanted to fuck a Lyston girl, you could go fuck...me." She sucked in a breath so hard she winced with the pain of it. "Then she said, 'Of course since you've had me, Bellamy will be a huge letdown.'"

She'd used that word today, so for all these years it must have been there in the back of her mind just waiting to be triggered. He cursed himself for being the one to do it. He hoped to heaven her recollection would stop there. "Who gives a damn what Susan said?"

But Bellamy seemed not to hear him. She was back at the boathouse, listening to her sister mocking her. "After saying that, she laughed. She smiled that smile that Steven remembers and described to us so well. That triumphant smile. That's when you left her."

She focused on him, seeking verification. Reluctantly, he nodded. "I couldn't stand the sight of her for one second longer. I wheeled my motorcycle around and was about to ride off. That's when I spotted you crouching there in the bushes. I knew you must have overheard what she'd said, and my gut sank. She always treated you like dirt. And you were—"

"Pathetic."

"I wasn't going to say that, but you were an easy target for her ridicule. It was an awful thing for her to say, in any case. But it was especially mean because she knew you were there and would overhear it."

"Yes, I'm sure she got double pleasure out of taunting you and humiliating me."

He watched her eyes, noting the shifting emotions they revealed. One second she looked abject and lost, like the awkward and insecure pre-adolescent who had been so cruelly insulted. Next, her eyes reflected the bewilderment she felt over that cruelty and the heartless nature of a sister who could inflict it. Finally, her blue eyes began to shimmer with tears of fury.

He'd watched from astride his motorcycle as the same transformation had taken place in the eyes of the twelve-year-old Bellamy.

Quietly, he said, "You had every right to hate her."

"Oh, I did." Her voice vibrated with the intensity of her hatred. Her hands closed into tight fists. "Knowing that I had a hopeless crush on you, she deliberately said the most hurtful thing possible. It was evil of her. I despised her. I wanted to claw her eyes out. I wanted to—"

He knew the instant the thought struck her, because he looked stricken by it. "I wanted to kill her." Moments ticked by while she gaped at him, breathing through lightly parted lips. "I wanted to kill her, and you thought I had. Didn't you? That's why you didn't tell the police that I'd seen you leaving the state park. You would have had to recount what was said between you and Susan in the boathouse, which the police would have seen as a motive for me to murder my sister. But you didn't tell. You protected me."

"Like hell. I was no hero, Bellamy. If it had come down to ratting you out or saving my own skin, I would have told. But when Moody came to my house the next morning and started questioning me, he never mentioned the quarrel at the boathouse, only the one Susan and I had had at your house that morning.

"It became clear to me that he didn't know about that second argument, didn't know I'd been with her at the boathouse, and that definitely worked in my favor. So I kept quiet about it." He took a step closer, but she took a corresponding step back, so he stayed where he was. "I couldn't figure why you didn't tell Moody about it."

"My memory of it was blocked."

"But I didn't know that. I thought you were holding back because—"

"Because I had killed her."

He hesitated, then reluctantly mumbled, "It crossed my mind."

"And now?"

"Now?"

"Do you still think I did?"

"I've got better sense. You were a scrawny kid. Susan outweighed you fifteen, twenty pounds."

She folded her arms and hugged her elbows. "She was clouted over the back of her head, remember? In a fit of rage, I could have hit her with something hard enough to dull her senses."

"I don't see that happening, do you? Seriously?"

"With a surge of adrenaline, people can perform physical feats that would be impossible for them at other times."

"Only in the movies and Ripley's Believe It or Not."

Furious over the quip, she cried, "This isn't funny!"

"You're right, it's not. It is, however, ridiculous to think that you—"

"Answer my question, Dent."

"What was the question?"

"You know the question!"

"Do I think you killed your sister? *No!*"

"How do you know? I was at the scene. I saw her before her purse was sucked into the tornado. How do you know I didn't kill her?"

"Why would you have taken her underwear?"

"Maybe I didn't. Maybe by the time I caught up with her in the woods, she wasn't wearing any. She could have given her panties to you."

"She didn't."

"To Steven. To Allen Strickland." Squeezing her eyes closed, she asked in a frightened whisper, "Did I see her do that?"

"Stop it, Bellamy. This is crazy. You can't force yourself to remember things that didn't happen."

She pulled her lower lip through her teeth, but now it didn't look sexy. It was the gesture of someone in torment. "Rupe Collier thought it possible."

"He was only trying to get a rise out of you. You know
that."

"I think Daddy suspects."

"*What?*"

"It's occurred to him. I know it has."

"What in God's name are you talking about?"

As she recounted their conversation of the day before,
Dent became increasingly agitated. "Be reasonable. If he
thought you'd done it, he sure as hell wouldn't have asked
you to grant his dying wish and expose the murderer."

Past listening, she threaded the fingers of both hands
through her hair and held it off her face. He could practically see her mind wildly spinning. "When we were with
Moody and I described the crime scene, you got nervous. You were biting the inside of your cheek. You looked
tense, tightly wound, like you were about to spring off the
bed." He tried to keep his expression neutral, but she was
too perceptive.

"You thought that if I told too much I would incrimi-
nate myself. That's why you got anxious, isn't it?"

"Bellamy, listen—"

"You think I killed her and couldn't live with what
I'd done, so I blocked my memory of it. That's what you
think."

"It makes no difference what I think."

"Of course it does!"

"To who?"

"To me!" she shouted. "It matters to me that you think
I'm a murderer."

"I *never* said that."

"You did."

"I said that it had crossed my mind."

"Which is as good as."

"No it isn't."

"Thinking that, why would you want to go to bed with me?"

"What does one have to do with the other?"

She looked at him, aghast, speechless, and horrified.

He took a breath, blew it out, then said, "Look, after what Susan said about you, I wouldn't have blamed you for driving a stake through her heart. I don't believe you choked her, but if you did, so what? I don't care."

She hugged herself even more tightly. "You've said that repeatedly. You didn't care about your dad's indifference. You don't care what my parents think about you. You left the airline uncaring of people's opinion. You don't care if Moody blows his brains out. You don't care if I took my sister's life. You. Don't. Care. About anything. Do you?"

He remained stonily, angrily silent.

"Well, your not caring is a big problem for me." She held his gaze for several beats, then went to the staircase and started up. "I want you to go now, and I don't want you ever to come back."

Inside the master bedroom closet, Ray Strickland was beside himself. He'd overheard everything.

That bitch Bellamy had killed Susan and had got off scot-free! Allen had paid with his life for her crime, while she'd gone merrily on her way, living the good life.

"Not for much longer," he whispered.

He heard a door slam and figured it was Dent Carter storming out. Which was okay. Ray could catch up with him later. Right now, he wanted to feel the book writer's blood on his hands. He wanted to wash his face in it, bathe in it.

He slid his knife from the scabbard, thrilling to that hissing sound.

He could hear her tread as she made her way upstairs. Only a few moments now, and the injustice done to Allen would be avenged.

He heard her on the landing. Coming down the hall. She was steps away, seconds shy of entering the bedroom. She was mere heartbeats away from death.

The bedroom light flicked on.

He took a tighter grip on the bone handle of his knife and held his breath.

Chapter 24

Dent wasn't enjoying the kissing. Hers were sloppy.

He decided to skip the preliminaries and move things along. Reaching under the back of her top, he unhooked her bra strap.

"My, my. You're eager," she whispered and dug her tongue into his ear.

"I am."

"Okay by me. I'll just be a minute." She went into the bathroom and, after pausing to blow him a kiss, shut the door.

He went over to the bed and sat down on the edge of it to test its firmness. Not that it mattered. He wouldn't be there long. Just long enough.

He had tried to coax Bellamy out of her retreat upstairs, but it was as though the plug had been pulled on her emotions. She'd paused on the stairs to deliver a parting shot, spoken in a monotone, her expression closed, cold, removed.

"Look at it this way, Dent, if it turns out that I'm the

culprit, your name will be cleared. You do care about that."

He'd left, telling himself that his leave-taking was long overdue. He never should have become involved with her in the first place. Gall had tried to tell him, but had he listened? No. He'd plunged in and, now he was sick of everything associated with the Lystons.

He'd had it up to here with right versus wrong. He was no longer interested in who had said what, who had done what, and he was tired of trying to fit all the pieces together. To what end? Okay, exoneration for himself. But in the grand scheme of things, that wasn't much. He could live without ever being rubber-stamped innocent of killing Susan.

So if Bellamy wanted to end their affiliation here, this way, then it was fine and dandy with him.

While with her, he'd forgotten every life-lesson he'd ever learned. Like, don't become involved in someone else's mess. Don't offer advice to someone who obviously doesn't want it. Don't be a sap and admit to feeling anything, because what does it get you? Nothing, that's what. You wind up being not only rejected, but made to look like a damn fool as well.

He should have remembered that from all the times he'd cried himself to sleep for want of the mother who had cared so little as to have abandoned him. Or from the times he'd tried to get his father's notice, only to be ignored.

His father, the wizard of indifference, had taught him one thing: People could affect you only if you allowed them to.

So he'd told himself that Bellamy's problems were

no longer his, that he was done, finished, and had sped away from her house in desperate need of diversion. He'd stopped at the first bar that looked promising. By the time he'd finished his second drink, she—he hadn't caught her name and didn't intend to—had taken up residence on the barstool next to his.

She was cute and cuddly. She hadn't talked about anything even remotely serious. Instead she'd been flirtatious, funny, and flattering, all excellent antidotes for what he'd been dwelling on over the past few days.

He hadn't noticed the color of her eyes, only that they weren't haunted. Or angry and accusatory. Or blue, and soulful, and deep enough for a man to drown in.

She didn't have a pale sprinkling of freckles on her cheekbones.

Her lower lip didn't make him think of sin and salvation at the same time.

Her hair wasn't dark and sleek.

Her main asset was that she was friendly and agreeable. No analyses, no whys and wherefores, none of that. In no time at all, her hand was making forays up his thigh, and he couldn't remember exactly who'd suggested the motel, him or her, but here they were, and he was waiting for her to come out of the bathroom so they could screw and get it over with.

Get it over with?

It suddenly occurred to him that he wasn't looking forward to it. Not in the slightest. So what the hell was he doing here?

And just where was he, anyway?

His searching gaze connected with his reflection in the mirror above the dresser opposite the bed. Mentally erasing the cuts and bruises from his face, he assessed the man looking back at him. With as much objectivity as possible, he decided that for a man nearing forty, he was holding up fairly well.

But ten years from now, would he still be looking at himself in the mirror of a random motel room, waiting for a woman he wasn't even attracted to, whose name he hadn't bothered to get? At sixty would he still be doing this?

It was a depressing prospect.

Not even realizing his intention, he left the bed, went to the door, and pulled it open. On his way out, he paused to glance back in the direction of the bathroom, thinking that maybe he should say something, provide some excuse for cutting out. But whatever he told her would be a lie, and she would know it, and that would insult her worse than if he just split.

Which was justification for letting himself off the hook easily. But at least he had the decency to acknowledge it this time.

He drove his Vette hard, but when he entered his apartment, he looked around and wondered why he'd been in such a hurry to get here. It was a shabby rathole, just as Bellamy had said. Sad and lonely, she'd called his life. She was right about that, too.

He stared into the emptiness of the room, but what he actually looked into was the vast, empty landscape of his life. The thing was—and it was the thing that bothered him most—he saw nothing in his future that was going to fill that wasteland.

Moving suddenly, he'd fished his cell phone from the pocket of his jeans and turned it on, then scrolled through the list of recent calls until he found the number he sought. He called it, and a woman answered by asking, "Is this Dent?"

"Yeah. Is Gall there?"

"Hold on. He's been trying to reach you."

Dent heard a muffled exchange, then Gall came on. "Where have you been?"

"Was that your lady?"

"Who else would it be?" he replied querulously. "I've called you a dozen times. Why didn't you answer?"

"I'd turned off my phone."

"How come?"

"I didn't want to talk to anybody."

Gall grunted. "How's Bellamy doing?"

"She's okay. Uh, listen, Gall, I want you to fix my airplane."

"Ain't that what I've been doing?"

"Yeah, but it's taking too long. What about those parts you've been waiting on?"

"I'm hounding them to rush the order."

"Good. I need to be flying again. Soon as possible."

"Don't I know that already?"

"Right. But I've also been thinking about—"

"Dent—"

"No, let me get this out before I change my mind. I've given more thought to the senator's offer."

"That's what you're calling about?"

"I know it's late, but you're the one who's been on my ass about it, so I'm calling now to tell you that I've decided to talk to him. Maybe...I don't know—it might not be that bad to have steadier employment. At least I can hear the guy out, see what he has to say."

"I'll set it up."

"An informal meeting. I'm not dressing up for him."

"I'll set it up."

Suddenly Dent felt good. Maybe a little proud of himself for the first time in a long time. He realized that he was smiling hugely. But Gall's restraint puzzled him. "I thought you'd be a lot happier."

"I'm real happy. You're finally acting like a grown-up, making a good decision."

"So, what's the matter?"

"I'm just surprised by your timing."

"Again, I apologize for the hour. Hope I didn't interrupt anything. But I reached the decision a few minutes ago and wanted to act on it immediately. Call the guy first thing in the morning, okay?"

"Yeah, yeah." A pause, then, "You talk this over with Bellamy?"

"I would have, except…" Dent took a deep breath, expelled it. "She's not speaking to me."

"Oh. I get it now. You don't know."

Gall's tone sent a chill through Dent. His happy bubble burst. "What don't I know?"

"Her daddy died. It was reported on the ten o'clock news."

Steven folded his dark pinstripe suit into his suitcase, which lay open on the bed, and looked over his shoulder at William as he came into the room. Steven asked, "Any problems?"

"None. All the shifts are covered. The chef will manage the kitchen. Bartender will oversee the dining room. No one will know we're gone."

"You hope."

"We've hired good people. Things will run smoothly, and if there is a hitch, it won't be the end of the world. Or even the end of Maxey's Atlanta."

Steven hesitated and, not for the first time, said, "You don't have to come with me."

William shot him a look as he pulled his own luggage from the storage closet. "I don't have to, but I am."

"For a decade I've protected you from my family and its woes. Why involve yourself now?"

"I'm not involving myself with your family. I'm involved with you. Period. End of discussion. What time is our flight tomorrow?"

Steven had made their reservation for the first flight out of Atlanta to Houston. "We'll be there by ten. The funeral home in Austin is sending a hearse to Houston to transport the body. We'll ride back to Austin with Mother in the accompanying limo, and then fly home from there after the funeral."

"Which is?"

"The day after tomorrow."

"Soon, then."

"Mother saw no reason to delay it. Howard's death has been expected for months. Actually, without her knowledge, he had already made most of the arrangements, even for the viewing, which will be tomorrow night." He laid several folded shirts in the suitcase. "Out of respect, Lyston Electronics will shut down for three days, although the employees will receive full pay."

"Who mandated that? Bellamy?"

"Mother. She thought it was a gesture that Howard would have approved. As for Bellamy, when I spoke to Mother, she hadn't yet notified her."

"Why, for godsake?"

"She dreaded having to tell her. Despite the time Bellamy has had to prepare herself, she'll be grief-stricken." He sat down on the edge of the bed, his shoulders slumping. Since receiving the news, he'd been busily attending to business matters, making travel arrangements, readjusting his schedule, packing mourning clothes.

Now the gravity of the situation seeped into him, and, along with it, profound weariness.

William came over to him. "What about you? What are you feeling?"

"I'm worried about Mother. She sounded as good as could be expected, but I'm sure she's keeping up appearances and holding herself together, being the strong, stalwart widow of an important man." He exhaled heavily. "But Howard was the center of her universe. Her life revolved around him. She's lost the love of her life as well as the purpose for it."

William acknowledged that the transition for her would be difficult. "Selfishly, however, I'm more concerned about your state of mind."

"I'm not leveled by grief, if that's what you mean. Whatever my relationship with Howard was or wasn't, it's too late now to change it, and in any case I wouldn't. Couldn't."

He took a moment to sort through his shifting emotions. "I think he would have been more of a father to me if I had let him. When they married he embraced me as his son, adopted me, made it legal. And it wasn't just for show or to please Mother. I believe he actually wanted to become my *dad*. But I couldn't have that kind of relationship with him. I kept him at arm's length."

"Because you blamed him for Susan's abuse."

"By extension, I suppose," Steven admitted. "Unfairly."

"Maybe, maybe not."

Steven looked at him sharply.

"Howard may have known what she was doing," he said softly.

Steven adamantly shook his head. "He would have stopped it."

"He would have had to acknowledge it first. For a man as principled, as devoted to family values as Howard was, accepting that his teenaged daughter was a conniving, malicious, unconscionable whore would have been out of the question. Rather than confront it, it's possible that he denied it, even to himself, and looked the other way while she continued her reign of terror over you."

It was only a theory, but upsetting nevertheless. Steven placed his elbows on his knees and buried his face in his hands. "Jesus. I fool myself into believing I'm over it, but I'm not."

"You should have had counseling."

"I would have had to tell first. And I couldn't tell."

William sat down beside him and placed his hand on Steven's bowed head. "Susan is dead."

"I wish," he said in a voice made raspy by anguish. "But I wake up in the middle of the night, feeling her breath on my face."

"I know. And the haunting has gotten worse since *Low Pressure* was published." William clicked his tongue with irritation. "For the love of God, why did Bellamy ever start this insanity? Why won't she stop?"

"Because she's haunted, too. She wants an end to it just as I do, and her approach is to dig for answers to questions that were buried with Susan." He raised his head and saw in William's eyes a foreboding that matched his own. "Until she has them, I'm afraid she won't stop digging." He added in a whisper, "But I'm equally afraid she will."

Ray figured he must be cursed or something.

Maybe some unknown enemy had a voodoo doll that looked like him, a thousand pins stuck in it. Maybe the stars that charted his fate were out of whack or had collapsed upon themselves.

It was certain that something was fucked up. Or else why couldn't he catch a break?

Bellamy Price had been seconds away from walking straight into his well-laid ambush.

When a cell phone rang.

Ray had heard it from inside the closet. Even as his jaw dropped with disbelief over his rotten luck, he'd heard her running footsteps going back the way she'd come. He'd heard her say, "Don't hang up!" as she raced down the stairs.

The phone stopped ringing. Breathlessly, she said, "I'm here, Olivia."

Then for a time, nothing, and Ray had thought to himself that if she was that absorbed by what her stepmother was saying, she probably wouldn't hear him. All was not lost.

He'd eased open the closet door, slipped out, and tiptoed to the double doors of the bedroom, where he'd paused to listen. She was speaking in a murmur. She'd made a sound like a sob then began crying in earnest.

He'd left the bedroom and crept down the hall, knowing that her weeping would keep her from hearing him. It had sounded to him as though she was at the foot of the staircase. That close. If he could reach the landing without alerting her, the noise he made going down wouldn't matter. By the time she'd registered his presence and reacted, she'd be dead.

Ray had heard her say, "I'll leave immediately and get there as soon as I can." Then more softly. "No, I'll be driving this time."

Some soft good-byes had been exchanged, and then she'd disconnected.

He'd peered over the banister and saw her snatch a large shoulder bag from the hall table, then go directly to the front door and pick up a suitcase. She'd paused only long enough to hit the light switch and plunge the first-floor rooms into darkness before she'd sailed through the front door and locked it behind her.

It had all happened so swiftly that Ray was still lurking on the landing, gripping his knife in a sweaty clutch and debating what his next course of action should be, when he'd heard her car starting. Headlights swept across the front windows as she backed out of the driveway and drove away. Just like that, she was gone.

Ray had had no choice except to punt. Again.

And that was why he was convinced that some bad mojo was working against him. He'd left her house and walked back to where he'd left his pickup. As far as he could tell, it had gone unnoticed. Just to be on the safe side, he'd switched out the license plates several times before driving to Georgetown.

Exhausted and out of options, he'd decided to go home.

Now, forty minutes after being thwarted again, he reached the duplex. He secured his pickup in the garage, then walked to the front door and let himself in. Groping his way around the living room, he lowered the blackout shades on both front windows. Only then did he move to a table and switch on a small-wattage lamp.

Turning toward the kitchen, he drew up short. "Jesus," he grumbled. "You scared the shit out of me. What are you doing here?"

Rupe Collier stepped out of the shadows and into the circle of feeble light. "I'm here because you don't do as you're told."

Chapter 25

————◆◆◆————

I don't take orders from you." Belligerently Ray shouldered past Rupe and lumbered into his kitchen. Rupe caught the full brunt of his body odor as he went past.

"You stink, Ray. Why don't you go take a shower?"

"Why don't you kiss my ass?" He took a bottle of beer from the refrigerator, twisted off the cap, which he dropped to the floor, and guzzled half of it before lowering the bottle and wiping his mouth with the back of his hand. Then he belched loudly and wetly.

Charming, Rupe thought. As soon as Ray's usefulness ran out, he needed to disappear.

From the outset their alliance had been an uneasy and tenuous one, fraught with mistrust on both sides. But for Rupe's peace of mind it had been necessary to forge the quasi-friendship.

Following Allen's fatal stabbing, Rupe had heard about Ray's attempts to scale the walls, both real and figurative, that protected the Lystons. As the prosecutor who'd gotten Allen convicted, Rupe figured he would also be a target for Ray's revenge. He had an idiot's IQ, but he was just pugnacious enough and stupid enough to be dangerous in a loose cannon sort of way.

Besides, Rupe was a firm believer in the adage that it was better to be lucky than smart.

He feared that one day Ray would get lucky and either kill, maim, or damage him in one manner or another. Rupe didn't want to be looking over his shoulder for the rest of his life, but he'd already made one attempt on Ray's life by staging the auto accident. He'd decided to take a different tack and befriend the man.

Because Rupe also believed in keeping his friends close, but his enemies closer.

He'd found Ray living in the same rundown house he'd shared with his late brother. Being limited in all capacities including his mangled left arm, he'd been unable to acquire gainful employment and was barely scraping by on welfare.

In rode Rupe Collier on a white stallion—actually in a flashy white Cadillac—offering Ray a new place to live rent free. He gave him a recently repossessed pickup truck and a job at a glass company, which Rupe had bought so windshield repairs and replacements could be done there cheaply.

Initially Ray had responded to the extended olive branch with a threat to bash in Rupe's skull. Playing meek and mild, Rupe apologized and said that he didn't blame Ray for his antagonism. Of course "antagonism" had to be defined.

Ray was mollified by the apology, but not entirely without suspicion. "How come you're doing this?"

"If I hadn't prosecuted your brother's case so well, he

would still be alive. I feel terrible about that. Even if Allen was guilty, he wasn't given a death sentence. He shouldn't have died in prison. And if he was innocent... well, that's a possibility I can't bear to think about."

"He was innocent. You and Moody cooked up a case against him."

"You're absolutely right, Ray," Rupe had said, oozing remorse. "Moody was keen on sending your brother to Huntsville."

"Even if he didn't do nothin'?"

Rupe sighed. "Moody couldn't make the charges stick with Denton Carter. He didn't have anybody else to nail that crime on, so..."

He made a helpless gesture and left the thought unfinished. Ray's beetled brow indicated that his pea-sized brain was trying to process it. Eventually he reached the conclusion that Rupe had hoped he would. "It's Moody's fault Allen got killed."

Rupe protested, but gently. "I must take partial responsibility. That's why I'm here. I can't bring your brother back, but I can make your life easier. Otherwise, I'll never be able to live with myself."

Ray accepted the arrangement. He would work for Rupe, live in a rented duplex paid for by Rupe, drive a new pickup every two or three years, and tell absolutely no one about his benefactor.

"I want to remain anonymous. Do you know what that means, Ray?" After explaining the concept of anonymity, he said, "That means I'll be like an invisible friend. No one can know about our friendship. Just us."

"Why don't you want anybody to know?"

"Because charity isn't true charity if it's advertised."

If Ray had thought it through, he might then have wondered why Rupe was often photographed handing over checks in sizeable amounts to local charities. The funds came from his employees, who were encouraged, even browbeaten, to contribute. Not a penny came from Rupe's private pocket, but he took credit for the generosity of Collier Motors.

Ray did as Rupe ordered and got a post office box, so that nothing was mailed to him at the duplex. He used a cell phone, no land line. Rupe's comptroller paid all his utility bills, and the relatively insignificant sums were so well hidden in the books of corporate entities and limited liability companies that an auditor would never find the link between the two men.

The only thing Rupe had Ray personally register to himself was the pickup truck.

"If you break the law while driving this truck, I don't want them coming after me." Rupe had said it with a smile, a wink, and a slap on the back, which had made Ray think that they were buddies.

They weren't. While the arrangement was indisputably beneficial to Ray, it served to keep him on a short leash, which Rupe held in a tight grip. It also provided Rupe with a facilitator who was as dumb as he was strong, and both traits had proved useful many times over. In a dispute, Rupe had often relied on Ray's violent streak to bring the other party around to his way of thinking.

Ray was dull-witted, obedient, uncurious, and malleable. For as long as their arrangement had been in place, he'd never once questioned Rupe's instructions or balked when told to do something.

Until this week. Which was why Rupe was now standing

in a filthy kitchen, watching with disgust as Ray folded a slice of cold bologna into his mouth. Chewing it, he asked, "What happened to your face?"

"We'll get to that. First I want to know where you've been and why you've ignored my calls."

"I've been busy."

"Not at work. Your foreman tells me you haven't shown up for several days."

"I've been following Bellamy Price. I thought you'd want me to keep doing that."

"Do me a favor, Ray. Don't do my thinking for me, all right?"

Her publicity blitzkrieg had annoyed and concerned Rupe. By happy circumstance, one of his most reliable repo men had an acquaintance, who had a cousin in Brooklyn, who knew of a guy, who, for a nifty fee, could send "messages with impact." Rupe had contacted him by telephone, and, after being given a menu of options, he'd selected the rat trick, which had actually sent chills down his own spine.

Soon after that, when he learned that Bellamy Price had returned to Austin, he feared that she hadn't been scared silent, only scared into moving her media carnival right into his backyard. That was when he'd instructed Ray to follow her for a few days and see what she was up to.

Apparently nothing. She'd spent time with her parents in their mansion, then she'd rented her own place, but she'd kept a low profile. No interviews, no lectures, no book-signing events. Relieved, he'd called Ray off. But Ray must have developed ideas of his own.

"It's a good thing I kept following her. You want to know why? Guess who she's hanging out with?"

"Denton Carter. And the reason I know that is because they came calling at my house around sundown tonight."

"Huh?"

"That's right."

The wind had been taken out of Ray's sails, but he retaliated with querulousness and a transparent indifference. "So what'd they want?"

"No, I get to go first with the questions. Tell me what you've been doing the last several days."

"I told you."

"What else?"

"Nothin'."

"I know better, Ray. One thing you did, you beat up Dent Carter."

He jutted out his lantern jaw. "What if I did?"

"Where?" Rupe asked only in order to compare Ray's version to Dent's. Ray's mumbled account more or less correlated.

"But he didn't recognize me. He didn't say my name or nothin'."

"Well, there you're wrong. He told me himself that you had attacked him."

Rupe could tell that worried him, but what Ray said was, "My word against his."

"You'd better hope so. What did you do after you left the pancake house?"

"I got the hell out of there." He told Rupe about tracking them, losing them, picking up their trail again at Dent's place, at her house, until Rupe himself got confused. It was clear Ray couldn't exactly remember the sequence.

"But he always goes back to that old landing strip

sooner or later. They've took off from there several times the last coupla days."

"In his airplane?"

"No. A bigger one. His is busted up. The old man was working—"

Suddenly Ray clamped his mouth shut and looked away from Rupe. He ran his large hand back and forth over that hideous tattoo on his left arm as though petting the snake.

Rupe tilted his head to one side. "'The old man'? Gall Halloway? He was working . . . ?" He ended on an implied question mark. "Ray? How do you know what he was doing?"

Ray remained silent. He looked around as though seeking the nearest way out.

Rupe sighed. Loath as he was to touch anything in the place, he propped himself against the counter, folded his arms, and crossed his ankles. "Just what have you been up to? And you'd fucking better not lie to me."

Ray wrestled with indecision for several moments, but then he blurted out, "She's got rich and famous. That's not right."

Then he talked for ten minutes, spraying bologna-flecked spit with every other word. Rupe listened without interrupting. He sifted out what he discerned were out-right lies or half-truths, filled in what he guessed Ray was omitting, and began considering how he could turn Ray's reckless actions to his advantage.

And when he determined a way, it was all he could do to keep from breaking into a wide smile. Instead, he pretended to be disappointed in his protege, angry over his independent actions, and deeply troubled by what the consequences of them might be.

As for Ray, over the course of his monologue he'd worked himself into a lather. He was perspiring profusely. Even his scalp was beaded with sweat, its sour stench contributing to his body odor. Reflexively he did curls with his left biceps and contracted and extended the fingers of that hand.

Through clenched teeth, he said, "She was only steps away from the closet. I could smell her. Then her phone rang." He'd been pacing like a caged bear. Now he came to a sudden halt and slapped his palm several times against his forehead. "So close."

Rupe made a tsking sound. "So close to getting justice for Allen."

Ray swiped his bare arm across his sweaty forehead. "Damn straight. Eye for an eye." He took another bottle of beer from the fridge, uncapped it with a hard twist, took a long drink, then faced Rupe and rolled his shoulders as though preparing for a fight. "Now you know what I've done, you gonna fire me? Kick me out of this place? Go ahead, see if I care."

"I should. But the fact is, I don't know what I'm going to do with you, Ray. I'm torn."

"Torn?"

"Between duty and obligation. Between the law and justice."

"I don't get it."

Rupe thoughtfully tugged on his lower lip. "Will you answer a few questions for me?"

Ray, pleased that he'd been given a choice, hooked his foot around the leg of a chair and dragged it from beneath the table, then flopped down into it. "Shoot." He slurped from the bottle of beer.

"Before Gall switched out the hangar lights, did he see you?"

"He could've. But except for the work light under the airplane, it was dark in there. That's how come I didn't notice it wasn't a real person."

Reasonable doubt, Rupe thought. Even if Gall Halloway swore on the Bible that his attacker had been Ray Strickland, it could be argued that it was too dark inside the hangar for him to make a positive identification.

"You didn't leave anything behind? Or take anything?"

He shook his head, but Rupe sensed he was lying. He let it go. It would actually be better if Ray did have something that could place him in the hangar that night. But Rupe didn't want him arrested just yet.

"You've changed the tags on your truck?"

"Five times," Ray said. "But the old man couldn't have seen it anyway, 'cause I parked a long way off."

For several moments, Rupe pretended to struggle with a decision and finally gave a deep sigh. "You should have checked with me before taking these actions. But you didn't, so now Dent Carter, and possibly Gall Halloway, are on the lookout for you."

"I'm not scared of them."

"What if they've notified the police? Aren't you scared of them? Do you want to go to prison and wind up like Allen?"

That subdued him.

"You've committed felonies, Ray. I can't protect you. In fact, I should turn you in myself."

"After everything I've done for you? Fuck that."

He had an excellent point. But Rupe didn't give him time to realize it. "Relax. We're friends, and I wouldn't betray a friend. Besides, I understand why you'd want to get revenge on Bellamy Price for writing that book and dragging your brother's name through the mud all over again." After a strategic pause, he said, "But she shouldn't be your primary target. She's not the one who destroyed Allen's life. And yours."

He left the counter and came to stand beside Ray, settling a hand on his shoulder. "Earlier you asked who'd messed up my face. I'll give you three guesses and the first two don't count. It was the same person who sent your brother to prison, to his death."

Ray snarled, "Moody."

Rupe squeezed the beefy flesh beneath his hand. "Moody."

The drive to Houston took Bellamy almost four hours.

Within seconds of receiving Olivia's phone call, she was out of her house and on her way. She hadn't even taken time to change out of the clothes that had been slept in while she was in Marshall.

Slept in with Dent while she was in Marshall.

Disallowing herself to think of him and the shocking discovery brought about by their last argument, she forced herself to concentrate on driving. She stopped twice for coffee, although her mind was far too troubled for there to have been any danger of her falling asleep at the wheel. The real hazard lay in the tears that continued to fill her eyes and blur her vision.

Her father was dead. She had failed to grant his dying request. And it seemed possible, even probable, that she had killed his firstborn daughter. He'd died possibly believing that she had.

When she arrived at the hospital she went directly to the room where he'd died. The lights had been dimmed, but they were sufficient to reveal her stepmother's grief. Deep lines of misery were etched into Olivia's face, making her appear to have aged drastically.

For several minutes, the two women clung to each other and wept, their shared heartache making words superfluous.

Eventually Olivia eased away and blotted her eyes. "The funeral director arrived ahead of you, but I wouldn't let them take him away. I knew you'd want time with him. Take all you want." She touched Bellamy's arm gently, then left the room.

She walked over to the bed and looked at her father's body for the first time since entering the room. People said kind things about the deceased. How peaceful one looked, how one appeared only to be sleeping.

Those were lies. Told out of compassion, perhaps, but lies nonetheless. Her father didn't look asleep; he looked dead.

In the few hours since he'd breathed his final breath, all vestiges of life had deserted his body completely. Already his skin had a waxy appearance. He seemed not to be made of flesh and blood or of anything organic, but of something artificial.

Rather than this upsetting her, she took comfort in realizing that what was left of him wasn't *him* at all. She wasn't prompted to embrace the still body or kiss the bloodless cheek, but rather to remember all the times she'd given him hugs or kisses when he was alive and warm and able to return them.

So she didn't address the body. Instead she spoke to

he spirit she knew still to be alive. "Daddy, I'm sorry. I
lidn't meet your deadline. And if... if... if I killed Susan,
orgive me. Please. Forgive me."

She whispered that plea over and over, turning it into a
:hant accompanied by harsh sobs that wracked her entire
>ody. They grew so loud that they summoned Olivia back
nto the room.

"Sweetheart, don't." She wrapped her arms tightly
round Bellamy. "He wouldn't want you crying over him.
That's the last thing he'd want. He's out of pain now and
t peace."

Bellamy knew that not to be true, but she allowed
Olivia to guide her out of the room and to comfort her
intil they were forced to deal with the practical issues
issociated with transporting his remains to Austin.

Bellamy dealt with the paperwork, welcoming the
listraction. She was simply too emotionally shredded to
:ontemplate that the culprit she'd been seeking, that the
ndividual who had caused her family so much turmoil
ind unhappiness, that the person her father had hoped to
dentify positively before he died, was herself.

Olivia had reserved a room for her in the hotel attached to
he hospital. It was four a.m. before she got to bed. Sur-
>risingly, she fell instantly asleep and slept dreamlessly.
She was too exhausted to do otherwise.

Olivia woke her at ten. "Steven and William are com-
ng straight here from the airport, and we'll leave for
Austin immediately after they arrive. I've ordered some
:offee and breakfast to be sent up for you. Can you be
eady by eleven?"

The water in the shower was wonderfully hot. She used

the toiletries provided by the hotel and had enough cosmetics in her bag to make herself look presentable. The stop at her parents' house yesterday had been fortuitous. She dressed in a pantsuit she'd packed in the suitcase. When she greeted her stepbrother and William in the first-floor lobby, she looked appropriately turned out.

"Do you have sunglasses?" Steven asked as he ushered her through the automatic glass doors and toward the limousine parked behind the hearse.

"Is that a kind way of telling me that my eyes are dark and puffy and that no amount of concealer will help?"

"What are brothers for?"

His gentle tease warmed her, and she smiled at him as she slipped on her sunglasses. However, she drew up short and her smile dissolved when she saw the man leaning indolently against a support column of the porte cochere.

Following her gaze, Steven asked, "Who's that?"

"Don't you recognize him from his byline photo? Meet Rocky Van Durbin."

"Good Lord," Olivia said.

"Jesus," William hissed. "Doesn't he have an ounce of sensitivity?"

"Not a drop," Bellamy said.

"This is too much. Steven, call Security."

"No, Olivia," Bellamy said. "That'll only give him the circus he wants." Steeling herself, she said, "I'll take care of it."

Before they could stop her, she walked toward Van Durbin, who pushed himself away from the column and came forward to meet her halfway.

She looked pointedly at the photographer, who was already snapping pictures. "Would you please stop that?"

He waited until Van Durbin gave him a sign, then lowered his camera and ambled off. When he was out of earshot, Van Durbin said, "Ms. Price, allow me to extend my condolences."

"Spare me the sentiment. The only thing my father's death represents to you is another provocative article based on rumor, speculation, and your own vivid imagination."

"Wasn't my imagination that I saw you and your former enemy coming out of his apartment. In dishabille," he added with a leer.

"Denton Carter was never my enemy."

"Aw, please," he scoffed. "He never had a kind word for your family. Your parents hated the sight of him even before your sister got killed. You gotta admit it's kinda kinky that you and he are all smoochy-smoochy."

"Hardly."

"Pictures don't lie. I'm partial to one taken at the airport, where he's got his hand in your hair. Very sweet. Very intimate."

Suddenly she realized that Van Durbin might actually be of help. From the bottom of her shoulder bag, she pulled out the envelope of photos he'd left on her doorstep. She took the one in which Jerry was in the background and pointed to him. "Do you know this man?"

Van Durbin looked closely and shrugged. "Just some guy."

"You don't recognize him?"

"No, should I? Who is he?"

"I was hoping you could tell me."

Steven called out to her and when she looked around, she saw that Olivia was already inside the limo. William was standing in the open door, and Steven was wearing an expression of consternation. He tapped the face of his wristwatch.

"Your stepbrother got here quick," Van Durbin said. "Having to come all the way from Atlanta. Who's that with him?"

"His business partner."

"*Business* partner?" He formed a lewd grin. "If you say so."

She stuffed the envelope back into her bag, removed her sunglasses, and looked at the columnist with censure and disgust. "If you have a grain of decency, you'll keep your distance from me and my family. At least until my father is laid to rest."

He mulled it over. "I could do that. In exchange for—"

"Bellamy. Olivia's getting anxious."

She glanced back at Steven and held up her index finger, asking him to grant her one more moment. To Van Durbin, she said, "In exchange for what?"

"Leveling with me."

"About what, specifically?"

"Dale Moody."

She kept her expression impassive. "What about him?"

"Have you seen him lately?"

"I wanted to interview him when I was researching my book, but had no luck locating him."

It wasn't a lie, but it didn't answer his question, and his grin told her he'd noticed. "The reason I'm asking, a little birdy told me that Moody might have bent some rules during his investigation."

"There were subtle suggestions of that in my book."

"Yeah, but my little birdy wasn't so subtle. My little

irdy practically accused Moody of *knowing* that he was ending the wrong guy to the pen."

"Does this little birdy have a name?"

He frowned comically. "You know better than to ask me to identify a source, Ms. Price."

Her money was on Rupe Collier, which seemed likely nd in character.

"Bellamy." This time Steven called to her with even nore irritation.

To Van Durbin she said, "I swear to you, on my father's casket, that I don't know where Dale Moody is. If I did, I vould be interviewing him myself. Now, I've leveled with ou. Stay away from me and my family and let us mourn ny father in peace. If you don't, I'll file a restraining order gainst you, then sue you and your cheesy newspaper."

Chapter 26

———◆———

Howard had specified that the visitation at the funeral home be kept private, limited to his company's executive and close personal friends.

His funeral was more public. Bellamy didn't realize just how public until the family limousine approached the church, where motorcycle policemen were needed to funnel the traffic into surrounding parking lots that were already overflowing. While the turnout was a moving and well-deserved tribute to her father, Bellamy dreaded having to endure the rite and all that it entailed.

She, Olivia, Steven, and William were ushered into the church through a side entrance and escorted into a parlor, where they waited until the church bell chimed two o'clock, then they filed into the sanctuary and took their seats in the front pew.

During the service, Bellamy tried to concentrate on the hymns being sung, the scriptures being read, and what was being said about her father and the notable life he'd led, but it all became a jumble. Superseding everything were the facts that her father was gone and that she had failed him.

And if she had killed Susan, she had committed a cardinal sin.

The four of them were led from the sanctuary ahead of everyone else. As they were climbing into the limousine, Steven remarked on the news cameras and reporters being contained behind a barrier across the street. "I see that Van Durbin is among the horde."

Bellamy spotted him and his trusty photographer. "As long as he keeps his distance."

"I suppose wild horses couldn't have kept him away."

At first Bellamy thought Olivia was also referring to Van Durbin, but then she saw that her stepmother was looking toward the main entrance of the church, where people were filing out and making their way down the steps.

He would be a standout in any crowd, but he looked particularly attractive in a dark suit and cream-colored shirt. Of course he would never bend to convention entirely, and he hadn't. His necktie was loosely knotted beneath his open collar, and his hair had been left to do what it did naturally, which was to be as unruly as he. He sported a day's scruff.

The sight of him caused Bellamy's heart to flutter.

His mouth was set in a grim line as he descended the church steps. When he reached the bottom one, he stopped and just stood there, staring hard at the back window of the limo, although she knew he couldn't possibly see her through the darkly tinted windows.

She turned away and looked out the opposite window. But several minutes later when the limo finally pulled

away from the curb, she couldn't resist glancing back.
Dent was still there staring after them.

Upward of five hundred people came to the reception at
the country club that followed the graveside service. Howard had stipulated that anyone who wanted to come was
welcome, because he didn't want to risk someone being
overlooked when a guest list was compiled.

None of his surviving family members was happy
about it, but they formed a stoic receiving line in the
club's foyer and welcomed people as they arrived. Steven
and William withdrew to the bar as soon as etiquette permitted. Bellamy remained at Olivia's side a while longer,
but when she was drawn away by members of her bridge
club, Bellamy gave up her post as well.

She made her way to the bar, where she joined Steven and William at a corner table. William stood as she
approached and held a chair for her.

"We couldn't stand the banalities any longer," Steven
said. "If I hear one more, 'Darlin', I'm so sorry, bless your
heart,' I'm going to hang myself."

"They mean well, Steven."

"What will you have to drink?" William asked her.

"White wine."

"Not nearly strong enough for this occasion." Steven
raised his glass of vodka.

"You're probably right, but I'll stick to white wine."

"I'll get it," William said, and left them to order the
drink at the bar.

"I like him," she said as she watched William walk
away. "He's very attentive and kind. Attuned to everyone's needs. He's been fantastic to Olivia."

"I tried to talk him out of coming. He insisted."

"He's your family, and I'm glad he's here for you. I know it was very difficult for you to come back." Steven had been nervously toying with his plastic stir stick. She reached across the table and covered his hand to still it. "If you can hold out for just a little while longer, you—" She broke off when she saw his expression change dramatically. Whipping her head around, she saw the cause of his alarm.

Dale Moody had just entered the bar from an outside terrace. They made eye contact. He acknowledged her by raising his chin.

Steven, noticing the gesture, looked at her with dismay. "You two are friendly now?"

"Not friendly. But I've met with him since I saw you in Atlanta."

"Jesus, Bellamy," he said under his breath. "What the hell for?"

"Answers." She couldn't address her stepbrother's disapproval now. Moody had stepped back though the doorway and out of sight. "Excuse me."

She rushed across the room and out onto the terrace. Moody was standing in the shade of a post that was wrapped in leafy wisteria, lighting a cigarette in defiance of the restrictions against smoking.

"My condolences," he said as he clicked off his lighter. He used it to motion toward the bar. "Looks like your stepbrother's done okay for himself. He has that air of prosperity about him."

"He has a strong aversion to you."

"Oh, that breaks my heart."

"When you were interrogating him, did you know he was gay?"

He shrugged. "Figured."

"Did you harass him about it?"

He flicked an ash off the end of his cigarette. "I was only doing my job."

"No you weren't. You were tormenting an underage boy."

His eyes narrowed angrily. "Don't make me sorry I came here to see you. Are you still looking for answers or not?"

She tamped down her resentment. "Most definitely."

"Then listen up. I left the case file with Haymaker. Go see him. He'll enlighten you."

He tried to turn away, but she reached out and grabbed the sleeve of his jacket. "That's it?"

"That's all you need. Everything's in there, including a statement from me, owning up to my machinations, as well as Rupe's."

"A signed confession?"

"Yep. And to eliminate any doubt or dispute that it's legit, I put my thumbprint on it. You won't have any trouble with Haymaker. I told him you'd be coming." He tried to pull away, but again she detained him.

"Two things," she said. "Please."

"Make it snappy."

"Dent and I went back to your cabin to warn you of Ray Strickland." She described the attack on Gall inside his hangar. "Strickland meant to kill him."

"Looks like he's going for broke."

"So it would seem."

"Warning noted," Moody said. "What's the second thing?"

She wet her lips. "Since I last talked to you, I've remembered something else about that day."

His attention sharpened. "Well?"

"I overheard Susan say something about me. Something nasty." She swallowed with difficulty, and her heart was beating so hard it filled her ears with its pounding. "During your investigation, did you find anything to indicate that possibly I had killed her?"

"No."

"But you would have dismissed me because of my age, my size. Did I ever cross your mind as a possible suspect? You know now that I saw her lying dead before the storm."

Moody studied her for a second or two, then pitched her his lighter. Reflexively she caught it against her chest. "What are you doing?"

"You're a lefty." He motioned down to the hand clutching his lighter. "After you described the crime scene the other day, I checked, just to make sure. You might have seen your sister dead, but you didn't kill her. Whoever struck the blow to the back of her head was right-handed."

The tension inside her chest began to lessen. She was virtually breathless with relief. "You're positive?"

He dropped his cigarette to the terrace and ground it out. "I still don't know who killed your sister, but I know who *didn't*."

He took his lighter from her, abruptly turned, and walked away. Bellamy struck out after him, but had taken only a few steps when one of her father's oldest friends stepped out of the bar and addressed her. She had no choice but to speak to him.

While the man was expressing his sympathy, Dale Moody once again disappeared.

*   *   *

Dent didn't go through the receiving line. He entered the club through another door and then blended into the crowd as well as he could. He didn't eat, didn't drink, didn't talk to anyone, and maintained his distance from the family, although he kept Bellamy within sight when at all possible. If she noticed him, she gave no indication of it.

She looked tired, beleaguered, bereaved. And gorgeous in a tragic heroine sort of way. Black suited her. Even the shadows beneath her eyes had a certain delicate appeal.

When the receiving line disbanded, he followed her as far as the double-door entrance into the bar. He didn't go in, but saw her sitting at a table with Steven. He loitered in the hallway, and the next time he drifted past, he saw her leaving the bar by way of a terrace door.

Seeing his opportunity to talk to her alone, Dent ducked out the nearest exit, circled the swimming pool, and rounded the corner of the building, which brought him to a shaded terrace where she was in conversation with an elderly man, who was pressing her hand between his.

As soon as he left her, and before she could reenter the bar, Dent spoke her name. He feared she might hightail it when she saw him. She didn't. She waited for him to come to her.

Up close, he could see that her eyes looked weepy. She could have stood a good meal or two. Always slender, she now looked fragile. After several moments of simply staring, he asked the question that had been torturing him for days.

"Why didn't you call me?"

Her father, the person she'd said she loved most in the world, had died. But she hadn't even called to tell him. He was surprised by how much that had hurt. She hadn't responded to his dozens of voice-mail messages, either. He would have thought... Hell, he didn't know what he thought. Or what to think now, because she still hadn't said anything.

"I had to hear it from Gall," he said, "who'd caught it on the news. Why didn't you call to tell me as soon as you got word?"

"We hadn't parted on the best of terms."

"But your dad died." He stated it like the settling point of an argument, as if nothing else need be said.

"Why would I bother you with that?"

"*Bother* me?" He stared at her with bewilderment for several moments, then turned his head away and looked out across the panorama of the golf course. "Wow. That speaks volumes, doesn't it? It says a lot about your opinion of me. Turns out you're even more like the Lystons than they are."

After a time, he turned his head back to her and looked into her eyes. Then he sniffed with disdain, brushed past her, and entered the bar through the terrace door. He shot a glance toward the table where Steven was sitting with William. They were absorbed in conversation.

Olivia was standing with a group of well-dressed men and women of her ilk. She appeared to be listening to what one of the silver-haired gentlemen was saying, but there was an absent look in her eyes.

Dent thought about staying and ordering a drink for himself. His presence would spoil their party, make the situation awkward, and he was feeling just ornery enough to do it. He even checked to see if there were any vacant stools at the bar. And that was when he saw him.

Jerry.

He was seated at the bar, hunched over a beer. But his gaze was fixed on Bellamy as she entered through the terrace door, looking upset, blotting her eyes with a tissue.

Jerry quickly reached for something beneath the bar.

All this registered with Dent in a nanosecond. He processed the potentially dangerous situation and reacted with immediacy, only one thought in mind: Protect Bellamy.

"Hey!" he shouted.

Jerry did as everyone in the bar did. His surprised gaze swung to Dent and, seeing that he was the person being addressed, he froze. But for less than a heartbeat. Then he bolted.

Dent charged after him. Jerry ran like the devil was after him. In his haste, he didn't see his way completely clear of the double doorway. He crashed into one panel of it, breaking several panes of glass and splintering the wood frame.

Women screamed. Men scurried aside.

Jerry, in a stumbling run, tried to get away, but Dent caught him by the collar, dragged him back into the bar, and slammed him face first against the wall. The man cried out in fear and pain as Dent crowded in behind him.

"What's your story, *Jerry*?"

"Let him go!"

Dent paid no heed to the shout coming from someone in the room. He wanted an explanation from the man who'd tracked Bellamy from New York to Texas. "What were you reaching for under the bar?"

"A b-b-book," Jerry stuttered.

"Dent." Bellamy was at his elbow, trying to pull him off the man. "It's nothing. He did have a book. See, it's right here. It was under his barstool."

Dent blinked the copy of *Low Pressure* into focus. Gradually, he backed away from the man. Jerry turned in the narrow space. He was bleeding from several cuts from the broken door panes. His nose was also dripping blood from being smashed into the wall.

Dent placed the heel of his hand over Jerry's sternum, keeping him pinned to the wall by stiff-arming. "Why have you been following her?"

Jerry's eyes bulged with fear. His lips were moving but he couldn't articulate a word.

"Let him go."

Dent recognized the voice as the one who'd spoken before. He turned his head in the direction from which it had come, and there stood Steven.

He motioned for Dent to remove his hand from the man's chest. "He's been following Bellamy because I paid him to."

Dent looked at Steven with disbelief. Then he turned to Bellamy, who stood there beside her stepmother, both of them frozen and mute and staring at him with horror.

He dropped his hand, and Jerry slumped to the floor. Dent made a gesture of supreme disgust that encompassed everyone in the room. "You people suck."

Then he stepped over Jerry and stalked out, crunching shards of glass beneath his boots.

The ten-minute drive in the limousine was made in absolute silence.

Bellamy was first inside the house. Helena approached, but Bellamy shook her head, and the housekeeper tactfully withdrew. Bellamy went into the living room, slung her handbag onto an ottoman, and turned to confront the other three as they filed in behind her.

"His name is Simon Dowd," Steven said even before she could demand an explanation. "He's a private investigator."

"Oh my God," Olivia groaned. "Steven, what in the world—"

Bellamy sliced the air, cutting off anything else her stepmother might say. She wanted only to hear what Steven had to say in his defense. "Why, in the name of God, did you hire a private investigator to follow me? I thought he was a stalker!"

"The whole business was distasteful, I assure you," he said. "His office is a third-floor walk-up. His desk is a card table. The morning I went to see him, there was a partially eaten bagel—"

"I don't give a damn about that! Why did you hire him to follow me?"

"For your protection." His voice had taken on an angry edge that matched hers. "You wrote a book about a true crime but left the ending open to interpretation. Then you started publicizing it, making you a target for anyone involved who had a problem with that."

"Like who?"

"Like Dent Carter. Who proved less that an hour ago that he's a thug. Not that that comes as any surprise."

"Scandalous behavior," Olivia said in an undertone. "I'll never be able to hold my head up in the club again."

Bellamy cried out, "He thought he was protecting me."

"Naturally you jump to his defense," Steven said. "He's

acquired those cuts and bruises on his face since I saw you in Atlanta. Who beat him up?"

"Don't try and change the subject. Tell me why you sicced this...this Simon Dowd on me."

"In your book you all but came out and accused Dale Moody of being a crooked cop. An incompetent one at best. He could have wanted retribution. Even Rupe Collier. Anyway, I became worried for your safety. William will tell you."

She glanced over at him. He nodded. "His motive was noble. He was terribly concerned about you."

"So I retained Dowd," Steven said, bringing her back to him. "His first love is the theater. He fancies himself an actor. He assured me that he would be perfect, that he could play the avid fan. That way, he could stay close to you when you appeared in public. And before you launch into a tirade, let me point out that my hiring him was validated when you told me about the rat, the vandalism done to your house, to Dent's airplane."

Olivia looked between the two of them with bewilderment. "What in heaven's name are you talking about?"

"It doesn't matter now." Wearily, Bellamy sat down on the arm of a chair and rubbed her forehead. As she thought back over the last several days, she now understood why Steven hadn't been all that surprised to see her and Dent when they appeared at Maxey's. Jerry—Dowd, whatever—had followed them from the park in Georgetown to the Austin airport. He'd given Steven advance warning of their trip to Atlanta.

"Which brings us up to today," he was saying. "I knew there would be a crowd at the funeral, and that made me nervous for your safety. For the safety of all of us. So I asked Dowd to be there, to watch our backs, and, again, I was justified in doing so. The funeral brought them all out. Moody. Rupe Collier."

"He was there?" Bellamy asked, raising her head. "I didn't see him."

"Seated two rows behind us in the church."

"And holding court in the country club's dining room," Olivia said. "Like he's a dear friend of our family."

"Let's not forget Dent," Steven said. "You and he are practically joined at the hip these days. I'm surprised you didn't go charging after him like you were twelve again, pining over your first major crush."

Bellamy's cheeks burned as though he'd slapped her. She left her perch on the arm of the chair and walked toward him. "Why do you say things like that?"

"Like what?"

"Hurtful things. Hateful things."

"Bellamy"—Olivia sighed—"please don't start something. Not today."

Ignoring her stepmother's plea, she kept her gaze fixed on Steven. "What's wrong with you? When you were younger, you were sensitive to other people's feelings."

"I grew up."

"No, you grew *mean*. Snide and scornful and mean-spirited like the people you once despised." She shook her head with perplexity. "I don't understand you. I truly don't."

"I never asked you to."

"But I *want* to." She reached for his hand. "Steven," she said with appeal, "I've always thought of you as a blood brother. I love you. I want you to love me."

"We're no longer children." He pulled his hand away

from hers. "It's time you grew up, too, and realized that life rarely gives us what we want."

She searched his eyes, saw how untouchable his heart seemed, and in that moment, she pitied him. Physically he was beautiful, but he was emotionally deformed. The effects of Susan's abuse had taken a tragic toll on his life.

But by refusing to let it go, he had prevented himself from healing. He'd let his hatred and resentment fester until he'd become critical, cynical, and slow to forgive. He had a mother who loved him with all her heart. He was adored by a patient and devoted partner whose love was visible in every gesture, grand or small. But Steven kept a part of himself separate even from them. He refused to wholly accept their love and to give his in return.

That, Bellamy realized, was the real tragedy.

Chapter 27

————◆————

The sun had set and dusk had settled in. The Corvette's headlights were on when Dent steered it into a parking space, but Bellamy remained unseen until he started up the metal staircase. When he saw her sitting on the landing, he paused for several seconds, then continued climbing the stairs in a steady tread.

He'd hooked his suit jacket on his index finger and was carrying it slung over his shoulder. His necktie had been undone and was lying flat against his chest.

She stood, dusted off her seat, and retrieved her high heels, which had become so uncomfortable she'd taken them off. He didn't say anything as he stepped around her and continued down the breezeway toward his apartment.

She fell into step behind him. "I hope you don't mind that I waited for you to get home. I didn't know when you'd show up. Or if you would come home at all tonight."

He unlocked the door and went into the apartment. She hesitated on the threshold. "May I come in?"

"Door's open." He pitched his key ring onto the coffee

table, tossed his jacket over the back of a chair, and followed that with his necktie.

She stepped inside and closed the door. "I don't think you're in the mood for anything elaborate, so I'll keep it simple. I'm sorry."

He went into the kitchen and took a bottle of water from the refrigerator. "Sorry for what?"

"For not calling you about Daddy. Honestly, I wasn't sure how you'd react to a call from me about anything. I'd said some harsh things to you." When he didn't say anything, she forged ahead. "I also apologize for not standing up for you at the club. I was...My only defense is that I was in shock."

"Don't worry about it. I'm not." He twisted the cap off the water bottle and took a drink. "That it?"

"Are you all right?"

"Why wouldn't I be?"

"You were awfully angry when you left the country club."

"Not for long. I blew off some steam."

"What did you do?"

"Went flying."

"I see."

"I doubt it."

The rebuke was succinct, but well aimed. She lowered her head and looked at the pair of designer pumps she was holding in her hands. She studied the black grosgrain ribbon across the toe. They were beautiful shoes, but they pinched. Why was it that she was drawn to things that were bad for her or that hurt?

"Moody showed up," she said. "I spoke to him just before I saw you. He said—"

He interrupted her. "I don't want to know what he said. I don't care what he said. I'm done talking about him or anything related to that subject." He looked her over from the top of her head to her bare feet. "If you want to take off your clothes and give me a lap dance, you can stay. If not, go back to the bosom of your rotten family and leave me the hell alone." He gave her about half a second to make up her mind, and when she didn't move, he snuffled. "I didn't think so. Don't let the door hit you on your way out."

Moving back into the living area, he picked up the TV remote. "Maybe I can catch the last few innings of the double-header I missed by going to your old man's send-off."

His rejection, coming so closely on the heels of Steven's, was crushing. A sob erupted from her as she turned and walked toward the door.

But before she could get it open, he was there, cursing under his breath, turning her to face him. He flattened his hands on the door, caging her between it and him, and pressed his forehead against hers. "That was a terrible thing to say."

"I guess I had it coming."

"No, it was a low blow. It was cruel. Because I know how much you loved him, how sad you are."

"When we're angry, we say things we don't mean. You're angry."

"As hell." He released a long breath and rolled his forehead from side to side over hers. "I don't know how you do it, Bellamy Lyston Price."

"Do what?"

"Make me so damn mad." He moved in closer. "And still keep me wanting you."

"Do you?"

"It's killing me."

He pulled away a few inches. She looked up into his eyes. He couldn't have mistaken her yearning when she focused on his mouth. But after having been turned down so many times, he wasn't going to initiate anything. What happened next would be up to her.

She whispered, "I'm afraid."

"Of disappointing me?"

She nodded.

"Not gonna happen."

This was what she'd come here for. Yes, she'd wanted to apologize, but what she wanted most was to be with Dent. While pitying Steven for refusing the love that was readily, unselfishly given to him, it had occurred to her that she had done the same. She hadn't allowed herself to love or to be loved.

Safe was a terribly lonely way to live.

She dropped her shoes to the floor and gingerly placed her hands on his chest. For a long time, they stood like that, neither moving. Then she undid a button on his shirt. After the first one, the others weren't quite so intimidating.

When she spread his shirt open, her desire was greater than her apprehension. She leaned in. His chest hair was soft against her face. It tickled her nose. She pressed a dry kiss on him, then opened her mouth. His skin was warm and slightly salty tasting.

He made a low sound, curved his hand beneath her jaw, and tilted her face up to his. His mouth was possessive and hungry, and the longer they kissed the more urgent the kisses became. His arms closed around her, bringing her up against him, and when she answered the pressure he applied with a corresponding grinding motion, he swore softly and broke the kiss to turn her to face away from him.

After gathering her hair in his hand and draping it over her shoulder, he unhooked the clasp at the top of her dress, then slowly pulled the zipper down past her waist. He slid his hands inside and settled them on her hips, pulling her back against him, and situating her bottom firmly against his erection.

Her breath soughed out as she weakly propped herself against the door.

He planted a tender kiss on the nape of her neck then sucked the skin against his teeth. Slowly his hands scaled up over her ribs to her bra strap. He undid it, then for agonizing seconds did nothing more.

She wondered later if perhaps he had been giving her a chance to stop there. If so, he had wasted a few precious seconds of lovemaking, because she wanted him, wanted this more than she'd ever wanted anything in her life.

His hands moved around to her front, up under the cups of her bra, and over her breasts. He angled her away from the door and back against his chest. She sighed and let herself be supported as he caressed her breasts, sweetly at first, and then erotically until she was restless and hot with wanting more. He knew it.

"Come here."

Turning her, he pushed her dress off her shoulders, and it dropped to the floor. Her bra followed. He slung off his shirt, then reached for her hand and drew her along with him as he backed up toward the bed. By the time they got there, he had his belt and trousers undone. A few seconds later, he was free of everything. Bellamy took him in, and she stared at his sex for so long that he said uneasily, "Okay?"

She laughed lightly, like *If only you knew how okay*, and he smiled. "Look at you," he murmured. His large hands reshaped her breasts. His fingertips played lightly over her nipples. After teasing them with his lips, he pulled back and smiled at her again.

Then his eyes turned dark. Because she had touched him. At first just a few tentative brushes with her fingers, to indulge her curiosity about the various textures, but, encouraged by his unsteady breathing and that smokiness in his eyes, she took him in her hand. Guided by his gruff whispers, and instinct, she pumped him until he grew incredibly tight. Hot breaths struck her hair as he bent his head over hers and groaned her name.

A drop of moisture leaked from the tip. She took it on her thumb, sucked it off, and pressed her thumb against the center of her lower lip, which he'd told her was sexy. Raspily, he said, "Disappointed, my ass," then covered her mouth in a fierce kiss that left her mindless. She was on her back on the bed before she realized how she'd got there. He bent over her and kissed her belly as he peeled off her panties.

She didn't know until later what had happened to them. They disappeared while she was held in thrall of the trail of kisses that brought his mouth to where she pulsed with need, in thrall of his stubbled cheeks against her thighs, in thrall of what he was doing with his lips, his tongue, with his gliding fingers, with his rumbled words of adoration and coarse carnality that she'd never found to be a turn-on until now.

In thrall of Denton Carter loving her.

* * *

"Are you back?" he whispered.

Her eyes opened partially. "Hmm."

"You sure?" It took all his willpower only to nudge her, not penetrate. But, damn, it was tough to hold back.

Her eyes came fully open. "Yes. I'm back."

He gave her a wicked grin. "Have fun?"

She blushed.

"Have fun?" He nudged her again, only this time pushing into her until the head of his cock was snug inside.

"Yes," she gasped.

"I'm glad." He rubbed his lips across the freckles on her cheekbone.

"Thank you," she whispered.

"The pleasure was mine."

"Really?"

All teasing aside, he angled his head back and looked into her beautiful eyes, which always looked slightly bruised. He wondered if they would ever be entirely rid of that haunted quality. "Really." They stared at each other for a meaningful moment.

He sank into her a little deeper and her throat arched up. "That feels amazing."

"To me, too."

"But you haven't . . ."

"Not yet."

"Why?"

"Because you were drifting in euphoria. And I want you to remember this. With perfect clarity."

She touched his rough cheek. "I could never forget this."

"Me either."

"Only because you had to work so hard for it."

"Nope. Because you're so damn beautiful." He pressed deeper still and grimaced with pleasure. "And because you feel so good. Now that I'm here, and I know just how sweet you are, I want to make it last. But damned if I can."

A second later, he was sheathed completely, his fingers were entangled in her hair, and his breathing was loud and ragged against her neck. Sliding his hands under her ass, he tilted her up and pushed into her as deep as he could possibly go.

"Jesus, Bellamy." He hoped that with that guttural moan he'd made her understand just how tight and hot and incredible she felt.

Because when he began to move, he was quickly lost.

"Hey, you? A.k.a.? Are you asleep?"

Bellamy snuggled against him and sighed with contentment. "No. Just thinking."

He had gathered a strand of her hair and was sweeping the ends of it across her nipple. "The way your hair brushes against them? Sexiest thing I ever saw. Drives me crazy. But I think I told you that already."

"That's driving me crazy," she said as he continued the idle whisking.

"Good crazy?"

"Wonderful crazy."

He tilted her head back and they kissed. When it finally ended, he asked, "What were you thinking about?"

"I was afraid of this because I didn't want to be compared to my sister. But I don't believe you were thinking about her at all."

He didn't say anything for several beats. Then, "You had a sister?"

She laughed and pressed her face against his chest. Her hand trailed down to his navel. "You're not wearing the bandage anymore."

"My back's okay. Stings a little sometimes."

"And these?" She leaned up and kissed the cuts on his face.

"They're gonna need a lot of that."

"And where's your gun?"

"I didn't think I should tote it to the funeral."

"Good thing you didn't. You might have shot Jerry. Although that's not his name."

"We'll talk about it later. Right now..." He pulled her over on top of him and when they were settled belly to belly she asked where he'd gone flying after leaving the reception. "Did you fly the senator's plane?"

He shook his head. "When I got out to the airfield, a buddy of Gall's was there. He has a Stearman. Know what that is?" When she shook her head, he described a vintage biplane that was originally used as a military trainer but was now popular for flying aerobatics in air shows.

"Ever since Gall told me about this guy and his plane, I've been wanting to go up in it. He took me for a spin, then he landed it, and we switched seats."

"He let you fly it?"

"And boy, did I. It's as fast and nimble as a waterfront whore."

"Isn't it dangerous?"

"I don't think about that. Only about how much fun it is." He winked mischievously. "I've got two favorite pastimes. Both are a lot of fun, and both start with the letter F."

Catching his meaning, she smiled. "But only one is dangerous."

"Depends on who you're doing it with."

"Why do you love it so much?"

"What's not to love? Being naked, skin to skin, feels good. You can't beat the view or the playthings." He touched the tip of her breast and smiled when it hardened against his fingertip. "Especially your playthings." He smoothed his hands down over her bottom and secured her more firmly against him. "But the best part is feeling you come."

Heat filled her cheeks. "I meant flying."

"Ohhhh, why do I love *flying*."

They shared a laugh, then he hugged her to him tightly. "I acted like a jerk when I got home, but I was actually glad to see you here."

"I was nervous."

"You thought I'd turn you down and kick you out?"

"I thought you might."

"Not a chance."

He slid his hands over her bottom all the way down to her thighs. He spread them apart until she was straddling him, then lifted her so he could push inside.

He was full and hard, but mostly he was Dent, and she pressed down on him with a satisfied sigh. Leaning forward, she kissed his mouth, long and slow, then squirmed down and touched the tip of her tongue to his nipple. He made a low, sexy sound and asked her to repeat that.

His arousal aroused her, but when she began to rock against him, he placed his hands on her shoulders and pushed her up to a sitting position. "I want to watch."

"What?"

He splayed his hand over her lower belly. "Lean back. Farther. Put your hands on my thighs."

She hesitated, then did as he instructed, making herself vulnerable to his hot gaze and to his thumb, which he slid down between their bodies. He watched the lips of her sex close around it, then looked into her eyes as he began to stroke her with a circular motion that caused her body to quicken and involuntarily thrust against his thumb. Tilting her face toward the ceiling, she closed her eyes and lost herself to the sensations.

Without inhibition, she gave over to her impulses, moved as her body was dictating, and allowed herself to be governed strictly by her senses. She heard Dent's hiss of pleasure, felt the fervent, wet tug of his mouth on her nipple, the flicking of his tongue in concert with his thumb's caresses.

She arched her back and cried out his name.

At some point during the wee hours, they grew tired enough to spoon. "You never did tell me," she said drowsily.

"Tell you what?"

"Why you love flying so much. You told me that you fell in love with it the first time Gall took you up. He told me you were enraptured."

"Gall said that?"

She laughed softly and turned to face him. "I supplied the word, but that's how he described you." She placed her arm around his waist and rested her cheek against the fuzziness on his chest. "Describe to me how you felt that day."

While collecting his thoughts, his fingers sifted through her hair. "For as far back as I could remember, I'd been trying to figure out why my dad didn't like me and what I could do to win him over. That day, when Gall took me up, it was like...like I left all that on the ground.

"During that five-minute flight, it stopped mattering to me whether my dad liked me or not. His indifference couldn't reach me in the sky. I knew I'd found something more important to my life than he would ever be because I loved it more. I'd found a new home."

He gave a light laugh. "Of course when we landed, nothing that poetic-sounding came to my adolescent mind. I've had years to think about that first flight and how significant it was. Even then, I knew it was life-changing, but, of course, nothing changed immediately.

"We landed, and I went back to that cold house and that unfeeling man. I remained angry and resentful, carried a chip on my shoulder just as I always had. The difference was, I now had something to look forward to. My dad couldn't lock me out anymore because I'd stopped wanting in."

He paused as though considering whether or not to continue. "This is going to sound as corny as hell. But"—again, he hesitated—"but during that flight, there was a span of time, maybe forty-five seconds, when the sun shone through a crack in the clouds. And I mean a slit. You know how it sometimes does just before sundown and there are clouds on the horizon?

"Anyway, we were flying at the perfect altitude to be level with it. That beam of sunlight was aimed directly at me. I was staring straight into it and I *owned* it. It was like a sign or something. For a kid who didn't have a mother, and a dad who looked through him, that was...Well, it was a lot.

"And I thought to myself, 'This is what it's about. It's never going to get better than this. This is my life's perfect moment. If I live to be a hundred years old, I'll remember this till the day I die.'"

Bellamy didn't move for the longest time. Eventually Dent mumbled, "Told you it was corny."

"No, it's lovely."

"You ever had a moment like that? Do you understand what I'm talking about?"

She raised her head, and a tear slid over her lower eyelid as she smiled down into his face and said softly, "As of right now, I do."

They slept for several hours and woke to make love again as they showered together. He was assembling the coffeemaker when she emerged from the bathroom, wearing only the dress shirt he'd discarded the night before, toweldrying her hair.

When he turned and saw her, an odd expression came over his face. "What?" she asked.

He shook his head slightly, then gave her a wolfish grin. "I was just thinking how good it looks on you."

"Your shirt?"

"Debauchery."

She blushed to the roots of her hair.

"Damn, that gets to me every time."

"What?"

"Your blush."

"I don't blush."

"Bet you will."

"*Will?*"

He sat down in one of the chairs at the table, caught her hand, and pulled her into his lap. It was a while before they got around to having their coffee.

Over steaming cups, she told him what she'd learned about the man they knew as Jerry. Dent muttered a few choice phrases. "Steven's the one I should have gone after."

"He retained the man to look out for me. He meant well."

He looked prepared to comment on that, but chose not to. "What was on Moody's mind?"

She related their conversation and, when she finished, she said, "Admit it, Dent. You must be a little relieved."

"To know that you didn't kill her?" When she solemnly nodded, he said, "I'm relieved for your sake. From a practical standpoint, I never really thought you had."

"But you had considered the possibility."

"Let's just say I hoped that when you regained your memory, it wouldn't be of you choking Susan. I'm glad you don't have to be haunted by that."

"Yes. But if it wasn't me, and it wasn't Strickland, then who? Moody claims only to know who didn't. Not who did. We need to—"

"Go see Haymaker," he said.

The retired detective looked as elfin as ever. "Sorry about your dad," he said to Bellamy.

She acknowledged the condolence but didn't linger on it. "Moody said you'd be expecting us."

He moved aside and motioned them in. They sat as before, he in the recliner, them competing with the dog for space on the sofa. Haymaker pointed down to the case file lying on the coffee table. "Recognize that?"

She nodded.

"Frankly, I can't believe Dale is ready to share this."

He held up his hands and gave an elaborate shrug. "But who's to say how a man's conscience works?"

"He told me that he left some kind of confession with you."

The former cop took several folded sheets of paper from the pocket of his shirt and spread them open. "Signed."

"And thumbprinted," she said, checking the last sheet, where Moody's signature was affixed along with the thumbprint.

"So what does he confess to, exactly?" Dent asked.

Haymaker settled more comfortably into his chair. "Ever hear of a Brady cop?"

Bellamy and Dent shook their heads.

"There was a Supreme Court case, midsixties, I think. Stemmed from a murder trial, *Brady versus Maryland*. The court ruled in Brady's favor. The upshot of it was that police officers and prosecutors had a duty, an obligation, to tell a defendant's attorney about any exculpatory material or information, even if they think it's hogwash.

"Even if they're damn near certain a witness is lying through his teeth on behalf of an offender, they're still required to share with the other side what they've been told. If an investigator discovers something on his own that favors the suspect, he's still obligated to share it."

"Which allows for lots of wiggle room," Dent said.

"And we—meaning cops—wiggle. But those who flat-out lie or deliberately withhold something are cheating the justice system and the law of the land. They're called Brady cops."

Bellamy said, "That's what Moody did?"

"With Jim Postlewhite. Moody questioned him early on,

as he did all the men at the barbecue." Leaning forward, Haymaker reached into the file and removed the sheet of paper bearing Postlewhite's name underlined in red.

He slipped on a pair of reading glasses. "Mr. Postlewhite told Moody where he was and what he was doing immediately before and after the tornado tore through the park. He described it in some detail. He told Moody about pushing some kids into a culvert before taking cover himself.

"If you can read Moody's chicken scratching, it's all written down here." He removed his glasses and looked at them. "Postlewhite's story eliminated Allen Strickland as a suspect."

"Why's that?"

"Because Allen had helped him shepherd those kids into the culvert."

"Where was this culvert?" Bellamy asked.

"A long way from where your sister's body was found. And Postlewhite said that Allen came running over to him and the kids from the parking lot, where he'd been looking for his brother."

Dent said, "He couldn't have been two places at once."

Haymaker nodded. "You had an alibi Dale and Rupe couldn't shake, so Rupe said they'd nail Allen Strickland instead. But Dale reminded Rupe that Postlewhite could testify that Strickland was somewhere else while the murder was taking place. Rupe told Dale to do whatever was necessary to get Postlewhite to forget that."

"Oh no," Bellamy said mournfully.

Haymaker patted the air. "He didn't have to do anything. Postlewhite had died of a heart attack three days after the tornado."

"Lucky for them," Dent said drolly.

"Rupe certainly thought so. Dale knew that the boy had at least a chance of beating that rap."

"But he never disclosed what Postlewhite had told him."

Haymaker paused and scratched his cheek thoughtfully. "Dale had been a good cop. Hard, maybe," he said, glancing at Dent. "But withholding exculpatory facts was stepping way over the line. There was also the so-called accident that prevented Strickland's brother from testifying. But by then, Dale was in so deep with Rupe he didn't see a way out."

"What happens to Brady cops when they're found out?" Bellamy asked.

"They're disgraced, exposed as liars. They're usually terminated. Some are put on a Brady list, which is basically a blacklist shared with other law enforcement agencies."

"Moody won't lose sleep over those consequences," Dent said.

"You're right," Haymaker said. "Poor ol' Dale hasn't got much to lose. But if it comes out that Rupe violated due process while serving as a state prosecutor, and knowingly sent an innocent man to prison, he might face charges. Especially since Strickland died there. At the very least, his reputation will be shot to hell. He won't be able to sell a secondhand tricycle."

Bellamy said, "Does Moody expect us to blow the whistle?"

Haymaker refolded the signed confession and handed it to her. "I made myself a copy, but I would never use it against my friend. Dale left it up to you what you do with the original. Turn it over to the Austin PD. To the DA's office. Attorney general. To the media."

"Why didn't he give it to me yesterday?"

Without compunction, Haymaker said, "He needed time to get himself out of Dodge. He won't be going back to where he was before, either. We've seen the last of him we're ever gonna see."

"He's a damn coward," Dent said.

"He told me you'd called him that to his face. He also said you weren't far off the mark."

Bellamy frowned thoughtfully. "Even if I do share this with the authorities, Rupe will claim it's all lies."

"No doubt. Dale's word against his. But Dale's notes in the file back up the part about Postlewhite. Every cop knows how important one's notes can turn out to be. And if that case file wasn't dangerous to someone, why'd it mysteriously go missing from the PD? Everything added together, it looks bad for Rupe. The King of Cars will be dethroned."

Then he leaned toward her and, speaking earnestly, said, "One last thing. Dale wanted me to emphasize to you that neither he, nor anyone, ever turned up a shred of evidence that implicated you."

"He told me that. He also knew that Allen Strickland hadn't killed Susan. Which leaves us still not knowing who did."

From deep inside Bellamy's shoulder bag, her cell phone dinged. She fished it out. "I've got a text." When she accessed it, she murmured, "It's a photo." She touched the arrow on her screen and then covered her mouth in horror when the enlarged picture appeared.

It was of Dale Moody. His throat had been sliced open from ear to ear.

Chapter 28

Ray smiled with satisfaction when he thought of Bellamy receiving that text message. Her number had been stored in Gall's cell phone, which Ray had found in the pocket of his overalls. How lucky was it that he'd taken the "dummy" with him when he ran from the hangar?

See? There was a reason why things happened the way they did. Allen had always said so. He should've listened better and believed.

Bellamy and Dent would see that picture of Moody and understand what was in store for them. Thinking how scared they must be made him chuckle. He just had to figure out how to close in on them. Rupe would help. He was good at planning.

Ray's first problem, however, was to dispose of the body and clean up the mess. He hadn't known a body could hold that much blood. Dale Moody had bled like a stuck hog, making one hell of a mess in Ray's duplex.

The last thing he'd expected was to find the detective lying in wait for him when he returned home around dawn. Ray had been trying to hunt down the son of a bitch all night, when Moody had been here all along, waiting to jump him when he came through the front door.

As planned, Rupe had called Ray from the reception following the funeral. Ray had wanted to go, but Rupe had said he would stand out in the ritzy crowd, and that that would be a disaster. Rupe had also suspected that Moody might show up at some point during the observances for Lyston, and he'd been right. Rupe was smart like that.

He'd spotted Moody skulking around the country club. "He had a brief chat with Bellamy. Your enemies are as thick as thieves with each other, Ray."

Rupe had given Ray a description of Moody's car and the license number, and had instructed him to be parked within sight of the country club gate, so that when Moody left, Ray could follow. He'd pulled out behind Moody in the car Rupe had loaned him from the glass company where he worked.

Rupe had told him to stay on Moody's tail and find out where he went, who he talked to, and what he did. But Moody's cop instinct must've kicked in, because they hadn't gone two miles before Ray lost him.

Rupe had called him repeatedly throughout the night, but Ray didn't answer. He knew Rupe was calling for an update, but, as far as Ray was concerned, Rupe could go screw himself. He was on a mission of his own. He wanted to find and kill the man who'd sent his brother to prison.

He'd spent the remainder of the night driving to all the places Rupe had called "Moody's old haunts," but with no luck. Moody wasn't to be found. It had shocked the hell out of him when he'd let himself into his duplex and was immediately caught in a headlock by the man himself.

With his other hand, he'd pressed the barrel of a pistol against Ray's temple.

"Why were you trying to follow me, Ray? Huh? I hear you've been up to some mischief lately. Slicing up Dent Carter, trying to kill an old man. Was I supposed to be next? Hmm? What's got into you?"

Ray rammed his elbow into Moody's soft gut and broke his hold. Ray spun around, and as he did so, he whipped his knife out of its scabbard and lunged. Moody saw it coming, but he was winded, and clutching his chest with his gun hand, and—Ray didn't think he was imagining this—he kinda smiled.

Ray's knife made a clean arc. The blade went through Moody's neck like it was warm butter. Blood spurted everywhere, on the walls, the furniture, on Ray, who leaped back but not far enough to escape the fountain.

Moody dropped his pistol but otherwise didn't move. He just stood there with that strange smile on his face, looking at Ray. Then finally his eyes rolled up into his head, his knees buckled, and he dropped like a sack of cement.

Ray, cursing the blood spatters on his favorite leather vest, stepped over Moody's body, went into his kitchen, rinsed the blood off his knife, dried it with a dish towel, and returned it to the scabbard. He then washed his hands and bent over the sink to scoop several handfuls of cold water into his mouth.

Killing was harder than it looked like in the movies.

He figured he ought to call Rupe, report this, get the man off his back. But Rupe didn't answer. The asshole was probably getting his beauty sleep while Ray was doing all the work.

Ray left him a blunt message. "Moody's dead. He made a mess of my place, so I may have to move."

He disconnected, made himself a potted-meat sandwich, and washed it down with a glass of milk.

When he went back into the living room and saw how funny Moody looked with his head lying to one side like that, he got the inspiration to take a picture and text it to Bellamy, using the old geezer's phone. That way she wouldn't have Ray's number, which Rupe had told him to keep just between them.

That done, he now realized how bushed he was. He'd had a long night and a busy morning. Before he addressed the problem of moving Moody's body, he decided to get some rest.

He went into his bedroom, opened the closet, and knelt down on one knee. To the naked eye, the corner of vinyl flooring looked like all the rest, like it was still glued to the concrete underneath. Only Ray knew that it could be easily peeled back because it was he who'd pried it loose the day after he'd moved in.

He'd chipped away at the concrete underneath, until he'd dug out a shallow depression. It didn't need to be deep, only large enough to hold a pair of panties, and there wasn't much to them at all. They were lighter than air. You could see through the material.

Taking them from their hiding place, he admired them as he had the first time Allen had crammed them into his palm. Ray remembered it like yesterday. Allen had been nervous. No, more than nervous. Scared. Moody and another detective had parked at the curb and were coming up the walk.

Allen was talking fast. He was sweating. "You gotta hide these, Ray. Okay?"

"That girl's panties?"

"Hurry. Take them. Hide them."

Ray stuffed them down his pants and into his own underwear, then patted his clothes back into place. Allen watched, nodding approval. "Soon as you can, get rid of them. Burn them. Promise me."

"I promise."

Then the cops knocked hard on the door. Allen wiped his damp upper lip, clapped Ray on the shoulder, and went to answer the door. Moody read him his rights while the other detective put cuffs on him. Then they took him away.

The whole time Allen was incarcerated, they never talked about the panties again. Allen never asked if he'd burned them, and he'd never admitted to breaking his promise. He couldn't bring himself to destroy them. They were his most prized possession. They were the last thing his brother had ever given him.

He didn't take them out of their hiding place very often. Not as often as he wanted to. But if killing Moody wasn't a special occasion, he didn't know what was.

He stretched out on his back on his bed and put his hand inside the panties, then held it up to the window and looked at his splayed fingers silhouetted through the sheer fabric. He sighed with contentment and rolled onto his side for a doze.

The cramped cockpit of a fighter jet had never made Den claustrophobic, but being inside an interrogation room a the Austin Police Department was an unsettling reminde of the last time he'd been here, being hammered by Dal Moody. It mattered little that Moody was dead. He stil felt like clawing at the walls.

Beside him, Bellamy looked pale and shaken, and often anyone speaking to her had to repeat what they said before it registered. Her distraction was understandable. Seeing the picture of Moody with his neck open had been a shock.

Because everyone in the department recognized her as a celebrity, and as the surviving daughter of the recently deceased Howard Lyston, the detectives were deferential.

Nevertheless, sweat had begun trickling down Dent's rib cage as soon as they were ushered into the interrogation room to give their statements. He kept a tight grip on Bellamy's hand, admittedly as much for his comfort as for hers.

Haymaker had called the police department from his house. Speaking to a homicide detective, he'd told him about the gruesome text message, identified the victim as retired police officer Dale Moody, and given the detective the number of Gall's cell phone.

"It's believed a guy named Ray Strickland has the phone, and that he's the one who sent the text. He's being sought for a suspected assault, so you've already got a report on him. The three of us are leaving now and will be there soon."

When they arrived at the police station, they'd been immediately met by the homicide detective with whom Haymaker had spoken, Nagle, and another named Abbott. To Dent they looked interchangeable. Same age. Same height and body build. Similar sport jackets.

They'd taken Bellamy's phone from her, looked at the picture that had been texted, and had admitted that they didn't yet have an address for one Ray Strickland, but that they were trying to locate him by triangulating the cell-phone signal.

"We've also issued a BOLO." Which Haymaker had translated to Dent and Bellamy as *be on the lookout.*

"Why would this Strickland want to kill Dale Moody?" Nagle had asked.

Haymaker had handed over the copied Susan Lyston case file. "It all goes back to this."

Now, more than an hour later, they were still talking, answering questions, painstakingly telling the entire story. At one point, a uniformed officer had stuck his head in and summoned Abbott into the hallway. Nagle urged Bellamy to continue.

She was retelling him about her conversation with Moody at the funeral reception when, suddenly, Abbott returned and announced, "Moody's body was discovered inside Strickland's residence."

"How'd they find it?" Nagle asked. "The cell phone?"

"No, we got a tip on where he lived."

"From who?" Nagle asked.

"Rupe Collier."

"What?" Bellamy and Dent exclaimed in unison.

"Yeah, seems Mr. Collier took pity on Strickland after his brother was killed in prison. He found him living on welfare. He gave him a job, set him up in a duplex, where he still lives. He said Strickland's never bothered anybody. A loner, but no troublemaker. Fairly good mechanic as well as a glass man. Does windshield work for him."

The detective glanced uneasily at Bellamy. "But, according to Mr. Collier, ever since your book came out and gained so much attention, Ray's been missing work days. He's been belligerent toward his boss and co-workers. Mr. Collier says he's talked to him several times by phone, trying to persuade him not to dwell on the past.

"But he says Strickland grew increasingly agitated and had recently made some threats against the two of you and Dale Moody. Yesterday, he took off with a car belonging to Mr. Collier. He made several attempts to speak with him by phone and talk him into returning the car before he was forced to report it stolen. Strickland didn't answer his phone and never called him back.

"Then, a short while ago, Mr. Collier retrieved a voice-mail message from Strickland, which had been left very early this morning. He said that Moody was dead and mentioned that he might have to move because of the mess. Mr. Collier called nine-one-one immediately and gave them Strickland's address."

"What a guy," Dent muttered. But the detectives didn't hear him because Nagle was asking Abbott about Strickland's state of mind when he was taken into custody.

"He wasn't."

"He's at large?"

"'Fraid so. We've got the license plate number for the car. Shouldn't take too long to bring him in. He's been upgraded to an armed-and-dangerous."

"How did he manage to get away?" Bellamy asked.

"According to the first officers in, they found him in the bedroom, asleep on the bed. They surrounded him. He was startled awake and launched an immediate attack with a knife, apparently the murder weapon. They said he was a wild man. Didn't heed their orders to drop the knife.

"One of the officers was wounded. He took the blade in the shoulder. Deep and dirty, but it looks like he'll be okay. That's the good news. The bad news is that Strickland made good his escape.

"There's something else," Abbot said, looking down at

Bellamy. "Strickland left these behind on the bed." From his jacket pocket he removed a sealed evidence bag and held it out to her. "Could these have belonged to your sister?"

Bellamy was loath to touch the bag, but she took it from the detective and looked at the article inside. Her throat seized up. Dumbly she nodded, then said, "That's the type she wore."

Abbott took back the evidence bag. "I'll get them to the lab, see if there's any forensic evidence to prove they were hers."

Haymaker said, "Dale always contended that the guy who had her underpants was the guy who killed her. If I'm remembering right, Allen was Ray's guardian. Maybe he took the fall for his little brother."

Bellamy ventured another theory. "Perhaps Allen gave them to Ray so he wouldn't be caught with them in his possession."

"We'll go digging in that case file," Nagle said. He seemed eager to do so.

"While you're at it, you may want to take a look at this, too." Bellamy passed Moody's confession to the detective. "I think you'll find it interesting reading. Especially in regards to Rupe Collier and why he was the first person Ray called after killing Dale Moody."

Steven disconnected the call and turned to address his mother. "She said she would stop by and fill us in on the details. She sounded tired and a bit hoarse from talking for hours to the police, but she says she's basically okay." Wryly, he added, "She also said it will be a long time before she'll open a text message."

"How awful that must have been for her," Olivia said.

"'Ghastly' was the word she used."

"I'm worried about her. She's had to endure so much the last several days."

"And I'm partially responsible. Is that what you were about to say?"

"Not at all."

"Well, it's true." He sighed and sank back into a chair. "I'll never forgive myself for hiring Dowd, who only gave Bellamy something else to worry about."

"You made a mistake," William said. "Your intention was good. You didn't foresee how it would be perceived or turn out. You've apologized. Let it go."

Steven smiled across at his partner. "Thank you."

William returned his smile, then asked to be excused. "I should call the restaurants and check in, make sure no crises have arisen."

Steven saw through the ruse. William was sensitive to the family matters Steven and his mother needed to discuss and was giving them the privacy to do so.

As soon as he'd cleared the door, Olivia let down her guard. Her shoulders slumped with fatigue, which Steven knew was a holdover from the days she'd stood vigil over Howard's deathbed. She was also suffering equal parts of grief and mental anguish.

"As soon as this Strickland character is caught, it will be over, Mother. Finally and forever."

"God, I hope so."

He laughed mirthlessly. "It will be strange to wake up and not dread the day and what ugly surprises might be in store. From the day Bellamy's book went on sale, I haven't welcomed a single dawn."

"I know what you mean. Neither have I. I just wish…
Well, I wish a lot of things that can't come true."

"Such as?"

"I wish Bellamy hadn't received that hideous text."

"She has Dent's broad shoulders to lean on."

"That's another of my wishes. I wish he weren't in her life."

"It's not official."

Olivia looked at him and arched her brow.

"Yet," he added ruefully.

"Do you think it's inevitable?"

"I've seen the way they look at each other."

"Which is how?"

"The way you and Howard looked at each other just after you met."

She smiled sadly. "That bad? Well, in any event, there's nothing I can do about it. Just as I can't stop you from going back to Atlanta tomorrow. I wish you didn't have to leave so soon."

She would be hurt to know just how badly he wanted to escape this house that held so many horrible memories for him. He'd stayed this long only because he didn't want to leave her alone in her grief. But he wouldn't breathe easily until he was miles away.

"Mostly," she said on a sigh, "I wish that Howard had lived long enough to see the end of all this."

"I wish that, too. But thank God it'll soon be over for the rest of us. Bellamy's quest, for lack of a better word, came to an end when Susan's undies were found in Ray Stickland's house. Case closed."

Olivia put her elbow on the arm of her chair, leaned her head into her hand, and massaged her forehead. "The recovery of her panties will be in the news. It will be written about, talked about, speculated on. For days."

"But not forever. Another scandalous story will soon come along."

"That little trick of hers cost us all so dearly."

Steven went perfectly still. He stopped breathing, and he would have sworn that his heart stopped also, except that his body was infused with an incredible rush of heat. His eyes remained fixed and unblinking on his mother.

Eventually she lowered her hand, raised her head, and looked over at him, smiling wanly. "We have no choice but to get through the coming media blitz. God knows I—" She broke off and looked at him curiously. "Steven? What is it?"

He swallowed. "You said that little trick of Susan's cost us all so dearly."

Olivia's lips parted, but nothing came out.

"What little trick were you referring to, Mother?"

She still didn't speak.

"Mother, I asked you a question. What little trick? Her little trick of taking off her panties and giving them to men?"

"I—"

He shot to his feet. "You *knew*?"

"No, I—"

"You knew, didn't you? You knew she'd done that little trick with me. Many times. Did you also know about everything else?"

When she stood up she was wobbly on her feet and had to grab the back of her chair for support. "Steven, listen to me. Please."

"You knew about...everything? All of it? And didn't do anything about it?"

"Steven—"

"You didn't stop it. Why?"

"I couldn't," she whimpered.

He trembled with rage. "It ruined my life!"

She covered her mouth to stifle her sobs. Her entire body was racked by them, but he bore down on her mercilessly. "Why didn't you stop it?"

"I—"

"Why? *Why?*"

"Because of Howard!" she cried. "It would have destroyed him to know."

For long moments, Steven stood there, staring into her stricken face. "It would have destroyed Howard, and you couldn't have that. But it was okay for me to be destroyed."

"No," she wailed, reaching for him.

He slung off her hand.

"Steven! *Steven!*"

She was still screaming his name as he took the stairs two at a time.

Chapter 29

⟡

Dent pulled his car to a stop in the semicircular driveway in front of the Lystons' house. "Gall's timing couldn't be worse, but I asked for the meeting, so I feel like I should go."

"You definitely should," Bellamy said.

"I'll make it short and sweet."

"This is important to you, so don't rush it on my account. Besides, I'll be busy mending fences. When I left here yesterday everyone was upset and angry."

"You came to me and spent the night. For that alone, they probably scratched you out of the will."

"It was worth it," she said softly.

"Yeah?"

They exchanged a warm look, then, remembering why they were there, she said, "They'll want to hear about everything that happened today, and there's a lot to tell."

"Which is another reason why I don't want to leave you. I hate letting you out of my sight with Strickland still at large."

"There's a police car parked outside the gate."

"I'm glad of that. If the detectives hadn't suggested it, I would have." He looked up at the sky through the windshield. "It also looks like rain. Maybe I should wait out here while you go inside—"

"You'll do no such thing. You braved the police station for me all day today. I appreciated your presence, especially knowing the discomfort it cost you to be there. The least I can do is brave a rain shower."

Their parting kiss left them wanting to get their separate obligations done with so they'd be back together sooner. She waved him off, went up the steps and into the house. No one was about on the lower floor, which was surprising since she'd notified Steven that she was on her way.

She called out to him and Olivia, but it was the housekeeper Helena who appeared, coming from the direction of the kitchen. "I'm sorry, Ms. Price. I was just about to leave for the day and didn't hear you come in."

"Where is everybody?"

"Mrs. Lyston is upstairs in her room. She asked not to be disturbed for a while."

"And my brother?"

"He left."

"He went out?"

"No, he and Mr. Stroud are flying back to Atlanta."

"I thought they weren't due to leave until tomorrow."

"He told me they'd had a sudden change of plans."

Sudden was an understatement. Steven must have left shortly after their telephone conversation.

Seeing Bellamy's disappointment, the housekeeper said, "He left a note for you on the desk in Mr. Lyston's study."

A note. That was all she warranted? He couldn't have delayed his departure long enough for them to say a proper good-bye?

"Do you need me for anything before I go?"

"No, I'm fine, thank you, Helena."

"I'll say good night then."

Bellamy went directly into the study. The built-in bookshelves were filled with memorabilia that chronicled her father's life, from a black-and-white photograph of him with his parents on the day of his christening to a picture taken of him just last year playing golf at Pebble Beach with the president of the United States.

But for all its comfortable clutter, the study seemed empty without him. She and her dad had enjoyed long talks in this room. It put a lump in her throat just to walk into it. Usually it represented warmth and security. Today, it was gloomy and oppressive, its dimness unrelieved by the open drapes. Outside, the sky had grown increasingly overcast.

She switched on the desk lamp as she sat down in her father's chair. The squeak of the leather was familiar and, again, she was almost overwhelmed by a wave of homesickness for him. She was made even sadder by the envelope with her name written on it lying on the desk.

She broke the seal and read Steven's brief note.

Dear Bellamy,

Had the circumstances of our lives been different, maybe I would have been the brother you wished for and I wished to be. As it is, I'm doomed to disappoint and hurt you. I apologize again for Dowd. Honorable intentions, but a bad idea. I wanted to

*protect you, because I do love you. But if you have
any love in your heart for me, for both our sakes,
please let this good-bye be final.*

Steven

The message pierced her heart, making her hurt as
much for him as for herself. She held the note against her
lips and fought back tears. They were heartfelt, but to cry
was futile. She couldn't undo the past that had left such
deep scars on her stepbrother's soul.

Her eyes strayed to the framed photograph on the
corner of her father's desk. She wondered if Steven had
noticed it when he left the note. If so, he'd probably found
it as disturbing as she did.

Once, she had asked her dad why he kept this particular photograph where he would see it every day. He'd
told her that it was the last picture taken of Susan, and he
wanted to remember her as she looked in it: smiling and
happy, alive and vibrant.

It had been taken that Memorial Day before they left
for the state park. They were all decked out in their red,
white, and blue clothing, which Olivia had mandated
they wear for the occasion. They'd assembled on the
front steps of the house, and when they were posed, their
housekeeper at the time had snapped the picture.

It was similar to the Christmas family portrait only
in that it revealed so much about their individual personalities. Steven look sulky. Susan was radiant. Bellamy
appeared self-conscious. Olivia and Howard, standing
arm in arm, smiling, looked like the embodiment of the
American dream, like tragedy couldn't touch them.

A low rumble of thunder caused Bellamy to turn her head and glance nervously out the window. Rain was spattering the panes. She rubbed her chilled arms and got up to pull the drapes. A masochistic bent forced her to look up at the sky.

The clouds were malevolent looking and greenish in color.

She closed her eyes for several seconds, and when she opened them again, saw that the clouds weren't green at all. They were gray. Scuttling. Moisture-laden rain clouds. Nothing more.

Nothing resembling the apocalyptic sky on that afternoon eighteen years ago.

She turned back to the desk and picked up the framed family photograph, holding it directly beneath the lampshade to maximize the light, tilting it this way and that so she could look at it from different angles.

What was she looking *for*, exactly?

She didn't know. But something was eluding her. Something important and troubling. What was it? What was she missing? Why did it seem essential that she find it?

A bolt of lightning struck close by, followed by a sharp crack of thunder.

Bellamy dropped the picture frame. The glass inside it shattered.

Dent entered the Starbucks near the capitol building where the state senator had suggested they meet. Most everyone in the place was pecking away on a laptop or talking on a cell phone, except for the two men who were waiting for Dent. Gall had dressed for the occasion, trading his greasy coveralls for a clean pair. He was nervously gnawing on a cigar.

The man who stood up with him as Dent approached their table was sixtyish and balding. He wore a plaid shirt with pearl snap buttons. It was tucked into a pair of pressed and creased Wranglers held up by a wide, tooled leather belt with a silver buckle the size of a saucer. His broad, sunburned face was open and friendly, and the hand that clasped Dent's as Gall made the introductions was as tough as boot leather.

He pumped Dent's hand a couple of times. "Dent, thanks for coming. I've been looking forward to meeting you. Have a seat." He motioned Dent into the chair across the small table from him.

Just then a clap of thunder rattled the windows. Dent looked out and saw that it had begun to sprinkle. When he came back around to the two men, he said, "I can't stay long."

His rudeness caused Gall to glower, but the senator smiled genially. "Then I'll make my pitch quick. Gall has already laid out your terms to me, and, frankly, I don't think they're fair." He paused, then laughed. "I can do you better."

Dent listened as the senator proposed a sweet deal, which only a damn fool would walk away from. But most of his attention was on what was happening outside. The wind was buffeting the sycamore trees planted at intervals along the sidewalk. The sprinkles had turned into a heavy rain. Lightning and thunder had grown more frequent and violent.

Bellamy would be afraid.

"Dent?"

He realized the senator had stopped speaking, and that
natever he'd last said necessitated a response of some
nd, because both he and Gall were looking at him
pectantly.

"Uh, yeah," he said, hoping that was a suitable reply.

Gall took the cigar from his mouth. "That's all you've
ot to say?"

Dent stood up and addressed the senator. "Your air-
ane's a wet dream. And I can fly it better than anybody.
ut right now, I've got to go."

As he wended his way through the tables he heard the
nator chuckle. "Is he always in that big of a hurry?"

"Lately, yeah," Gall said. "He's in love."

Dent pushed through the door, which the wind caught
d jerked out of his hand. He didn't stop to close it, but
wed his head against the pelting rain and took off running.

ith trembling hands, Bellamy shook the shards of bro-
n glass from the frame, then ran her fingertips across
e photograph itself. She looked carefully at each family
ember individually, trying to figure out what was both-
ing her about the picture.

Lightning flashed. She cringed. And for that instant,
e was twelve years old again, in the wooded area of
e state park, petrified with fear as she crouched in the
derbrush. She needed to take cover from the weather,
t she was too frightened to move.

The flashback was so intense her breath started coming
loud, rushing gasps. Taking the photograph with her,
e scrambled around the desk to the nearest bookcase
d dropped to her knees in front of the cabinets beneath
e shelves. Inside were all the research materials she'd

collected while writing *Low Pressure*. She'd had Dext
send her all the files, which she'd left behind when s
fled New York. When they arrived, she had asked her d
if she could store them here in a space he wasn't using.

Moving unsteadily, she stacked the bulky folders
the floor in front of her and began rapidly sorting throu
them until she found the one containing photographs of t
tornado and its aftermath. She'd clipped them from mag
zine write-ups and newspaper articles, and printed them
the Internet, until she had dozens of pictures that had be
taken that fateful Memorial Day in Austin.

But she was searching for one in particular, and h
search was so frantic she flipped through all the photograp
twice before she located it. It had been captioned: *Prom
nent family searches for loved ones among the rubble.*

A Lyston Electronics employee who'd had his came
at the barbecue had taken the picture within minutes
the tornado. In the background, the devastation look
surreal. The snapshot had captured people in tears, in t.
ters, still in the throes of panic.

In the forefront were Howard, Olivia, and Steven.

Howard was clutching Olivia's hand, his face streak
with tears. Steven's arm was raised, his face buried in t
crook of his elbow. Olivia's expression was stark, vast
different from the smile she'd been wearing in the phot
graph taken that morning on the front steps of her home

Bellamy held the photographs side by side.

Yes, the contrast between Olivia's facial expressio
was pronounced.

However, not so noticeable was the difference in h
blouse. In the photograph taken earlier, it had a bow at t
neck. In the second photo . . .

Bellamy dropped the photographs and covered her face with her hands as the memory jolted her. As though she'd been propelled supersonically through a time warp, she was suddenly back there picking her way through the woods, looking for Susan, who'd left the pavilion with Allen Strickland.

Bellamy wanted to find them together so she could embarrass Susan the way Susan had embarrassed her by saying what she had about her and Dent.

But when she came upon her sister, she was lying face-down on the ground, the skirt of her sundress flipped up, showing her bottom. Clutched in her hand was her small purse. She wasn't moving. Bellamy knew she was dead.

As shocking as that, Olivia was standing over her, looking down. In her hand was the tie that belonged around the neck of her blouse. The end of it was trailing on the ground.

Bellamy wanted to cry out, but she was frozen with fear and shock. She remained perfectly still and held her breath. It would have been hard to breathe anyway, because the air had turned so thick. The woods had become preternaturally silent and motionless. Nothing moved. No birds or insects, no squirrels, not a single leaf. It was as though everything in nature had stopped to watch Olivia choke her stepdaughter to death.

Then suddenly the stillness was interrupted by a strong whoosh of wind, and the silence was split by a roar that knocked Bellamy to the ground. The change galvanized Olivia, who turned and thrashed her way through the trees and underbrush at a run, moving in the direction of the pavilion.

Bellamy clambered to her feet and stumbled blindly

through the woods as the wind beat at her and stole her breath, as the charged atmosphere caused her hair to stand on end. The noise was unlike anything she'd ever heard. It was like the roar of a dragon bearing down on her.

But she hadn't been running from the terrifying elements of the storm. She'd been running from what she'd seen. She was blindly seeking not shelter from the wind and natural debris that was whipping around her, but rather refuge from the unthinkable.

When she finally reached the boathouse, lungs bursting and heart racing, she stumbled inside and instinctually sought a corner in which to cower, even as a section of the metal roof was ripped away and another sliced through the cavernous building like the blade of a guillotine, cleaving a boat in two. Weeping uncontrollably, she covered her head with her arms and made herself as small and invisible as possible.

Rain was lashing at the study window now. A jagged fork of lightning struck close. Following a loud explosive pop, the lamp on the desk flickered, then went out.

She wanted to seek cover and hide, as she had that day in the boathouse, but she was no longer a child, and if she gave in to her fear now, she might never learn what even her unlocked memory couldn't tell her.

Reaching up from her place on the floor, she grabbed a corner of the desk and used it as leverage to pull herself to her feet. She closed her eyes against the lashing fury of the storm, took several deep breaths, then let go of the desk and walked from the room.

All the lights in the house had gone out, but she found her way to the main staircase. Gripping the newel post, she paused. Its curving length seemed rife with menace.

It was so dark she couldn't even see where it ended at the top, but she forced herself to plant her foot on the bottom tread and start up.

She was blinded by periodic flashes of lightning, causing her to grab the banister and wait until her vision returned. When she reached the second-story landing, she looked down the long hallway. It was dark. But a faint light shone beneath the door of the bedroom Olivia and Howard had shared. Bellamy walked toward it and didn't even pause to knock before turning the doorknob and going in.

A candle votive flickered on the nightstand. Olivia was lying on the bed, the covers pulled up to her chest. "Olivia?"

She raised her head from the pillow. "Bellamy." Then, more weakly, "Steven left."

Bellamy crossed the room to stand at the foot of the bed. Olivia glanced down at her hand, in which she clutched the two telling photographs. When her gaze moved back to Bellamy's face, she looked deeply into her eyes for ponderous moments. Finally, she said, "You know."

Bellamy nodded and slowly sat down on the edge of the bed. For a time they just looked at each other, saying nothing. Olivia broke the taut silence. "How did you piece it together?"

"I didn't. With the help of these photographs, I finally remembered."

Olivia looked at her quizzically.

Bellamy explained her memory loss. "Even when I was focused on that day and writing the book, I couldn't remember snatches of time. Not until just now did it all come back."

"You saw me do it?" Olivia asked quietly.

"I saw you standing over her body with the tie to your blouse in your hand."

"It was detachable. After the tornado, no one noticed that it was missing. People had had their clothing blown off. One child was found completely naked. The funnel had literally sucked her clothes off her."

"You just dropped the tie amid the rubble. The murder weapon vanished when the storm debris was cleared."

"All this time it's been assumed that she was strangled with her underpants."

"So the pair of panties that was found in Strickland's house today—"

"Oh, I'm certain they're hers. Allen could have given them to his brother before his arrest, so he wouldn't be caught with them."

"You knew he had them?"

"Oh, yes. Of course I couldn't tell, because I couldn't say how I knew. I was sure the police would find them, which would have clenched his guilt. But they didn't. I can't explain why Ray kept them all these years."

Bellamy couldn't believe the calm and detached manner in which Olivia was relating all this. "Olivia, what happened out there in the woods?"

Her chest rose and fell on a deep sigh. "I saw her leave the pavilion with that boy following her like she was in heat. She was, you know. Constantly. She gave off an animalistic...scent. Something. I don't know. But it was unmistakable to men. Anyway, I followed them. I didn't want her shenanigans to spoil our big day.

"I heard them before I saw them. Disgusting noises. Like animals in rut. His heavy breathing, her moans.

Susan's back was against a tree. The top of her sundress was pulled down. He was at her breasts. His hands. Mouth. He seemed totally absorbed, but Susan looked bored. She was staring up at the sky.

"She remarked that it looked funny, that it looked like a storm was coming. But either he didn't hear her, or he ignored her. She said his name and gave him a slight push away from her. 'I don't want to get rained on,' she said.

"He laughed and said, 'Then we'd better hurry.' He undid his pants and jerked them down over his hips. She looked down at him and giggled. 'Put that thing back.' And he said, '*Back* isn't where I'm gonna put it.'"

Olivia gave a shudder. "I was disgusted to the point that I thought about turning around and leaving. I didn't want to watch them. But then Susan slapped at his groping hand. 'I mean it. I'm not going to stay out here and have my dress ruined.'

"He tried to cajole her, playfully at first, and then more angrily. Finally, he called her names, yanked up his pants, and started walking away. Laughing, she told him not to go away mad.

"Then I watched her take off her panties and shoot them at him, like they were a rubber band. She told him to use them while he pleasured himself, and to think of her while he was doing it." Olivia closed her eyes for a moment. "Of course she used much cruder terminology."

She paused for a moment and drew a deep breath. "She straightened her clothing and fluffed her hair. As beautiful as she was, I was sickened by the sight of her. My expression must have conveyed it because when she saw me, she said, 'What do *you* want?' You know the inflection I'm talking about. She wasn't embarrassed, or even curious to know how long I'd been there and what I'd seen. She just asked the question in that hateful tone.

"I told her precisely what I was thinking, that she was a disgrace, that she was unspeakably vile and amoral. She sighed theatrically, pushed herself away from the tree, and said, 'Spare me.' When she sauntered past me, she pulled her skirt aside so it wouldn't come into contact with me. That was the last straw.

"Before I knew it, my hand had shot out, and I'd taken a tight grip on her arm. She told me to let go, but I only moved in closer. And that's when...when...when I told her to leave Steven alone."

Bellamy gasped. "You knew about her and Steven?"

"So did you, it seems."

"Not until this week. He told me when I went to Atlanta. You knew back then, when it was happening?"

She turned her head away so that her cheek was resting on the pillow. "God help me."

Bellamy was more astounded by this than Olivia's confession to killing Susan. "Why didn't you do something to stop it?"

"Susan knew why," she said, barely above a whisper. "I told her that if she came near Steven again I was going to tell Howard. She laughed in my face. 'Who do you think you're kidding, Olivia?' She knew I wouldn't tell him because it would have shattered him, and our family.

"She was Howard's daughter. He would have felt an obligation to support her. My loyalty would have been with Steven. It would have torn us apart. Our marriage. Everything. I wouldn't let that little tramp destroy us."

"But—"

"I know, Bellamy. I know. She destroyed the family

anyway. But on that day, I tried to make my threat believable. I told her again to leave Steven alone. She got right in my face and said, 'Not as long as that broody little faggot can get it up.'"

Olivia stared blankly at the opposite wall for a long, silent moment, then slowly brought her head back around to look at Bellamy. "She walked—sashayed—away, swinging the skirt of her sundress.

"I didn't plan it. I just reacted with rage. I bent down and grabbed a broken tree limb that was lying on the ground, and hit her in the back of the head with all my might. She fell facedown. I untied the bow at my neck and took it off." She raised her shoulders in a slight shrug. "It was like watching someone else. It was remarkably easy. When I realized that she was dead, I insulted her by flipping up her skirt."

Neither said anything for a while. Bellamy stared at Olivia's composed face. Olivia stared at the ceiling.

Bellamy stirred. "I must ask. Did Daddy know? Or have so much as an inkling?"

Olivia's face crumpled. "No, no." Then in a mournful tone, she added, "Sometimes I would catch him watching me. Thoughtfully. Frowning. And it caused me to wonder..."

"He never asked?"

"No."

Bellamy wondered if perhaps he hadn't asked because he didn't want to know. Maybe he had commissioned her to get to the truth in order to vindicate not Allen Strickland, but Olivia. He hadn't wanted to die with even a midgen of suspicion that his beloved wife had taken his daughter's life.

They would never know his mind, and Bellamy was actually relieved that they wouldn't.

"Does Steven know?" she asked quietly. "He told me himself that he was glad Susan was dead."

"No. But I let it slip today that I knew what she was doing to him. That's why he left."

Bellamy's heart sank as Olivia described the scene. "I begged his forgiveness, but he refused to listen. He locked me out of their room and when he opened the door, their bags were packed, and a taxi was waiting to take them to the airport. I pleaded with him to stay and talk it out, but he wouldn't even look at me. Which is the worst possible punishment for what I did."

She took a moment as though collecting her thoughts, then said, "I deceived myself into thinking that Allen Strickland's conviction was a sign from God that he was granting me a second chance.

"Steven suffered, and so did you to some extent, but Howard and I had almost two decades of happiness. I made myself believe that killing Susan was justified, and that's why I'd gotten away with it." She sighed. "But things don't work that way, do they?"

"No they don't," Bellamy said softly. "Because you have to tell the authorities, Olivia. Allen Strickland deserves to be exonerated. So does Dent, Steven, anyone who came under suspicion. You must clear them."

Olivia nodded. "I'm not afraid anymore. I've lost Howard. Now Steven. Nothing worse can happen to me."

Bellamy suddenly realized that, except for her head, Olivia hadn't moved. Her face was wet with tears, yet she hadn't pulled a tissue from the box on the bedside table.

"Olivia?"

Her eyes had closed, and she didn't respond.

"Olivia!"

Bellamy whipped back the covers, and, although she'd never been a screamer, she screamed now. Olivia was drenched in blood. Both wrists had been slashed.

Bellamy frantically slapped her cheeks, but her only responses were faint murmurs of protest.

Bellamy snatched the cordless phone from its charger on the nightstand, punched in 911, and began babbling as soon as the operator answered. She shouted the address. "She's bleeding to death! Send an ambulance. Hurry, hurry!"

The operator launched into a series of questions, but when Bellamy saw headlights cut an arc across the ceiling she dropped the phone, rushed to the window, and flung back the curtains.

Despite the downpour, she recognized the Vette's low profile as it came speeding through the open gate. She cried out in relief.

She returned to the bed, touched Olivia's cheek, and was startled by how cool it was. "Don't die," she whispered fiercely, then left the room at a run.

The hall was darker than before, but she didn't slow down even when she reached the stairs. She practically flew down them, tripping on the last tread and barely catching herself on the newel post before she fell.

She reached the front door just as the Corvette rolled to a stop. "Dent! Help me!"

Heedless of the downpour and the lightning that filled the sky with a blue-white glare, she ran across the porch and down the steps. She rounded the hood of the car just as he was alighting.

She launched herself at him. "Dent, thank God! It's Olivia. She's—"

Strong arms went around her, but they weren't Dent's.

"'Bout time we met."

She looked up through the rain into Ray Strickland's leering face.

Chapter 30

When Dent reached the parking space where he'd left is Corvette and found it empty, he made a three-sixty turn, hinking that the cloudburst had thrown him off and that he'd one to the wrong space. And then for several seconds more e stood there, confounded, while rain beat down on him.

The possibility that his car had been stolen from the arking lot made him gnash his teeth. But then his heart tuttered when it occurred to him who the thief might e. Could it be a coincidence that his car had been sto- en while Ray Strickland was at large? Strickland was a mechanic. He would know how to break in, hot-wire, and lo anything else necessary to steal any vehicle.

All this ran through Dent's mind in a millisecond, and e acted on his fear instantly. Ducking beneath the nar- ow overhang of the building, he pulled out his phone to all Bellamy and warn her. He punched in her number efore remembering that Nagle and Abbott had confis- ated her phone to hold as evidence in Moody's murder. No one answered it.

Dent burst into the Starbucks looking like a ma[n] deranged, startling the customers and staff. Heedless o[f] the fact that he was soaked to the skin, that his hair wa[s] plastered flat to his head, and that his eyes looked feral, h[e] shouted, "Gall, your truck. Where's it parked?"

Gall, who was still in conversation with the senato[r,] gaped at Dent. "Where's your car?"

"Not where I left it. Give me the keys to your truck[.] Call nine-one-one and tell them to send police to th[e] Lystons' house. The cops at the gate need to be alerte[d] that Ray Strickland may try to get onto the property b[y] driving my car. Bellamy hasn't got her phone, so I can[']t call her directly, and I don't know the land line numbe[r.] Now for godsake, pitch me your keys."

Gall did as told, and Dent snatched them from the ai[r.] "West side of the building," Gall yelled at Dent's back a[s] he plunged back into the thunderstorm.

He ran to the parking lot and spotted Gall's relic c[of] a pickup. He climbed into the cab and cranked it or[,] then, pushing it as fast as it would go, jumped a curb an[d] bounced into the street.

As he drove with one hand, he dialed 911 with hi[s] other. By now Gall would have called the emergenc[y] number, but it wouldn't hurt to put in a second call.

He gave the answering operator his name and th[e] address of the Lystons' house. "Bellamy Lyston Price i[s] in danger of her life."

"What's the nature of the problem, sir?"

"Too long to tell. But there are a pair of cops stationed a[t] her front gate. They should be notified to be on the looko[ut] for a red Corvette. They shouldn't open the gate becaus[e] Ray Strickland might be driving it. And call Nagle an[d]

Abbott. They're homicide detectives. They'll know what this is about." He was out of breath by the time he finished.

"Your name again, sir?"

"What?"

"Your name again?"

"Are you fucking kidding?"

With infuriating calm, she began again with the question about his name. Cursing, he tossed his phone onto the seat of the pickup so he could use both hands to steer around a slow-moving minivan. He blasted through a red light, blaring the pickup's horn.

Ray's luck had changed, and it was on account of him killing Moody.

There had to be a correlation, because that was when things had started going good for him.

First, he'd escaped the two cops who'd showed up at his place. One's blood was still on his clothes, along with the splotches Moody had sprayed on him. He didn't think he'd killed the cop, but he hadn't hung around to find out.

Dodging the second cop's bullet—another stroke of luck—he'd barreled his way through his duplex and out the back even as other squad cars were squealing to a halt in front.

He'd lived in the neighborhood for a long time, so he knew the twisty streets well, knew which ones were dead ends and which provided a quick way out of the maze, even for someone traveling on foot.

Yes sirree. Luck had definitely been on his side. Running between houses and going over fences, he'd made it to the back of a strip center where there was a doc-in-the-box.

Knowing that the staffs of these minor emergency clinics usually worked long shifts and figuring that this early in the morning one would be starting, he deduced that a stolen car wouldn't be missed for hours. He'd waited behind a Dumpster until a young woman dressed in scrubs parked in the employee lot and entered through a back door. Breaking into her car had been a piece of cake.

Was he one lucky bastard, or what? Within minutes of leaving his duplex, he'd been miles away from it. Pumped. Exhilarated. Wanting to spill more blood. Bellamy Price's blood.

Ever since her old man's death, she'd been staying with her stepmother in the family mansion. Ray made that his destination, reasoning that she would eventually turn up there. Driving past it throughout the day also gave him an opportunity to plan how he might get through the gate and onto the property.

It was going to be doubly difficult now that a patrol car was posted outside the gate.

But, again, luck smiled on him.

He just happened to be on one of his reconnaissance drive-bys when he saw Dent's red Corvette leaving through the gate. He was alone, meaning that Bellamy was inside and, for the time being, inaccessible.

Ray decided to follow Dent. And when he parked his car and went into a Starbucks, Ray realized that he wasn't just lucky, he was brilliant, because he saw the answer to the problem of how to get past that damn gate.

He left the car he'd stolen earlier in an adjacent parking lot and helped himself to Dent Carter's sweet ride. And, as if good fortune wasn't already with him, it began to

in buckets, which would make it difficult for the policemen at the gate to see who was behind the wheel of the
'ette. To make it even more difficult for them to see into
he car, Ray turned the headlights on high beam.

It was so easy he'd wanted to laugh. The two cops
who'd waved to Dent when he drove out waved to Ray
when he pulled up to the gate, which opened even before
e came to a full stop. Abraca-fucking-dabra. He figured
he cops had been given a transmitter so they could con-
ol who went in and out.

Getting inside the house posed no problem. Bellamy
erself ran out to greet him. He had her in an inescapable
ear hug before she realized he wasn't Dent.

She seemed too shocked even to scream, which was
ood. It saved him from having to hit her. He didn't want
er unconscious. He wanted her awake and terrified.

But as he lifted her off her feet and started up the front
teps with her, she began to struggle. "No, please, my
tepmother is upstairs."

"I'll get to her. Two for the price of one. But you first."

She doubled her efforts to wiggle out of his grip and
icked him solidly in the shin. It hurt so bad that as soon
s they were across the threshold and he'd pushed the
ont door closed, he thrust her from him so hard she went
urtling forward and landed on the stone-tile floor.

plintering pain shot from Bellamy's shoulder and hip,
hich had sustained most of the impact. But she had no
me to dwell on the pain because Ray was whipping a
nife from its scabbard.

He brandished it at her, and she saw that the blade
as already streaked with dried blood. Moody's? Bile

filled the back of her throat as the image of his open nec
flashed into her mind. That was what Ray would do to he
if she didn't prevent it.

He grinned down at her and took two lumbering step
forward.

She put a hand up. "Listen, Ray, you don't want to d
this."

"Hell I don't. You killed Susan and let..."

"No. No I didn't."

"I heard you. I was hiding in your closet when yc
admitted it. I should've killed you then."

Hiding in her closet? She didn't take time to sort th
out. Stammering, she said, "I didn't kill my sister, but
also know that your brother didn't, either. He was inno
cent. I'm going to tell everyone that he was innocent."

"Too late for that."

"I know," she said wetting her lips. "There's nothir
anyone can do about what happened to him. But I wa
people to know that he was unjustly sent to prison. Yc
were wronged, too. I want to tell about it. But I won't l
able to do that if you kill me."

"I'm gonna kill you." He reached down, grabbed a fis
ful of her hair, and pulled her up by it. She cried out i
pain, and did the only thing she knew to do. She knee
him hard in the groin. It wasn't a direct hit, but his gr
on her hair relaxed slightly, enough for her to jerk herse
free.

She ran for the staircase. If she could lock herself insic
Olivia's room only long enough for the 911 responders
arrive, there was a chance that both of them could surviv

But she was still a long way from the second floo
when Ray's arm hooked her around the waist. He pushe

her face first onto the stairs and landed hard on top of her, knocking the breath out of her. Slapping his hand over her forehead, he pulled her head back against his shoulder. She felt the blade of his knife against the soft area beneath her jawbone.

"I told you you'd be sorry."

When Dent fishtailed Gall's pickup onto the Lystons' street, he saw two silhouettes inside the squad car. What were they doing just sitting there?

He braked hard, leaped out of the truck, ran up to the police car, and smacked the driver's window with both hands, startling the officers inside. He yelled, "Have you seen my Vette?"

The officer lowered the window. "Sure. When you drove it in a few minutes ago. But how'd you get—"

"Wasn't me. It was Strickland."

"Strickland? In your car?"

"Where's the transmitter Bellamy gave you?"

"Right here, but—"

"Open the gate." He ran toward it, shouting over his shoulder. "And call for backup."

The second officer alighted from the passenger side and shouted through the rain. "Dispatch just reported a nine-one-one from the house. Said a woman's bleeding to death."

Dent, fear clutching him, gripped one of the iron bars and shook it. "Open the fucking gate!"

The officer retrieved the transmitter from inside the car, but as he fumbled with it, he hollered to Dent, "Stay where you are. This is a police matter."

Dent remembered the gate code from earlier in the

day, but the patrol car was between him and the column where the keypad was mounted. He made an about-face and began scaling the estate wall, using the wet, clinging vine for footholds.

"Hey! Stop there!"

"You'll have to shoot me."

He got a knee onto the top of the wall and, without even looking to see what was on the other side, flung himself over. He landed in a hedge of evergreens, breaking branches as he worked his way free, then sprinted toward the house, which seemed to be miles away and in total darkness.

His chest was burning with exertion and fear for Bellamy as he hurdled the steps, skidded across the rain-slicked porch, and put his shoulder to the front door as he pushed his way through it.

He couldn't see a thing until lightning flashed, then he took in the scene at once. Strickland had Bellamy face-down about midway up the staircase. Strickland's knee was planted in the small of her back and he had her neck arched and exposed.

"No!" Dent bounded up the stairs.

Ray's head came around and, seeing Dent, he released his hold on Bellamy, spread his arms away from his body like wings, and launched himself down the remaining stairs, catching Dent on the fourth one.

They tumbled together down onto the floor of the foyer in a jumble of arms and legs. Dent was the first to disentangle himself and sprang to his feet, but Ray surged out of a crouch with his knife aimed at Dent's belly. Dent bowed his back, making his abdomen concave enough to escape a fatal uppercut.

By now his eyes had better adjusted to the darkness. When Strickland lunged at him again, Dent went after his knife hand, risking his own hands in order to gain control of the weapon. His fingers clamped around Strickland's wrist and, using fury as his propellant, drove him backward against the wall. He slammed Strickland's knife hand into the paneling.

But Strickland had enough leeway in his wrist to turn the knife toward Dent's face. The tip of it was level with the corner of his left eye. One jab would blind him.

"I'm gonna mess you up, pretty boy. Then I'm going to cut her head off."

Dent bared his teeth. "I'll kill you first."

"Drop it!"

The order must've come from one of the cops. Dent didn't turn his head, but Strickland looked in that direction, and Dent used that momentary distraction to flip the knife away and, with his free hand, give the man's Adam's apple a hard chop. "That's for my plane, you son of a bitch."

Strickland, stunned and suddenly breathless, tried to suck in air. Dent squeezed his wrist so hard he released the knife and it clattered to the floor. Then four police officers swarmed them.

But, even gasping for breath, Strickland wasn't going down easily or quietly. Dent fought his way past the policemen trying to subdue him and bolted up the staircase to where Bellamy was weakly crawling up the steps.

Panicked, he bent over her. "Are you hurt? Did he cut you?"

"No. Olivia." Using handfuls of his wet clothing, she climbed up him until she was on her feet. "Up there. Help me."

He put his arm around her waist and practically carried her up the remaining stairs and along the dark hallway to a bedroom.

The moment he saw Olivia Lyston on her bed, ghostly pale, lying in an ocean of blood, he knew she was dead.

A few minutes later, EMTs confirmed it.

Ray Strickland's bellowed invectives against Bellamy and Dent echoed through the house. It took several officers to restrain him, and all the while he was hollering about injustice. But he bawled like a baby when his hands were secured behind him and he was led outside to the waiting squad car.

"I gotta kill them because it was on account of them that Allen died," he blubbered. Bellamy heard him ask one of the arresting officers if he could have Susan's panties back. "My brother told me to keep them."

She and Dent were questioned separately, and the investigating officers, Nagle and Abbott among them, began linking together the bizarre chain of events. Dent's Vette was towed away as evidence.

"I'm sorry," she told him as they watched the tow truck's taillights leave through the gate. "First your airplane, now your car."

He shrugged. "They can't bleed."

She turned her face up to him.

"When I got here, the cops told me that a woman inside the house was bleeding out."

"I'd called nine-one-one for Olivia."

"Yeah, but I didn't know that." He placed his hand on the back of her head, pressed her face against his chest, and kissed the crown of her head.

"I can't believe she killed Susan," she whispered. "All these years..."

"Yeah," he said on a soft exhale. Then, in an even quieter voice, "Steven's here."

Austin police had found him and William at the airport, where they were waiting for a flight that had been delayed due to the weather. One of the officers had called Nagle, who'd handed over his cell phone to Bellamy, who'd had the unwelcome task of telling Steven about his mother's suicide.

For a long time he'd said nothing, then, "We'll be there soon."

Now, as he and William entered through the front door, she went to embrace him. It was evident that he'd been crying. Given the way he and Olivia had parted, Bellamy knew he would bear responsibility for her taking her own life.

He allowed her to hold him close for several moments before easing away. "We heard about Strickland from the policemen who drove us here. Are you all right?"

"Bruised, but otherwise okay. Dent got here just in time."

He looked at Dent. "Thank you. Truly."

Dent acknowledged the thanks with a nod.

Coming back to Bellamy, Steven asked, "Where is she?"

"In her bedroom, but don't go up. The coroner is in there now. In any case, she wouldn't want you to see it."

"You don't understand. I must go to her. When I left—"

"She told me. But don't blame yourself. I think she was looking ahead to life without Daddy, and simply couldn't stand the thought of it."

"Howard was her life."

"Yes. She would have done anything for him." She hesitated then said, "She did. She killed for him."

Steven, who'd been staring at the top of the staircase, brought his gaze back down to her. He said quietly, "Susan."

She glanced at William, who hadn't even flinched at the revelation. Looking back at Steven, she stated what seemed to be obvious. "You knew?"

"No, I swear it. But I suspected."

"Since when?"

"From the start, I think. When did you find out?"

"My memory of it came back tonight." She related everything that had happened since Dent had dropped her there. "She was already dying. I think it must have been a huge relief to her to tell someone about it."

She paused as a realization struck her. "I understand now why you were so opposed to my book. You didn't want anyone—me—to find out."

"As much for your and Howard's sake as for Mother's. At least she died without having to admit it to him. That would certainly have killed her. I, perhaps more than anyone, knew how much she loved him. More than anything. Or anyone." His voice cracked. William placed a comforting arm across his shoulder, and Steven smiled at him gratefully.

"Steven?" Bellamy spoke his name softly, and when he was looking at her again, she said, "I told the police." At his pained expression, she said, "They were reinvestigating the case. I had to tell them. It was only right. The record had to be set straight."

He didn't dispute that, but he looked extremely unhappy about it.

She placed her hand on his arm. "Once it becomes known, the backlash won't be easy or pleasant for me, either, but we've been shackled to this lie for eighteen years. I refuse to be for the rest of my life."

A short while later, Olivia's body was carried out and placed in an ambulance bound for the morgue. As they watched it pull away, Steven said to Bellamy, "William and I will be at the Four Seasons. There'll be no folde-rol like there was for Howard. We'll bury her beside him. Privately."

"I understand and agree."

"As for the other..." He looked away briefly before coming back to her and saying, "You did what you felt you had to do. In a way, it's a relief, isn't it?"

She hugged him tightly and whispered, "For you, too, I hope."

With tearful eyes she watched him walk down the steps and get into the waiting taxi with William. Her relationship with Steven would never be what it had been when they were young teens. She'd been naive to believe it could be. Their personalities, their destinies, had been reshaped by what had happened on that Memorial Day.

But she would continue to hope for a relationship with him.

Detective Abbott asked that she make herself available to answer questions that would invariably arise. "Ray Strickland will be charged with a laundry list of felonies. You'll be called to testify."

She had expected that, but she didn't look forward to it.

Just as the detectives were leaving, Nagle passed her a business card and said, "Specialty cleaning service."

Considering that and all the other unpleasant responsibilities facing her, she would have been disconsolate if Dent hadn't been there with her to lock up the house and then walk with her toward the front gate. It had stopped raining, the storm having moved off to the east.

There were still several police cars on the street. Officers were having to move along gawkers who'd been drawn to the scene of the emergency. As soon as they got past the bottleneck, Dent said, "That son-of-a-bitchin' vulture."

Sitting on the hood of Gall's pickup was Rocky Van Durbin.

"No, wait," Bellamy said, putting out her arm to hold Dent back. She kept walking until she was no more than a foot away from Van Durbin, then she said in a tone that meant business, "Get off the truck."

Shit-eating grin in place, Van Durbin slid off it. "I didn't mean any harm."

"Of course not," Bellamy said, meaning the opposite.

"Seriously," he said. "I was just waiting to ask you about Mrs. Lyston's suicide. Was it grief over your father that drove her to it?"

She took a deep breath. "Van Durbin, you're a sly, sneaky, bastard who thrives on the misfortunes of other people. You're a bottom-feeder, the lowest life-form I can think of. But actually..." She paused for emphasis. "I'm glad to see you."

She felt Dent's startled reaction.

As for Van Durbin, his ferret grin wavered, as though unsure he'd heard her right. "Where's your photographer?" she asked.

The columnist hesitated, then pointed toward a hedge that separated the Lyston property from their neighbor's.

"If he takes a single picture, this conversation is over," Bellamy said. "Tell him."

Van Durbin assessed her for a moment, then turned toward the hedge and drew a line across the base of his neck, a gesture that caused Bellamy to shiver. She hadn't had time or opportunity to think about Strickland's near fatal attack on her, knowing that when she did, she would likely have an emotional breakdown. She was postponing that until she could be alone.

She told Van Durbin to get out his notebook.

He took it from his pocket along with a pencil with a gnawed eraser.

She said, "I have a proposition for you, and these are the terms. You're going to write them down, word for word, using no shorthand or symbols, and sign it. Agreed?"

"No, not agreed. What kind of terms, and in exchange for what?"

She simply stared back at him. After a moment, he grumbled, "What're the terms?"

"You'll never reveal me as your source for anything I'm about to tell you."

"That's a given."

"Write it down." She waited until he did so before continuing. "You're to write nothing, and I mean not one allusion to, not one syllable, about my stepmother's death."

He gaped at her. "Is this a joke?"

"Shall I call the *National Enquirer*?"

He stuck the eraser in his mouth and chewed on it while he deliberated, then wrote down a line in his notebook.

Bellamy said, "You're also never to reference my brother, Steven. His name is not to be mentioned in any article you write about this."

"This, *what*? So far you've given me squat."

Dent said, "If I were you, I'd shut up and do as the lady says."

Van Durbin tilted his head toward him. "I guess he's off limits, too?"

"Not at all," Bellamy replied smoothly. "He's to be hailed the hero he is for saving my life. He's to be completely exonerated where my sister's death is concerned. But you'll write nothing about our personal lives. His or mine. Singly or together. Ever. And no more photographs of us."

Van Durbin looked ready to balk. "This had better be good."

"It is." She took the notebook from him, read what he'd written, then passed it back to him. "Sign it." Once she had the signed sheet in her possession, she motioned toward the stub in his hand. "You're going to need a bigger pencil."

"You can imagine my shock when I learned yesterday that a man in my employ, one to whom I had extended a helping hand, had taken another man's life in such a gruesome manner."

Rupe had decided to conduct his press conference in the showroom of his flagship dealership. His sales team provided a captive audience. Customers who'd come in to shop cars this morning were being treated to a show.

He had set up a small podium with a built-in microphone system. He didn't want anyone to miss a single heartfelt word. All the local television stations were represented. Because of the popularity of *Low Pressure*, the story about Ray Strickland and Dale Moody—the electrifying final chapter of an eighteen-year saga—would no doubt make national news. The King of Cars could very well be appearing on network TV tonight.

He didn't even lament his disfigured face. It added drama. He was feeling so good it was hard to maintain the solemn demeanor that the situation called for.

Things couldn't have worked out better. Strickland had taken care of Moody, and the police had taken care of Strickland. He was under lock and key, ranting and raving like a lunatic. The things he'd been quoted in the newspaper as saying—such as asking for Susan Lyston's panties back—made him sound like a total whack job.

He also continued to issue threats of vengeance against Bellamy Price, Denton Carter, and just about everybody else on the planet. Nobody would listen to a madman's allegations against a former assistant district attorney, upholder of law and justice.

Thinking quickly, Rupe had preempted any questions that might arise about the telephone calls to and from him on Ray Strickland's cell phone, which would have been noticed. He'd admitted to having helped support Ray, which now appeared to have been an act of Christian charity rather than a means of maintaining control over a potential threat.

And that crap about a copy of the case file? Moody hadn't died with it on him, and it hadn't been found in his car. Rupe figured Bellamy Price had been bluffing about its existence.

Rupe couldn't ask for things to be any tidier. Moody, gone. Strickland, as good as. Bellamy Price and her book made to look incredible by Olivia Lyston's staggering deathbed confession.

To capitalize on the hot news story, he'd called his own

press conference to clear up any questions regarding his relationship with Ray Strickland, to express his regret over the grisly death of Dale Moody, a police officer for whom he had the fondest memories and utmost regard, and to convey his sympathies once again to the Lyston family, to whom the fates had been so grossly unkind.

He laid it on thick and the reporters were eating it up.

He was just about to close when Van Durbin and his photographer walked into the showroom.

National coverage! he thought.

The columnist gave him a jaunty little wave. While Rupe was answering the last question posed to him, the two elbowed their way forward until they were standing directly in front of Rupe. When Rupe stopped speaking, Van Durbin raised his hand.

"Ah, I see our friend from *EyeSpy* has joined us. Mr. Van Durbin, you have a question for me?" He flashed a smile toward the cameraman, who was rapidly taking shots of him.

"No question. I already have all the answers. In a signed confession Dale Moody left with Bellamy Price."

Rupe's bowels loosened. But he blustered and flashed another smile. "Moody was a delusional drunkard. So whatever he said—"

"What he said was that you and he sent Allen Strickland to prison for killing Susan Lyston, knowing full well that he hadn't committed the crime. You're accountable for his death, as well as for Moody's. Your bad, Rupe."

"You print that and I swear—"

But Van Durbin was looking at a point behind him.

He spun around and found himself face-to-face with two grim-faced men. "Who're you?" he demanded.

"I'm Detective Abbott. I spoke to you yesterday on the phone when you reported that Dale Moody had been killed. This is my partner, Detective Nagle. Pleased to meet you, Mr. Collier." Then, after a beat, "You have the right to remain silent."

Nagle stepped behind Rupe and fastened a pair of plastic restraints on his wrists.

Van Durbin's photographer got some great shots.

Epilogue

----◆◆◆----

One week later

I need a pilot."

"Yeah? Happens I'm a pilot."

"I hear you're good."

"You heard right. Where do you need to go?"

"Anywhere."

"That narrows it down."

"Can we talk about it?"

"Sure. What did you have in mind?"

"Can we talk about it in person?"

"I guess. I mean, sure."

"I'm still at the Four Seasons. Do you mind meeting with me here?"

"Fine. When?"

"How soon can you get here?"

An hour later, Dent knocked on the door of her suite. She looked at him through the peephole and, even distorted by the fish-eye lens, he looked wonderful. He was dressed as she'd seen him that morning when she'd first chartered his plane. Jeans and boots, a white shirt, black necktie loosely knotted beneath his open collar.

He obviously regarded this as a business meeting.

She took a deep breath and opened the door. "Hi."

"Hi."

He came into the suite and, standing in the center of the parlor, slid his hands into the back pocket of his jeans and took a look around. Finally he came around to her. She said, "Thank you for coming on such short notice."

"I still need the charters."

"You didn't take the job with the senator?"

"Yeah, I did."

"How's it working out?"

"Okay. I've flown him back and forth between here and his ranch. Easy breezy. Less than an hour with a tailwind. On Saturday, I ran him and his wife down to Galveston to meet some friends for dinner. Was home by one a.m."

"So it's going well."

"It's only been a week, but so far so good."

"I'm glad. Meanwhile, how are the repairs on your airplane coming?"

"That's why I need the charters. My deductible is high. Even with Gall doing the labor, replacement parts are expensive."

They were killing time, avoiding what they really needed to talk about, and both were aware of it. Her heart was about to burst out of her chest. She gestured to an armchair. "Sit down. Can I get you something to drink from the minibar?"

"No, I'm good, thanks."

He took the chair. She sat down on the sofa. He looked round, noticing how lived-in the room was.

"You've been here all week?"

"Yes, since you dropped me off."

Her long conversation with Van Durbin had moved from the street outside the mansion to an all-night diner. When it had finally concluded in the wee hours, she'd asked Dent to take her to the hotel. He had, without argument or comment. He'd given her a good-night hug but hadn't offered or asked to stay with her.

She hadn't heard from him again until she'd worked up the courage to call him an hour ago.

"After Olivia...I didn't want to stay in my parents' house."

"Understandable."

"It was hard enough for Steven and me to go through it, room by room, seeing what we wanted to keep. He took some of Olivia's things. I kept some of Daddy's which held special memories for me. Everything else, even Olivia's jewelry, has been turned over to an estate liquidator. Steven and I agreed to donate all the proceeds of that sale to a homeless shelter. We'll sell the property."

"Are you sure you want to do that? It's been in your family forever."

"It holds as many painful memories for us as good ones."

"What about the Georgetown house?"

She hugged herself. "Knowing that Ray Strickland had been inside it, lurking in my closet, handling my things—I could never spend another night there, so I bought out my lease. I'd rented it furnished. It's fortunate that I never completely unpacked my personal belongings."

"So that leaves New York. When do you go back?"

That he could ask so dispassionately was crushing

but she kept her voice level. "Actually, I haven't decided where I want to light. My apartment up there isn't really my *home*. It's a solid investment. I'll keep it as a pied-à-terre, but—"

"A pita what?"

She smiled. "A place to stay when I have to go to New York for business."

"You're gonna keep writing?"

"Strictly fiction next time," she said ruefully. "But I can write anywhere."

"Is that why you called me? You want me to fly you around till you see someplace you like?"

"No," she said slowly, "I called you because it appeared that you were never going to call me. I figured that if I ever wanted to see you again, I'd have to invent a reason."

He shifted his weight in his chair. He propped one foot on his opposite knee, then immediately returned it to the floor. He ran his hand over the length of his necktie as though smoothing it down, although it didn't need to be.

Reading the signs of his unease, she asked, "Is this where you'll say all the things that guys say when they don't really mean them?"

"No."

"You came on strong until I shared your bed, Dent. You broke down barriers that no other man had been able to break down. Was winning that prize all it meant to you? Were my orgasms trophies?"

"Jesus," he said, shaking his head. "No."

She continued looking at him and then raised her shoulders, silently asking, *Then, what*?

He fidgeted some more and finally said, "I don't know how to do this."

"Don't know how to do what, exactly?"

"Be a...a half of something. A partner, or boyfriend, or significant other, or whatever you want to call it. And that's presumptuous for me even to say, because that might not be at all what you have in mind for me. Us.

"But, if it is, I'm telling you, fair and square, that I'll probably suck at it. And I'd hate that. Because I wouldn't want to be the asshole who hurt you. Again. More than you've already been hurt. You deserve to be happy."

"Would you be happy?"

"If what?"

"If you were a half of something, a partner, boyfriend, significant other, or whatever."

"With you?"

She nodded.

"I don't know how to answer because I've never done it. All I know is that when I left you here last week, and it looked like everything was going to work out okay, I thought the best thing I could do for you was to back off and let you get on with your life. Swear to God, it was a sacrifice because I still wanted to be all over you. And I could have been. And I knew it. But I didn't think it would be the best thing for you. So I left, thinking, 'Well, take a bow, Saint Dent. You've done a good deed.' I've never felt that good about a decision. Or that lousy."

He left the chair and went to stand at the window that afforded a view of the hotel's landscaped gardens and the river beyond. "I've thought about you every freakin' minute. My apartment was crap before, but I really can't stand it now, because everywhere I look, I see you. It's gotten so bad I've spent the last two nights in the hangar. Gall isn't speaking to me."

"Because you slept in the hangar?"

"Because I'm too stupid to live."

"He said that?"

"He did. He, uh..." It was several moments before he came around slowly to face her. "He said falling in love would make a person stupid. But I, being me, had taken stupid to a new level and let you go."

Her eyes went misty. "You don't want to have Gall mad at you."

Later, they argued over who moved first, but the important thing was that they came together in an embrace that fused their bodies and mouths. Eager hands opened articles of clothing, but when he pressed her up against the window, she appealed to his reason and said that anyone on the hotel grounds could see them, and he asked, "Who cares?" and when she said she did, he pulled her to the floor, where her few remaining inhibitions were stripped away as swiftly as the rest of their clothes.

Eventually they moved to the bedroom, where they made excellent use of the king-size bed, then lolled, temporarily replete, stroking each other.

"That morning," he said. "When you came out of the bathroom, just out of the shower, wearing my shirt."

"Hmm. You looked at me funny."

"Well I was feeling funny."

"Why?"

He rubbed his lips against her temple, started to speak, then paused before saying, "I was about to say that that was the first time I'd ever been glad to see a woman on the morning after. But it was more than that. I also realized how much I'd miss waking up with you if you weren't there."

She closed her eyes against the emotion welling up in them. "I don't know where it will go, Dent, or what will happen," she whispered against his throat. "I only know I want to be with you like this as often as I can be, for as long as I can be."

"I can live with that. In fact, I *want* to live with that." He angled his head back so he could look into her face. "You don't mind that I'm poor and you're rich?"

"Do you?"

"Hell no. Despite what Gall said, I'm not stupid."

She tweaked a chest hair. "Are you after my money?"

"Absolutely. But first things first."

He touched her in a way that caused her to gasp, and then he was above her again, moving inside her, not as frenzied as before but slowly and with feeling. Teasing aside, cupping her face between his hands, he kissed her closed eyelids, and when she opened them, he said, "They don't look sad anymore."

"That's because I'm deliriously happy."

"Then that makes two of us."

"So you cared about whether or not I called you?"

Looking deeply into her eyes, he reached for her hands, positioned them on either side of her head, and, palm to palm, linked their fingers tightly. Resting his forehead on hers, he settled his weight on her and said gruffly, "I cared. I cared like hell. Thank God it only took you a week."

Softly she kissed his mouth. "A week and eighteen years."

Acknowledgments

During the writing of this book, I needed a lot of help with the flight sequences for both a twin-engine private aircraft and commercial airplanes. My thanks to Ron Koonsman, my friend and first go-to person, who provided so much valuable information, including an introduction to Jerry Lunsford. He patiently and painstakingly answered my many questions and acquainted me with the totally alien landscape of a cockpit. Jerry Hughes advised me on technical aspects and terminology. Others, who asked to remain anonymous, know how grateful I am that they shared their personal experiences and vast knowledge.

I apologize for any mistakes, which are mine entirely and not the fault of the above-mentioned pilots.

Sandra Brown

June 2012